The Big Snow

By,

Robert A. Boyd

Cover Illustration Courtesy Ryan Wilkerson

Dedication:

For the men and women who work The Hill.

Prologue:

Donner Pass...

Ever since men laid rails across the Sierras, the mountains fought them tooth and nail, giving no quarter in a relentless struggle between man and nature. Nature's weapon of choice is snow, or as men came to call it, the Big Snow: blizzards marching in one after another from the Pacific creating white-out conditions which can go on for days. Men fight back with grit and determination, steam and steel, shovels and bulldozers, snow plows and dynamite. Men suffer, equipment breaks down, trains stall or are swept away by avalanches, but somehow they always manage to keep the traffic moving.

This year would be the worst yet. The Weather Service scientists in San Francisco crunched their data, studied their computer models, and made dire predictions. Nature-lovers noted how the birds flew south early that autumn, and the animals had thicker fur than usual. Old-timers studied the dirty gray skies, and shook their heads, and muttered to themselves. This was going to be a bad one.

The storms came early that autumn, driven by a disastrous shift in the jet stream and a catastrophic rise in ocean temperatures. The world was heating up, to hear it told, overturning the traditional patterns and creating more bad weather than *ever*. The old snow record—884 inches—fell by early November as the mountains were relentlessly pounded, and the Weather Service made dire warnings of more than that—far more.

900 inches...

The crews read the bulletins and shook their heads in disbelief, wondering if *this* was the year nature would win the ancient battle. The Big Snow kept coming: wave after wave of storms, often blending into each other so the blizzards went on non-stop. The battle went on non-stop as well, men working until they dropped from exhaustion. More men—road crews, clerks, shop personnel —were pulled in and the battle continued, pushing mortal men as hard as human flesh could endure. They barely managed to keep ahead for all their efforts, and sometimes even that wasn't enough.

1000 inches...

The National Guard was called in, but this was something they never prepared for. They were needed down in the lowlands to deal with the disastrous flooding anyway, so good intentions were about all they could offer. The railroad struggled on. The men developed a grim, weary determination to *beat* this muther if mere human flesh could do it. As time went on that seemed more and more doubtful.

1100 inches...

Trains had to feel their way by GPS reckoning and radio dispatching, since they often ran in white-out conditions. The signals were erratic at best, anyway, and no one trusted them. Traffic slowed to a crawl as the trains groped blindly across the Sierras and the snow crews struggled against hopeless odds.

1200 inches...

Lineside buildings collapsed. Turnouts froze. Trains stalled more frequently. They ran out of helper engines, and had to bring power up from Southern California, who could ill-afford the loss. The new year arrived in a blinding blizzard. The exhausted, frozen crews hardly noticed, but went on because they simply didn't know what else to do.

Down in San Francisco, the Weather Service scientists crunched their data and studied their computer models, and were grimly silent.

And the Big Snow kept coming...

*****

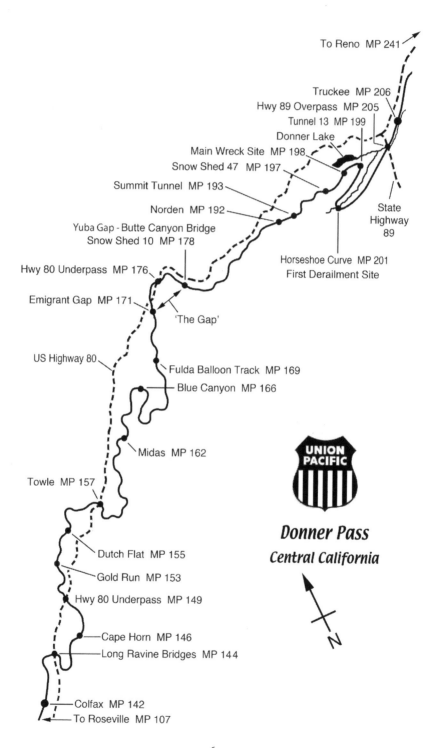

To Reno MP 241

Truckee MP 206
Hwy 89 Overpass MP 205
Tunnel 13 MP 199
Donner Lake
Main Wreck Site MP 198
Snow Shed 47 MP 197
Summit Tunnel MP 193
Norden MP 192
Yuba Gap - Butte Canyon Bridge
Snow Shed 10 MP 178
Hwy 80 Underpass MP 176
Emigrant Gap MP 171
'The Gap'
US Highway 80
Fulda Balloon Track MP 169
Blue Canyon MP 166
Midas MP 162
Towle MP 157
Dutch Flat MP 155
Gold Run MP 153
Hwy 80 Underpass MP 149
Cape Horn MP 146
Long Ravine Bridges MP 144
Colfax MP 142
To Roseville MP 107

State
Highway
89

Horseshoe Curve MP 201
First Derailment Site

UNION
PACIFIC

Donner Pass
Central California

N

January One, Midnight:

Milepost 142, Colfax, California:

The insistent buzzing of the alarm clock failed to penetrate Dan McGuire's exhausted slumber until the guy on the next bunk got tired of the racket, and threw a pillow at him. "Hey! Rise and shine, sleepy-head!"

"Awright, awright." He groaned to a sitting position on the edge of the bunk and tried to collect his wits, leaving the alarm running for the moment as petty revenge. Midnight: a new year, a new day at the same old grind. Right then he couldn't care less. He had a grand total of five hours exhausted slumber, and felt like he could use another fifty. He ached. It took an effort to focus his eyes and his thoughts, his arms were shaky, and he felt weak. He wondered vaguely if standing up was a good idea. He needed to hit the john.

He thought briefly about laying down again and telling the world to go to hell, but he knew better. The world out there was in crisis, blizzards sweeping across the nation, and everyone had to pitch in to the desperate, endless struggle to keep the railroad open. Guys like him got the bare minimum of legally required down time, some of which went to eating and other necessities, not to mention waiting around on your own time for a reliever to arrive. Exhaustion was all part of the lifestyle, though never so much as these days.

Officially, legally, he was 'off the law' and could be sent out again, but for the life of him, he couldn't see why he should give a damn. Right then he was *sick* of railroading, *hated* Donner Pass, and was fed up to *here* with the Union Pacific railroad. He was weary of the erratic hours, the lack of sleep, of eating too many hash house meals and sleeping in too many railroad dorms. Right then it was all just too much. But this was what he did for a living: twenty-five years as an engineman. At fifty-one, with a pension only nine years away, it was too late to think about another line of work. No, like it or not, he was stuck with the job, and as much as he hated it, he could see why they drove the crews so hard.

It was a mess out there—a National Disaster, the TV news called it. There was more Goddamned snow than you could *dream* of, and it *must* be cleared—somehow. Donner Pass bore an evil reputation going back over a century, and it was well deserved. Winters in the Sierras were always bad, but these last few years set new records for misery. He didn't understand all this talk about climate change, and for the life of him he couldn't figure why 'global warming' could produce so *many* blizzards, but that wasn't his problem. Getting through the next twelve hours was.

Besides, his wife left him long enough ago that it didn't hurt any more. The railroad was 'family' now, and he needed to do his part in a family crisis. He was resigned to the long hours, anyway.

His bladder was demanding attention, which the chill in the dorm didn't help. He shut off the travel alarm, tucked it in his kit with a weary sigh, and headed for the restroom.

§

Milepost 171, Emigrant Gap:

Fred Roth paused for a moment to rest and scan the scene around him, and wondered vaguely if they were *ever* going to get a break from this weather. His arms ached from the relentless effort digging packed snow out of the turnout points. Was it his imagination, or was the snow worse? He studied the white cascade in the glare of the hi-rail truck's headlights, the only way he could tell. Yeah, it was worse. Between the dark and the snow he couldn't make out the other three men on his crew who were (hopefully) just yards away. Their truck stood at the head of the crossover shining its high beams south down the line to help keep his people from getting lost. There was very real danger out here where there was nothing for miles but the railroad itself. Hypothermia is tricky, especially as tired as they all were, and he kept after his men to be sure they were safe.

Maintenance of Way is a thankless job at the best of times, and this year was the worst *ever*. It wasn't natural; couldn't be. There were all those fires last summer, when men dropped like flies from heat stroke. After the drought came the autumn rains with the floods and mudslides as the torrents came roaring down the denuded hillsides. And now snow. Endless snow. No one was under any delusions about what it meant to work Donner Pass, but each succeeding year lately was worse than the last.

He looked up, watching the snow as it glittered in the headlights. It was definitely getting worse, which meant they'd be even harder pressed to keep these turnouts cleared. It was a hopeless task, pretty much a fool's errand, but if the working parts got jammed with snow and ice, the line would be paralyzed. Worse, a jammed turnout could cause a huge pileup and then they'd *really* have a miserable time.

It used to be the blizzards would blow over and they'd have several days to dig out before the next one came. That was back in 'the good old days'. *This* year the storms were all but endless, white-out conditions which went on for weeks at a time. Even the UP's Donner Crossing, famed for their snow removal expertise, was overwhelmed. How they would cope was beyond him.

He strained to check his watch in the faint glow of the truck's headlights. Another hour: time to call his people in for a few minutes to warm up and have some hot coffee. He headed wearily for the truck, dragging his shovel behind him.

§

Milepost 142, Colfax, California:

It was too nippy in the dorm for a shower, not that Dan cared any more, so he headed for beans, the one thing which mattered right then. At the entrance to the dorm there was a sign-in desk with a telephone and a portable TV tuned to the Weather Channel. A couple other crew types were watching the latest word silently.

"The President extended the state of Disaster to include most of the Central Valley, with extensive flooding in Sacramento and Stockton. Airline travel into San Francisco remains disrupted by the storm conditions, with thousands of holiday season travelers stranded. With the highway over Donner Pass blocked, and rail travel being severely impacted by the blizzards, the Red Cross anticipates it may be weeks before travel can be resumed."

9

"Shit, tell us somethin' we don't know." Dan turned to find Murphy standing behind him, watching the TV over his shoulder.

"So what's the word?"

Murphy scowled. "Twelve-hunnert-twenty-eight *mutherfuckin'* inches at Summit." He was the crew caller, third trick, for the Maintenance of Way forces here in Colfax, and a thankless task it was to drag exhausted men out of warm beds and send them up the Hill in this weather. The other idlers drifted away or tried to look inconspicuous as Murphy focussed on him. "And this storm ain't done yet, an' we got another one due."

Dan sighed, but said nothing. Those who fought to keep Donner Pass open didn't need explanations. Those who weren't there wouldn't understand. Murphy examined his clipboard. "You're good, ain'tja?"

Dan nodded silently. He knew what was coming. 'Good' meant he was 'off the law' with the crew rest requirements, and able to go out again. 'Good' didn't mean he was actually fit to take a train over the pass.

"Grab some chow. You're booked on *SPMW* 207. They're down in the service yard refueling, so you got about thirty minutes."

Dan nodded again, too weary to argue the matter. Another snow extra; like he should be surprised. Twelve hours shoving a rotary snow plow back and forth over the Hill with everyone from the Conductor to the VP Operations griping about their slow pace. And it was number 207 no less; the oldest rotary still in service. The Southern Pacific was absorbed into the Union Pacific years ago, but the SP men insisted on maintaining 'tradition': all former SP equipment still ran as 'Southern Pacific Maintenance of Way', as did most of the old-timers. Dan was an SP man himself.

At least he could avoid the worst cold in the steam-heated cab, not like his last trick on one of the flangers. It wouldn't do any good to complain anyway. As far as the railroad was concerned he was a lost soul, condemned to a frozen eternity on the Hill. Once Maintenance of Way got their clutches on a man, they never let go.

Murphy consulted his clipboard again, then pointed at a notice on the bulletin board. "And the FRA just issued a special ruling.

'Cause of the emergency here, they relaxed the Hours Of Service law. You'll still do your twelve, but if sumpthin' comes up, you can go to sixteen. You'll get time-and-a-half for it."

Dan stared at the notice printed on crisp Department Of Transportation stationery without really seeing it. Sixteen hour days: things must have really gone to smash. This weather... It wasn't natural. Twelve hundred and twenty-eight inches of snow, and it was still snowing. Unbelievable. The worst of it was they couldn't close Donner Pass and wait for spring. As much freight as could be was being rerouted south, but the routes south had their own snow problems. Donner Pass was too critical to give up on, even if they only got a trickle of traffic over the Hill.

He heard from an old friend the other day, someone he crewed with several times the last few years, who was on a regular run south down the Coast Line into Los Angeles. Those brown hills would be rich green by now, with warm golden sunshine and a mild breeze coming in off the Pacific. Instead he was stuck here, on snow duty, on the *mutherfuckin'* Hill. He thought briefly about pleading with Murphy to send him back to the general pool, but it would be useless. Keeping the Hill open was the most urgent mission on the road, so crews who got roped in were stuck here for the winter, if it ever ended. In any case Murphy was a hulking brute, and his none-too-steady temper was badly frayed by the strain they were all under. No sense in pushing his luck.

§

Milepost 206, Truckee, California:

"So hows it look?" Jeff O'Brian asked Reggie Greenbaum when he returned from the Stationmaster's office.

Greenbaum ignored him long enough to force the door shut against the stiff wind, then pulled his gloves off and rubbed his hands together. Even if the distance from the Truckee station to the 'City Of San Francisco' wasn't much, conditions were horrid. It was pitch dark out there, with a raw wind from the west, but at least it wasn't snowing for the moment. He gave his brakeman a weary glare. "Oy, such a mess! I wish I was back on the 'Palmetto'. I could use some Florida sunshine!"

11

"You and me both!" In fact the two of them, along with several cars from the Florida train, were hijacked to beef up the 'City' for the holiday crisis.

"What about groceries? The cattle are getting restless." They were so far behind when they reached Reno that George Reinsbach, the regular conductor in the forward double-decker section decided not to wait for provisions. It wouldn't have mattered if they could have sailed over the Hill to Emeryville. No such luck: as bad as things were on the High Plains, it was nothing compared to the chaos here in the shadow of the Sierras.

It'd been like this the whole trip. Chicago was a nightmare; only to be expected with the lake effect snow and bone-chilling cold. But that was merely the beginning of their ordeal. All across the northern plains they'd faced bottlenecks and delays from blizzards coming down from Canada. The whole country was struggling in this unnatural winter, and the railroads were not the only ones to suffer. Airline travel was severely curtailed, and the highways were a dreadful mess, all of which forced holiday season travelers onto Amtrak's already overworked trains. They tried: Amtrak tried their damnedest to uphold the old tradition that the trains would always get through. And they *did* keep running, somehow, but it was a constant battle as trains ran late and suffered breakdowns, logistics were fouled up and crews were overworked.

Greenbaum rubbed his weary, aching eyes. "George told 'em we're out of everything. They said they'd hustle up as much as they can." George Reinsbach, their regular conductor, had come to regret passing on provisions at Reno, and present efforts to make amends were hampered by the ongoing storms. They were down to serving canned stew over rice, and even that was all but gone. "I don't know how long this'll take, but don't make any dinner plans." He kept a supply of instant coffee in his kit—he'd learned some important truths on this run—but even he was running low.

"Shit. We'll be stuck here for hours, likely."

The 'City' was already a day late due to the weather when they got to Reno, which didn't bode well for Amtrak's newest reborn streamliner. Even aside from this holiday crisis, the demand for rail travel had skyrocketed in recent years. Amtrak managed (somehow) to pull enough cars out of repair shops and dead lines to field lean consists for a three-times-a-week west coast service. Those had been supplemented in turn by cars pulled off eastern trains during this 'transportation emergency' to handle holiday season crowds stranded by the weather. It was a far cry from the 'City' of old, but it was the best they could do.

Greenbaum sighed. "Hell, at this rate the 'Zephyr' will overtake us."

O'Brian replied with a woeful snort. "They're probably as bad off as we are."

"Not my circus. Not my monkeys." Greenbaum pulled his gloves on and tugged his Conductor's cap firmly down on his head. "I got to see how things are forward." These 'eastern' single-deck cars were mismatched against the 'western' double-deckers. There was no direct connection between the two sections, so he had to trudge up the length of the platform to check in with the other half.

"Yeah. Watch out for polar bears."

§

Milepost 142, Colfax, California:

'Beans'—there was no way to tell which meal this was supposed to be, not that it mattered—was scrambled eggs, sausage and potato hash, sliced bread, and all the stale coffee you could chug down. At that they were lucky: the railroad set up this ad-hoc kitchen to run round the clock supporting the road crews and work gangs going out into that frozen hell. The staff were mostly volunteers, many of them family members stepping up to help their men out on the line, and they focussed on churning out solid fare in quantity rather than getting clever. Most of their customers, like Dan, were too tired to worry about what they ate anyway, as long as it was hot and filling and plenty of it.

Dan took one of the metal cafeteria trays and filled it with whatever was in front of him without really noticing what it was. He knew from experience hot chow would be a rare luxury out there on the Hill, and a full belly could make the difference in a long, wearing day. If it was anything other than horse shit, he'd eat it. Horse shit he could get anywhere around here.

13

*'Cause of the emergency here, they relaxed the Hours
Of Service law. You'll still do your twelve, but if sumpthin'
comes up, you can go to sixteen.'*

Murphy's warning came back to him as he contemplated the
future with no pleasure. He knew, sure as shootin', he'd wind up
doing sixteen, maybe more. These storms weren't about to let up,
and neither would the Union Pacific, so they pulled some strings in
Washington which made him dance. But there was nothing he
could do about it, so he grabbed a mug of hot cocoa and headed for
the trestle tables.

"Hey, Dan." He'd hardly settled in when his distracted haze
was interrupted by a familiar voice.

He looked up to see Davy Burns, another of the SP's lost souls
headed his way. "Hey," he grunted, not that he was thrilled by the
interruption.

Burns settled on the table next to him. "I hear-tell you're on the
207."

"Yeah."

"I'm afraid you're in for a long night. We were told we'll be 'off
the law' for the foreseeable future. Sixteen hour days! Can you
believe it?"

Dan sighed. He didn't much care for Burns and really didn't
want to be having this conversation. Still, anything he could get on
conditions on the Hill would be all to the good. "Yeah, I can, with
how things are out there. How you guys managing?"

Burns looked vexed and weary. "Not so hot. It's getting so
deep our flanger can't handle it any more. They had us work west
toward Roseville, and we were pushing our limits. I hear spreader
4034 will be back from th' shop soon and they're gonna send it up
the Hill. I pity the poor bast'ds they stick on that job!"

Dan paused his fork full of hash. "Why am I not surprised?
How do they expect us t' make do in these conditions?"

"Lord knows. I sure don't. How we'll manage is beyond me
with this *freakin'* weather. Global warming? Yeah, right!
Somethin's goin' on here they don't want us t' know! I tell ya, this
ain't natural!"

14

"Neither is hauling ten thousand tons of freight at sixty per."
Dan shut Burns down fast before he got off into one of his
conspiracy rants. "So why you here if things are so bad out there?"

Burns gave him a hurt look. "I came in t' fill up on coffee." He
hefted one of the large stainless steel crew thermoses. "Damned
crew goes through it like nobody's business, and none of them
bothered t' bring any." He stood up and gave Dan a sympathetic
grimace. "Gotta get back. Eight more hours of this shit! Hope it
goes smooth out there."

He moved on, and Dan went back to stuffing his face
mechanically, not even noticing the taste of what he ate as he
pondered his shift ahead.

> *'Cause of the emergency here, they relaxed the Hours*
> *Of Service law. You'll still do your twelve, but if sumpthin'*
> *comes up, you can go to sixteen.'*

Yeah, things would go *real* smooth between the weather and
equipment breakdowns. He dismissed it because if he worried
about it it'd give him a headache. He glanced at the clock: time
was running out, fast. He needed to get moving.

On his way out he stopped at a table with a couple coffee urns
and a pile of individually wrapped sandwiches, there for the crews
to take along. After filling his thermos, be examined one of the
sandwiches: ham and cheese. He grabbed one of the paper grocery
sacks, filled it with a dozen sandwiches, added several bags of
chips and some pudding cups. At least he'd eat adequately out
there, even if it wasn't hot.

§

Milepost 171, Emigrant Gap:

Fred stopped once again to ease his aching back, his shovel
drooping in the pile he'd already dug. This was hopeless. He
pondered his remaining strength, and realized he was trembling.
The wind picked up again, tormenting him. Hypothermia is
treacherous, and with how they all labored like mules he couldn't
be too careful. He was hungry too, which didn't help.

15

He stopped to collect his wits and size up the situation. This seven mile stretch was one of the worst spots on the Donner Subdivision, so much so that they had their own Maintenance of Way base station, which also served as a spot where trains waited their turn to enter 'The Gap'. A short way east of there the line narrowed to a single track where it passed under Highway 80, using the underpass as a snow shed. 'The Gap' ran through a winding gully so narrow only a single track could fit, and only by twisting back and forth like a snake. Toss in some major storms, and winters became an ongoing nightmare. In a year like this, with these impossible snowfalls, the situation was hopeless. The spreaders were useless here, and even the rotaries did good to throw the snow far enough to clear the right of way.

All this made 'The Gap' one of the worst snow challenges on the western slopes, and a permanent Maintenance of Way crew was stationed here in the winters. It was his damned luck he and his seven men were condemned to this paradise.

But they were completely outclassed, and needed to budget their limited resources of time and strength to what *had* to be done. Right now they were focussing on the multiple turnouts serving the three track passing zone which ended here. His people were in two hi-rail crew cab trucks at different points on the passing zone to their immediate west trying to keep the turnouts clear of snow and ice. It was all they could do in these conditions.

The radio in his truck crackled to life, the tinny transmission coming faintly to him. He listened, trying to catch the faint signal. It came again; they were definitely calling him. He set aside his shovel and climbed into the cab. Any excuse to get warm.

"Maintenance of Way at Milepost 171 to UP dispatcher, over?"

"*Roseville dispatcher to Maintenance of Way at Milepost 171, be advised SPMW 207 is due your location in about three hours. Over?*"

"Copy. We'll be ready for them."

Great: a rotary, just what they needed to deal with this mess. Even with the two freights which passed here in the last few hours, snow levels were climbing fast. He and his men couldn't begin to fight the accumulation, but a rotary could. And that new development—a localized dispatcher in Roseville—said things would soon get worse.

He changed frequencies and picked up his radio mic again. "Ernesto? Did you copy that last from dispatch?"

"Si, Jefe. We need a rotary sumpthin' awful!"

Fred was not pleased with how quickly he responded. His people tended to goof off in the hi-rails unless he rode herd on them, Ernesto in particular. "How are the turnouts at your end?"

"They're good, Jefe."

Sure they were. "Will I like what I see when I come down there?"

"¡Si, Jefe! We're doing fine here."

He knew better, but was too cold and too tired to care. Just to be sure, he decided not to mention his plan to head up to Yuba Gap. "Alright, keep at them for the next hour and a half, then shift up here and take care of the turnouts at this end. And make sure they're clear! *You* don't want to explain derailing the rotary to the home office. I'll be down later to take a look-see. Over?"

"Si, Jefe." Resentfully.

Not one of his best hands, Ernesto, a bad example who tended to take over whenever Fred wasn't around. Hopefully that threat would keep him on his toes. Fred hung the radio mic on its hook and honked the truck's horn to call his three in.

"What's the word, Boss?" Elwood, the only black on his crew, asked when they piled in.

"There's a rotary coming in three hours. I'll leave Ernesto here, and we'll position at shed 10 to cover the far end of The Gap."

"What about the spreader?"

Fred racked his memory, trying to piece together where UP's thin assets were. "4032 went east to help that last freight through to Truckee. 4034 is still in the shop, last I heard. We won't likely see a spreader for a while, but they're sending us the 207, which is even better."

Spreaders can only do so much, and the UP only had four on the Hill. With these endless blizzards the snow was coming down faster than the spreaders could keep up. Worse, since Truckee also dealt with the grade east to Reno, they were forever borrowing one of theirs. The Gap was the worst spot on the division, where the spreaders were pretty much useless anyway.

"Hey Boss, we out-a coffee." One of the hands hefted the large crew thermos and shook it for emphasis.

Fred was reminded that he was starving, and a hot coffee would be a Godsend right then. "Okay, we'll stop by the shack for a refill and sandwiches before we head east."

§

Milepost 142, Colfax, California:

It was still snowing when Dan left the crew shack and headed out to his assignment. He could remember when it rarely snowed this far down the Hill, and when it did, Colfax rarely got much. But that was back in 'the good old days', which made him feel positively ancient. The present storm already dumped something like two feet of snow here in Colfax, which didn't bode well for up the line. A Bobcat was dancing back and forth to clear the accumulated snow swept aside by the flanger assigned to the yard, and faint lights in the distance marked where weary men with shovels and wire brooms were clearing the turnouts.

The wind buffeted him, sending icy knives through his heavy parka. Wind was one of the ugly realities of winter here, and you couldn't wear enough clothes to keep warm. He sighed in resignation and headed for the yard. The easiest way to get anywhere in this mess was to walk on the tracks, so he headed down to the wye while keeping a wary eye out for moving trains. A couple men had been hurt this season already.

SPMW 207 sat on a stub track when he arrived, just as a tanker truck from a local fuel distributor pulled away. Rotary 207 was an old familiar sight, not that Dan was thrilled. This beast was built way back in 1929, fer Crissakes. At least they replaced her steam boiler with electric power years ago. Behind the plow was its 'snail', an ancient diesel 'B' unit used to provide power for the rotary's enormous scoop. Behind them in turn were an ancient heavyweight sleeper for a crew dorm, one of the old World War 2 troop kitchen cars, a box car for supplies and a fuel tanker, followed by two elderly GP 38 diesels and finally another rotary and snail facing the other way. The sight of those camp cars was not comforting, nor was he pleased to have those two dinosaurs as their only road power, but the snow crews long since learned to take what they could get.

Marcus Chang, their conductor, was talking to a group of men in bulky work gear when he arrived. "Glad you could join us," he greeted Dan, shortly. "Word is these storms are getting worse, if you can believe it, and it's getting too bad for the flangers to handle. There's still no word on either of our spreaders, so we're it for keeping the line open."

Snow removal normally started *after* the storms had passed, except these storms didn't 'pass'. Snow equipment and methods meant for kinder, gentler winters couldn't keep up.

"They're sending us up to Norden for a little camping adventure. We drew supplies for a week." He gestured at the box car, which brought on a round of weary cursing. "We'll be in charge from Fulda to Summit Tunnel. Once rotary 211 gets out of the shop, they'll work Fulda to Roseville, and we'll do the high country. Truckee'll handle everything from Summit east."

"Any word on when we'll get the 211 back?" Dan asked.

Marcus frowned. "No, nothing. My guess is it'll be several days yet." Rotary SPMW 211 was in for repairs after trying in ingest a large rock, and its partner, UPMW 18161, was benefiting by some much-needed minor work. The four survivors were on their own. "All the snow crews will stand watch-and-watch until further notice. Can't afford the down time for fuel and supplies. I hear they'll send a supply train up rather than us coming back."

This was not welcome news either. Up to now, they could keep ahead of the snow accumulation, but lately it was so bad the higher-ups must have decided to further split up the work load and commit their last reserve of heavy snow gear—as soon as it could be repaired. Their hard luck was to draw the garden spot of the Hill, and if the road was sending out supply trains, they could be stuck out there for the rest of the winter.

"Okay, crew assignments. We got Dan, here, and Jesus for primary crew, Margret and Willy for relief crew."

She was short and stocky, half-way decent looking, enough so for some of the guys to hit up on her, although she made it clear she wasn't interested. A lot of the older hands resented a woman intruding into their world, although she'd shown she could handle train duties. Still, she was awfully low on the seniority list, and her Number Two, Willy, was still in training. The road must be scraping the bottom of the barrel to send these two out by themselves, even on a plodding rotary.

"And we got Joey, here, as maintainer."

He and Dan exchanged polite nods. Joey was in his fifties, thin, balding, with the hang-dog expression of those seconded from the Roseville shops to the snow extras to keep those ancient diesels turning if at all possible.

"As for the rest, we got the usual camp crew and some gandy dancers, and there's a signals truck at Emigrant Gap, so keep your eyes open when we get there," He added with a stern look at Dan and Margret. "Finally, I just got word dispatching for th' Hill has been localized in Roseville; you all know what *that* means. We'll be operating on verbal orders until further notice, with the poor visibility and the signals still being screwed up. So remember to call out your mileposts whenever you move. Alright, we're ready to head out as soon as we get word from dispatch, so saddle up."

Margret and Willy overtook him as he headed forward. "Any word on what it's like up the Hill?" she asked.

He paused and considered the two of them for a long moment, trying to marshal his thoughts and wondering if they were up to this. "It's bad. Real bad. I never seen th' like. My guess is we'll have t' dig the whole line, every time we move."

"It can't be any worse than being stuck on a flanger," Willy protested. "At least we'll have the power we'll need."

Dan was on the flanger Burns ran now, last trick, and knew better. Willy had a lot to learn about life on the Hill; hopefully the lessons wouldn't be too expensive. At least Margret had the sense to keep her mouth shut and not make a fool of herself. "Yeah, well, we'll see how that goes when the next several storms hit."

§

Milepost 206, Truckee, California:

"We'll be dead on the law in a couple more hours." The engineman of Amtrak 15 was adamant. "Even if we're cleared now, there's no way we can make Colfax before we outlaw, to say nothing of Sacramento. You'll need a new crew before this train can go any further, and, dammit, we need something t' eat!"

Reinsbach couldn't argue. They were lucky to get this far in the last ten hours between the weather, backed-up traffic, and extra movements by snow fighting gear. What was worse, the railroad prioritized what little capacity Donner Pass could deliver for eastbound freight—to clear the logjam in Roseville, so he was told. Progress since leaving Reno was glacial, and they finally wound down here in Truckee, thirty-five miles from where they started.

In any case, both men were frazzled and exhausted, and the law was clear. He wasn't thrilled about trying the Hill unless the head end were on their toes anyway. "Alright, I'll call it in, but who knows when, or if, a relief will get here. As for beans, I'm afraid you're out of luck. The diners are empty."

Both men greeted that with weary curses. Just because they would officially be off duty didn't mean they could leave the train. Someone had to remain with the locomotives in case a problem arose. (It was not unheard-of for an untended locomotive to be stolen, too.) That meant they were stuck in the cab of their diesel until someone relieved them, and that someone had to come from Sparks, Nevada, thirty-eight ice-and-snow-bound miles away.

"Can't we at least see what we can find locally?" one of them asked. "One of us can stay on the units, and the other can bring something back."

"At this hour? What's gonna be open now? In any case, d'you want to risk it out in this?" The wind was raw, and it was starting to snow again.

The two Amtrak crewmen pondered the weather silently for a moment. "I don't suppose we could phone for pizza?" That earned them a stony glare from Reinsbach, who was already in hot water for the diner foul-up. "I guess not," one said at last. "Still, we need relievers, and we need food."

"As if we don't have enough problems," George grumbled after sending them back to their units.

"Yeah, well, you were the one who passed up reprovisioning in Reno," O'Brian muttered.

"You need to get on the horn to Reno before that load of groceries heads this way," Greenbaum added. "Have 'em bring a bunch of deli sandwiches with the reliefs."

George gave him a withering glare as he buttoned up his overcoat. "I should-a stayed in freight service."

"We all should-a stayed in bed," O'Brian sighed after he left for the station.

"Or in Florida, anyway," Greenbaum said.

§

Milepost 142, Colfax, California:

Dan read the fuel gauges, made sure the brakes were free of ice, and checked the air and electrical connections between units on his way forward. Methodical was the only way to survive out here, and he'd learned some hard lessons over the years. At last, satisfied for the moment, he climbed up into the cab of rotary 207. Jesus Romano, a brakeman he knew well, greeted him in the doorway. "*Hola*, man-o. Some weather, eh?"

"Yeah, somethin'," he muttered. At least the cab of the rotary was warm, the radiators fed by the steam generator in the rear of the unit hissing softly in the background. They'd need every bit of heat they could get once they reached the higher elevations.

"D'you believe it, *amigo?* My aunt Esmeralda, she told me they got snow in San José Viejo! Snow that fuckin' far south! It ain't right. It's gonna play hell with the tourists, man!"

"Well, I hope she's dressed warm," he mumbled as he studied the electrical control panel. San José Viejo and Jesus' aunt could fend for themselves; they had more than enough to deal with. The engine readings *looked* normal, but you never could be sure of these old diesels, not the way they were pushed these days. One thing he *sincerely* didn't want was to have to crawl under a dead unit to drain the radiator. That would be Joey's job, he decided. Might as well get some use out of those shop pukes. The steady rumble of the big sixteen cylinder power plants from somewhere aft was reassuring, even if it was an illusion.

He settled in the ancient engineman's seat, adjusted the height a bit, then dug up the GPS unit. The railroad started installing GPS in the road units years ago, but it only came to the Maintenance of Way in the last couple years as conditions on the Hill became impossible. These hand-held sets weren't as reliable as the installed units, but they were better than nothing. Trains were moving at a crawl, relying on GPS and radios for traffic orders in a dangerous game of blind-man's-bluff. He waited impatiently while the unit dithered and argued with itself before finally settling down. The final fix showed them in Colfax: which was promising. Without these units, traffic on the Hill would be impossible.

Jesus interrupted to hand him a bundle of train orders. He dug through them slowly, trying to comprehend each in his bleary mind. It was all the usual: extreme snow conditions; bad signals; the radio repeater at Emigrant Gap was acting up with a signals crew on their way to deal with it; effective white-out conditions; work crews scattered everywhere. One update said the line from Emigrant Gap over Summit to below Horseshoe Curve was all single track: no reason given for why, but rumor held that Maintenance of Way at Truckee was dogging it. He shook his head in despair: it used to be they could cope with the snow pack east of Summit; the western slope was the traditional trouble spot. But that was ordinary winters in ordinary times. He dismissed it with a silent curse, and kept reading.

There were a half-dozen snow trains scattered along the line, although he suspected the flangers were about at their limit of usefulness. Sadly there were just two rotary lashups, one on this side of the Hill, the other based out of Truckee. Add in spreaders and flangers at Colfax and Truckee, and any real train would have a hard time threading their way over the Hill. Their own plodding Extra would add to the clogged conditions, although without the rotaries the situation would be hopeless.

The weather reports were the worst: another storm due by mid day tomorrow, with at least three more lining up out in the Pacific. The word from the home office was the latest guesstimate called for a seasonal total of at least 1600 inches—perhaps as much as 1800. He dismissed it with a weary sigh. If it got that bad, there was nothing they could do about it.

The radio crackled to life, disrupting his chain of thought:

> *"Roseville Dispatcher to SPMW 207?"*
> *"SPMW 207."*
> *"SPMW 207, you are cleared to depart Colfax. Proceed via track two to Norden and hold for instructions."*
> *"SPMW 207, via track two to Norden and hold. Did you copy that, Dan?"*

Dan settled in the engineer's seat and peered up the track. A red light down low, faint in the snowy gloom, had changed to yellow. He grabbed the radio mic with one hand and the train brake lever with the other. "Ah, copy, Marcus."

"Low yellow, man-o," Jesus muttered. Dan nodded to acknowledge his confirmation of the trackside dwarf signal, and twisted the brake handle.

The air brakes hissed down the length of the Extra. The last of the section hands climbed into the sleeper as everyone settled in for the long slog up the Sierras. Dan opened his side window enough to peer over his shoulder to check his consist, quickly pulled the window shut again, and cranked the throttle up a couple notches. The chant of the big EMD diesels quickened. The rotary shuddered, stirred, and crawled slowly ahead. Jesus fired up the huge rotor, and a stream of snow began flying off to one side. Even this far down the snow pack could clog their scoop unless disposed of, and they *were* all about snow removal.

The rigid trucks banging over the turnouts, sending shocks through their seats as they crawled out onto the high iron. Up ahead, the next signal bridge showed a red light for the adjacent track and a yellow for them. That was all they'd likely get from the dispatcher, since these rotaries weren't designed for speed. It was fifty *freakin'* miles to Norden; uphill all the way, through the forest, in a blizzard, at night. The old joke about the complaining old-timer came back to him. He wasn't amused. He hated to think of what it was like further up the line.

As they cleared the last turnout, Dan opened the throttle a couple more notches, and the Snow Extra trundled along at a sedate ten miles per hour, about all they were good for. He remembered to reach up and turn on the rotating windscreen which kept his view clear by tossing off any muck which landed on it. Shame he couldn't grab a nap. This was going to take *forever*.

Another trick on the Hill had begun.

*****

Early Morning:

Milepost 206, Truckee, California:

It was getting on toward dawn—what passed for dawn these days—before a company crew van pulled onto the platform and stopped next to the single-deck diner. Reggie rousted the dining car crew out of their quarters, and they set to eagerly. The dining cars were empty, so much so that the stewards were afraid the passengers were about ready to eat *them*. Plus they were hungry too, so it wasn't long before the galley fires were lit and the big coffee urns bubbling.

"God, this feels good!" O'Brian sighed after his first chug of fresh brew. "Almost makes a fellow feel human again."

"Almost," Reggie said, sullenly. "A hot shower and twelve hours sleep, in Miami, would help, too."

O'Brian answered that with a theatrical sigh. "Oy, Reggie, such conniptions! Where did your mother and I go wrong?" For a dyed-in-the-wool Mick, he had a knack for that Brooklyn Jewish accent, which he used to keep his boss grounded when it would help.

Reggie reacted with a sheepish grin, but his retort was interrupted by the van driver. "Hey, you the conductor? You gotta sign for all this stuff." He shoved a clipboard with a thick wad of triplicate forms at him.

"Took your own sweet time getting here," Reggie groused as he signed the chit.

"Hey, mean night out there, ya know?" In fact this load of groceries was hustled here from Reno since Amtrak didn't service diners in Truckee. Aside from the time needed to shake down the local grocery distributors, highway 80 was a nightmare. The only reason the van was let through, with a state police escort and a snow plow, was because of their situation.

"Yeah, well, drive safe going back." No sense in hassling the poor schmuck. Reggie handed the clipboard back and turned to the chief steward here in the single-deck section rather than face O'Brian, who too-obviously said nothing. "How's it look, Otis?"

26

Otis pondered the pile of bags and boxes his crew were still struggling to get stowed while at the same time coping with three cars worth of hungry passengers. "I'd say we got enough fo' a couple days, maybe a bit more."

"It's likely to take that long to reach Emeryville, what with this weather," O'Brian grumbled.

"Yassah, might be so with all this-here snow. But don't you worry none. Th' eatin' won't be *luxurious*, but we'll keep folks fed."

"Good work..." Reggie was interrupted when his portable radio crackled to life:

"Amtrak train 15 to all crew, we have a hold waiting for a freight coming down the pass. After that we're clear to proceed."

Otis shook his head in dismay, but said nothing.

"I swear, if it isn't one thing, it's another," Reggie sighed. He looked askance at O'Brian. "Helluva way to run a railroad, huh?"

"Oy!"

§

Milepost 149, Highway 80 Underpass:

"I tell you, man-o, I'm thinkin' I'm gettin' too old for this." Jesus had to speak up to be heard over the steady whine of the motors turning the huge rotor. "This is work for young men, for *hombres*. Maybe I ought t' see about becomin' a clerk. At least they got steady hours."

Right then Dan could sympathize. "I hear you. Honestly, I think you'll miss it, though."

Jesus was silent for a bit as the rotary trundled along spewing snow. The night outside was a swirling blindness reflecting their headlight back in their faces, not that there was anything to see anyway. The wind buffeted them, shaking the massive rotary. The sense of isolation drew them together, lowered their barriers, helped them to voice their inner fears, to reach out for the only source of comfort available.

27

"*Si*, maybe so," Jesus said at last. "Maybe I take my retirement in two more years, then no more trips up the Hill. What I do after, I don' know." He was passed over for engineman training several times in recent years, leaving him stranded as one of a dying breed of brakemen, pretty much limited to yard work and locals. Despite his doggedly sunny disposition, that failing got to him at times.

"Hey, you're a good *hombre*, Jesus. I'm glad you're with us on this run."

Jesus didn't respond at first, but sat slumped in his seat staring out the forward windows. "*Gracias, amigo,*" he muttered after a bit.

Most new hires don't realize that railroading is mostly endless boredom. They cruise along as the consist more or less runs itself with nothing to do but call out the signals. Occasions where throttle and brakes must be used to maintain a steady pace are a welcome relief from the boredom. All those hours glued to their seats watching the same scenery and the same track passing for the umpteenth time gets to the men after a while, and they naturally turn to each other for some diversion.

You learn a lot about your fellow railroaders on the long runs: their hobbies, family problems, politics, likes and hates. You learn who the stand-up guys are, and the slimeballs. You learn about the smart ones and the slackers; who's easy to get along with and who's an asshole; the steady ones and those who will panic in a pinch. You learn a lot talking to the guy sitting across the cab, and talking is about the only thing to do on the long runs.

"Middle yellow." Jesus nodded at the next signal coming into view ahead.

"Middle yellow."

The rotary ground along, spewing a steady stream of snow to one side. As they entered a long curve, Dan gazed across the cab through the far side window, expecting to see Interstate 80 on their left. Usually they would be greeted with a flowing river of headlights; now there was nothing. The highway was closed and deserted. He got the eerie sensation that the whole world had been abandoned, that they were alone out here in the middle of nowhere, seven miles from Colfax.

"God, that's creepy," he muttered.

"*Si.*" Jesus crossed himself nervously. They both could feel the utter desolation around them. The icy wind found its way in through every crack, chilling them to their souls, stifling any conversation.

The underpass came up on them by surprise, they were so distracted. In an instant the ghostly highway vanished and the snow quit abruptly, leaving them in a dark cavern lit by their powerful headlight. In moments they emerged on the other side to be deluged by the storm once more. The spectral highway was behind them, the headlight revealing nothing but swirling white again.

The track curved to the left as it clawed its way upward following the contour of the mountain slopes. For a while there was nothing to see until the track curved back to the right, and the highway slowly came into view again. The sight dismayed them both, which the chill in the cab made more visceral. Dan wanted to say something to break the spell, but the words wouldn't come. They sat there enthralled by the ghostly sight.

The track curved away left once more, all but reversing course, leaving the highway behind, breaking the spell. Both of them were left troubled and alone.

"Middle yellow." Jesus gestured at the next signal, faint and blurry in the snow ahead.

"Middle yellow."

§

Milepost 178, Yuba Gap:

Fred Roth and his gang finally arrived at the far end of The Gap, and he was thankful *that* trip was over. It was a scary ride through some wild, uninhabited country where they couldn't see ten feet ahead of them. The snow was deep enough to bog down their hi-rail truck more than once, forcing them to turn out and dig themselves clear. There were moments where it looked like they might never get unstuck, with the nearest help miles away, but they made it—to the only shelter for miles around, the concrete Snow Shed 10.

"Safe at last." Elwood managed to stretch in his cramped passenger seat, then turned the heater up to its highest notch. The blast of warm air helped curb the all-pervading chill, but they could feel the icy presence waiting out there patiently, like some unearthly predator.

"Until we run out-a gas," one of the others grumbled as a blast of arctic wind shook their truck.

Startled out of a half doze, Fred glanced at the gas gauge: a bit less than half a tank; enough for now. Still, he better keep an eye on it. "Alright, let's do a quick check of the bridge and the shed." That earned a chorus of groaning protests. "The sooner we get this done, the sooner we come back in out of the cold, so lets hustle."

They turned to with no small amount of grumbling, feeling their way along the track by flashlights. A quick inspection showed the Butte Canyon bridge, at the entrance to Shed 10, needed some work, but wasn't too bad. As for Shed 10 itself, there was some ice buildup from snow blown in by the wind, but it wasn't bad either. They could deal with it with a minimum of time and energy. Having finished their inspection, they crowded into their hi-rail truck to try to warm up.

"Th' rotary should get here shortly," Fred told his crew. "And we got an Amtrak due later this morning. We need to get off the line and wait until the rotary clears. After that, we'll tackle the bridge."

Thankfully, that meant simply switching onto track two, which needed a lot of work east of there since the snow removal efforts were hard put to keep track one open. That was a job for the rotary. There was some argument over who would have to get out and work the turnout mechanism, which Fred finally settled by pointing to one of the guys in back, and they inched the hi-rail off the number one main deeper into the shed to await events.

§

Milepost 206, Truckee, California:

"You guys took your own sweet time getting here," the Amtrak engineman complained when Bobby Mayfield and Karl Olson climbed into the lead unit's cab.

30

"Yeah, well, we stopped off at the casinos," Bobby told him. "We won big: we're gonna buy Amtrak, and I'll *personally* appoint you traffic manager here in Truckee."

His predecessor greeted that with a snort of contempt. "Yeah, a fool and his money. What about food for the diners?"

"T'hell with them! What about food for us?" his partner griped.

"They loaded the van right up to the roof. Made for a rough ride," Karl said as he handed over a paper sack with some deli sandwiches. "The crew chief in Reno said to give you these."

"Wonderful." The lead engineman grabbed the sack. "We were hoping for a turkey dinner with all the fixin's."

"Yeah, well, that's waiting for you back in Reno, *if* you can get there."

"Figures," the lead man griped. "We've been on the law two hours already."

"Thankfully we don't get paid by the mile!" his partner complained. They signed onto this same train at Reno, in fact, some fourteen hours ago, only to wind down here due to track and traffic conditions. The two crewmen grabbed their kits and pulled their coats tighter. "She's your headache now. We're out-a here."

"Yeah, thank heaven for small favors," the other said. "I wasn't lookin' forward to going over the mountains in this weather!"

"Who would be?" Karl grumbled.

§

Milepost 178, Yuba Gap:

After about an hour while Fred and his crew waited with perfect patience, the gloom to their west was lit by the glow of an approaching headlight. Elwood nudged Fred's shoulder, snapping him out of a light doze. "It's them, boss."

"Huh?" Fred scanned the white darkness, trying to pick out details. Something was moving in the distance, shrouded in a halo of light. "Yeah." He grabbed the radio mic. "Maintenance of Way at Shed 10 to rotary at Milepost 178, good to see you guys."

The approaching rotary ground to a halt half way across the bridge, its huge rotating scoop spinning fruitlessly, a vague motion in the snowy dark.

"Ah, copy that, Maintenance of Way. You guys out of our path?"

"We're in the clear. Come on up. How's the line west of here?"

"It's in good shape, now. But at the rate it's coming down, it won't be good for long, so if you want to head west, you better get a move-on."

SPMW 207 rumbled past, the throbbing engines reverberating off the roof of the snow shed in an impressive display of antique power. It took a couple minutes for the sound to fade into the distance.

"Okay, let's get the bridge cleaned up," Fred said at last. "We got a passenger train coming."

"How soon we gonna head back, *Jefe?*" Ramon asked. "You heard the man; th' track ain't gonna be good for long."

Honestly, Fred was about fed up with all the whining by then. "Keeping this track open is *our* job! We'll head back when the job is done, *not* before!"

§

Milepost 142, Colfax, California:

"What you doin' in here, Burns?" Murphy demanded when he caught Davy lolling at one of the tables in the mess hall.

Burns reacted as if he'd been stung, jumping to his feet. "I was just catching my breath, Murphy. I came in t' get some more coffee for my crew." He held up the battered crew thermos as proof of his innocence.

"Uh huh. Your crew drinks a heck of a lot-a coffee. It's a wonder you don't all pee your brains out!" The look he gave Burns would intimidate stronger men. "For *your* information, while you're in here goofing off, you've been reassigned to spreader 4034, which just arrived. I'll trouble you t' spend a little less time *catching your breath* and a lot more time on your rig!"

Burns was not thrilled by this news, since it likely meant a trip up the Hill. "Hey, we'll be outlawing in a few hours! The snow's coming down something awful. You need a fresh crew! I'm not sure we can do much more the way things are!"

"The way things are ain't gonna change with you in here holding that chair down! You got snow? Plow it!"

Burns knew when it was time to cut and run. He grabbed the thermos and headed for the door, pausing to grab a couple sandwiches off the table. Murphy watched him go in ill-concealed contempt, then sagged once he was gone. Sad to say, he knew all too well how conditions were out there. Burns was right: the flangers were useless by now, and the spreaders were working near to capacity. And according to the weather report, this storm was far from over. As much as anyone on the Hill hated to admit it, they may have met their match. A lot of their equipment, none too adequate for these conditions, was either overwhelmed or down for repairs. Worse, they were running out of men, else he'd have written Burns up by now.

He glanced at his clipboard with its all too short list of names, and headed for the dorm, shaking his head in despair.

§

Milepost 206, Truckee, California:

"So *when* are you going to get this train moving?! I was supposed to be in Tokyo by now, but *you people* can't get *anything* right!" Of all the frustrations and misfortunes conductor Greenbaum endured on this trip, Wilbur Harkness, International Anointed High Muckety-Muck, was the most unbearable. "It's not bad enough the airlines have cancelled all flights west because of this weather, now you people can't deliver either!"

Greenbaum tried to be correct and polite with this blowhard over the last four days—dear God, did he try!—but he was at the end of his rope. "I am not in charge of the airlines," he said, curtly. "Or the weather, either. Some things simply can't be helped."

Not that his protest made a difference. His Nibs kept up a steady stream of complaints from the get-go in Chicago, griping about everything from the size of his seat to the price of drinks in the buffet car to a litany of imagined slights from the crew. His biggest gripe, beyond having to be here at all, was he couldn't get sleeper accommodations—preferably a full drawingroom—and had to settle for riding with the common herd in coach. He made sure *everyone* felt his displeasure, which made a seemingly endless trip seem even longer.

"You can bet my Congressman will hear of this! If I lose this deal because of you people's incompetence, you'll never hear the end of it!

That pushed Greenbaum once too often. "Yeah? Well tell your Congressman to get rid of all this snow, and we'll have you in San Francisco *tout suite*. But unless he can work miracles on demand, you're shit-out-a luck!"

"That's what you bought him for, after all." Charlie Parkhurst and his girlfriend Barbara Jean Howard were enjoying the show here in the buffet, since there was nothing else to do. Most of the passengers didn't share their amusement.

"I didn't ask your opinion!"

Parkhurst shrugged. "Free country. Besides, word is Frisco's airport is closed, so it looks like you're double shit-out-a luck."

"So sad," Barbara snarked with a mock-bemused shake of her head. "Poor little rich guy, still can't buy the weather."

"This is ridiculous! What do we waste all these tax-payer dollars for since you can't even keep this train moving! This is a *monumental* fraud, and I'll make sure the whole *world* hears of it!" He also favored the young couple with some scathing remarks of their own. "And I *don't* need any lip from some...crazy hippies!" He stomped away, angry enough to chew railroad iron, headed for his seat in the second car.

"Hippies?" Barbara laughed. "Gawd, how retro!" Truth be said they looked the part, although one of Parkhurst's cards in Reggie's pocket stated he was a software engineer with Apple.

Parkhurst offered Reggie a bemused look. "What's wrong with being crazy? Sanity is *boring!*"

"Yeah. I hear you," Reggie muttered.

Actually he sympathized, in spite of himself, with how uncomfortable Harkness was. The total passenger count this trip was four hundred seventy-six—a capacity load including the one-hundred-thirty-two in the three coaches and buffet/dorm of his single-deck section—as well as a crew of twenty-four. It made for crowded conditions, with overworked food service, overworked toilets, precious little distraction, and precious little room to move around. In Harkness' case it was even worse since he was unable to get a sleeper berth, and clearly viewed coach passengers as having cooties.

The much-delayed four day trip just made it worse. The passengers in this section were restless and miserable (and some of them did have cooties). The buffet being exhausted added to their misery. Truth, the one hundred thirty-two passengers in the single deck section should have a full diner, but those were in short supply so this old buffet/dorm was pulled out of dead storage and given a new lease on life.

Nor was Harkness Reggie's only problem. There was a *very* pregnant woman in the third car who worried him, and someone whose insulin was running low, and several bratty, frustrated kids. It all kept him jumping despite his exhaustion. His one solace was that things in the forward double-decker section were no better.

O'Brian came up. "You okay? I heard His Highness was at it again."

Reggie scowled at the memory. "I guess I shouldn't have barked at him like that."

"What you *should* have done was bite his leg!"

"Gawd! Don't tempt me!" He sagged as his fatigue overtook him. "This has been a miserable trip! I don't recall anything like it before."

"Me neither. But you can take some comfort: at least we aren't running SRO."

Reggie gave him a severe look. "Not *yet*, you mean. Don't jinx it; we may be doing that headed back east."

§

Milepost 142, Colfax, California:

Burns was fuming by time he reached the siding where he left the flanger. It was *just* his damned luck to receive a new assignment which would send Murphy looking for him at the *worst* possible moment. He was well known on the railroad as a

35

malcontent and slacker, although he thought of himself as put-upon by an unfeeling world, and he had been written up several times for minor infractions and careless behavior. The one thing he *didn't* need was for Murphy to catch him napping; that bastard would grab any excuse to turn him in. He had the sure instinct of someone who didn't pull his weight, and it said he was pushing his luck. Murphy scared him, which fueled his rage.

Sure enough, the flanger was gone, parked at the end of the wye to get it out of the way. Its place was taken by his new assignment, SPMW 4034, backed up by a large road diesel.

"You took your own sweet time!" Lee Marris, his conductor, griped when he climbed aboard the locomotive.

"You're lucky I came back at all!" Burns snarled. "It's a jungle in the mess hall."

"Uh huh, I'm sure. We got orders to clear the yard, so let's get to it."

"Yeah, whatever."

His next destination was the cab of the spreader, taking the crew thermos with him as petty revenge. His brakeman, Pietro, greeted him at the door with little enthusiasm. "*Hola.* We got orders to scrape the yard."

"So I heard." At least they weren't going up the Hill, which was *some* good news anyway. Burns dropped the thermos next to his seat where Pietro couldn't get at easily. "Where's our third guy?"

Pietro shrugged. "Nobody said nothin' about no third guy."

"Shit!" Burns grabbed the radio handset. "Lee? Where's my third guy?"

"We don't have one. Murphy said they're short-handed, so you'll have t' make do."

"This is bullshit! There's supposed t' be three guys on a spreader!"

"There's lots of things 'supposed t' be' in this world. You'll just have to cope."

It was no more than what he could expect. This was Murphy's little game. Bastard. But there was nothing he could do, not when Murphy had it in for him. "This is some kind-a fucked!" He threw the radio mic down and turned to Pietro. "You got her ready t' go?"

"*Si.* I filled the oilers and topped off the hydraulics while waiting for you to return." He was usually a placid sort, but turned sullen around Burns, like a lot of people did.

"Marvelous." Burns grabbed the radio mic again. "We got clearance t' enter the main?"

"Ah, copy. We have the yard for the next four hours, so lets make the most of it."

He keyed the mic again. "Yeah, yeah. I'm doin' it." Just like that bastard Lee to camp out in the locomotive with his paperwork while they were short-handed here at the pointy end. He dropped the mic, settled in his seat, and grabbed the brake handle. "Extend to full width," he ordered as he released the brakes.

"What? Ain't we gonna check her out first?" The practice was to do a walk-around to give their unit the once over looking for possible problems before heading out.

Burns gave him an icy glare. "You wanna check 'er out, you just help yourself! It's too damned cold out there!"

Pietro hesitated, then shrugged.

§

Milepost 192, Norden:

Finally, at long last, *SPMW* 207 sighted the entrance to the snow shed at Norden. Five *freakin'* hours it took them to get here! They had to run the big rotary scoop continuously to dig their way through, and were slowed more than once to clear wind-blown drifts. Dan halted them just inside the western end of the show shed while Jesus climbed down to cut the rotary off from the rest of the consist. He took the moment to stretch his aching back. The shift was nearly half over, and his commute wasn't even done yet. Margret took over the two power units and shoved the camp cars

37

onto one of the covered sidings. Back on the main, the two rotaries were recoupled and moved onto the other siding to await their first assignment. As soon as they ground to a halt, the radio crackled to life:

"Okay, Dan, you and Jesus grab some chow. We'll likely get called soon. Margret will take over for now."

"Copy that."

"This is good, man," Jesus said as they hit the ballast. "Maybe you get some sleep, huh? You look like you need it."

Dan vented a weary sigh. "God, I hope so. I could use it!"

The snow shed was a boxy cave, dimly lit by the equipment lights, its walls and roof stained by countless locomotive exhausts. There were faint traces of snow blown in by the wind, but what they needed to be wary of were patches of ice: snow melt dripping in through cracks in the aged concrete and freezing again. The crew dorm and kitchen car were a lighted oasis ahead of them in the gloom, but that was cold comfort. They drew housekeeping power from hookups in the shed, which were vulnerable to outages. It was remarkable they had power at all in this weather.

"How long you think we'll be here, man-o?"

Dan pondered wearily. "Too long." For all they knew, they could be stranded out here until the spring thaw, if it ever came.

§

Milepost 178, Yuba Gap:

The wind was shrill and constant in their exposed position on the Butte Canyon bridge. It cut through the thickest layers of clothing and seeped in through every cuff and zipper to chill them to the bone. Breathing was painful. It wasn't possible to dress warmly enough in this wind. An article of faith among them was the only thing which could keep them warm would be space suits.

Fred paused to rest his aching shoulders, set the end of the heavy pry bar on the ties and leaned into the stiff wind. That wind made walking on the icy ties in the dark even more dangerous. They were trying, with great and wearing labor, to clear the worst

38

of it by chopping it up with ten pound pry bars. They broke the ice up nicely, but this sort of labor was an endless workout even worse than shoveling.

The wind kicked up, sending a chill through him, and he had to wonder if this was another fool's errand. The ice didn't matter since no one was likely to walk over this bridge; it certainly wouldn't interfere with train movements. He was beginning to think this was a wasted trip.

The snow was still coming down relentlessly, only to be blown off the bridge by the endless wind. He shifted his gaze, and saw the landscape around them was dimly lit. Dawn was approaching. He sagged in his weariness, realizing he worked through the night. It robbed him of what little enthusiasm he started with

He paused to check out the others. They were all suffering from this damned weather. He walked cautiously down the length of the bridge shining his flashlight on both sides to see how the work had progressed. It wasn't in tip-top shape, but it would do. The icy wind whipped at him, making him cringe. Fuckit.

"Alright everyone!" he called out. "Enough of this shit! Back to the truck!"

The truck's heater was a welcome blessing. Elwood hefted the crew thermos and doled out the last of their coffee, which was only lukewarm by then. Someone produced a flask of Tequila, and after some hesitation, Fred agreed to a hit all round.

"Boss, ah don't know how much longer we can keep this up," Elwood said. "We're all plum tuckered out, and it's gettin' close to outlawing time anyway."

"You're right, Elwood. We're not needed here. We'll wait until the Amtrak clears, then we'll head back to Emigrant Gap."

§

Milepost 206, Truckee, California:

The last few cars of an eastbound freight rumbled past followed by their helper engines, which created a minor stir among the passengers. Needless to say, the biggest stir was created by the much-endured Wilbur Harkness, who accosted Greenbaum and O'Brian when they came through the second of their four cars.

"We've been sitting here all day while this lousy railroad runs *freight trains* past us! Are humans less important than containers? *When* are you going to get this train moving?"

Reggie gave him an icy glare. "I'll check my social calendar. My secretary will get back to you, sometime."

"I have had *enough* of your insolence, mister! You can be sure I will file complaints against you—*all of you!*—when I reach San Francisco!"

"Man, you need t' chill," Charlie Parkhurst grumbled. "You're gonna bust an artery, you keep your little 'tude going."

"Yeah. And we'd appreciate a little peace and quiet, too," another passenger added.

"Helluva way to run a railroad!" Harkness stomped back to his seat and plopped in it, clearly determined to have his mad.

"Man just doesn't go with the flow," Parkhurst observed.

"So how soon will we be going?" Barbara asked, politely.

"Well, I..." Reggie was interrupted when his radio crackled to life:

"Amtrak train 15 to all crew, we got our clearance, and we're ready to get under way. Are you set back there, Reggie?"

Reggie keyed his handset. "Yeah, we're good here, George." He turned back to the two passengers. "To answer your question, I'd say right now."

"Cool."

"About fuckin' time," O'Brian muttered as the air brakes hissed. "How long d'you figure to reach Emeryville?"

Reggie sighed as he looked out the window at the dim light soaking through the cloud cover. "You tell me, then we'll both know."

"Hey, don't sweat it, man," Parkhurst said. "As long as we got life's little essentials, it's no biggie."

"Yeah," Barbara added. "A little wine, a little weed, something t' eat, some snuggle time, we're in no hurry." She cuddled next to Parkhurst, who affectionately nibbled her ear.

"God, I envy them," Reggie mumbled as he and O'Brian headed toward the buffet car.

"Yeah. At least *someone* has their heads straight!"

Even with clearance, the trip ahead would be endless as they crawled up the Sierras at a walking pace due to the white-out conditions. The latest word was more snow up ahead, and it was even snowing lightly here in the lea of the mountains. They warned him the signals on the Hill were acting up and the Signals department couldn't always find the relay boxes to make repairs. They needed to depend on railroad-issued GPS locators—assuming they worked—to report their positions so the dispatcher could guesstimate train movements. It was the lame leading the blind, and damned risky, but the alternative was to shut the railroad down until spring.

There was a faint lurch, and the 'City Of San Francisco' was moving for the first time in ten hours.

§

Milepost 192, Norden:

The kitchen car was a throwback to another era. Built for troop train service during the war, hundreds of these converted box cars were sold off to the railroads afterwards, where they became a staple of the Maintenance of Way forces.

The service was functional: foam trays, plastic utensils, paper napkins, and you took your meal back to the dorm car and ate at your berth. But for all that they provided essential hot meals for men who labored like pack mules under horrific conditions.

There was a narrow passage down one side running along the serving line. The rest of the car was filled with a remarkably compact kitchen, with a dry stores locker at one end, and a refrigerator at the other. A three-man crew worked these cars; the quality and selection depending on who was behind the counter, but at least it was hot and filling.

"How you doing, Dan?"

It took him a moment to focus in on the plump little woman on the other side of the serving line. "Oh. Hi, Trudy. Doin' okay, I guess. How're the grandkids?"

41

"They're having a great time being off from school with this snow. Better than you fellows are, I'd say."

"You got that right!" Dan was dismayed by how tired he was. It took an effort to marshal his thoughts. "It's good t' have you with us."

She gave him a mock-stern glare. "And where else would I be? At home tending to my knitting?"

Trudy was popular among the MoW crews: a widowed retiree, she worked with the Forest Service handling communications during the summer fire season, and recently started helping the snow crews in the winters. The railroad had its own dispatchers, thank you very much, but she proved priceless in the camp cars, where the chow was always hot and tasty and on time.

"Heaven forbid! I swear, Trudy, without you this ol' railroad would just curl up and die."

"You shouldn't swear, it's not polite." She spooned out a generous helping of beef stew (canned, but she performed miracles with spices), added a helping of lima beans, then waved her serving ladle menacingly. "Now you eat your greens, or I'll mop the floor with you!"

"Yes, ma'am!"

§

West Of Truckee, California:

Breakfast on the 'City Of San Francisco' was pancakes, little sausages, orange juice and hot coffee. The passengers descended on it like locusts, with enough pushing and shoving that the crew had to intervene. The panic subsided by time they got under way, and buffet car operations had pretty much returned to normal.

"Damn, it feels good to be moving again." Greenbaum fought off a cavernous yawn and rubbed his eyes to relieve the constant ache. "Lets pray the rest of the trip goes smoothly."

"Amen!" O'Brian said, fervently.

The 'City of San Francisco' rocked gently in the stiff wind, and they could tell from the faint vibrations coming up through the floor that they weren't traveling very fast. But they were traveling; a vast relief to them all.

"You look beat," O'Brian added. "Why don't you grab a nap? I'll cover for you."

Greenbaum found himself staring vacantly at the snow hitting a nearby window, and had to forcefully shake off the distraction. He *was* beat, in fact, especially after wrangling the chow line. Truth, he couldn't remember how long he'd been on his feet. "My own Irish mother hen. Truly I am blessed." He was interrupted by a jaw-breaking yawn. "Yeah, I'll do that. Thanks." He was distracted again by the snow on the window, about at the end of his rope. "Give me a couple hours," he said over his shoulder as he headed for the dorm section.

"Sure thing." O'Brian settled by the window after he left, watching the pale pre-dawn and enjoying the reassuring rumble and sway of the car. All was right with the world, for once. They were moving again, and Emeryville was finally within reach.

*****

Dawn:

A couple hours sleep didn't help much, but it was better than nothing. Conductor Greenbaum did a quick washcloth bath on his face and neck in the crew dorm section of the buffet car before donning his dark blue coat and rejoining the world of the living.

He ran into O'Brian in the corridor near the kitchen, who asked, "How you doing?"

Reggie gave him a baleful look. "I'm alive, I think." He glanced out the aisle window, but couldn't see much except the silhouettes of passing trees against a pale background. "What's our progress?"

O'Brian replied with an angry scowl. "We were held over an hour for a trackside warning; the dispatcher stopped us until they were sure about a slide. We're moving again, but we're only now coming up to Horseshoe Curve."

"Five miles? Is that all?"

"Yeah, well you'll be pleased to know we're now rocketing along at a blistering five miles per hour. Can't see shit out there, so we're groping our way on dispatcher's verbal orders."

Reggie gave him a dismayed look. "It's really that bad around here?"

"So I'm told. I heard from some regulars that getting over the Hill these days is as much a matter of luck as anything else. The signals can't be trusted, so we have to keep reporting our GPS position to the dispatchers so they know where everyone is."

"And hope everyone else does, too. Helluva way to run a railroad!"

"You got that right. I heard the only reason they keep the Hill open is they're desperate for freight movement. If this wasn't the main line to Chicago, they'd shut everything down and wait for spring."

"Thank God for GPS; we might never be seen again otherwise." They both felt the car sway gently and slowly rotate as it dug into the Curve. They'd reached the end of Cold Creek

44

Canyon, and were starting to climb back along the far side. It was progress of a sort, every bit of which was treasured.

"Hell, when we get to Emeryville I may just put in for retirement. It'll take that long!"

"Yeah, if we live to see the day..."

...The car gave an odd lurch. "What th' hell?" Reggie muttered. Before they could react, the car began shaking violently, bouncing up and down in a sickening see-saw motion.

"We're on the ground!" O'Brian staggered forward, bracing himself against the car's gyrations, and yanked the emergency brake handle in the vestibule. There was a shuddering, grinding crash as the car scraped against a stone cut. A window in the dining section shattered as dishes and chairs flew around the dining section and a chorus of panicked voices filled the car.

That shook Reggie out of his confusion. He keyed his radio mic while bracing himself on the bulkhead. "City train to forward section! We're on the ground back here!"

The air brakes came on before a reply came back:

"How bad is it? Anyone hurt?"

"I don't know yet. Checking." After an agonizing moment while they wondered if the car would roll over, the train came to rest. Reggie and O'Brian looked at each other in dismay, shaken by going through one of any railroader's worst nightmares. "You okay?" Reggie mumbled at last.

"Yeah." O'Brian's hands were shaking.

Otis came by from the dorm headed for the dining section. "Otis! Get your people together and check the passengers! Help anyone who's hurt!"

Otis gave him a distracted nod. "Right, boss."

Reggie and O'Brian stood uncertainly for a moment, trying to collect their wits. Through the door at the end of the car, they could see the next car was sitting at an odd angle compared to the buffet. "It could-a been worse," Reggie said at last. "Come on. Let's check the damage."

§

45

Finding a way off the train took some doing. The buffet car, first in line, didn't have vestibules, and reaching the steps in the first coach meant braving the buckled coupling between cars. The two sat at such an angle that the weather-tight diaphragms between cars were forced apart, leaving a gap wide enough for a foot to slip through, and letting a raw wind into the car. The two of them stepped gingerly across the gap and tried to open the coach door. It was stuck on that side, buckled in its frame, the window cracked. After trying to force it failed, they headed further aft through a swarm of confused, apprehensive passengers.

One elderly lady in particular seemed on the verge of panic. "This is terrible!" She clung to Reggie's hand, trembling. "We're lost in the middle of nowhere!"

"Don't you worry, ma'am. We can handle this weather," Reggie assured her, speaking out loud so everyone could hear. "It's like this all across the country. The highways are a mess and the airlines are grounded, but the trains are still moving. That's our greatest strength. We've had a minor accident, but the railroads know how to deal with these things. We'll have it straightened out shortly."

"But...we're in Donner Pass..."

O'Brian put on a bold front. "That was the old days; we tamed this pass over a century ago. Some of the very best snow-fighting equipment and crews are assigned here. It's not like we're lost at sea or something. They know where we are, and what to do."

Reggie's portable radio crackled to life:

"Amtrak Train 15 to UP dispatcher, we are stopped and derailed. Two cars partly off the track, no word yet on casualties."

"Roseville dispatcher to Amtrak 15, what is your position?"

"Ah...our GPS position puts us at about milepost 201."

"There. You see?" Reggie turned up the volume so everyone could hear. "They know we're stuck, and they'll be up shortly to retrieve us."

"Copy, Amtrak 15. Roseville dispatcher to train 5614 West. The train ahead of you is derailed. Be prepared to stop and render assistance."
"UP 5614 West, we copy."

"See? No problems," O'Brian added. They'll be along presently, and for the moment we're sitting pretty."

The mighty Wilbur Harkness didn't share his optimism, and wasn't shy about expressing his frustration. He jumped up from his seat and confronted the two mid-car. "*Look* what you've done now! Can't you even keep this train on the rails? We're trapped out here in the middle of *nowhere* thanks to you incompetents! It wouldn't surprise me if we all wind up freezing to death!"

That was *exactly* the wrong thing to say and *exactly* the wrong moment to say it. O'Brian grabbed his lapels and got up in his face. "Standard equipment on these trains includes a straightjacket for unruly passengers," he hissed. "Now you *sit down* and *shut up*, or we'll have you bound and sedated!"

That took the starch out of Wilbur Harkness, who plopped in his seat and sulked, grumbling to himself. The rest of the passengers didn't seem to share his alarm, and since everything was under control, the two of them moved on. A bit farther along they came by Charlie Parkhurst. "Straightjacket, huh?" he muttered. "You wish."

"Yeah. We may need it with that panicky bastard."

§

Somewhere it must have been a bright, sunny morning; here at Horseshoe Curve the cloud cover and swirling snow reduced visibility to a matter of yards. The two of them hit dirt, flashlights in hand, and worked their way forward as the icy wind cut them like knives. They quickly saw the extent of the damage. The coupled ends of the first and second cars were wedged up against an outlying bluff protruding from a cut made for the right of way.

They scrambled up on the rock outcropping to examine the damage. The rear of the buffet car and the vestibule of the coach were crumpled, but intact. Both cars were well off the track centerline. The rear-facing truck of the buffet car was twisted

47

sideways, and the coach next behind had one wheel off, but the couplers kept the first car from careening totally out of control.

"Aw, Jesus...Frog on a lily-pad!" O'Brian griped. "Talk about bad luck!" They *would* derail in the one spot where a rocky bluff hemmed in the right of way. "We'll never get to Emeryville!"

"It...doesn't look too bad," Reggie said, hollowly. Their earlier bravado didn't seem so convincing now. "Those rocks likely saved us from goin' down into th' valley.."

"Dammit! This'll be *at least* another day's delay!"

"At least they know where we are. They'll come t' get us."

To their right, the land opened out into the Cold Creek Canyon, now tapering sharply downward from the grade as the right of way climbed into the mountains. To their left was a solid wall of snow, the uncleared right of way for track two, and beyond that the ground rose sharply. Track one ran along a narrow shelf cleared by ongoing snow removal efforts.

"I don't know what we'll do for food service," Reggie grumbled. "It'll take weeks to repair these two, and I doubt there's another buffet car on the west coast."

"And we can't run with 'em boarded up."

The center door of the last double-decker just forward opened, and George Reinsbach jumped down and struggled aft to where they were. "Wot th' hell happened?"

"We must-a hit some ice, or maybe a rock."

"It's these lightweight cars," O'Brian added. "They weren't designed for these conditions. Those hulking battleships of yours rolled over whatever we hit, but we couldn't."

"I wouldn't be surprised if this wind had a part in it too," Reggie said. The gusts must have been doing thirty miles per hour or better, driving the snow into them like a sand blaster.

Reinsbach pondered the sight for a moment, then shook off the distraction. "Okay, check your people t' make sure no one's hurt, and get a flagman out. We got a freight comin' up behind us." He turned and headed back to his half of the train. "I called it in," he yelled over his shoulder. "They should be here to help us soon."

"I hope so," Reggie grumbled. "It's freezing out here."

§

Back inside, the passengers had already retreated to the forward part of the dining section where Otis and one of his stewards were treating an injured passenger while the two cooks were sweeping up the broken glass and trying to improvise a blanket over the window. When Otis spotted them, he left the work to his assistant and came to report.

"We got one with some facial cuts, ain't too bad. We got a few bumps and bruises, and a lot of folks shook up, but it ain't much. We was lucky."

"Yeah." Reggie and O'Brian could both breathe a sigh of relief. "What about further back?"

"Ah looked already. It's just this car and the next. They's a few folks bruised up a bit, but they alright."

"Okay." Reggie pondered for a bit, trying to collect his wits. "Issue free drinks to anyone who needs it."

Otis nodded and went back to his passengers.

With the immediate crisis under control, the two of them stood there indecisively for a moment before Reggie said, "Well? You heard the man. We got a freight coming up behind us, and we sure as *hell* don't want t' get cold-nosed out here."

O'Brian sighed. "Yeah. That's why I get the big bucks, I guess." He stopped at the dorm section to retrieve his overcoat and some flares, then set off reluctantly into the storm.

§

Milepost 192, Norden:

Due to some odd quirk of radio acoustics, the message from the 'City' came in loud and clear on board the Snow Extra:

> *"Amtrak Train 15 to UP dispatcher, we are stopped and derailed. Two cars partly off the track, no word yet on casualties."*

"Shit," Marcus muttered as they listened to the byplay. The conversation in the office caboose ended abruptly as everyone strained to hear. Earl Jenks, laborers' crew lead, scowled, but said nothing. There was a nervous murmur from the others.

"Roseville dispatcher to Amtrak 15, what is your position?"

"Ah...our GPS position puts us at about milepost 201."

"Copy, Amtrak 15. Roseville dispatcher to train 5614 West. The train ahead of you is derailed. Be prepared to stop and render assistance."

"UP 5614 West, we copy."

"That's *just* what we need," Marcus grumbled. "Instant Cluster Fuck, in this weather."

Earl shook his head in dismay. "At milepost 201, too; right on the Curve. That's a bad spot."

"It sure is. Go wake Dan and Jesus."

§

Dan was drifting off in one of the double berths when Earl shook him awake. "Huh? Wha?"

"We got word of a derailment up the line. Marcus wants t' see you two."

"Aw fer Christ's sake! Doesn't it ever end around here?"

"If it did they'd lay you off, so consider yourself lucky."

§

Dan and Jesus arrived in the office caboose a few minutes later, still groggy and half asleep. "What you got, Marcus?" Dan asked. Marcus shushed him and turned up the radio volume:

"Amtrak 15 to Roseville dispatcher, we're right on the Curve with two cars in the rear of the train down with one truck each off. We have some minor damage, and only a few minor injuries we've already treated."

"It doesn't sound so bad," Dan muttered.

"Still, they'll need the big hook," Jesus said.

Marcus turned to him. "Yeah. I contacted Colfax, and they said Roseville is already getting their shit together. I want you two to take the rotary up to clear the way for them."

"Huh? What about the tractor-mounted hooks?" Dan objected. "Truckee is closer, and that doesn't seem like such a big deal."

"Yeah, man," Jesus added. "Let them deal with it. We don' want t' hog all the glory."

Marcus gave them both a somber look. "They can't get track mounts in there in this weather, so we'll have t' do this the old-fashioned way. In any case, it's not ours to wonder why, so get a move-on."

Dan was about to protest, but the radio cut him off:

"Copy, Amtrak. We're sending the hook from Roseville your way, but figure it will take several hours to get there in this weather, depending on track conditions."

"That's our cue," Marcus said as he turned to Dan and Jesus. "Take Earl and some of his guys along to help get the train moving again. We'll flag the wrecker here so the Amtrak can bring their forward part over the Hill; then the big hook can get in there."

"I'll take Antonio with us," Earl said. "We might need his fireworks." Antonio was the team's explosives expert, helpful when fallen trees or rock slides must be dealt with.

"Yeah, right. Draw some of your dynamite from the supply car. Let's get you guys moving."

"Why us?" Dan demanded. "We've been on since leaving Colfax, and this is likely to put us over our hours. Margret's on duty now, why not send her?"

Marcus hesitated for a long moment, then glanced at Earl, who shrugged. "I know you guys are tired, but honestly, Margret is too inexperienced at this, especially going up where slides are happening. It's only nine miles. This'll be a simple out-and-back, after that you can sign off for twelve, I promise."

Dan glanced at Earl, and sighed. "Yeah, right. Talk about a Cluster-Fuck!" His nap proved shorter than he'd hoped.

§

Milepost 201, Horseshoe Curve:

Reggie returned to the buffet car after checking the rest of his section, and ran into Parkhurst and Barbara, who were helping tend to the injured. "How's it look?" Parkhurst asked.

51

"Fortunately it was just these first two cars. The damage doesn't look too severe."

"Bummer, man. At least there weren't many people hurt."

Reggie gestured at Barbara, who was resetting the bandages Otis applied to their facial injury earlier. "I appreciate the help, but she shouldn't..."

"She's an Emergency Room RN. She knows her stuff."

"...Oh."

"So what now, man? This is gonna hold us up even longer, isn't it?"

"Well, I..." His radio crackled to life:

"Reggie? This is George. Bring your passengers up to the double-deck section. We'll go on over the Hill, then they can bring the big hook in to deal with your two cars."

Reggie keyed his portable. "Copy that, George." He turned back to Parkhurst. "There you have it. The worst is over."

"Uh uh." Parkhurst jerked a thumb at the next car. "You still have to deal with Mighty Mouth."

Reggie glared at him, then waved an admonishing finger. "You know, I think I'll have to hate you."

§

Sure enough, Mighty Mouth, the regrettable Wilbur Harkness, turned up a short while later in a rare mood. "You people ought to be in jail!" he shouted. "The way you run this railroad is criminal! *Criminal!* I'll report this *disaster* to the highest authorities! I'll see that all of you are fired!"

Right then Reggie was in no mood to put up with him, and honestly didn't care about his threats any more. "Yeah? Well for *your* information, you are interfering with an interstate transportation emergency; that's a *Federal* offense! So if there's any reporting to be done around here, *your* name will be at the top of the list!"

That took Harkness aback, but only for a moment. "Are you threatening me, sir?" he snarled. "If so, my lawyers will make mincemeat out of you!"

52

"That was no threat, that was a plan of action! And I'll put that plan *in* action as soon as we get to Emeryville unless you *sit down* and *shut the fuck up!*"

Harkness was duly scandalized to be talked to in such a manner. "You're nothing but a public servant! Who the *hell* do you think you are to come that tone with me?"

"I am the *captain* of this train, and I can have you put off it, right here, in the middle of nowhere, in a blizzard, if you pose a threat. And I guaran-*damn*-tee you that's *exactly* what I'll do if you don't *pipe down!*"

"Threat? You're the one making threats! This'll look mighty bad for you in my complaint!"

"Yeah? Well it'll be your word against mine, and *my* word is the *official* word!"

"Hey, Mighty Mouth," Parkhurst called out. "He's got plenty of witnesses, so don't push your luck!" That was greeted by a rumbled chorus of approval from the other passengers.

Harkness turned to him in confusion. "Mighty Mouth?"

"Yeah, that's right: Mighty Mouth." Parkhurst addressed the other passengers. "Seems appropriate, doesn't it?"

The people in the buffet began chanting, "Mighty Mouth! Mighty Mouth! Mighty Mouth!"—a few at first, but the chant quickly filled the car as everyone joined in. Harkness fumed in impotent rage, then beat a retreat with the chant ringing in his ears.

"Next contestant!" Parkhurst called out, evoking a round of laughter. He gave Reggie a sardonic grin. "That guy takes all the fun out of being in a train wreck!"

"Yeah, he does." Reggie realized his hands were shaking. One thing he *didn't* need was all this stress. "Thanks."

"It's cool, man."

One good thing to come of the confrontation was the mood in the buffet car seemed lighter and more relaxed afterwards.

§

Milepost 192, Norden:

"This isn't fair!" Margret protested when Dan gave her the news. "I'm on duty now. I should go!"

53

"Marcus is worried about slides..."

"There's slides everywhere! I don't need t' be babied! I can handle this run just as well as you can."

Dan retreated before her outrage, arms out in a defensive posture. "Hey, this was Marcus's idea! I don't like it any more than you do."

"Marcus! That arrogant, sexist bastard needs t' be taught a lesson!" She was working up into a mood to deliver it, too. Her brakeman, Willy, hovered in the far corner of the cab watching the drama in wide-eyed dismay. "I won't stand still for this! He'll answer for it!"

"Well you can rip him a new one for me while you're at it!"

"Damned right I will! You watch!" She left in a blue cloud; everyone knew she could swear like a mule-skinner when upset. Willy hesitated for a long moment, gave Dan and Jesus a nervous look, and followed her.

"I tell ya, man-o, I don' want *ever* t' get on *her* bad side!" Jesus was awe-struck by her command of the language, as were most of those unfortunate enough to earn her wrath.

"Yeah. You and me both." Dan *almost* felt sorry for Marcus.

There was a knock on the far side door, and Earl looked in. "All clear?"

"For the moment."

"I got my guys in the rear rotary. Let's get th' *hell* out-a Dodge before Hurricane Margret comes back!"

They were making ready to get under way when Jesus said, "Hey, man-o? We need t' leave one of the diesels behind t' provide power for th' camp cars."

Dan hesitated, then groaned. "Yeah, dammit!" Without one of the diesels to provide power, the camp cars would freeze if Norden's utility connection failed; all too likely in these conditions. But that meant they'd have to face the worst part of the Hill with one aging locomotive. He sighed in frustration. "Why don't we have an erupting volcano as well, just to make things interesting?"

Jesus got up and pulled on his gloves, ready to uncouple the consist. "Yeah, man. That way we be warm, huh?"

§

Milepost 201, Horseshoe Curve:

"Alright everyone, we're going to move everybody forward to the main part of the train." Reggie's voice of calm authority coming over the PA system throughout the four cars of the single-deck section helped to calm the jittery passengers. "Please be sure to collect your belongings, and dress warmly. As you can see, it's pretty cold out there." The passengers needed a lot of calming down, as did Reggie, not that he would show them his frazzled nerves. "We will start the evacuation in a few minutes. Please remain on the train until we can escort you forward. Thank you."

"Well, that's the 'easier said' part." Parkhurst was lounging in the dining section while Barbara finished up with the last of the injured.

"Yeah. I'll get back t' you on the 'done' part."

§

Milepost 178, Butte Canyon:

Fred was shaken out of a pleasant drowse when Elwood said, "That passenger train is sure taking their own sweet time, ain't they, boss?"

He was right, now that Fred thought about it. He glanced at his watch: time was getting on. "Yeah, they are." He shook off his drowsiness, sat up straighter, and reached for the radio mic. "Maintenance of Way at Butte Canyon to the Roseville dispatcher, over?"

It took several minutes before the reply came back:

"Roseville Dispatcher to Maintenance of Way Butte Canyon."

"Dispatch, how soon will that Amtrak get here? We're running on the law, and need to sign off."

Again, the reply was delayed for several minutes, which had Fred wondering if something was up.

"What's the holdup?" Elwood grumbled.

Finally an answer came:

"Maintenance of Way at Butte Canyon, be advised the Amtrak is derailed east of Summit. There's no telling how long it'll take to clean it up, so you might as well sign off."

Fred greeted that with a weary curse for all the time they spent out here twiddling their thumbs. "Ah, copy that, Dispatch. We're returning to Emigrant Gap where we'll sign off duty."

"Copy that, Maintenance of Way, but shag your butts on it. We'll be sending the hook up in a bit, and there's a work train already en-route."

"Copy that, dispatch. Maintenance of Way at Butte Canyon departing for Emigrant Gap. Out."

"Shit, man," Elwood grumbled as Fred put the hi-rail in gear. "This railroad's falling apart."

"At least we'll get some sleep," one of the others said. "And something t' eat."

"Which reminds me, who's on kitchen duty?" Fred asked as he gunned the hi-rail and headed into the storm.

"I am," Elwood said. That was one bit of good news.

§

Milepost 201, Horseshoe Curve:

O'Brian was half-frozen when the headlights of the approaching freight lit up the snowy gloom. He managed to ignite a flare, and stood waving it until the lead engine ground to a halt twenty feet short.

"How's it look?" the freight engineer asked when he made it to the *heavenly* warmth of the cab.

"Two cars derailed, one truck each, some minor damage. No serious casualties." He pulled his overcoat open and stood in front of the heater vent like a flasher exposing himself. "We must have hit some ice."

Just then the radio sputtered to life:

"Roseville dispatcher to UP 5614 West?"

The engineman grabbed the radio mic. "UP 5614 West, we've made contact with the derailed Amtrak. Over?"

"UP 5614 West, you are authorized to return to Truckee. If they have any critical casualties, bring them with you. Over?"

"Wonderful," the second engineer grumbled. "We'll be stuck there forever."

"So how many injured do you have?" The leading engineman peered through the forward windows trying to spot the distant lights of the 'City', but the headlight's glare turned the swirling snow into a white wall.

"Nothing much. We only have a few bumps and bruises."

"Pretty tame, as derailments go, huh?"

"Thankfully! It was enough excitement for me, thank you!"

The lead engineman peered into the gloom ahead. "How far up are you?"

"Maybe a thousand feet." The two enginemen didn't say anything. Company rules required a flagman to go three thousand feet back, but it must have been a monumental grind to get this far. Plus, at the speed the freight moved, a thousand feet was ample.

"So what will you do here?" the other crewman asked.

O'Brian sighed. "We're moving our passengers to the forward part of the train, beyond the derailment. We'll go on over the Hill so the hook can come in and clean up."

"You gonna leave a flagman here?"

"If they do, it won't be me! Mark this on your GPS; I'm not gonna stay out here in this slop." It was against the rules, but the only traffic likely to come this way would be the Truckee rotary.

"Yeah, I hear you. Sorry about what happened. We need to get back down the Hill." He picked up his radio mic. "UP 5614 West to Roseville dispatcher. Amtrak reports no serious casualties. We are ready to come back down to Truckee. Over?"

"Roseville dispatcher to UP 5614 West. You are cleared to come back down the Hill."

"Copy that. UP 5614 West, proceeding east to Truckee." The engineman punched the button for their tactical frequency. "Bert? You still back there?"

"Ah...that's an affirmative, head end."

"We got orders t' head back to Truckee. You take over and lead us down, over?" Their retrograde move would be handled by the last set of helper engines on the rear of the train.

"Yeah, copy that. We're heading out."

O'Brian climbed down and watched as the freight crawled slowly back down the track until it vanished in the swirling white. It left him feeling awfully alone. He finally sighed, hefted his switchman's lantern, and trudged up the track toward the 'City Of San Francisco', lost somewhere in the distance. This was one train he sincerely did *not* want to miss.

§

Milepost 201, Horseshoe Curve:

Reggie was the only one left available to guide the passengers forward after he posted the dining car staff in each vestibule to keep people from leaving the train on their own. There was nothing for it, so he called the people gathered in the buffet to order. "Alright, everyone. We're going to start the evacuation. Let's have the first ten people. We'll take ten at a time so we can be sure no one gets lost out there. The rest of you, please wait here until I come back for the next lot. You don't want to go wandering around in this weather, believe me."

The first batch pulled themselves together, including their injured passenger, who didn't seem all that bad. Barbara went along to tend to him and the other minor casualties while Charlie Parkhurst remained behind after they shared a brief hug and kiss.

Before they left, Reggie took him aside. "I need a hand here, will you? Please keep things orderly, and set up the next batch of ten. I'll be back in a few."

Parkhurst nodded. "Sure, but what do I do about Mighty Mouth?"

Reggie offered an aggrieved look. "Give him a mirror and let him argue himself to death!"

Parkhurst grinned. "You got it, boss. But I get my Railroading merit badge for this."

"Hell, I'll get you a conductor's hat!"

"Deal!"

§

Reggie and Otis helped the passengers into the next car where they could start their journey at the first vestibule, opposite the jammed door. The two derailed cars blocked the right of way on the open side, so they had to go the back way through the narrow gap between the train and the snow bank. It was a dark, treacherous, unnerving journey over icy, uneven terrain with only the lights of the car windows to guide them. At least they were out of the worst wind, although there was a steady trickle of blown snow coming down from the overburden next to them.

"Alright everyone, stay together." Reggie tried to sound calm and reassuring for people who had been through a lot lately, a train wreck being only the latest hassle. "Watch your step. This is very uneven, so watch your footing." Truth be known, he needed the reassurance as well.

Fortunately it wasn't that far from the vestibule of the first coach along the buffet car to the last double-decker in line. When they got there, George Reinsbach and two of his porters were waiting for them.

"Are these your casualties?" Reinsbach asked.

"Yeah. These are our only significant cases." Included was an elderly gentleman with his face obscured by surgical tape, three more with miscellaneous bandages and a large bruise on one forehead, and the elderly woman still teetering on the edge of hysterics.

Reinsbach studied the lot by the light of a trainman's lantern. "Not too bad," he muttered. "It could-a been much worse."

Reggie summoned Barbara forth. "This young lady is an emergency room RN. She treated our injured."

Reinsbach looked her up and down. "Good. At least we have *someone* with more than first aid training!"

§

Milepost 171, Emigrant Gap:

It seemed like forever before the odometer on the hi-rail said they'd gone the distance to their base. Fred stopped the truck and peered around uncertainly. "Anyone see anything?"

"Not a damned thing, boss," Elwood said.

That was unnerving. They were lost in the middle of nowhere, in white-out conditions, the wind was picking up, and they were running low on fuel. Fred grabbed the radio mic. "Ernesto, this is Fred. Are you guys in at base?"

"Si, Jefe. It's snowing like a bugger out there."

"Yeah, we noticed. We should be right outside, but we can't see anything. Light us up, huh?"

"Uno momento, Jefe."

A few minutes later they saw a faint glow in the gloom on their right: the headlights of the other hi-rail. They'd come up a hundred yards short.

"Damn, that was close," Elwood said. Close, but no cigar: if they didn't have that light, they could wander lost in this blizzard until they all froze to death.

It took a few minutes to get the hi-rail down off its track wheels and pull off the right of way next to the other truck, and the crew gratefully turned in for the first rest they'd had in fourteen hours.

§

Inside the crew shack was a haven of light and warmth which felt heavenly to the weary men. In the center was a lounge-cum-classroom where maintenance operations could be planned. To the left, a trestle table and folding chairs separated the kitchen from the rest of the room. On the right were some improvised showers and

60

a bunk room with lockers and double-tiered metal framed beds. It was rude and crude, but effective as a forward outpost for the ongoing effort to tame the Hill.

Most of them either crashed at the large table, or headed for the double bunks at the far end of the building. Elwood headed for the kitchen and started sorting through the refrigerator and cabinets to see what he could scare up, while Fred collapsed at his desk.

"You guys looked like what the cat dragged in." Their shelter also paid host to two electricians from the Signals department. "I thought we had it bad!"

"Yeah, well, some of us answer to a higher calling," Fred grumbled. "How's it with you?"

"We got the repeater fixed, for now at least. We decided to stay right here where it's nice and warm until we get called t' fix something else."

"Half the time we can't even find the signals boxes," his partner said. "Stuff's buried under *yards* of this shit! You ask me, we won't have this railroad running right until spring."

"Ain't that the truth!" Fred slumped on his elbows and sat staring at the schematic map on his desk. The more he stared at that map, the more his earlier doubts began to nag him. Finally he turned to the rest of them. "Ernesto? Did you clean those turnouts like I said to?"

"Yeah, man," Ernesto growled. "We cleaned 'em, jus' like you told us."

"You know how important that is. So what shape are they?"

Ernesto turned combative at his badgering. "Hey, *puto*, we worked our *asses* off out there! We cleaned them turnouts like they never been cleaned before!"

The others on his team nodded their agreement, so Fred figured he was telling the truth for once, and he was too tired to argue it anyway. "Alright, you say so. But we got the wrecker coming up from Roseville, and if the big hook goes on the ground, we're gonna be shit-out-a-luck!"

"Yeah? Well you don' believe me, you can go clean 'em you'self!" Ernesto wasn't satisfied by Fred's reluctant concession, and he had a temper.

"Hey guys, it's all cool, ya' dig?" Elwood said. "Let's chill and get some dinner. We still got them chicken parts; what-say t' some of my jambalaya?" Elwood learned to cook from his momma in New Orleans. His offer was eagerly accepted, and put any arguments to rest.

*****

Mid-Morning:

The trip from Norden was an ominous portent for the men who worked snow removal on the Hill. Norden was high enough that they were socked in by the low-lying cloud cover. The snow was relentless, and rotary 207 shook constantly from the buffeting winds. Despite the steam generator in the rear of the unit, the temperature dropped steadily until their breath came in clouds of steam, and their hands and faces ached. Once they left the shelter of the Norden snow shed, the wind found its way in through every crack and opening, bringing arctic chill with it.

"It's doin' the best it can, man-o," Jesus said as he fiddled with the steam heater's controls. That steam was there to keep the machinery from freezing up; crew comfort was secondary.

"Yeah," Dan grumbled. "I sometimes think we'd be better off with the old steam-driven plows."

"No lie, *compadre.*" Jesus resumed his station peering out the portholes for obstacles ahead, although they couldn't see much of anything with the snow and fog.

"Where are we?"

Jesus examined the portable GPS unit. "We're about to hit the Summit Tunnel."

No sooner did he say it then the snow abruptly quit, and their headlight showed them the long bore through solid rock ahead of them. Dan cut the rotor back to idle, and the consist trundled along, safe from the weather for the moment.

"How bad d'you think the wreck is?" Jesus asked after a bit.

Dan pondered the question as they waddled through the narrow darkness. "Two trucks off, minor damage, doesn't sound so bad."

The sound of the diesel behind them changed pitch, and their speed crept up. With one of their two locomotives left behind to provide power for the camp cars in the snow shed, their singleton was working on this grade. Neither of them was happy with the situation. These old locomotives were too weary for the relentless service they were being called upon to deliver. If their unit quit now, they'd be in a bad way. The engine's sound shifted further, and their speed picked up a bit more. They were across the Summit and on the downgrade for Truckee and beyond.

"*Si,* that wreck don' sound so bad. Still, in this weather, getting those cars back on the rails is gonna be a miserable job."

"Yeah. Thankfully we're not with the wreckers!" Neither of them wanted to talk about what *really* worried them.

The snow returned abruptly as they emerged from the far end of the tunnel, blinding them once again. Dan was caught by surprise, and kicked the rotor back into action as they slowed like they'd run into a sand bank.

Jesus examined the GPS again. "We coming up on Milepost 196, man-o. Only another five miles to go."

Dan didn't answer. They were on single track now, starting back at the western entrance to Summit Tunnel. Like a lot of this road, the right of way wound along the side of the hills and through occasional cuts. There was always high ground on one side or the other, or sometimes both, with the attendant danger of avalanches. Actually this stretch wasn't as bad as some—further east, around Snow Shed 47, was where it got gnarly. But the danger was real nonetheless, as the moments when the consist faltered and dug into snow drifts showed.

The huge rotor blade dug in once again. The whine of the motors became more labored as the WHEEL SLIP buzzer sounded. Dan eased a notch off the throttle and hit the sanders as Jesus added more power to the rotor. Rotary 207 staggered, seemed to choke for a bit as the drive gears whined, then the sensation eased as they dug their way clear. The two of them settled in their seats and went back to their vigil. Five more miles to go.

§

Milepost 107, Roseville Shops, California:

"You wanted t' see me, boss?" Walter Karns asked the Roseville Yardmaster when he reached his office in response to a beeper alert.

"Yeah, Walter." The Yardmaster set his clipboard aside and gave him his undivided attention. "We got a wreck up at

Horseshoe Curve. Passenger train. It don't sound too bad, but they'll need the big hook. I'm calling Gus in, but there's no telling how soon he'll get here. You go ahead and get set up so you can get out of here as soon as he arrives."

Walter took the news calmly enough. One of his duties was as the foreman of their enormous wrecking crane. He dealt with this sort of thing all the time, especially in winter. "So what we got there?"

"I hear two cars, one truck each, plus some minor damage."

Walter greeted that with a snort. "Shit, is that all? What about using truck cranes? Truckee's got a couple of 'em."

"Yeah. Word is the weather's too rough for them fancy civilian contractors, so it looks like you're elected."

Walter took a high attitude. "Clear over t' Horseshoe? Ain't hardly worth my time. You might as well send some Cub Scouts up there t' take care of it."

The Yardmaster matched his bravado with a wry grin. "Yeah, but we don't have any Cub Scouts, so we'll have t' make do with your toy. Think you can manage?"

His bluff called, Walter got serious. "We'll have a job on our hands in this weather. This might take a while, but we can do it."

"Good. I'm putting together a work train to get out of here PDQ with some grunt force. You can follow as soon as you're ready."

Walter nodded and turned for the door. "On it, boss."

§

Milepost 197, Snow Shed 47:

They finally reached the comparative shelter of Snow Shed 47, and Dan brought the rotary to a halt as they studied the landscape ahead. The line had dropped to where they were below the clouds again, and this was a good place to pause and take stock. The stretch ahead was known for its slides and wind-blown drifts. The snow let up a bit for the time being, and the pale light filtering through the clouds let them see ahead maybe a quarter mile. Neither of them was thrilled by the sight which greeted them; it wasn't reassuring.

As soon as the track left the safety of Shed 47, it vanished under a smooth layer of snow flowing down hill toward Donner Lake, somewhere off to the left. There'd been an avalanche here; some time ago from the look of it since new snowfall covered the uneven, tumbled pack. It was likely the Amtrak train wouldn't have made it through here even if they hadn't been delayed.

"That's got to be...what? Twelve feet in spots?"

"*Si*, man-o. It don't look good." Twelve feet was about the limit of what they could handle, and only for short stretches at best.

"No, it don't." Dan studied the pale landscape ahead with deep misgivings. "At least that slide'll take some of the pressure off. We *should* get through without trouble."

Jesus turned and gave him a solemn look. "There's many things *should* be in this universe, *compadre*."

"You got *that* right!"

Just then Earl came climbing into their cab. "So how's it look?" He studied the sight ahead, solemn and tight-lipped. "What d'ya think? You gonna risk it?"

"That's what we're here for," Dan said, unhappily.

"And we gotta get t' them passengers so they can come out," Jesus added. "We can't jus' leave 'em up here."

That was the trump card in anyone's game. Earl nodded. "Okay, why don't I get our guys off the train in case you get hit? We'll be able t' help you then." He was right, damn him. He climbed down again, leaving the two to contemplate the risky move ahead.

"You know, man-o, Marcus was right: this ain't no place for Margret. She ain't ready yet."

"Yeah. But who would be?"

Dan opened his window and peered aft to see if Earl had his half-dozen off the consist. The snow shed was shrouded in stygian darkness, and he couldn't see much beyond the end of the rotary. A quick toot on the whistle brought a distant flashlight waving a 'go ahead' signal.

"Okay, here we go." He shut his window, released the brakes and goosed the throttle, and rotary 207 started moving again; digging into the snow bank.

Jesus leaned out the cab door and studied the way ahead, then waved him forward cautiously. "Alright, dead slow, man." Dan opened the throttle a couple more notches, and the huge rotor dug into the slide, throwing a spray of snow to their left, down hill. They came out from under the shed roof into the pale light, the rotary bucking and choking on the heavy load it tried to ingest. Jesus gave the rotor more power, the snow flew in a solid arc, and their pace steadied as the rotary found its balance...

"Hold it!"

Dan slammed the throttle shut and hit the air in one swift move. "What is it?"

"We got a tree down on the track." They'd managed to gain all of fifty yards.

"Wonderful. I don't know why I thought this would be a routine trip."

Jesus pulled the door shut. "This *is* a routine trip, *compadre*."

"Yeah, more's the pity." Dan called Earl on his hand-held. "Earl? We got some business for you. Roust Antonio out, will you?"

§

Milepost 201, Horseshoe Curve:

They finally managed, somehow, to get all the passengers from the single-deck section tucked away in the double-decker cars; but it wasn't easy. The diner and lounge cars couldn't begin to absorb one hundred thirty-two passengers between them, so people were crowded in everywhere they could find an odd corner to sit on their carry-on luggage or plop on the floor.

It soon turned into a monumental game of musical chairs as they tried to reserve too few seats for those who needed them most. Needless to say, the priceless Mighty Mouth demanded priority seating, and reacted predictably when he didn't get his way. George Reinsbach told the porters to distribute all the spare pillows and blankets, but there weren't nearly enough to go around.

"How soon are we goin' t' get moving?" Reggie asked Reinsbach when the last passengers were safely aboard. "This place is turning into a zoo!"

"Ain't that the sad and sorry truth?" Reinsbach grumbled. They paused in one of the vestibules and Reinsbach keyed his radio. "Amtrak 15 to Roseville dispatcher, over?"

"Roseville dispatcher to Amtrak 15."

"We've transferred our passengers and are ready to proceed over the Hill. Over?" They waited for some minutes before the reply came back:

"Roseville dispatcher to Amtrak 15, be advised rotary 207 reports a major snow slide near Milepost 198. They're working to clear it now. Hold until they make contact."

"Wonderful," Reinsbach muttered. "I should know better." He keyed his radio again. "Amtrak 15 to Roseville dispatcher, copy your hold until rotary 207 makes contact. Out."

§

Milepost 197, Snow Shed 47:

There was a brief burst of garbled Spanish over Earl's hand-held radio. *"Eso es bueno mi amigo,"* Earl replied, then turned to Dan. "Antonio says he's about ready."

Earl and the rest of the track gang returned to the shelter of the snow shed, leaving Antonio to set his fuses. Antonio was a vague shadow at the edge of visibility, all of a hundred yards ahead, lost in the swirling snow.

"Three separate obstacles to be blasted," Dan grumbled. "In a hundred yards. And four miles t' go. We're in for a long day."

"I hope not," Earl said. "I didn't bring very much dynamite."

"Wonderful." If they ran out, they'd have to tackle fallen trees with axes and chain saws, or shift boulders with pry bars. It'd be faster to go back to Norden for more explosives.

The radio crackled in Spanish again. *"Comprendido. Estamos listos aquí,"* Earl replied as Antonio came sprinting down the right of way. "Alright, here we go."

§

68

Milepost 201, Horseshoe Curve:

The distant *BOOM!* echoed faintly across the hills, stirring the 'City' passengers out of their lethargy. "What was that?" someone asked.

There was nothing to see out there, and interest was dwindling when another faint *BOOM!* came to them.

"Thunder?" someone asked.

"In a snow storm?"

Then Reggie realized what was happening. "That's dynamite! There's a work crew trying to clear the track up ahead!" The news galvanized the passengers, raising their morale at the prospect of impending rescue.

Charlie Parkhurst was nearby, and overheard Reggie's remarks. "Dynamite?" he asked softly when Reggie came by. "Why would they be blasting?"

Reggie considered him soberly, then decided he could be frank. "There was an avalanche up ahead. They use explosives to clear fallen rocks and trees."

There was a third faint explosion in the distance.

"Hmmm, maybe we were lucky we stopped here," Parkhurst said, somberly.

"Yeah. Maybe so."

§

Milepost 197, Snow Shed 47:

Antonio stepped out from where he took cover behind the rotary's scoop, moved ahead up the track to check his handiwork. Three scorched areas littered with debris showed where his explosives cleared wreckage out of the way. He clambered through the disturbed snow, examined the area, then clambered back and waved them forward. "We got the go-ahead, man-o," Jesus said.

"We're lucky he didn't start another avalanche," Dan groused as he released the brakes and inched the throttle up a notch. The rumble of their diesel kicked up, making them uneasy. The rotary, facing down hill, began drifting forward.

69

Jesus scanned the high ground nervously as they emerged from the snow shed. "I don't see nothing." That wasn't much reassurance. The snowfall seemed a bit thinner, but between it and the pale gray twilight filtering through the clouds, they couldn't see more than a few hundred feet.

The rotary dug into the snow pack, almost stalling until Dan reluctantly gave it a couple more notches. Two large pine trees lay shattered in the snow on either side of the right of way. They inched past these and dug deep into the snow slide, buried up to the top of the rotor housing, causing the rotary to stall. Dan reluctantly gave her another notch as Jesus added power to the rotor, and they started moving again. A third shattered tree crept past. The rumble of their diesel and the 'snail' had their nerves on edge. The racket could set off another avalanche, and in this limited visibility they'd have no warning. Not that seeing it coming would make any difference.

The rotary trundled ahead, spewing a steady stream of snow off to their left, down slope, while they divided their attention between the rising slope on their right and the track ahead. If they could just make it another half mile, they would enter the cut leading to Tunnel 13 and safety—if there were no more obstacles.

§

Milepost 107, Roseville Shops, California:

"You can pick up the spreader at Colfax," the Yardmaster told Parker Lee at a last-minute meeting before the relief train went out. "There's a rotary at Norden which is plowing the way up to the Curve, so you should have smooth sailing all the way."

Parker Lee knew there was *never* 'smooth sailing' on the Hill, but was enough the old Southern diplomat not to contradict his boss. "Yassah, we're all set t' roll. Don't you worry none; we'll get them out." Everyone who knew him was enchanted by his soft Magnolia accent; everyone who knew him knew he was a driver who got the job done.

"You have all your equipment?"

"Yassah. We got ever'thing we need, plus twenty-five men. Good men; we'll have that ol' train out-a there in two-twos."

70

"Alright, then. Get moving. Walter will follow you shortly with the wrecker."

Parker exchanged nods with Walter, and left.

§

Milepost 142, Colfax, California:

Davy Burns was pissed at the world in general, the Union Pacific directly, and the Lord-almighty Murphy in particular for this meaningless, demeaning job he was stuck with. As he told Murphy—*told* him, dammit—the snow was just too much to deal with. He'd been following the dispatcher's calls, and knew another train wouldn't come out of Roseville for some time. There was only an Amtrak coming down the Hill, but beyond that the road was out of commission.

They were too short of equipment for weather like this, so until rotary 211 came back from the shops, only the most urgent high-priority freight even tried to get over the Hill. But that didn't keep Murphy from finding demeaning make-work to keep *him* hopping.

Leave Colfax northbound and scrape to the Long Ravine Bridge a couple miles away, then back up, go through the wye (clearing the yard trackage as they did so), then south on track 2 to Tunnel 32. Back up to Colfax, go through the wye again, and repeat on track 1. Endlessly. It was enough to drive him to tears, but he got madder and madder instead.

This was Murphy's doing; he knew it as sure as the sun rises. That bastard had it in for him! It was meaningless: scrape one short stretch of track and a couple sidings while the rest of the road went to hell. It never occurred to him that the Colfax Stationmaster had a penchant for neatness, so since the spreader was short-handed, he kept them busy doing busy-work instead of trying to do more than they were equipped for. Illogical, but the Union Pacific has their bureaucracy the same as anywhere else.

It was all too much! Burns fancied himself as capable a railroader as any, and if he bowed to the inevitable in this weather it wasn't fair to ride *his* ass. But here he was, trundling back and forth keeping one short stretch clear while he shivered from the cold, his fingers ached, and his ill-mood grew hotter and hotter.

71

Pietro stoically endured his ill-temper and occasional outbursts all shift, knowing Burns was one the higher-ups looked down on, but he retreated into surly silence some time back, watching his side and adjusting the left spreader wing as needed while pretending Burns was just a vulgar rumor. It kept the lid on.

They were approaching Colfax from the south for the umpteenth time when the radio crackled:

> *"Colfax Stationmaster to spreader 4034, over?"*
> *"4034."*
> *"Be advised your track warrant in Colfax yard is cancelled. Move onto the wye to clear the way for a work extra. Over?"*
> *"Yeah, Colfax, when's it due?"*
> *"About twenty minutes."*
> *"4034, copy. Davy, put us on the wye."*

Davy Burns grabbed the radio mic. "Yeah, yeah, I heard you."

> *"Cut the 'tude, Burns, and do your job!"*

Burns petulantly goosed the throttle up several notches, causing the spreader to jump as its diesel shoved from behind, and bringing another angry blast from Lee:

> *"Burns, you either quit your tantrums and do your job right or I'll have Pietro take over!"*

An uneasy silence returned as Burns drove the spreader consist toward the yard throat where they could switch off onto the wye. "A work extra? In this weather?" Pietro muttered at last. "What's that about, you think?"

"I'll tell you what I think: I think I don't give a shit!" Burns was smoldering over Lee blasting him over the radio where everyone could hear. Pietro retreated into silence once again as the resentment grew.

§

72

Milepost 198:

Progress was slow, with one major setback when Antonio spotted another tree and a large rock in their way. Earl called out the section hands who set to work digging in the hard ground so Antonio could plant some more dynamite. Dan and Jesus watched the slope above them while the dancers did their thing. The bitter mountain wind came seeping in through every crack, chilling them, and the thin mountain air made each breath a gasping exertion. They knew the section hands endured far worse, and pitied them. Both were painfully aware of the risk they all took standing out in the open like this. At the rate the snow was falling, another avalanche was inevitable. Dan focussed on the snow building up on the side window sill: it looked thick and solid; 'rubber snow' the men called it. That shit would hold together for a long time before it let go, but when it did, woe betide anyone caught in its path. Neither of them felt safe out here in the open, but then none of them were.

Finally Earl called:

"207, we're ready here. We'll come aboard, then you better move back under the shed again before Antonio sets off his charges."

Dan grabbed the radio mic. "Yeah, copy you, Earl." The section hands were already tromping along the cleared right of way, leaving Antonio to set his fuses.

Once they were aboard, the rotary moved back some three hundred yards to the shelter of Shed 47, about at the limit of how far they could see in this slop.

"This is gonna take forever, man-o," Jesus grumbled. He watched the snow drifting steadily down, creating a shroud which obscured everything more than a couple hundred yards away. Only Antonio was left out there, a vague figure in the gloom. "These winters keep gettin' worse all th' time. I heard maybe they build some more snow sheds next summer, enough t' cover th' whole road."

"That'd be a big help," Dan said, wistfully. Normally he couldn't see the Union Pacific spending so much money, but after this winter who could say?

"They used t' have them, all across the Hill. That'd be somethin', huh?" One could only hope.

"Sure would. We can't cope with this as is. If it gets any worse, we'd be useless."

"Here we go, man-o." They caught a vague image of Antonio sprinting down the right of way...

BOOM!

...there was a hazy view of a fountain of dirt and debris, with two halves of a huge pine tree flipping end over end...

BOOM!

An enormous rock hung balanced on the rail for a moment before it toppled down slope and vanished.

"Neat," Dan said, approvingly.

"*Si*. That Antonio, he know his stuff, man."

"Okay Dan, let's wait a bit to see if we stirred up anything."

Dan grabbed the radio mic. "Yeah, good idea, Earl."

No sooner did he say it then an avalanche came pouring down on the right of way. Antonio just made it to the shelter of Shed 47, and stood gasping as he watched the slide flowing past in a cloud of stirred up snow. It took a couple minutes for any obvious movement to end, and several more as they anxiously watched the high ground on their right. The rotary was sitting with its nose just far enough out of the shed so they could look through the side windows at the landscape above.

"Dammit, I *hate* this shit!" Dan said at last. He was leaning out the side window, ignoring the biting cold, to study the high ground. "Can't see any movement."

74

"This weather is *El Diablo*, man-o. We can't be too careful."

"How's it look up there, Dan?"

Dan settled in his seat and grabbed the radio mic again. "That was a fairly small one, I think. It looks like it's over for now."

"Alright, if you think it's safe, let's get this over with."

"Copy that. Here we go."

Dan slid his side window shut, settled in his seat, hit the air brakes, and gave the throttle a couple notches. The rotary crept ahead, and began digging into the snow cover in front of it as Jesus fed power to the rotor.

The slid reclaimed some fifty yards of their three hundred yard progress thus far. They dug in, slogging relentlessly along, spewing an arc of snow to their left. There was a brief rattle-bang as some smaller rocks were caught up in the rotor. They held their breaths, hands hovering anxiously over the controls until the rocks went flying and the racket subsided.

Jesus settled in his seat and gave Dan a weary look. "I swear t' you, man-o, I'm gonna put in t' be a clerk. I'm gettin' too old for this."

"Yeah, you and me both."

They went on, snow flying to one side. There were no more obvious obstructions, although they both hovered over the controls anxiously. The snow seemed to be getting worse again, reducing visibility to less than a hundred feet or so. At this rate, the track behind them would already need to be dug out again on the trip back.

After another hour of butting heads with nature, the rotary started into a long curve as the ground on either side started closing in. They'd reached the end of the cut leading to Tunnel 13, out of sight ahead. They breathed a bit easier; the risk of being caught in an avalanche was greatly reduced, and in another thirty minutes or so they'd reach the comparative safety of Tunnel 13.

§

Milepost 142, Colfax, California:

No sooner were they safely off the main and parked then the radio lit up again.

"Spreader 4034 to Colfax Stationmaster. What's the situation with the work extra? Over?"

It seemed Lee was wondering about such an unusual move, too. That extra couldn't be a snow train unless rotary 211 was released sooner than anyone expected, and if it was for anything else, it must mean trouble on the Hill.

"Stationmaster to spreader 4034. We got a derailment near summit. They're sending a work train up to help out."
"Ah...yeah, copy. Who's on the ground?"
"Amtrak 15. They said it wasn't anything major."

There was a brief silence as Lee, in the cab of their diesel, pondered this development.

"Colfax, do you want us to go back to work once the work train is passed?"
"Ah...no, they might need you. They're due soon. Wait till they get here, and we'll see what develops."

'See what develops' the man said! Davy knew all too well what would 'develop'. They'd get sent out to scrape the too-long-neglected right of way, which would be a major hassle and put them well over their hours. And they were due to be relieved, too! This was to his mind only the latest insult in a long, tiring day of abuse and ill-treatment, and right then he was too cold and weary to take it with anything like good grace.

He sat for a time staring at the control column, wallowing in self-pity. This railroad treated him like shit because he was the only one who saw how useless all these heroics were. He knew they despised him as not being the *Manly Snow-Buster* they were

76

—Murphy in particular, power-mad bastard—and he despised them in turn. There was no good reason why he should put up with this bullshit, especially as it was a fool's errand. He ought to quit; climb right down from this cab, march right up to Murphy, and tell him to go to hell. He'd never find the nerve to do that, which he instinctively knew even if he didn't recognize it, and it just added to his angst.

After stewing in his resentment for a while, his thoughts turned to the crew thermos at his feet. Right then he was wound up and hyper, and like he usually did when this way, he craved coffee. That would only make him worse, but he didn't understand his self-destructive nature, or his caffeine addiction, and right then he wouldn't have cared if he did.

Pietro watched as he drew down on their dwindling supply. Thus far he hadn't had any since Burns sat on it so close. Now he was tired and cold, and needed it badly, so he decided to speak up. "Hey, I'd like some of that too."

His protest goaded Burns into one of his fits of petty vindictiveness. "Like hell!" He cradled the thermos, holding it away from Pietro. "I dragged this thing out here, and I didn't see *you* lift a finger t' help. You want coffee, you get your own!"

Pietro was on his feet, bristling with long-contained anger. "Hey man, that coffee is for all of us!"

Burns hesitated under his angry glare. Pietro was a hulking brute; getting physical with him wouldn't end well. More than that, he had a solid reputation among the maintenance crews. Burns *knew* how Murphy would spin any confrontation between them. His petty tantrums weren't enough to face very real anger, so like he did all too often, he folded. "Here!" He shoved the thermos at Pietro and collapsed in his seat, wallowing in bitterness and shame. "I hope you choke on it!"

§

Milepost 201, Horseshoe Curve:

Rotary 207 finally emerged from Tunnel 13 and ground to a halt about a hundred feet from the lead Amtrak locomotive. Dan set the brakes and climbed down to meet with the train crew.

"It's good to see you," Bobby told him. "This mountain railroading is gettin' old."

"We were starting to worry with all this snow," Karl added. "Hopefully we don't get snowed in."

"Yeah, well your worries are over. You got good track down to Norden, and usable track on into Colfax. The wrecker should leave Roseville before long, so we got to get you guys down the Hill. You ready to roll?"

"Ah...no." Bobby gestured, and led Dan back to their locomotives. "Actually, our worries aren't over yet."

A minor avalanche had come down the hillside and piled up against the two locomotives, blocking them in. "This happened when you guys were blasting, the other side of the ridge."

Dan stared at the mess in dismay. "Oh...darn."

§

Milepost 107, Roseville Shops, California:

The arrival of Gus Vincincegorough at the service yard in Roseville was fair warning to all and sundry that things were *not* good on the Hill. He'd been at this longer than most UP crewmen had been on this earth, and what he didn't know about clearing train wrecks wasn't worth knowing. He was semi-retired, with seniority to sit out the weather thus far since the railroad wouldn't fritter away his unique skills on lesser tasks, but that was no more. There was a wreck to clear, which interrupted his football game, and Gus was in a mood. Even the Sierras should be worried.

He paused to look around when he hit the service line, which was all but obscured in the swirling darkness. He didn't bother cursing the weather; acknowledging an old enemy was beneath his dignity. All that mattered was getting this done.

Walter Karns, his Number Two, was easy to spot in the snowy gloom because those around him *hustled*. "What you got, Walter?"

Karns wasn't one to waste time on pleasantries, either. "We got Amtrak 15 off the rails at Horseshoe Curve; two cars, one truck each. Rotary 207 is at Norden plowing the line up to Summit with their work crew. A work train left here about half an hour ago. They'll pick up spreader 4034 at Colfax, and head on up. Rotary

78

207 is based out of Norden, and they have a work train with them; Earl Jenks is in charge. Our best bet is to coordinate out of there. No word on what Truckee's doing from their end."

"Right." Short, sweet, and to the point: just how Gus liked it. "Don't sound so bad. So what about your baby?"

Walter's 'baby', SPMW 910006, 250 tons of brute lifting power, sat on a siding near the Roseville engine shops, its diesel rumbling steadily, its dark mass towering over the tiny figures moving about in the harsh glow of its spotlights making ready. A switcher was putting the last touches on the work train, adding a crew dorm behind the crane tender and tool car.

"We should be ready to go as soon as we get a work party together," Walter said. "We sent one batch up already, and I got the caller ringing 'em up."

Gus stepped out to where he could look down the length of the work train. A group of about a dozen figures appeared faint in the swirling darkness as they waited to board the crew dorm. As they watched, a couple more headlights appeared in the distance and drew up to the parking lot. "How many'd you send out on the work train?"

"Twenty-five, including Parker Lee."

"Good." Gus pondered the situation for a bit. The latest weather reports were ugly, and he knew all too well what conditions were like at Summit. "This'll take too long. Did th' doctor get here?"

"Yeah. He showed up a few minutes ago."

"Alright, we don't got a plow, so we need to get a move-on before this snow buries the track again. The extra hands can come up later. Right now we need to make a move."

"Right."

§

Milepost 201, Horseshoe Curve:

"Aw...shit," Dan muttered as they examined the slide blocking the Amtrak in. "Sorry about that, guys."

"Hey, it's part of the game," Bobby said. "Thing is, can we get dug out before this storm snows us in?"

79

That was a critical point. The longer they stood there, the more likely wind-blown snow would build up around the train until they couldn't pull free. They were strictly on the clock, and it was snowing steadily. Dan turned to Earl, who had just joined them to see what the delay was. "What d'you think, Earl?"

"I only got a half-dozen men." He pondered the piled snow bank with no enthusiasm. His men were already tired and chilled, and this looked to be a tough job for so few. "But we either do it now or bring everyone and his dog up here and do it later, so we better get to it."

"Hell, if you got a couple extra shovels, we'll pitch in," Bobby said. "We don't want t' get stuck here any more than you do."

Earl considered him somberly. "Yeah, that'd help. What'd help even more is if your diner could scrounge some hot food for us."

"You got it!"

§

Milepost 107, Roseville Shops, California:

Gus Vincincegorough climbed onto the rear platform of the old caboose which would serve as his office, glanced up the consist to make sure everything was in order, then waved his lantern to signal the locomotive to head out. There was no need to call the dispatcher for clearance, few of whom would argue with him anyway. There was a wrecked passenger train at Milepost 201: he owned the road, and everyone knew it. The big diesel revved, its turbochargers howled, and the Wreck Extra began moving.

SPMW 910006, Walter Karns' 'baby', came right behind the locomotive, which plowed doggedly into a half-foot of new snow which fell since the last freight train went up the Hill. The wrecker groaned and squealed and swayed through the turnouts, a hulking shadow in the gloom dominating everything around like some prehistoric monster. The rest of the train, impressive in its own right, was merely a cheering section for the real Titan at the head of the consist. Gus Vincincegorough was on his way.

*****

Noon:

Milepost 201, Horseshoe Curve:

Antonio paused to rest his weary back, cursing the winter for the who-knows-how-manyth time. Shoveling snow was the hardest, most frustrating task the section hands had to cope with, and he wondered—not for the first time—about blasting the locomotives clear with some quarter sticks of dynamite. He was certain he could do it; he learned explosives in the Army, but he was sure Earl would never agree to it.

At least they got a hot meal out of it: beef stew over rice; add some Tabasco sauce and it wasn't half bad. Thus fortified, they set to work digging a narrow trench in the snow along side the two diesels. They pretty well had them freed, but the snow was coming down thick and fast now. They were in a race against time and the elements, and all of them did their best knowing failure now could mean *days* of this miserable labor.

He considered the others strung out in a loose line, each responsible for some twenty feet of snow which was five feet deep in spots. Just getting to where they were to dig was all but impossible, with show forced up their pants legs and boots saturated. These were hard, tough men, born to a life of manual labor, but even they had their limits. If this went on much longer, Earl would have to call them in or risk frostbite. His own feet were numb, his hands ached, and his lungs burned from the thin, bitterly cold mountain air. But there was nothing for it. They needed to do this now or the alternative would be much worse. He hefted his shovel with a weary sigh, and went back to digging.

§

"*Esos pobres diablos,*" Jesus muttered as he watched the work party from the rotary's cab. After a bit he turned to Dan. "Man-o, I thank *El Dios* I'm not a track man, especially now."

"Yeah, I hear you, Jesus."

Not that their situation was much better. The icy wind filtered in through the tiniest openings, with the steam heater going flat-out, not altogether successfully, to keep up. The air in their cab was brisk, their breath clouded with steam, the windows decorated with delicate traceries of frost. Worse, they were out of coffee.

"How much longer you think it'll be, man?"

Dan pondered the work party's progress with a critical eye, not that he could tell much from this distance. His attention shifted to the sky: the cloud cover barely cleared the right of way, and the snow was falling so fast it was hard to tell where clouds, sky and land met. "Not much longer, I hope. They'll be snowed in soon, if they aren't already."

They had their own snow buildup worries as well. Blowing snow binds all trains with fine impartiality, and if the freakin' *rotary* got snow-bound they'd be in a righteous pickle, not to mention they'd never hear the end of it. So every half hour or so, they would back up to the entrance of Tunnel 13 and dig their way forward again; as much for the exhaust heat from the rotor drive as to prevent being snowbound. They just completed their fifth or sixth such run when the radio crackled to life:

"Maintenance of Way at Norden to Rotary 207?"

Dan grabbed the handset. "Rotary 207."

"How's it going up there? Is Earl available?"

"Ah...Earl is out with the track crew. The Amtrak engines are snowed in, and they should have them dug out shortly." There was a brief pause, no doubt for Marcus to express his frustration in private, then:

"Ah, copy that. Tell him the weather report says this storm has been overtaken by the next, so don't expect the weather to clear for another thirty-six hours. Over?"

Now it was Dan's turn to express his frustrations privately. "Copy, Norden. We hope to have the Amtrak moving shortly."

End of discussion. Jesus sighed in exasperation. "*Madre Dios,* man-o, *when* is this winter gonna quit, huh?"

Dan gave him a sour look. "What makes you think it'll *ever* quit? We done died and gone t' hell, my friend. Forget your Eternal Fire, *this* is damnation for them what work the Hill!"

Jesus crossed himself nervously. "You scaring me, man; scaring me maybe you're right."

§

Milepost 142, Colfax, California:

"Hey, they're here." Pietro was leaning out the rear door peering into the snowy gloom, which glowed from the approaching headlights.

"Yeah, okay. Shut the damned door, will you?"

A road unit came rumbling by just then with a bunk car, a flat car with a bulldozer, a fuel service tank car with its truck springs fully compressed, and one of the old cabeese used by the MoW forces as an office. The bunk car was loaded with men. As the last car passed, the newcomer ground to a halt. The radio lit up:

> *"Extra 3209 to Spreader 4034, over?"*
> *"4034."*
> *"It's getting pretty bad. You guys need to go on ahead of us if we're gonna get to Norden."*
> *"Yeah, copy that. Burns, take us up to the yard lead and put us on the main. And get your spreader ready. We'll have to plow all the way up there."*

"No shit, Sherlock," Burns grumbled. Lee, their conductor, was sitting pretty in the cab of their diesel, bastard, while they made do with a jury-rigged oil heater. He keyed his radio mic. "What about my third man?"

> *"What about him? Murphy would-a sent someone if he could, so you'll just have t' suck it up."*

"This is bullshit!" Burns threw the mic down, causing it to clatter around the cab on its cable. "*Damn you,* Murphy!" he shouted. "Damn you, you arrogant prick!"

"Long day, man," Pietro sighed. They'd both been looking forward to putzing around in the yard until their shift was up. Now they faced a fifty mile trip in the worst blizzard conditions, with the line no doubt in dire need of scraping.

"Yeah, and even longer thanks to God-Almighty Lee Marris!"

"Hey man, you got no call t' go blaspheming!" Pietro was a devout Catholic, and took his faith seriously.

Burns rounded on him. "I'll Goddamn well blaspheme if I Goddamn well please! You wanna make somethin' of it?"

Pietro shut up; his was a Faith of peace, and he wouldn't let Burns goad him into a fight. "I wish we could get some relief," he griped. "That way I don' gotta listen t' your shit no more."

Good point. Burns keyed the radio. "Hey, Lee? What about some relievers? We'll be on the law in a couple more hours."

"Fraid not, Burns. I checked with Murphy, but there's no one available right now. He authorized us to go overtime. We should reach Norden before too long, and they can assign a crew to bring this lashup back."

Dammit! Murphy again! It was obvious, now that he could connect the dots: the Almighty Murphy was jacking him around! His rage boiled up, almost getting the better of him before he tamped it down. There was nothing he could do: he couldn't protest, he couldn't ask for reassignment, and if he quit what other road would hire him with all the dirt being spread around? Murphy owned him as sure as if he was bought and paid for. Of all the endless insults and slights he endured, being Murphy's bitch was the worst of all!

Pietro pulled up his parka hood and grabbed his hand lantern, ready to hit the ground to handle the turnouts. "Looks like we gonna collect some more overtime pay."

"Hell," Burns grumbled. "We'll be too damned tired t' spend any of it." Publicly he was resigned, determined not to give them the satisfaction of knowing they got to him. But privately, he fumed.

§

84

Milepost 201, Horseshoe Curve:

It was hard to tell what time of day it was, the snow was falling so fast now. It took most of the morning for the section hands to dig the last of the snow from around the Amtrak diesels and climb wearily back into the cab of rotary 207, making themselves comfortable as best they could in the crowded space. The last passengers from the back of the 'City of San Francisco' were camped out in the diner and lounge car of the forward section, and everything was set to lead them over the Hill to Norden. From there they would proceed on to San Francisco and the big wrecker could come in to rerail the two cars. The only question now was could the Amtrak's two diesels get the train moving with all the blown snow piled up around it.

"God, I hope she'll come loose," Dan grumbled. "We'll spend days digging them out otherwise."

"No lie, man-o."

If trains stand still any length of time in these conditions, wind-blown snow would build up underneath until they are unable to move, and the Amtrak was here over-long already. If the delay resulted in them becoming stuck, they'd have to bring up anyone they could scrounge and dig the train out shovel by shovel. The line would be tied up *forever*.

Dan and Jesus shifted to the other end of the Snow Extra and took up residence in rotary 18146, a far more modern and comfortable unit than their previous dinosaur. Earl and the section hands were back at the (new) rear trying to warm up while the Amtrak got ready to roll some hundred feet away.

"Hey, this is nice," Dan said as he admired the up to date fittings of the 18146. "We get the chance, we need to turn the consist around so we're using this end."

"Oh, I don' know, man. This ain't so fancy. Its got no air conditioning, for one."

"Well, yeah, there is that..." Dan realized Jesus was grinning at him. "Clever, dude." He dropped into the engineman's seat and rubbed his face with both hands. "You think they'll get her to move?"

"I hope so, man-o. We been at this too long already."

"This is Amtrak 15 to the rotary. We're ready to go here. How about you guys?"
"Ah. copy that, Amtrak. Let's make sure you can move before we head out."
"Yeah, copy that. Wait one."

Both of them moved to the rotary's door and looked back down the track to see what would happen next. The only indication they got was when the lead unit's headlights brightened. With their modern anti-pollution gear, they didn't produce enough exhaust to be visible in the gloom.

"Come on, guys," Dan prayed. "You can do it."

The weather was really nasty by then, the wind picking up, the snow falling faster and faster. At this rate, it was now or never for the 'City'.

"How's it look, Amtrak? Can you work your way free?"
"Yeah, she's loose. We're moving."

"Thank heaven for small favors," Dan sighed.
"*Si*. Maybe we get some sleep soon, huh?"

"Alright, great. Those hills ahead of you look like bad news all the way up to Summit Tunnel. You better give the rotary about a ten minute head start. That way if there's an avalanche, you'll have plenty of warning."
"Yeah, copy that. Good luck to you guys."

The lights on the radio changed as Earl switched to the dispatching frequency:

"SPMW 207 to Roseville dispatcher, we're ready to move west to clear the 'City' train."
"Roseville dispatcher to SPMW 207. You are cleared to move west to Norden and clear the main. Amtrak 15, you

86

are cleared to follow Extra 207 at minimum speed, violating the limitations of order, to Norden. Hold there for the wreck extra, holding the main, then proceed to Colfax at track speed."

"Copy, dispatch. Extra 207 to Norden and clear the line."

"Amtrak 15, we copy. Follow Extra 207 at minimum speed to Norden, hold for the wreck train, then proceed to Colfax."

The lights changed as Earl switched to the tactical frequency:

"Okay, Dan, take us back."

Dan keyed the mic. "Copy that, Earl." He dropped the mic and took one last look to make sure Earl and the others were aboard the other rotary, then released the brakes. The rotary shifted slightly as the air sighed out.

"We better be careful, man-o," Jesus muttered. "Them hills must be ready to go."

"Yeah." Dan edged the throttle up a notch, then another, and SPMW 207 stirred. "I love the way he said we're the ones to go out there and trip an avalanche. Makes a fellow feel really loved, ya know?"

"*Si*, but someone got to do it, and we're first in line."

"Ain't that the sad truth?"

Starting on the stiff grade was not easy, even with their relatively light train, but they managed to do it. They crawled up the grade toward tunnel 13, making more noise than either of them was happy about. Both of them kept a nervous eye on the high ground to their left. Fortunately it wasn't as steep as on the other side of the ridge, but the danger was real nonetheless.

But this was taking forever, and they were in danger of stalling. Dan goosed the throttle up another notch, and the rotary trundled ahead toward the inviting darkness of Tunnel 13. It seemed like forever, but was really only a few minutes until they plunged into the darkness and they could breathe easier.

Tunnel 13 curved steadily to the left, doubling back on itself as it pierced the ridge line. When they emerged, they were headed west again, traveling through the cut on the side of the mountain which seemed like such a haven earlier. Now they felt naked once again, exposed to the evils lurked on the high ground above. Dan cut back his throttle, quieting the diesel. The land to their right rose sharply to a jagged, tree-studded ridge line high above. On their left the cut faded away to a cut-and-fill shelf which normally offered a great view of Donner Lake in the distance, but now was empty whiteness fading into the gloom. The cloud cover was nearly down to the railhead; a churning gray menace.

Dan noticed their speed had dropped off to nearly nothing. He muttered a curse and inched the throttle up another notch. The snow extra slowed even more, ready to stall. Another notch. The rumble of their diesels quickened, the speed steadied and started crawling up again. The extra crept along, its power unit pouring out black smoke as they watched the hills above. The racket their diesels generated was deafening. They watched nervously as they crept along, wondering if the pounding noise would shake loose a million tons of snow and ice to bury them.

"This is some bad shit, man-o." Jesus crossed himself as he studied the hillside rising above them. If they were caught in an avalanche, they'd wind up in Donner Lake, far below on their right.

"Yeah. Thankfully we only got the one diesel."

The steady thunder of their diesels sent vibrations pulsing along the length of the slope overlooking the right of way, where the unprecedented snow pile already teetered on the brink of giving way under its own weight. They eased around the next turn at a walking pace, and Dan spotted Snow Shed 47 ahead of them. "Come on," he muttered. "We can do it."

§

Milepost 166, Blue Canyon:

> *"The wreck train is about half an hour behind us, and my guess is they'll catch up to us when we reach Norden."*
>
> *"Copy that. They'll have a lot easier time than we are. This track is the pits!"*

Davy Burns listened to the gossip between Lee and the supervisor on the work extra in tight-lipped silence. He could tell they were talking about him, indirectly blaming him for all their troubles. There was nothing he could do about it but listen as the cats yowled at his expense.

> *"Yeah, that's a big mia culpa at you, buddy. Sad to say we wasted most of this shift doing busy-work."*
> *"So what's the story? I'd think they'd send you guys out since you're the only snow unit down here in the lowlands."*

Sure. Burns could see where this was going; blame *him* for Murphy's fucked up vendetta. What was worse was how everyone seemed to pile on when this shit started.

> *"Beats me. We spent the day in Colfax 'cause the Stationmaster couldn't bear the thought of us getting lost, I guess."*
> *"What? He figured you guys'd take off for Las Vegas or something?"*
> *"More likely he figured we'd come across some real snow and get all unhappy and poopy-drawered over it."*

This was too much! He grabbed the radio handset, hand shaking in rage. "You don't know from shit, Marris! It's not *my* fault there's more snow than we can handle!"

> *"I never said it was, Burns. You just tend to your driving and don't get all poopy-drawered over things you can't deal with."*

That stopped him in his tracks, leaving him tongue-tied in rage and humiliation. Pietro said nothing, but he was too-clearly gloating at the slam he received.

> *"Whoa! He's a touchy one, ain't he?"*
> *"A real prima-donna, him. Doesn't like the cold."*

And it seemed they weren't going to let up on him.

"Is he like this all the time?"
"Well, not all *the time, but you could say he has issues."*
"It sounds more like he's got a lifetime subscription."
"Ain't that the truth!"
"Roseville dispatcher to the work extra, can the yammer and focus on doing your jobs!"

Silence returned as they trundled through the swirling void, and Burns simmered at this latest slap. 'He has issues', the man said! That catty school-girl snark was *exactly* the sort of thing haunting him wherever he went. This is what he got for simply accepting the truth about this ungodly weather! It wasn't *his* fault they were buried under this endless blizzard, so why pick on him? He knew Lee hated him, considered him a slacker for his common sense, but did he have to go spreading that filth to everyone on the road? He was mortally tempted to stop the whole parade right here in the middle of nowhere, go back to the diesel, and punch Lee right in his smart mouth. He instinctively knew he could never do that— he was a scrawny runt, picked on by all the high school bullies— and his lack of brawny machismo, which he *knew* was a license for these thugs to pick on him, grated on him almost as much as his helplessness in the face of such unfeeling abuse.

"Extra 3209 to Spreader 4034. What's the holdup? You guys are taking forever. Over?"
"It's our prima donna again. Come on, Burns, move it up. We got work to do. You want us t' stall on this grade?"

He looked at his speedometer for the first time since leaving Colfax: they were down to a walking speed. "Yeah, yeah, hold your water, Big Man," he mumbled. He shoved the throttle up a couple more notches and the speedometer crept upward again, which ended the complaints for the moment. They rode on in angry silence as his rage and bitterness simmered.

§

90

Milepost 198:

The rotary made it safely to Snow Shed 47, but unknown to them the damage was done. The vibrations from their diesels weren't much—most people would consider it mildly annoying—but it didn't take much to upset the delicate balance on the mountains already destabilized by the earlier blasting. They were just entering Shed 47 when a dollop of snow fell from a pine tree high up on the slope. It knocked loose a minor slide, which gained strength as it flowed down hill. By time anyone would have seen anything, momentum and gravity were firmly in control. The slide kept building, knocking more and more of the overburden loose until what started as a trickle became a white tidal wave carrying rocks and broken trees with it as it thundered down on the right of way.

As luck would have it, the avalanche reached the track just as the lead Amtrak unit rounded the curve and took the blow square on its chin. The wall of snow engulfed the two locomotives, lifting the first bodily, tumbling it on its side and carrying it down slope. The second unit was dragged along by the first, as was the baggage car before the coupler shank was ripped bodily out, leaving the car dangling sideways over the cliff. The rest of the train, mercifully, was sheltered from the worst by the cut leading to Tunnel 13. The first two passenger cars were rocked to one side, throwing the passengers to the floor in a heap, but remained on their wheels. Further back, passengers were thrown off their feet by the sudden stop.

§

Milepost 197, Snow Shed 47:

Their first warning that something was amiss was a frantic radio call:

"City train to head end. What happened? Where's the power? Why'd the brakes come on?"

Dan and Jesus looked at each other in surprise and dismay.

91

"Head end, you there? Answer up!"

"It's sumpthin' bad, man-o."

"Extra 207, Dan, stop us! The Amtrak is in trouble!"

"Copy that, Earl!" Dan killed his throttle and hit the brakes, and the rotary ground to a halt. The next couple minutes offered little solid information since they were forgotten for the moment, but the frantic radio traffic spelled out the pandemonium somewhere behind them.

> *"Amtrak 15 to UP dispatcher! We been hit by an avalanche! Both engines are gone! We need help up here!"*
> *"Copy that, Amtrak 15. What is your position?"*
> *"My...uh...I dunno. We just cleared a tunnel..."*
> *"Snow Extra 207 to Roseville dispatcher, they're somewhere about milepost 198. It's a real bad spot."*
> *"Copy, Snow Extra. Can you assist?"*
> *"We're ahead of them in Shed 47. We'll backtrack and see if we can reach them."*

"That's us, man-o." Jesus zipped up his jacket and leaned out the side door to look back down the track as Dan set the controls to reverse.

"Rotary 207, Dan, back us up, slow and easy."

"Copy that, Earl!" Dan released the brakes and opened the throttle a couple notches, sending a cloud of diesel exhaust through the snow shed. The consist ran in with a series of thumps, and started crawling back the way it came.

"*Madre Dios!* Both locomotives gone! It's gotta be bad, man."

Dan spared a quick glance at Jesus, still standing in the door. "We'll know soon enough." At the very least there were the head-end crew to worry about: if the locomotives vanished completely it meant they were swept away some distance down slope or were buried. As for the rest of the train, no one said anything yet, and the lack of information stoked their worst fears. How many passengers could a modern train carry? What condition were they in? How many were hurt? He was sick with anxiety...

"Hold it, Dan!"

...he hit the brakes and killed the throttle just as a solid *thump* came rumbling up the length of the consist. He grabbed the radio mic. "What's happening up there, Earl?"

They were ignored once again in the press of more urgent matters:

"SPMW 207 to Roseville dispatcher, the end of the snow shed is blocked by the avalanche. We can't get to them."
"Copy that, Extra 207. What do you recommend?"
"We need more manpower than we have. We'll need the rest of our work crew at Norden."
"Copy that. You have the road down to Norden. Do what you can."

"Great!" Dan grumbled. "That slide must be a half-mile wide at least if it hit the Amtrak *and* blocked the snow shed!" Earl hadn't seen the obstruction in the gloom until they were almost on top of it.

Jesus gave him a somber look, and crossed himself. "That's one monster slide, man. I ain't never heard of one so huge. Maybe we lucky they only lost the locos."

"Dan, take us over the hill to Norden. We need the rest of the work crew."

"Copy that, Earl!" Dan shifted the controls to forward and released the brakes. "Maybe so," he said to Jesus. "We'll play hell getting them out-a there. I can't think of a worse spot for this to happen!"

§

Milepost 192, Norden:

"Holy shit!" Marcus was dismayed when Earl related what happened. This was friggin' unbelievable! He keyed the mic. "How bad is it, Earl?"

"It looks about as bad as it can get. The end of Shed 47 is blocked, so that must be a monster avalanche. We should be back there in about an hour. Get everything ready so you can move up as soon as we arrive."

"Copy that, Earl!" Marcus dropped the radio mic and turned to Joey, the shop puke, his *defacto* number two for the moment since Earl was out on the rotary. "You heard him, Joey. We got a deep-shit-no-lie emergency here. Shake our people out, fill 'em with hot coffee, and be ready t' move as soon as the 207 returns."

Joey nodded grimly and headed for the door. "I'm on it, Marcus!"

"And tell Trudy t' start cooking! Anything, as long as its hot and plenty of it!"

"You got it!"

Once he was gone, Marcus turned his attention back to the radio. "Maintenance of Way at Norden to the Roseville dispatcher, over?"

It was some minutes before he got a response:

"Roseville dispatcher to Maintenance of Way at Norden, over?"

"We just got a report of a major wreck at milepost 198. We're getting set to move up. How soon will the wrecker get here?"

"Ah...copy your report on the Amtrak. We're already aware of it. Latest positions show the relief train approaching Emigrant Gap. The wrecker is stopped at Milepost 144 for repairs. No word on how soon they'll get moving again."

94

The news left Marcus stunned. It was more than twenty miles to Emigrant Gap; it would take hours for the relief train to get here, not to mention all the way to where the wreck was. And the wrecker...stopped for repairs? Out on the road? That couldn't be good. He and his handful of men were all they had to rescue the passengers of the 'City'. It left him feeling awfully lonely.

§

Milepost 198:

Aboard what was left of the 'City Of San Francisco', George Reinsbach was shaken and spooked by the sudden disaster which overwhelmed them just as it seemed the worst was over. It was all a blur: one moment they were rolling along, then came a horrendous jerk which threw everyone off their feet. The lights went out as the air brakes hissed and the train shuddered to a halt, creating panic in the already crowded cars. He was caught by surprise, sent sprawling in the aisle of the first sleeper with several people piled on top of him. It took him a moment to recover his wits, and some effort to drag himself out of the scrum before he could key his portable radio.

"City train to head end. What happened? Where's the power? Why'd the brakes come on?"

There was no answer. The sharp tilt the car had taken as well as the sudden disappearance of the head end power was alarming. The battery powered emergency lights came on, driving home the feeling something terrible happened.

"Head end, you there? Answer up!"

Nothing. Fearing the worst, he scrambled to his feet and down the aisle to the forward end of the car, shoving people out of his way. The passage door which normally would lead to the next car looked out instead onto open air since the double-deckers were coupled to a single deck baggage car. The window was glazed over with a sheet of ice, evoking a bitter curse as he fumbled for his keys. He finally got the door unlocked, pulled it open, and was appalled at what he saw. The baggage car was twisted around sideways, laying nose down on the steep slope. There was nothing beyond. Both locomotives had vanished into a white wilderness.

There was no sign of them, their crew, or the railroad itself, since everything was buried in a tumbled mass of snow and wreckage. He noticed movement; the slide was still under way, the last bits catching up to the earlier part and settling against the baggage car.

Shaken, he slammed the door and keyed his portable. "Amtrak 15 to UP dispatcher! We been hit by an avalanche! Both engines are gone! We need help up here!"

It seemed to take forever, but was only a few seconds until he got a response:

"Copy that, Amtrak 15. What is your position?"

That tinny voice was his first hint of hope. He keyed his portable again. "My...uh...I dunno. We just cleared a tunnel..."

"Snow Extra 207 to Roseville dispatcher, they're somewhere about milepost 198. It's a real bad spot."
"Copy, Snow Extra. Can you assist?"
"We're ahead of them in Shed 47. We'll backtrack and see if we can reach them."

Those words brought tears of relief to his eyes; they weren't alone out here in this desolate wasteland.

"George? This is Reggie. Where are you?"

That spurred him with new hope. He keyed his radio with shaking hands. "Reggie! I'm forward, in the first sleeper. Where are you?"

"O'Brian and I are in the diner. What happened?"

"We...ah...we got hit...avalanche. Both locomotives are gone." His tongue was tied in his panic, making it hard to talk. "T-take charge back there a-and check for casualties."

"You got it!"

96

Reinsbach leaned against the bulkhead as his trembling got to be too much. His breathing was fast and shallow, and his stomach was threatening to rebel. Right then he doubted he could take a step without falling on his face. One thing was clear: he needed to pull himself together, right now. He was in charge of a massive train wreck in one of the worst *possible* spots they could be stranded in. They had to depend on the railroad to rescue them no matter how impossible the weather was, and it was up to *him* to keep things from falling apart until help arrived.

The passengers around him were beginning to recover, coming out of their compartments to find out what was going on. At least there didn't seem to be any panic—yet. They'd be turning to him for answers and reassurance, which he had no idea how to provide. "God," he mumbled as he watched the people gathering in the narrow corridor. "What do we do now?"

§

Reggie and O'Brian were helping passengers in the crowded dining car to their feet when they overheard Reinsbach's frantic radio call. Their brief conversation didn't improve anything. They looked at each other in dismay for a long moment before O'Brian said, "God! What do we do now?"

That helped Reggie shake off his stunned dismay. "We gotta get organized." He needed to raise his voice over the swelling tide of panicked passengers. "We got t' get these people calmed down or they'll explode."

"Right. Let's get to it." O'Brian forced his way to the waiters' station in the center of the car and reached for the public address handset. "May I have your attention?" Nothing. The PA system was out of commission without the head end power. Next best option, he climbed up on a chair to address the crowd. "Your attention, everyone!" It took a few tries to get them focussed on him. "It's obvious we've been in another accident," he said once he had them. "From what we were told, both locomotives were swept away, which is why we don't have the main lights. I won't deny this is serious, but the railroad knows what happened and where we are, and they are mobilizing all their resources to come get us." He paused to size up the mood of the crowd; they seemed pensive, but were responding to the voice of authority. "I think it's fair to say we will be late arriving at Emeryville." That brought a few nervous chuckles. "But we *will* get there! This pass..." (he almost said the name, but checked himself in time) "...is the last major barrier between here and California. I won't lie to you: this is the toughest part of the whole road, but the Union Pacific concentrated their *best* men and equipment here for that very reason. They *will* come to rescue us! So all of you, please remain calm and work with us. We'll do our best to make you comfortable until help arrives."

The crowd seemed nervous, but was under control after he finished, which was the best they could expect under the circumstances. O'Brian climbed down, and the two of them and Otis moved off into a corner to figure their next move.

"We need to check the rest of the train," Reggie said. "And we need to connect with George so we can figure out some sort of plan. We need t' get all our people together, porters, stewards, you name it. We need t' set up some sort of supervision in each car. One thing we *don't* need is for panicked people to jump off the train and try to reach safety!"

"Hell, that's something we can't let happen!" O'Brian scanned the uneasy mob around them. "We'll need to treat the injured, as well."

"Shit..." Casualties had completely slipped his mind in the confusion. He noticed some familiar faces, Parkhurst and Barbara, sitting at a nearby table. "You two alright?"

Parkhurst comforted Barbara for a bit before answering. "I think so, man. This is some kind-a fucked up, huh?"

"You know it!" Reggie faltered, completely lost for what to do next. The sight of Barbara offered a feeble thread to cling to. "Look: I need your help. Set up an aid station here. Otis and his people will pitch in. Otis, have your people check the train, bring anyone hurt here." Otis nodded, and moved toward the kitchen to assemble his stewards and cooks. Reggie turned to O'Brian. "We need t' see if we can find the head end crew. They're likely in bad shape."

"Right."

"We'll be ready." Barbara's calm assurance was a welcome sign of stability in their world of hurt.

As Reggie and O'Brian headed forward, Parkhurst sighed. "I gotta tell you, dude, getting there *isn't* half the fun!"

Reggie paused to give him a peeved look. "No, but you have t' admit, it is entertaining."

*****

Mid-Afternoon:

Milepost 144, Long Ravine Bridges:

No sooner did the wrecker extra clear Colfax then it was halted when an air hose carried away. Gus Vincincegorough was pissed by the delay, but there was nothing for it. Walter and his crew were adept at minor repairs, and he figured it wouldn't take more than a half hour or so and they'd be on their way again. So while they waited, Gus spent the idle time in the bunk car enjoying a mug of coffee 'fortified' by one of the section hands and griping about the delay.

"Damn brake hose was rotten. They need t' take better care of this equipment. Ya never know when we might need it."

"Well, boss, them things happen," one of the hands said. "They fix it and we be on our way soon."

True enough. Unlike most maintenance of way gear, the big wreckers often sat idle for years at a time, kept in working order by routine inspections and an occasional startup to turn the diesel over. That was no substitute for being out on the line, so just to be safe, they carried a goodly selection of spare parts—such as air hoses—in the supply car. It was less than perfect, but a broken rubber hose was a small price to pay for long idleness.

"Yeah. Well, I guess it could be worse. Still, it bugs me. We have enough trouble with the rotaries as is."

The snow equipment received the same routine inspection during the summers, but were pushed a lot harder than usual these days. Much of their gear was old and worn, too. The early part of the season was rife with breakdowns.

Frank Morgan, foreman of their work crew, came forward from the office caboose, and he wasn't happy. "The Amtrak got wrecked again, Gus."

Gus looked at him in surprise. "Huh? What?"

"They tried to bring the forward section over the Hill, but they got hit by a slide at Milepost 198. Both locos were swept away 't hell and gone; no word on the crew. The baggage car is sitting cock-eyed on the road, but the rest of the train is alright."

"Aw, fer Christ's sake!" Gus griped. "Can't the snow crews do *anything* right?"

Frank turned defensive at his outburst. "It's this weather, Gus. We've never been hit like this before. There's nothing anyone can do about the buildup on the mountains. We're lucky we can keep traffic moving at all in these conditions."

He had a point, and Gus was forced to back off and consider just how bad this arcane weather really was. From what he'd already seen, it was clear he'd spent too much time in the comfort of his home lately. Time to get his game on. "Yeah, well, I guess you're right." The hinted resentment on the faces of the gandy dancers around them said just how far off-base he was. "This ain't a minor job no more, is it?"

"Doesn't look like it."

Gus pondered the situation with no pleasure: time he came up to speed on the new reality of the Hill. "We're gonna need *beau coup* manpower. What do we have?"

"There's the relief train, about an hour ahead of us; twenty five plus a bulldozer. There's also a work party at Norden; another twenty. I expect they're already moving up. And we have a dozen with us."

"That's not all that many. We got anything more?"

"I hear there's a track detail at Emigrant Gap, eight men."

It'd have to do. "It's better than nothing. Any word on the weather?"

"They're saying gale force winds and heavy snow for at least the next twenty-four hours, maybe longer."

"Wonderful. Things'll be hell up there at Summit." Gus sighed in frustration; this weather sure wasn't like back in the good old days. He couldn't help but wonder how much worse it *could* get. "Alright. Get on the horn and give Emigrant Gap a heads-up. Then contact Roseville and tell 'em t' shake as many men as they can out-a the bushes."

Frank nodded and headed to the office caboose. "You got it."

"And tell Walter t' hustle his sorry ass!"

"Right!"

§

101

Milepost 192, Norden:

Their base was a bee hive of activity by time they made the six miles back to Norden. No sooner did they grind to a halt under the snow shed than Margret and Willy turned up. "We'll take it from here," she said, abruptly. "You two grab some chow."

"We gotta get moving," Dan protested.

"You guys are long since dead on the law. You're relieved."

Dan had to work through a cavernous yawn before he could answer. She was right about them being exhausted. They'd already put in far more than Marcus called on them for earlier, and they had a twelve hour layoff coming. The look she gave him said arguing was useless anyway, so why was he fighting this?

"Okay, she's yours." He struggled up from his seat with his back and legs protesting. "The track is clear to the east end of Shed 47, which is blocked by the avalanche. The Amtrak got hit solid, so you'll have a helluva job digging your way to them."

"Yeah, we've been following the radio. The engine crew are missing, but no word on other injuries so far. They're putting together another extra down in Roseville to bring up more people."

"Well, that's some good news, anyway."

"We'll need 'em," Jesus added.

§

Trudy was waiting for them when the made their way to the kitchen, and shoved heaping plates of franks and beans at them. "Here, you eat."

There wasn't much going on in the kitchen car at the moment, so both of them ate right there at the counter, too weary for the mental effort of finding some place to sit down. At least they were warm. Trudy watched them silently for a bit, her face drawn by worry. "It's bad...isn't it, Dan?" she asked at last.

"God, Trudy." Dan shook his head in dismay, reflecting on what happened. "It's bad, real bad. We'll have a helluva job getting those people out."

"You know it has to be done, Dan; which means it *will* be done, which means it *can* be done. You need to keep faith in yourselves, is all."

Dan paused with a forkload of beans in front of his face. "I hope so, Trudy."

"That avalanche was somethin' terrible," Jesus added, somberly. "I ain't never seen the like. Them mountains, they loaded up somethin' awful. We gonna see more slides before this is over. Maybe we get them out, but I don' see how."

"Have faith in yourselves. You know you can do it if you only keep trying to find a way."

"*Si*. Faith is all we got right now." Jesus finished his plate, killed the last of his coffee, and waited while Dan finished his. "We gotta get some sleep."

"Good beans," Dan murmured as they headed for the dorm car.

As they made their way between cars, they felt the deck rocking gently; they were moving up. That wasn't their problem right then. Marcus promised them twelve hours on the law, and they'd for *damned* sure take every second of it. They found a couple empty bunks, and were asleep in moments.

§

Milepost 171, Emigrant Gap:

"You're fuckin' kidding me!" Ernesto was not pleased when Fred told his crew the latest from the dispatcher. "We're on the law! We all dead tired from shovelin' all day! They can't send us out there again."

"I don't like it either, but them's the orders," Fred snapped. He was dismayed by how what seemed like a minor problem a few hours earlier had blown up into a major crisis. The railroad was mobilizing every resource, and from his recent experience every man and piece of equipment would be urgently needed. "We got a passenger train wrecked, and you know we always turn out for emergencies like this."

"We got civilians to help, man," Elwood said. "Can't leave 'em up there while we sit here all warm and cozy." That evoked a general chorus of approval from the rest of the team. Ernesto wasn't satisfied, but was forced to back down in the face of public opinion.

"So what's the plan, boss?" one of the others asked.

"There's a relief train due shortly. We'll be picked up by them. Pack an extra set of clothes if you want; we're goin' 't be there a while." The others scattered to make last minute preparations. "And Ernesto? You can sleep on the train until we get there."

§

Milepost 144, Long Ravine Bridges:

Gus Vincincegorough was back at his station in the caboose when Walter Karns turned up. "She's all fixed, Gus." He helped himself to the coffee pot simmering on the stove. "We can move on whenever you like."

Gus confronted him in a dark mood. "About damn well time! You heard about the Amtrak?"

Walter cringed; Gus's black mood would scare anyone. "Yeah, Frank told me. This is turning into a helluva mess!"

"And it ain't gonna get better until we get there, so let's shag our sorry asses up the Hill before we get snowed in!"

That was a very real danger since they were traveling in the wake of the work extra, now nearly ninety minutes ahead of them. Without a spreader of their own, they were vulnerable to every wind-blown drift and minor snow slide.

Walter gulped his coffee and set the mug down hastily. "Right away, Gus!"

§

Milepost 198, on the grade:

For a miracle the baggage car was still coupled to the rest of the train, which may have kept it from sliding down hill into oblivion. It was all but buried on the uphill side, but the car's mass sheltered the downhill side, leaving most of that side exposed and forming a slight overhang which offered partial shelter. O'Brian followed it down slope through the swirling darkness, one hand touching at all times, partly to give him some frame of reference in this blinding wilderness. He prayed the two diesels would lie just beyond. That hope was shattered once he reached the end of the car. There was nothing but the tumbled snow mass fading into nothingness in less than a hundred feet distant.

104

It took him a moment to realize the coupler was missing; the massive metal saddle supporting it was bent outward, giving some clue about the force it endured before solid cast steel gave way. The thought scared him and filled him with awe at the same time. He hesitated for a long while, probing the blowing snow around him with his flashlight, but there was no sign of the locomotives. Finally, with the cold getting to him, he gave up and reluctantly headed back.

"Can't see a freakin' thing," he said when he managed to climb back to where Reinsbach and Greenbaum were waiting. "They must-a slid quite some way down, but you can't see your hand in front of your fuckin' face out here." In fact he only found his way back to the 'City Of San Francisco' by clambering up the treacherous snow pack and following the flashlights of the two conductors.

"They may have survived," Reinsbach insisted.

"Maybe. But I'm not going down there again. It's way too easy to get lost in this hell. Besides, this'll take more equipment and know-how than we have." The icy wind was picking up; he was shivering. "Let's get back inside."

§

'Back inside' wasn't much better. Without the absent diesels and their head end power, the train was rapidly cooling. Already the air was damp with condensation, and the windows decorated with delicate patterns of frost. The stewards and porters distributed all the available blankets, sheets, and towels, and the passengers huddled in small groups for mutual warmth and emotional support. The only thing they had going for them was the combined body heat of five hundred people. How long they would last in this cold and without food was problematical.

Otis greeted them when they arrived in the diner, and he was not happy. "We got some people hurt bad. Miss Barbara says some of them gotta get to a doctor right quick."

"Oh, shit," Reggie said.

The dining car looked like a war zone. The upper deck had been transformed into an emergency ward, with one table serving as triage and their major casualties laid out on the other tables as

105

improvised beds. Barbara was busy treating a young child's scraped face while a steward held a flashlight to illuminate her work and the mother hovered anxiously nearby. The train's medical kit sat open on the table, the area around it littered with discarded wrappers showing how badly depleted their medical supplies were. When she saw them, she quickly finished up with the youngster, offered the mother a few encouraging words, and came to report.

"We had people thrown around like rag dolls all over the train," she said. "I have a dozen serious injuries. The first one we got is a broken collarbone and probable spinal injury with partial loss of motor control in the legs. Right behind that is an elderly lady with a possible hip fracture, and another with what looks like internal injuries. We have two head trauma, one unconscious, the other disoriented. There's a wrenched knee, a couple broken bones, and several with significant cuts and abrasions. I've managed to stop the bleeding, but some of these people need transfusions, including our internal injury case."

"Jesus!" Reggie muttered.

"We were lucky, considering."

Reggie looked around the diner where people lay on the tables with whatever pillows and blankets could be found to comfort them. Aside from their bed cases, several more sat at the far end of the car after having been treated for lesser injuries. The air was heavy with sweat, humidity, and the smell of disinfectant. This was his first major train wreck, for all his years with Amtrak. He was appalled at their suffering; it made him feel guilty for their predicament somehow.

"What about these other people?" Reinsbach gestured to the walking wounded gathered at the far end.

"There's another couple dozen minor injuries, one wrenched shoulder, one has a bad knock on the head, and there are any number of bruises and cuts, but it could have been worse."

"Did...anyone die?"

"Not yet, but I can't promise anything. Some of these people need to be hospitalized immediately, and there's little more I can do for them." Despite what one saw in the disaster movies, there were no doctors on board. Barbara, an RN, and some first aid training was all they had.

"Thank heaven it wasn't worse!" It seemed Reinsbach shared Reggie's sense of guilt.

"We're practically out of supplies," she added. "I had the porters cut up a sheet to make slings and bandages, and I've been handing out Tylenol and liquor as our only pain killers. If nothing else, severe pain can worsen our serious cases. You people really should carry more medical supplies!"

Reinsbach winced. "We try not to have major train wrecks..."

"Still, it happens: you need to be ready for the worst." They were all intimidated by her full-on-medical-professional mode.

"Well, there's nothing we can do about that now. Right now we need to get some medical help up here, and evacuate your wounded if at all possible."

"Can they be moved?" Reggie asked.

Barbara hesitated. "Most of them. Some will need special handling. In any case, we need a full trauma team up here to check out our serious cases before we try moving them."

They pondered that in nervous silence. "At least no one has died," Reggie said at last.

"What about the engine crew?" she asked.

That fell on O'Brian. "There's no sign of the locomotives. The end was practically torn off the baggage car, so they're probably some way down slope. There's no way we can find them; this'll take specialists and rescue gear."

She nodded somberly. "You should be prepared to mark them off as fatalities, then."

Charlie Parkhurst and Paul, the chief steward in the double-deck diner, joined them. "Things are pretty well settled down, boss," Paul reported. "We got the last of the real injuries treated and resting comfortably, and I just got back from another sweep through the train. Aside from a few minor bruises, all the injured are here and taken care of."

"Our big danger now is this cold," Parkhurst said. "It must be down to zero out there, and that wind has to be gale force or better. This place'll be a freezer in short order."

107

"I'm afraid there's nothing we can do about it," Reinsbach said. "We were relying on the locomotives to provide power. Without them, all we have is the batteries." Now that he brought it up, the emergency lights did seem a bit dimmer.

"They go, and we'll have no communications to the outside," Reggie said. "Our hand-helds don't have the range to reach very far in these mountains." That was a disturbing thought: being cut off from contact with the outside world could mean the death of all of them.

"Then we better call in right quick before we lose contact," O'Brian said. "Tell 'em t' send up a portable generator along with the doctors."

"That'd take a pretty big generator," Reggie said. "Nothing less than a locomotive could supply that much power."

"What about the baggage car?" Paul asked.

"It's sitting sideways, and it looked pretty beat up," Reinsbach said. "I'm not interested in that; we have more urgent problems right now."

"No...what about the auxiliary generator?" The five of them looked blank. "I happened to notice it's one of the old units, the ones with the auxiliary power. Can we get it running?"

§

Milepost 166, Blue Canyon:

"Come on, Burns, let's pick up the pace. We'll never get there at this speed."

Burns figured their slow but steady five miles per hour was good enough; they'd get there eventually, and that passenger train wasn't going anywhere. Lee's cheap shot was uncalled for and unwise in this weather, and was one cheap shot too many. He grabbed the radio mic. "I'm being careful! I can't see a thing out there!"

"There's nothing t' see out there! We got the road up to Emigrant Gap. Them passengers need our help, so get a move-on!"

108

His rage got to be too much for him, overriding his secretive nature. He gripped the radio mic with both trembling hands like he was trying to strangle Lee. *"Why do you always pick on me!?"* he yelled. "I'm just doin' my job, and you all piss on me, like this weather is *my* fault! Don't think you'll drive me t' quit! I'm on t' your little game! I'll *never* give you that! *I hate you! All of you!"*

Pietro finally had enough, and turned on him angrily. "Man, you some kind-a *paranoid* or sumpthin! Why don' you quit your bitchin', huh? Why would *anyone* conspire against you? You ain't worth the bother!"

"You tell 'em, Pietro! Burns, I've had it with your petty shit."

Burns realized he still held the radio mic in a death grip. He was humiliated to realize Pietro's complaint went out over the air; likely the whole road was laughing at him now!

"Roseville dispatcher to SPMW 4034: you guys quit your bullshit and do your jobs or you're all gonna get a month's layoff!"
"Sorry about that, dispatcher. We got us a troublemaker here."
"Well you straighten things out up there or I will!"
"Yes sir! Burns? You heard the man. You quit your shit or you'll be back in Colfax and Pietro will be in charge!"

A tense silence returned. Pietro returned to his seat and stared fixedly into the blinding snowfall, his features stony with anger. Burns sagged in his seat, choking on bitterness and rage. It was so unfair! Now even the dispatchers were piling on him! His guts were churning; he wanted to puke; he wanted to cry. But he would never do it, break down and cry, no matter how much he longed to. He wouldn't give them the *satisfaction* of seeing *him* crumble! Like he did all too often, he kept it bottled up inside. The pressure was building.

§

Milepost 198, on the grade:

Getting into the baggage car was not easy since it lay at a thirty degree angle half buried in loose snow. The left—up hill—side was buried, but Paul and O'Brian managed to work their way along the right side, which was sheltered from the avalanche, until the reached the middle of the car.

They were thankful to find a fuel tank slung under the floor, mid-car; so there *was* a generator on board! It was half buried, but O'Brian was able to brush the snow and crud off the fuel gauge, and studied it by the glare of his flashlight. "It's full!"

"Thank Heaven for that!" Paul said, fervently.

"Thank the shops in Chicago; the car was empty, so they filled it. A triumph of bureaucracy."

"Yeah, well, this doesn't look so good." Paul shown his borrowed switchmans' lantern on a dark stain flowing down hill from the tank. "I'd say we got a leak."

"Shit." O'Brian was at a loss for the moment. "Well, we just have t' hope it isn't a bad one, and get as much out of it as we can."

§

Milepost 196, East end of Summit Tunnel:

"Did you get that, Norden? Please pass it on. Our battery power is low and we can't reach anyone else. Over?"

Marcus was appalled at the casualty report they just received from the wrecked 'City' train. "Copy that, Amtrak! We'll get the word out right away!"

"Tell 'em some of these people are in bad shape. We need t' get them to a hospital ASAP."

"Got it. We're already headed in your direction, so hopefully we can get to you in the next few hours."

"Good God!" Earl muttered after Marcus signed off. "This is turning into a disaster!"

"This whole winter is a freakin' disaster!" Marcus growled. "How soon will your guys be ready t' move?"

"As soon as we get there."

"Right. You go stir some shit, and I'll pass the word."

Earl nodded and headed for the caboose door. "Got it!"

§

Milepost 146, Cape Horn:

"Aw, sweet Jesus, what next?" Gus groaned when he received the call from Marcus.

"We're moving up t' Shed 47, and we'll start tryin' t' dig our way to them. You want us t' do anything different?"

Gus hesitated for a moment, trying to build the mental picture in his mind. "Ah, no, Marcus. Move on up and get to it. We'll base out of Norden when we get there."

"Copy that."

"How's the weather?"

"Lousy! We got clouds down t' the rails, and the wind is somethin' awful. Snowin' like a muther, too. Can't see more'n a hundred feet, tops."

None of them were happy with the news. "Okay, Marcus. Do your best. We're comin' along as fast as we can."

"How soon d'you think we'll get there?" Walter asked once the conversation ended.

"Gawd, I don't know. We're doin' good as is." The wreck train already met with a couple of snow drifts which they needed to batter their way through with the diesel's pilot plow. "How far behind are we?"

"Last I heard, the work train was passing Blue Canyon."

Gus nodded glumly. "They must be at Emigrant Gap already. Twenty-five miles: nearly two hours at this rate."

111

"That's if we hold them at the Gap until we can catch up."

Gus pondered the idea with mixed feelings. Without a spreader they were falling further and further behind, and it would only get worse as they went further up the Hill. But those twenty-five men would be invaluable to the rescue effort, and the wrecker wouldn't be needed at first. "No, let 'em go on. If we get stuck, we'll call for Norden's rotary."

§

Milepost 198, on the grade:

Getting the side door open took both their strengths, and they had to claw their way up into the car; Reggie boosting Paul up, and he hauling Reggie up in turn. Inside was a mess. The passengers' baggage, carefully stowed in the wall racks, had gone flying as had some of the racks themselves. Many suitcases were burst open, clothing and personal articles scattered everywhere. The traditional wrecking gear—pry bar, ax, shovel, and stretcher— were still clamped firmly in place. Their first step was to break those out and stack them next to the door.

The generator, a bulky six cylinder diesel, was in a wire cage against the wall mid-car. They looked it over with their flashlight and lantern: it seemed serviceable, if dusty with age. Paul checked the service card in its wall rack. "It says the last service date was in May, '95.

"This must be one of the dead line cars."

"Yeah." Paul surveyed the car with his brakeman's lantern. "I thought they scrapped all these long ago."

"Thankfully not. It's still in pretty good shape."

"Or was, anyway." Paul scanned the room again. "The miracle of stainless steel; they knew how to build 'em back then."

"Let's see if we can get this dinosaur running."

There was an engraved instruction placard mounted on the circuit box, but some helpful fool painted it over back in the mists of the past. They studied it by flashlights which were starting to fade, but couldn't make out anything.

"We'll just have t' wing it," O'Brian said at last. "It's a diesel, so starting it should be fairly simple."

The next few minutes went to tracking down the fuel cock and rummaging through the circuit box to find the starter. They finally got the fuel pump working, which set off an alarm buzzer. "That's the 'engine stalled' alarm," Paul said. "It should be ready to go."

The start button was big and centered on the console, easy to identify. Next to it was a power meter registering in the yellow— almost in the red. "Shit," O'Brian said. "We may not have enough battery power."

"Diesels don't have spark plugs," Paul said, doubtfully.

"But we'll need power to crank the starter, and they take a lot of juice, especially how cold this unit is."

"Can we...hand crank it?"

O'Brian gave Paul a jaundiced look.

"Well then, we'll just have to hope for the best."

§

Milepost 169, Fulda Balloon Track:

"We're passing Fulda now, and should be at your place in about fifteen minutes. You guys ready t' go?"
"Yeah, we're ready."
"You hear that, Burns? Let's keep up the pace."

Burns didn't bother to answer, but stared fixedly into the blizzard while he simmered. Lee wasn't gonna let up on him, and he *knew* the dispatcher's earlier threat would only fall on *his* back if he protested further.

His nerves, already strained, were giving him a monumental thirst. Without thinking, he reached for the crew thermos and poured himself another shot, now lukewarm and running low. He didn't care. His caffeine fixation drove him to chug the bitter brew almost without tasting it. He went back to staring out the window at the blizzard, not really caring where they went, leaving Pietro to adjust the spreader arms to avoid any obstacles. He didn't feel any better. He still boiled with angst and resentment, and although no one, least of all him, realized it, his rage and the excess caffeine had him slightly unhinged.

§

The whole atmosphere aboard the 'City' was dramatically changed when they returned. The lights were back on, which had an immediate effect on passengers and crew alike. O'Brian and Paul met with the others in the diner.

"It's not really enough power, but it's better than nothing," O'Brian explained to the conductors. "The heaters are gonna suck up power somethin' awful, so there may not be enough for the diner as well."

Right then all that mattered was the lights were back on and the clammy chill was starting to thaw as the air ducts pumped out lukewarm air.

"We'll manage," Reinsbach said. "If need be, we'll cut the heat for short periods while the kitchen makes up stuff in bulk lots like stew and soup."

"Coffee," Greenbaum added.

"Coffee." They were all relieved the latest 'worst' was over. "Now all we have to do is sit tight and wait for them to come and rescue us."

"Yeah, well let's hope they get here soon. The fuel tank is leaking, so there's no way t' know how long it'll last."

That amped the tension in their group. "How long do those auxiliaries normally last?" O'Brian asked.

They focused their attention on Paul. "If I recall correctly, they carried enough fuel for twelve hours. They were supposedly refueled en-route."

"Great," Reinsbach muttered. "So twelve hours is the *best* we can hope for!"

"We'll just have t' hope they can get to us by then," Reggie said.

§

Milepost 206, Truckee, California:

"D'you copy, Jim? You're a lot closer to them than we are, plus we got a shitload of snow t' move before we can get to 'em."

Jim Mortensen was appalled by the report he'd received from Gus Vincincegorough by radio. He gave an uncertain look at Herb Mokowski, then picked up the radio mic again. "Ah...copy your report, Gus. We'll do whatever we can here."

"This is important, Jim. Give it your best."

Mortensen stared at the radio with a deep sense of the walls closing in after Gus signed off. He knew his own limitations, perhaps all too well. They simply weren't prepared for something like this, and it was largely his fault for not anticipating this ungodly winter. But how could *anyone* anticipate this mess?

"What do we do, Jim?" What Herb was really asking was 'Can you do anything'?

That hurt. Mortensen knew he was in over his head, and everyone around him knew it too. Gus's last remark showed how little faith they had in him. It made him want to throw up his hands in despair and leave it to someone more capable to figure out. But he couldn't do it, not now, not right in the middle of the crisis. He was in charge; he had to take the heat.

"We...have to get those wrecked cars out of the way. Then we can send a relief extra."

"Then we'll need a crane." Herb picked up the phone and pointedly shoved it at him.

§

Milepost 244, Maintenance of Way Office, Sparks, Nevada:

"Ah... Yeah, Jim, we got a crane." Phil Collins, the MoW Super in Sparks, was not surprised to hear from Mortensen since he was *forever* calling to beg for help, but this was the first he'd heard about a wrecked passenger train. "But it's only a dinky little forty tonner; would that do you any good?"

"It'll do, Phil." Mortensen sounded scared, which made Collins wonder just how bad things were up there in the mountains. *"How soon can you get it over here?"*

Collins pondered the situation, and was not pleased. UP 903052 was actually in storage pending a scheduled overhaul.

115

They'd have to do a hasty patch job, fuel and service it, put together a support train, and get a crew together. There'd be no *end* of mechanical bugs to iron out, which was why it was waiting for a slot at the Cheyenne shops in the first place. "It'll likely be tomorrow morning before it gets there, Jim, depending on the weather and traffic. D'you still want it?"

There was a brief hesitation. "*Yeah, Phil. We need it. Please get it here as soon as possible.*"

"Okay, Jim. It's on its way."

Collins hung up and sat pondering this development. A wrecked Amtrak near Summit: no wonder Jim sounded flustered. Normally he'd be happy to help, but a passenger car would be a mighty big challenge for that little crane. It *could* be done, but it would take some finesse handling. It would take someone who knew crane work like he was born to it. It would take... He picked up the phone and started dialing.

§

Milepost 171, Emigrant Gap:

It was perhaps half an hour later that the relief train came crawling out of the swirling snow and ground to a halt in front of the way shed.

"You took your own sweet time getting us here, Burns!"

Burns was still on edge, having brooded over the abuse he endured earlier. Without thinking, he grabbed the radio mic. "Yeah? Well in case you haven't noticed, it's snowing outside!"

The complaints ended for the moment since both of them took the dispatcher's earlier threat seriously. Pietro didn't say anything, but his expression said volumes. Burns simmered in the following silence. *He* couldn't help the delays caused by a couple deep snow drifts they had to batter their way through. Normally the trip here from Fulda would take maybe ten minutes, even on this stiff 2.43 percent grade, but that didn't figure on how they spent all day putzing around in Colfax, neglecting the rest of the Hill. *Of course* it was *his* fault!

The snowy gloom around them was lit up by the locomotive's headlight. Vague figures were moving in their direction, coming out of the dark from the way shed invisible only a couple hundred feet distant.

> *"How's it look up there, 4034?"*
> *"I can see your people now. They're headed in your direction."*
> *"Yeah, copy that. I got 'em."*

Pietro watched them go from his perch at the spreader's rear door, letting in a blast of bitterly cold air; doing it deliberately, Burns was convinced. Bastard. Damned Mex *puto* bastard! *Of course* it was his, Burns, fault! Never mind the weather, or Murphy jacking him around: it was blowing a goddamned *blizzard* out there, so *of course* they blame him! And to rub it in, he was saddled with *puto*-Pietro, good company man Pietro, hold the door open to freeze his ass Pietro. Right then the stress and his fevered imagination had him right on the edge of losing what little self control he still had.

Fred and his seven climbed aboard and settled on the aged Pullman berths which were kept made down for the weary crews who preferred use their free time to get some sleep.

"They're all aboard, man," Pietro said.

"Wonderful. *Shut* the fuckin' door!"

> *"Okay Burns, wake up and get the show on the road, huh?"*

Burns bit back on an angry retort, hit the air brakes, and shoved the throttle four notches over in frustration. The WHEEL SLIP alarm buzzed; he backed the throttle off, hit the sanders, and opened up again. The alarm quit and the spreader moved forward with an abrupt jerk.

"Hey, easy, man," Pietro cautioned.

Burns angrily kicked the throttle up two more notches. "Shut the fuck..."

...the spreader hit a detracking point, where the space between the rails was filled in with boards so the hi-rail vehicles could exit the right of way. Despite his earlier claims, Ernesto had *not* cleaned the narrow flangeways, where the snow was compacted into a hard mass. Before anyone knew what was happening, the spreader hit that patch at *precisely* the wrong angle. Their momentum caused the lead wheels to bounce, climb the rail, and fall off onto the roadbed, banging along as Burns and Pietro hung on in confusion.

"We're on the ground!" Burns froze in panic, so Pietro lurched across the small cab and hit the air brake handle. Before the brakes could come on the spreader hit the overpass where the service road ran under the right of way. The spreader staggered, its lead truck twisted sideways, then the whole unit toppled bodily off the bridge into the roadway below. The massive left wing, fully extended, crumpled under the impact, ripping one of the hydraulic extender pistons loose and sending it crashing through the spreader's cab.

*****

Sunset:

Milepost 171, Emigrant Gap:

"The engineman is in bad shape," Jack Whitacre reported to Fred and Parker Lee. "I'd say he has internal injuries, possibly a ruptured spleen. The other one has a broken arm, back injuries and a concussion. They both need to be hospitalized right away."

"Can't you do anything for them?" Fred asked.

Jack shook his head. "I'm just an EMT. We got plenty of supplies, but this is way above my pay grade. They need real doctors in a real hospital, right away."

"Shit!" For once Parker Lee lost his magnolia charm, he was so upset. "Why'd this have to happen?" The relief train left Roseville so fast that the company doctor was left behind. He was coming on the wrecker, to hear it told, but Jack was all they had for the moment, and that only because he was a holiday temp hire for snow work.

Fred was at a loss. "How we gonna get them to a hospital? There's nothing around here, and we can't back the whole train down to Colfax!"

"What about the hi-rails, boss?" Elwood suggested. "We can get those Signals guys to take 'em down."

It was the one real option available, and Fred was happy to grab it. "Good idea!" He summoned the two Signals maintainers out of the pack gathered around. "We need you guys to take 'em down to Colfax PDQ. The track's been scraped so you should have smooth sailing."

The two exchanged uncomfortable looks. "Yeah, okay, if they can be moved safely," one of them said.

"We don't have a choice," Jack said. "They need to get to a hospital."

"What about the wrecker?" someone asked. "They're on the way, and there's no place for the hi-rail t' pull off for 'em."

"Yeah." Parker Lee pondered the dilemma with no pleasure. "We need t' call in."

§

119

They retreated to the office caboose, and Parker Lee got on the radio. "This is SPMW 4034 to Roseville dispatch, we have an emergency. Over?"

"This is Roseville dispatcher to SPMW 4034, what is your emergency? Over?"

"Roseville, our spreader derailed and overturned at Emigrant Gap. The two crewmen are badly hurt, and we need to get them to Colfax by a hi-rail unit. Thing is, we got the wrecker train headed this way, with no way to get around them."

There was a brief hesitation:

"Can't you wait for the wrecker to clear?"

Lee gave Jack a searching look; he shook his head. There was no telling how long it would be before the wrecker arrived, and minutes counted. "Ah...dispatch, we can't wait. These guys are hurt bad. Over?"

"Aw, Jesus. Okay, get them moving. I'll contact the wreck train and figure something out."

Lee dropped the radio mic and turned to the two signalmen. "Alright, you heard the man. Let's get those guys moving. We'll update you when we hear from dispatch."

§

Milepost 197, Snow Shed 47:

About that time SPMW 207 came trundling up to Shed 47. Margret brought the train to a halt just inside the shed's entrance, and they went back to consult with Marcus on their plan of action.

"As I recall, we have enough track to park the work train and one locomotive on track one," Marcus said. "Then we can start digging our way to the wreck." Shed 47 also served as the point where the single track from Summit Tunnel split into dual trackage on east into Truckee.

"More playing musical chairs," Margret grumbled. Nonetheless everyone was pleased they had a safe spot to park the vulnerable work train where it was out of the wind and possible avalanches.

"How we gonna work this?" Earl asked. "Last time, we had t' blast trees repeatedly, and we can count on a lot more junk mixed into the mess this time."

That drew everyone's attention to Margret and Willy, since without saying it in so many words, he'd touched on the doubts they all felt about them. They'd had an easy trip thus far since the line was dug out earlier, but from here on in the rotary would be hard pressed in the jumbled snow pack. Worse, they couldn't risk the 207 being damaged; it was their last real hope to getting to the stranded Amtrak in time.

"They hit a rock, and they'll wind up in Roseville, like the 211 did," someone muttered.

"*Si*, we gonna risk more slides when we start blasting, too," Antonio added.

There was an uncomfortable silence as they pondered the risks.

"You want me t' wake Dan and Jesus?" Joey asked. Margret bridled at that; Willy looked mournful, but said nothing.

Marcus was sorely tempted, but he couldn't do it. He promised them twelve hours on the law, which both of them needed badly. More than that, if he couldn't put his trust in their two rookies, there was no sense in them being here at all.

"No," he said at last. "Margret and Willy have the assignment." He turned to them. "Just take it slow and easy. Better a slow trip than no trip."

For once, Margret said nothing. She and Willy headed back to the 207. Marcus watched them go with some apprehension, then turned to Earl. "Post some of your guys where they can see what's ahead of the rotary. They can warn Margret of anything in their path."

Earl nodded. "You got it. Antonio? Start preparing your charges."

"*Si*, boss."

§

121

Bret Johansen, Maintenance of Way foreman, was a frustrated, angry man, and he was not shy about sharing his angst with his boss. "Damned radiator's drained, damned oil's drained, damned fuel's drained, and it's got no sand, either! Why'd they even bother keeping her on the roster if they ain't gonna keep her up?" UPMW 903052 was sitting in the service yard about as useless as teats on a boar hog, to hear him tell it, which made for an unpleasant conversation for Phil Collins.

"You know she's on her way to Cheyenne, Bret. She's all we got, so we need to put her back on line for this emergency. You'll just have to get her ready."

"Get her ready! Have you *seen* the log book on that piece of junk? I could do better with a rock and a long two-by-four!"

Collins could understand his frustration. The road had chronically shorted them on heavy equipment for years—like the big, beautiful 180 ton crane Truckee *used* to have—and now they were paying the price. But there was no sense in whining about it. "We don't have any two-by-fours, so you'll have to get her up and running. It shouldn't take more than a few hours."

"Oh, sure! As soon as we can get to her! The damned snow removal crew didn't bother t' keep the service area cleared. We got two feet of snow t' dig through!"

"Shit," Collins muttered. Just when they needed a big hook the most... "Look: I'm sorry about that, Bret. I'll chase up a front-loader to help clear your unit, and I'll chew out the snow crew about it, too."

"Yeah? Well you can run over and chew Mechanical Department's leg while you're at it as well!" He stormed out of Phil's office in a mood which didn't bode well for any Mechanical Department people who crossed his path.

Collins sat for some time fuming about this unexpected slackness on his people's part, then took a deep breath and picked up the phone. It seemed he had a whole lot-a leg-chewing to get caught up on.

§

Milepost 170:

"God, d'you believe this weather?" The hi-rail driver was hunched over his steering wheel trying to see something, anything, through the white torrent which shook their truck. They were inching along down the line in total white-out conditions, their headlights surrounding them in a swirling white fog.

"You can pick it up a little," his partner said. "There's nothing ahead of us but the wreck extra, and we know where they are."

"Yeah, only we don't know about any drifts and slides 'cause they don't call in t' the dispatcher."

His partner sighed. "There is that." He turned to the two in the back seat. "Still, these guys aren't doing so good," he said, softly. "We should maybe take a few chances."

The driver pressed down in the gas a bit more. "Maybe."

"Speaking of which..." His partner examined their GPS, then picked up the radio mic. "...This is the emergency hi-rail, passing Milepost 170."

§

Milepost 149, Highway 80 Underpass:

"Gus, we got a problem." Walter Karns was not a happy camper, as he had to bring Gus more bad news. "The relief train derailed at Emigrant Gap. Spreader 4034 toppled over and was damaged. Both crewmen were injured, and a Signals unit is bring them down the Hill in a hi-rail."

Gus stared at him in amazement. "Dammit! How d'you tip over a spreader?"

"They derailed and rolled off the overpass." Gus's tone made Walter flinch like it was *his* fault they wrecked the only snow equipment available to them. "It was a one in a million shot."

"Aw, fer Christ's sake! What *is it* with this road?"

"It's this weather, Gus. Our people are exhausted, and the snow removal is far behind."

"I don't want excuses, I want action!"

"I'm sorry, Gus! There's nothing we can do until we get to Emigrant Gap."

123

Gus sighed in frustration. "Ain't this the pits?" He stewed for a bit, then said, "Alright, but when we get to th' Gap there's gonna be some reckoning!"

That sounded bad: Walter knew he meant every word of it. "Okay, Gus, but what about the hi-rail?"

"What hi-rail?" He'd overlooked that altogether.

"The one bringing the two injured crewmen down to Colfax."

Gus stared at him, confused. "Oh, shit," he muttered at last. "There's no place they can pull off, is there?"

"Emigrant Gap was the only spot they might have got clear."

Gus sighed in very real frustration. "Alright, contact the dispatcher and have him set us up a meet. We'll transfer those two to our doctor and send the hi-rail back up the Hill."

"You got it, Gus!" Walter beat a hasty retreat for the office caboose.

§

Milepost 198, aboard the 'City of San Francisco':

Reggie returned to the diner after making another tour of the rear part of the train, and stopped to check with Barbara on her patients. "How are they doing?" he asked, softly.

Barbara was busy changing a saturated bandage, and took a minute to reply. "We need help," she said once they were off to one side where no one could hear. "Our conscious head trauma patient seems to be stabilizing, but the old woman with the hip fracture is slipping. There is evidence of abdominal bleeding. We'll lose her if we don't get help soon."

That was an agony to contemplate. "How long?"

She pondered the old woman for a bit; she was resting silently, her hips and back supported on pillows, but she was clearly suffering. "I don't know," Barbara said at last. "But it won't take much for her to be beyond saving."

Reggie rubbed his eyed to fight off his exhaustion. "God...what a mess!"

"It's not your fault," she said. "It was just bad luck."

"Yeah. It's never anybody's fault." He brooded as he scanned the rest of the room. "What about the others?"

"Our minor cases are alright. Our unconscious head trauma is touch-and-go. Our broken collarbone is resting comfortably, but there's no improvement in his leg sensation." Her exhaustion was showing as well. "I hoped his nerve condition was traumatic, but it looks more and more like a dislocated spine. He might even have a shattered disc."

"That's not good."

She looked at him evenly. "He might never walk again."

Reggie sighed, and turned toward the lounge car where he could get some coffee. "You're doing a great job. Hang in there."

"Any word on when help will arrive?"

He paused. "Nothing. I'll call them and ask."

§

Milepost 206, Truckee, California:

"They say they got several people in bad shape, including at least one possible fatality. They need medical help up here as soon as possible. Word is the train from Roseville is still at Emigrant Gap. We're only now clearing the way to the wreck, and we can't do them any good until the relief train gets here anyway. Can you do anything from your end?"

Jim Mortensen was appalled at the latest word from Summit. As much as he worried about all those people, he felt deep down there was nothing they could do. But now it seemed Roseville was washing out as well; not surprising in light of how far they needed to travel and the conditions they faced.

"Please hurry! It's hell up here! I don't know how much longer they can hold together."

There was genuine fear and anguish in Marcus's voice, clearly heard even over the radio. Mortensen *wanted* to help, sincerely he did, but he was out of his depth in this miserable weather, and knew it. He tried to come up with something to say, but his thoughts were in a turmoil of indecision and shame.

125

"Plus at the rate it's snowing, we could be looking at more avalanches before too long. We need t' get them out of there ASAP. You there, Truckee?"

It was too much. Mortensen gripped the radio mic. "Copy that, Marcus! Hang in there, and tell the train people we're doing everything possible from this end."

"Well? That settles it," Herb said after the radio conversation ended. "We can't sit by and do nothing! Not now!"

"But what *can* we do?" Mortensen was practically in tears. He pulled himself together with an effort. "We'll...have to call in the company doctor from Reno..."

"It could take hours to get him here. And once he does, how do we get him up the Hill?"

"I...don't know. We can send an engine..."

"But they can't get past the first derailment until that damned crane gets here, and it must be a couple miles from there to the second wreck. How can they walk that in this weather? It could take *days* before we can clear that first derailment!"

A painful silence returned as they tried to come up with some bright idea for this seemingly hopeless situation. Herb pondered the question as he watched the snow swirling past Mortensen's office window. He had precious little sympathy for his boss, although he agreed this seemed hopeless. But this was no time to call the game on points: lives were at stake. This was no longer a what-if, and there could be no excuses for failure. There *had* to be an answer, and it looked like *he* had to find it.

The snow was blowing across the rail yard. He could feel the numbing cold in his mind, imagining what those poor souls up there on the Hill must be going through. Mortensen couldn't do the job; was overdue to be put out to pasture anyway. It fell to him to come up with an answer. The weather was deteriorating steadily. If they were going to do anything, they had to do it now.

Finally he turned to Mortensen. "Forget Reno, forget the crane, forget your engines. You get me a doctor, *I'll* get him up th' Hill!"

§

126

Milepost 153, Gold Run:

"What you got now, Walter?" Gus's tone was ugly when he arrived in the caboose in response to Walter's summons.

Walter gestured at the radio on his desk. "We just got word from the dispatcher. The 'City' train has several serious casualties on board. Some of them might die. They want t' know how soon we'll get our doctor there."

"Awww...DAMMIT!" Gus was sick with agony over the endless delays, and now this... He stewed over this mess for some time, trying to come up with some solution. There was only one answer. "Alright, we got t' get there come hell or high water. I don't want any more excuses! We roll on through as fast as we can. No breakdowns, no delays, no nothing!"

"We still gonna meet the hi-rail?"

Gus hesitated, caught between two crises. "No, we can't wait. We gotta get the doc and his supplies up there as soon as possible."

"What about the hi-rail? Send 'em back to Emigrant Gap?"

Gus pondered that with no joy. If they were bringing people down the Hill in the face of the wrecker, those two casualties were likely severe. It was situations like this which gave dispatchers on the Hill ulcers. "Tell 'em to pull off at the Fulda Balloon. It's the last spot where they *might* be able to get off the line."

"They'll have to hurry, we'll reach Dutch Flat before long."

"Then tell 'em t' shag their sorry asses and *get it done!* Tell 'em t' get clear no matter *what* it takes!"

Walter turned to the radio without answering.

"We ain't *never* gonna get there at this rate!" Gus muttered.

§

Milepost 206, Truckee, California:

The first step in Herb Mokowski's grand plan was transportation, which he could arrange by phone. "Alicia? This is dad. I want you to get both the Sno-Cats ready; make sure they're fully fueled and get them down to the rail yard, pronto." A brief silence. "Tell your mother I said so!" He reined in his temper. "Let me speak to your mom."

127

There was a brief pause, then, "Jan? Hi, babe. This is an emergency. We need the Sno-Cats for a rescue mission." Further silence. "Yes, hon, it's urgent. I'll be late this evening."

He hung up, confident that least *this* part of his plan was going smoothly. "Alright, that's your transportation," he said to Mortensen. "Now you need to get me a doctor."

Mortensen shook his head in dismay as he picked up the phone. "I hope you know what you're doing."

"Yeah, so do I," Herb mumbled to himself.

§

Milepost 198, aboard the 'City of San Francisco':

"I got word from the dispatcher," George Reinsbach told Barbara, quietly. "The relief train from Roseville is stalled at Emigrant Gap, several hours away at this rate, and Truckee made some big promises, but there's not much they can do. I'm afraid medical help won't get here for some time."

"That's bad," she said. "We may lose one, maybe two if we don't get help soon."

"God! I *wish* we could do something!" Reinsbach fumed in frustration.

"There's nothing we *can* do, except hang on, and hope." Barbara sagged against the bulkhead and fought off a yawn.

"You okay?"

She straightened up. "I'll manage."

"You've been going nonstop. You need some rest."

She shook her head. "I can't. I'm all they have." She stared vacantly at the tables crowded with injured people and littered with used bandages and medical wrappers. Her exhaustion was showing. "We're used to the long hours anyway," she said at last.

§

Milepost 206, Truckee, California:

An ambulance arrived at the Maintenance of Way office about forty-five minutes later, bringing a Doctor Menendez from the local hospital. He was not thrilled to be there, and hastily retreated into the Maintenance of Way building.

128

"Good Lord, it's cold out there!" He pulled off his gloves, threw back his hood, and looked around at the people assembled. "So what is your emergency? Can't you bring them to the hospital?"

"We're still working on getting them out," Mokowski told him. "For now they're stranded up near Summit."

"Summit? You mean up in the mountains?"

"That's right. We have a passenger train wrecked up there."

Menendez was dismayed. "How bad is it? Why haven't we heard about it until now?"

"We just got a report from them. They have several severely injured passengers, and they need a trauma surgeon." Mokowski considered him skeptically; Doctor Menendez was in his fifties, overweight, and didn't look at all athletic. "You *are* a trauma surgeon?"

"Well...actually...I'm a general surgeon, the best we have locally, I suppose. We're a small hospital, and I also do a lot of work in the ER. But how can we get to them?"

Herb caught movement through Mortensen's office window. "Here comes our ride now."

§

They made their way outside as two Sno-Cats came roaring up and skidded to a halt, showering them with icy muck. "Hi, daddy!" fifteen year old Alicia said. "Where we going?"

"*You* aren't going anywhere!" Herb said, sternly. "And what have I told you about hot-dogging? This isn't a joy ride; we need these for an emergency up on the Hill."

"Up in the mountains?" Alicia was thrilled. "I wanna go!"

"Me too!" twelve year old Angela pitched in. "Can we, dad? Pleeaasee?"

Herb was exasperated by his daughters' arguing. "No sweetie. This is serious business, plus your mother'd kill me if I let you two go along."

"Awww daddy!"

"It'd serve you right," Angela pouted.

"Alright, enough! You two stay here and mister Mortensen will arrange for someone to take you home."

Menendez studied the Sno-Cat with obvious misgivings. "I don't know how to drive one of those things."

"I'll take him," the ambulance driver said.

"The hell you will!" the attendant barked. "Two wallowing hippos like you would bog down for sure. I'll take him." He looked askance at her, but backed down.

Herb eyed her skeptically; she was half the size of the hulking driver. "This'll be a tough run," he said, doubtfully. "D'you have any experience on these things?"

"I ride a ZR 9000 Thundercat. Those kiddie cars are for amateurs." She was a petite five foot nothing, moved with the swift grace of an athlete, and seemed like she'd been sculpted out of piano wire. Her assertive no-nonsense look stilled any possible argument.

"Really?" Herb was surprised and impressed. "We're heading up the Hill, nearly to Summit. It'll be a rough ride in this weather. Sure you can do it?"

She gave him a chilly look. "Time's a-wasting. You in or out?"

Herb's eyebrows crept up. "Maybe you'll do after all." The driver nodded ruefully in confirmation.

"Plus I'm an EMT3-trauma specialist; you'll need all the help you can get up there."

This was no time to debate; the recent message from up the Hill erased any doubts about this gamble. "Okay. So what's your name, anyway?"

Having gotten her way, she flashed an engaging smile. "I'm Jamie Kirk."

"Really? Why am I not surprised? Alright then, let's do it."

His two daughters didn't share in their consensus. "Awww daadddeee! This isn't fair! We wanna go!"

"Yeah!"

"I said enough, you two! Inside, both of you." They went, reluctantly. "Jim, make sure they get home, will you?"

"Beware the female of the species," Mortensen muttered as they set to work.

Herb gave him a peeved look. "Gawd, you know it!"

§

"How bad are they?" Everyone in the office caboose followed Marcus's conversation with the relief train in strained silence, each of them praying for their friends down the line.

"The spreader crew were injured, we're sending them down to Colfax. Everyone else is okay, but we can't go on without the spreader. Can you send your rotary down?"

Marcus gave Earl an anxious look. "Ah, copy that, relief train. They're on their way down to you."

"I do *not* believe this!" Earl grumbled after their conversation ended. "How many wrecks can one railroad have?"

"As many as it takes." Marcus shifted his attention to the radio. "Marcus to rotary 207?"

"207."

"Margret, we got a problem. The work train lost their spreader at Emigrant Gap. I need you to run down and bring them up."

"So you finally got a job simple enough for a mere girl to handle?"

Marcus bridled at her dig, but let it go. There were more urgent things to worry about. "We need those section hands. I want you to go down and clear the way for them."

"What about the wrecker?"

"My guess is they'll have caught up by time you get there, so you can bring everyone up. Bring 'em back to Norden so they can sort things out."

"Right. On our way."

§

"Do you believe this?" Willy grumbled. "We were just getting warmed up, too!" They managed to dig precisely one car length into the snow pack when Marcus' radio call came in.

"If you call this 'warm'," Margret said. What little they accomplished came from monumental effort as the overloaded rotary tried to swallow more than it was designed for. "A lesson for you, my young padawan: *nothing* ever goes as planned on the Hill!" She set the controls in reverse, pulled on her gloves, and headed for the door. "Alright, let's get this fuster cluck on the road."

§

Milepost 169, Fulda Balloon Track:

"What d'you think?" The two Signal maintainers surveyed the situation with deep misgivings. The balloon track hadn't been scraped in several days and was hopelessly buried in snow. The tiny track wheels of their hi-rail could hardly wade through that mess. What was worse, there was a five foot bank of snow displaced by the spreader a few hours earlier, and there was no way they could climb it. They were stranded in the narrow lane cleared by the spreader, with the wreck train bearing down on them.

"I think we're screwed," the driver replied. They just received the call from the wrecker, somewhere to their west and coming on strong, and they were still a bit off balance.

"Well we gotta do something!"

There were precious few options. Fulda was in the middle of nowhere, its only significance being a loop of track used to turn snow equipment around, and a detracking point where they could supposedly exit the right of way. A row of tin sheds housing Maintenance of Way supplies, now collapsed under the weight of snow, was the only sign of civilization for miles around.

There *was* a safe spot, a paved area right in front of the maintenance shacks, which could still be driven onto—but it was blocked by the wall of snow shoved aside by the work train's spreader. They were dead in the wreck extra's sights, and there was nowhere to go.

"Shit," the driver muttered.

"We gotta go back to Emigrant Gap," his partner said, doubtfully.

The driver shook his head and gestured to the two injured men in the back seat. "They won't last that long." Just then their truck radio crackled to life:

"This is the SP wreck extra, passing Dutch Flat."

"That's fourteen miles, man. They'll be here within the hour. What do we do?"

The driver reached into the back of their truck and grabbed a shovel. "We dig." He handed the shovel to his partner and grabbed the other one. "We dig like two sumbitches!"

§

Milepost 206, Truckee, California:

Preparing for their rescue mission meant stripping the ambulance of every last bit of medical gear, much to the driver's dismay. "Jeez, Jamie, why don't you take the spare tire, too?" The vehicle was solidly pillaged.

"You are *such* a fuss, Will!" Jamie gave him an engaging smile as she pulled the portable oxygen bottle free from its bracket. "You can reequip when you get back to the hospital. We'll need this stuff up there."

"Are you sure this is a good idea?" Doctor Menendez clearly didn't think so. "I've been following the weather lately, and it's a disaster up there, by all accounts."

Herb Mokowski paused stuffing the loot into borrowed backpacks to give him a somber look. "It's our only choice. We can't get to them any other way."

"Yes, but..."

"It's eight miles on a good grade. We follow the tracks so we'll have an easy run and can't get lost."

"But I..."

"Don't worry, Doc!" Jamie gave him her smile; she apparently could wrap any man around her little finger. "I'll get you there, no problem." Her smile faded. "They need us. We have to do this."

Menendez hesitated, torn between his fear and his sense of duty. Finally he bowed to the inevitable with a weary nod.

Herb went back to his packing. "Is this everything?"

"It's everything we have," Jamie said. Their loot was in three backpacks plus the oxygen bottle. She hefted one of the packs. "I'll take one of these and the doctor, you take the other two and the oxygen."

"Good." Herb fixed her with a stern look. "I'm the trail boss." He cut off her protest. "I know the terrain and the situation, and the weather."

She hesitated, then nodded. "Right. Let's do it."

Alicia and Angela came bouncing up as they were getting ready. "We wanna go, daddy!" Alicia insisted.

"We've been up in the mountains before, and we both know how to ride!"

"Why does she get to go?" Alicia aimed a hostile finger at Jamie. "I'm bigger than her! I should be the one!"

"No, me!"

"N-uh uh! I'm the big sister! I get first pick!" She turned on Doctor Menendez and the ambulance crew. "You tell him!"

Will, the ambulance driver, backed off with a show of hands. "Don't look at me!"

"Enough!" Herb barked. "This is serious business, and we'll take care of it. You two go home to be with your mother."

"Awwww daaadddeeee!"

Jamie was amused by their outburst. "Spirited. I like 'em."

"I'll make you a package deal for 'em," Herb grumbled.

§

Milepost 198, aboard the 'City of San Francisco':

O'Brian completed another patrol down the length of the train, and paused in the lounge car to grab a cup of coffee from the snack bar downstairs. Right then there was a limited selection of drinks, soup and sandwiches available in the snack bar and the diner since the diner's kitchen was shut down for lack of power. It wasn't really enough, as the frenzied crowd in that tiny space showed, but at least it was something.

"How's it going, Claire?" he asked the much-harassed snack bar attendant.

She brushed back an unruly strand of hair and gave him a frenzied look. "They're coming out of the woodwork! We're just about out of everything!"

"I know!" He had to shout to be heard over the noise level. "Things are getting worse. People are afraid. Try to keep some order down here!" She looked askance at him, and turned back to the customers competing for her attention.

Paul came down just then with one of the large coffee pots from the diner. "Hey, Claire, got some more hot soup for you. Beef and barley this time." He managed to slide the heavy pot onto the condiment table and plugged it in before the mob descended on it. Paul fought his way clear of the shoving mass, and handed her a paper sack. "Got some sandwiches for you, too."

"Thank you, Paul!" She seemed relieved at this timely gift, not that they would last long.

Her and O'Brian fought their way to a less crowded spot by the stairs. "How are things with you folks?" O'Brian asked.

Paul sagged from fatigue, and rubbed his eyes. "We're managing for now in the diner, but we're down to hamburger buns for sandwiches. Chips and candy and stuff are long gone, and my guess is we'll be down to soup in another hour or so."

"At least we're providing *some* food." They'd long since given up charging for meals under the circumstances.

"We've been debating whether to turn the heat off long enough to cook up some stew, but with the weather what it is out there, Reinsbach is reluctant."

"Who can blame him!" It was blowing a full gale out there, and even the part of the train still inside Tunnel 13 was chilly. In fact the auxiliary generator was straining to provide lights and enough heat to take the worst edge off the chill as is.

"These people are losing it..."

...the lights flickered and faded just then, evoking a wail of dismay from the mob. "Oh, shit!" They looked wildly around, trying to contain their own panic as the lights came up again. The lights flickered once more, fading almost to dark before recovering. O'Brian dug his flashlight out of his pocket and turned with his back against the bulkhead next to the stairway. "Everyone remain calm!" he yelled. A blackout now would set off a panic in this crowded space.

"The generator out of fuel already?" Paul asked.

O'Brian checked his watch. "We shouldn't be; it's only been about five hours..."

The lights flickered again, then were steady once more. Everyone stood wire tense, not moving or making a sound as they wondered what would come next. The tension in the crowded space was electric. Another flicker; the lights dimmed for several seconds, evoking a chorus of moans and whimpers before returning to normal. They stood there for a couple more minutes before people began unwinding. The voices rose once again, although more subdued than before.

"Water in the fuel, maybe?" Paul suggested.

"God...I hope that's all it is." O'Brian forced himself to relax, fiddled nervously with his flashlight, then tucked it in his pocket again. "Tell the kitchen to do as much as they can while they can, just in case," he said, confidentially.

"Yeah," Paul muttered. "We need to start making plans for when the power finally does go."

"Gawd, I don't even want t' *think* about that!"

§

Milepost 169, Fulda Balloon Track:

The last forty-five minutes left the two Signals maintainers aching and gasping for breath, hearts pounding from their efforts. They'd managed to knock the worst of the snow barrier down, but there was still a lot to move, and they were running on sheer adrenalin, which can only take a man so far. They both knew the wrecker could come out of the gloom at any moment. It was too late to cut and run for Emigrant Gap, so digging was their only option, but there is only so much human flesh can endure. Finally the cold and the thin mountain air caught up with them, forcing them to pause for breath.

That was when their truck radio crackled to life:

"This is the wreck extra, passing Blue Canyon."

"Shit, man!" the helper gasped. "That's three miles! They'll be here any moment now!"

"It's now or never, dude!" The driver staggered to the cab of the truck as the faint sound of a diesel horn came out of nowhere. "Pull the track wheels!"

His partner flung his shovel aside with a curse and tackled the front wheelset, trying to get the small track wheels to fold up so they could drive off the right of way. They were stuck! The release lever was caked with ice from snow melted by the motor. He kicked at it futilely, trying to knock it loose, with no luck.

The horn came again, closer this time.

Frustrated, he hammered the lever with his shovel, sending ice chips flying, then wedged the shovel blade in and heaved. The front track wheels came loose; the hi-rail settled with a *thump* as the driver gunned the engine, cut hard right, and floored it.

The horn sounded again, right on top of them as the hi-rail swerved right and climbed the reduced snow bank. The rear track wheels hung up on the rail, then the truck dug in and bounced over the snow embankment as they were bathed in light from the oncoming train. The truck hung up on the mounded snow and stalled, just barely clear of the right of way as the wreck extra bore down on them. The swirling gloom throbbed with the sound of diesel power, the darkness glowed as the headlights grew closer, then all of a sudden the wrecker was there; the massive diesel looming over them like a dark cliff.

As the locomotive passed, its massive pilot plow clipped the rear fender of the hi-rail, shoving the truck aside and breaking the tail light. The engine was followed by the crane, its tool car, then its service train and finally the office caboose.

They got a brief glimpse of Gus Vincincegorough glaring at them as the caboose went by before the apparition was blurred out by falling snow. The red running lights faded into the gloom and vanished as the rumble of the big diesel dwindled into the night. It was that close, but they survived. Nothing lay between them and Colfax now but twenty-seven miles of blizzard.

The two Signals men were shaken by their near miss, staring numbly at each other for the next few minutes before a low moan broke the spell. Davy Burns was out cold; Pietro was semi-conscious, and moaned faintly as they checked him.

Finally the driver stirred. "Alright." His hands were shaking as he put the truck in reverse. "Lets get the *hell* out-a here!"

*****

Mid-Evening:

Consciousness returned, slowly.

The first thing Bobby Mayfield was aware of was pain. His left arm throbbed and his back ached. He lay on his side for a long time wondering about that pain; what caused it, why he was hurting, but he couldn't make sense of it. Gradually he became aware of a new sensation: cold. Wherever he was, it was bitterly cold. The thin air burned in his lungs, making every breath an effort. Something was wrong, but his thoughts were fuzzy, unreal. He couldn't make sense of what was happening, but he knew this wasn't right.

After reflecting on these sensations for a while, he stirred, rolled over on his back, evoking more pain, and managed to open his eyes. He couldn't see anything at first. The world around him was formless blackness, well out of focus at that. Vision came slowly, bit by bit, helped on by some small red lights in the distance. He tried to focus on them as he wondered where he was and how he got here. His head ached, along with his arm and back. He blinked his eyes several times, and the lights came into focus. He was staring at the power panel, lit up with red emergency lights. That didn't make sense, either. Power panel? What was it, and why did it matter? And why would it be above him? It should be behind him...

...then his mind came into focus: they were hit by an avalanche. He was in the wreck of the locomotive laying in the nose staring up at the rear bulkhead above him. It took a long time for it to make sense, but at least he had a clue he could work with. The picture gradually emerged...the locomotive lay nose down...on a steep mountain slope...on its side. The cold...was because they were high up in the mountains, just about to crest Donner Summit. The pain...he was injured...in the wreck. That alarmed him, and it took him a moment to understand he was still alive. He could still move, however painfully. That brought a glimmer of hope. He might just get out of this yet.

Then the thought came to him: what about the rest of the train? There were five hundred passengers and crew on board; what became of them? That goaded him into action. He tried to stand...

...the pain in his arm grew into a fiery agony, evoking a whimper. He settled on his back as his vision dimmed, and lay gasping for breath until the pain subsided. After who knew how long, he used his right hand to feel along his left, trying to scope out the damage. Above his elbow the sleeve was sticky wet, and a new wave of pain welled up when he touched something hard protruding through his skin. His left arm was broken.

§

Milepost 204, Highway 89 Overpass:

The overpass spanning State Highway 89 marked the effective end of civilization at the boggy delta where Cold Creek met Donner Creek, both coming down from the high country. Ahead lay Cold Creek Canyon and the climb to Horseshoe Curve.

The two Sno-Cats labored on through the thick snow pack, both heavily enough loaded to make it tough going. Herb Mokowski hung doggedly onto the handlebars, trying to see the track all but buried ahead of him. The snow was getting pretty severe, and while it wasn't white-out conditions, yet, visibility wasn't good. The wind tore at him, finding its way in through every cuff and opening, chilling him. He used to love going out on the Sno-Cats; he and Jan took the girls out regularly when they were younger, and lately the two girls would double up on one while he rode the other. But they never went out in these conditions! People got lost in weather like this. People died. A couple of the road's regulars were volunteers with the local search-and-rescue, and were often called away in this kind of weather, but he never imagined himself going out willingly in this.

But he wasn't here for the hell of it. They were on an urgent mission, and he had to wonder if this was even do-able. It wasn't possible to dress warmly enough in these conditions. The cold was starting to sap his strength, blunt his will. Even if he could manage, their doctor was no outdoorsman. That thought preyed on his mind; filling him with doubts.

140

He threw a quick glance to his rear: the other Sno-Cat was about fifty feet behind, riding his trail doggedly. He had to admit that young woman was impressive, even if he wasn't sure she'd be a good role model for the girls. He shook that thought off: there were more immediate matters to deal with. The doctor was their weak link: how much of this could he take?

He checked the weather right before they left, and it wasn't promising. The blizzard pounding the western slopes was finally leaking over to the east. The forecast was for as much as two feet of fresh snow. The right of way was already buried; even the rails were covered, not that he could see much in the gloom anyway. Navigation was strictly by following the smooth, even grade ahead of them, and bumping up against one rail or the other every now and then. Thankfully they had this much to guide them; there was no way to navigate in this icy hell otherwise.

Something emerged out of the gloom ahead: a signal bridge spanning both tracks. Its lights were out, the superstructure buried under the buildup. *'That'll cave in if it gets much worse,'* he thought. They crawled under the signal bridge, receiving a shower of displaced snow for their troubles. The wind blasted bits of snow and ice in his face, building up around his goggles. The icy wind made breathing painful. Herb recognized it as the signal bridge at Milepost 203. Five miles to go.

§

Milepost 198, down slope:

Bobby lay on his back for some time trying to decide what to do next. His freakin' *arm* was broke, which spooked him something awful, his left leg was numb, and although he didn't know it he had a concussion. He never was one to endure pain, and now the pain was constant. It muddled his thoughts, distracted him.

"Bobby?" The voice was so faint he could hardly hear it, but it was definitely there. "Bobby? You there, man?"

That forced him back into focus. "Karl?"

"I'm hurt. Help me." The voice was fading and windy, tinged with pain.

141

"Where...where are you, man?"

"I...engin...eer station. I'm pinned."

Bobby struggled to his knees, ignoring the pain in his arm and back, and groped his way across the darkened cab. His knee hit something which skittered across the wall with a tinny sound. Instinctively he groped for it, finally finding what he needed most; a switchman's lantern. He thumbed the switch with a prayer, and the lantern lit up. The cab was a shambles. The locomotive lay on it's right side, nose down on the slope. The bullet-proof windscreen was starred, but held together, holding the snow at bay. The engineer's side window was shattered, and the entire control console had been ripped from its moorings. Karl was wedged between his seat and the console, sitting upright on his side against the right wall. There was a massive gash on his forehead, with blood oozing down his face.

"Help me, man," he wheezed. "I'm hurt bad."

"Okay...hang...hang tough, man."

Bobby struggled to his feet, which wasn't easy since his left leg didn't want to cooperate, and wedged his good shoulder against the console. Try as he could, and he couldn't do much, the console didn't budge. The thing weighed over a ton. Even if he was in good shape, he couldn't have moved it.

"God!" he gasped as he sagged against the console. "Can't..." He spotted the radio hand piece laying on the floor. He sagged to his knees, fumbled for the mic, and finally managed to corral it with his good hand.

"Mayday...mayday..." His voice was thin and wobbly, and it took all his effort to speak. "...Amtrak 15...calling anyone...help...we're wrecked. Can...you hear me?"

Nothing.

"Amtrak 15...anyone...help! We're hurt."

Nothing. No response. Not even the sound of static from the speaker. Then he saw a bundle of cables coming out of the base of the control panel: the wires were broken, frayed, their insulation torn. He gave up and dropped the mic. "Radio's no good, man."

Karl looked about gone. He stirred feebly, and his eyes held the gaze of a dead man. "We...ain't gonna...make it. Are we?"

142

Something in those eyes cut Bobby to his soul. Something inside him said no matter how bad off he was, he wouldn't give up; not while there was any way to continue the fight. "I gotta go, man. I gotta...get t' the other unit...see if its radio survived."

But first he needed to deal with his broken arm. He was pretty foggy, but instinct and his first aid training kicked in. His backpack lay nearby; he noticed the light bungie cord he used to keep the top closed. He managed to free it one-handed, and looked around for something to use as a splint. There were some fuzees in their rack next to the rear door. It took a lot of effort and several tries—the pain was horrendous—but he managed to wedge a fuzee against his side until he could loop the bungie cord around his arm, wrapping it around repeatedly and hooking it off. It wasn't much —it wasn't enough—but it was the best he could do.

That done, he sagged on his back against the forward bulkhead, breathing deep, rapid breaths to fight off the pain of binding his arm. For a moment he felt the urge to close his eyes and drift off to sleep, but some deep-seated survival instinct forced him back awake. If he passed out now, he might not wake up. There was nothing for it. Despite the pain, despite his injuries, he needed to reach the second unit. He struggled to his knees and crawled to the right hand door leading back into the engine compartment.

§

Milepost 149, Highway 80 Underpass:

"I don't know about you, but I'm fuckin' *lost*, man," the hi-rail driver muttered. "Can't see for shit."

"Me neither," his partner said. The snow was coming down thick and fast, leaving them to grope their way in total white-out conditions. "You might as well turn those damned wipers off. They're fuckin' useless." The snow was melting on their windshield and refreezing on the wiper blades, caking them and smearing their view ahead.

The driver shut them off. "It's not like I can see anything anyway."

His partner turned and looked back at their two injured passengers. "Those guys are in bad shape."

143

"I'm goin' as fast as I can..."

...Suddenly the snow stopped. Their headlights shown out ahead of them, revealing a dark passage dim in their snow-encrusted windshield. The driver instinctively hit the brakes and the hi-rail skidded to a halt.

They sat motionless for a moment, wondering what happened. "Where are we, man?" the driver said at last.

"It's the underpass! We're at...what?...Milepost 149!"

The driver was vastly relieved. "At least we know where we are now! Only seven miles t' go."

"Yeah, but how we gonna find Colfax? We'll be blind again once we leave this shelter."

The driver grabbed the radio mic. "We'll need some help."

§

Milepost 198, down slope:

The narrow engine compartment door lay on its side, so Bobby was forced to lay on *his* side and shimmy through the doorway into the back of the unit. Once through, he lay on his back against the right wall and held the switchman's lantern up. The faint glow showed him a scene of chaos.

The compartment was littered with the odds and ends which accumulate over time in such places. Some wire bundles were torn loose, hanging down in his potential path, which was blocked in any case by a dislodged sheet metal grille. The massive diesel was still on its bed mounts, its huge weight suspended in mid-air. Below it, a pool of engine oil rippled as sprung seals continued to drip. He'd have to crawl through that mess to reach the rear doors, but instinct held him back. These locomotives weren't designed to take this kind of punishment. What he could see of the engine compartment was devastation. There was no guarantee the massive drive components were still solidly held down. He couldn't see what shape the diesel was in, but noticed a couple of the bolts holding the electrical cabinet had sheered. That settled it: anything in here could sheer off at any moment. If he tried to take the easy route along the right—lower—side and something broke loose, they would both be dead.

144

That meant he needed to climb up over the drive equipment to reach the left hand gangway, ten impossible feet overhead. There was nothing for it, so he struggled to his feet, cradling his broken arm next to his side and clutched the lantern in his teeth. It took a monumental effort to crawl up the generator, hooking his good hand and both feet on relay boxes and cable loops to reach the other side of the engine compartment. That took all he had, so he lay draped over the end of the big diesel to recover his strength.

Once he lay still, he faded out, all but losing consciousness as he stared up at the left wall just above. He drifted for a time, not really thinking or feeling anything other than the cold and the pain in his arm. He might have quit then, would have if it wasn't for his friend Karl. This was hopeless. Karl was likely already dead, or would be soon, and he wouldn't be far behind. There was no sense in fighting it. The only sensible thing to do was give up, lay here quietly and let the cold take him.

But as battered and exhausted as he was, he couldn't do it. It didn't make sense to go on, but quitting just wasn't *right*, not when his friend was counting on him. He struggled to roll over, then crawled along the side of the big diesel on elbow and knees toward the rear of the unit.

§

Milepost 198, aboard the 'City Of San Francisco':

The dining car was a scene of quiet chaos when O'Brian returned from another sweep of the train. The injured were stable for the moment, enduring their pain as best they could while Barbara fussed over their three major injuries. The less seriously injured sat or lay wherever they could, while the center table in the dining section was set up to provide coffee, soup and sandwiches brought up from the kitchen on the lower level.

"How are things forward?" Greenbaum asked.

"Quiet, for now." He helped himself to a cup of soup. "I'm not sure how much longer the power will last."

"Yeah. There'll be trouble once that goes."

They didn't notice Charlie Parkhurst come in, speak briefly with Barbara, and they both left hurriedly.

145

"The kitchen is using their microwaves to heat up canned stew, so we're at least providing some hot food. I told them to go ahead and use it all up, since it'll be useless once the power quits."

"Any word on rescue?"

"Nothing yet. Maybe Reinsbach has heard something."

"Well they need t' get it up. We can't last much longer."

Greenbaum gave him a measured look. "They know we're here, and they know about our problems. They're doing everything they can t' get here as fast as possible."

"Yeah. I just hope their 'everything' is good enough."

Parkhurst came back just then, wading toward them through the crowded car. "Hey man," he said, quietly. "We got a problem." From the look on his face, his 'problem' would be ill-news.

"What is it now?" Greenbaum asked, wearily.

Parkhurst jerked a thumb over his shoulder toward the lounge car, next one over. "That pregnant lady, looks like she might be in labor."

§

Milepost 198, down slope:

The second unit was standing upright, its nose buried in the stern of the first unit. Bobby tried to force the rear door, but it was jammed, buckled by the impact of the second unit. His only way to get there was the rear left side door. He strained to reach the handle, caught it with his fingertips; the door gave way, flopping open and admitting a cascade of snow. For a moment he was afraid he would be buried alive, but the cascade soon ended, leaving the open door gaping above him. Getting to it took a superhuman effort. He managed to climb up on the air compressor housing and struggle through the open door with one good arm. How he made it was beyond him, but he did.

The sight which greeted him was grim: the lead unit was all but buried. The second was more or less upright, but it would be a tough slog through twenty feet of loose snow and a lifetime of forlorn hope to reach it. That was all he could see in the feeble light of the switchman's lantern. The rest of the universe was nothing but swirling white darkness.

146

His exertion left him feeling faint. He sat on the end of the lead unit and took deep breaths, trying to fight off his dizziness. If he passed out now, he'd freeze to death in minutes. It took a while before he felt strong enough to take the next step.

He left the brakeman's lantern propped on the end of the lead unit, grabbed the rearmost grab iron, and swung awkwardly down off the end of the unit. He sank nearly up to his waist, reluctantly let go of the handrail, and worked his way along the nose of the second unit, forging a deep trench as he went. It was brutal, exhausting work; he was only able to keep track of where he was going by following the second unit's nose. It wasn't long before his strength gave out again.

It took him a moment to realize the cab side door was just ahead, right above the snow line, which meant the second unit was buried something like six feet deep. He, in turn, was buried up to his waist, and his strength was giving out. He managed to find one of the built-in steps below the cab door, and pulled himself up by the vertical grab iron to where he could just reach the door latch— if he let go the vertical rail with his one good hand. There was nothing for it, and he had to act fast before he collapsed.

He was first-time lucky. He clung desperately to the door handle as it swung inward, and fell on the cab floor with a cry of pain, half inside. That was all he had. He lay there for some time, trying not to faint, before he recovered enough to raise his head and look around. The cab was intact, lit by the faint emergency lights glowing feebly on the rear power panel. Best of all, the engineer's station sat right in front of him.

§

Milepost 171, Emigrant Gap:

The only warning of their arrival at Emigrant Gap was the glow of the relief train's headlights lighting up the gloom. Fortunately they were only going at a walking pace. Margret killed the throttle and hit the brakes, and SPMW 207 ground to an abrupt halt. No sooner did that happen then Gus Vincincegorough climbed up to their cab. "*You're* the crew on this unit?" he demanded in surprise.

Margret was in a temper to start with, and bristled at his tone. "That's right, and if you want our help you better learn to like it!"

Gus stared at her in surprise, then backed down from her unexpected forcefulness. "What's it like further up?"

"It's bad. The snow shed is blocked, and you can't see ten feet in general. You guys ready t' head up?"

"Yeah. What you'll have t' do is dig out the crossover so we can get around that wrecked spreader. We'll back up to where we can follow you up on track one."

"You got the wrecker here? Can't you grab the spreader?" Willy asked.

She cut Gus off before he could answer. "We can't waste th' time. We gotta get that passenger train out before they're buried alive. They can worry about the spreader another day."

Willy retreated. "Yeah, okay."

That wasn't what Gus was going to say, but she was right. "We'll stop at Norden so we can get everyone sorted out."

She gave him a hard look. "That's the idea. So what are you standing around with your thumb up your ass for? Let's get this show on the road!"

Gus climbed down, duly chastened and thankful to escape her temper, and Margret took SPMW 207 back up a short way to where the track passed under highway 80; where the double track from Colfax narrowed to a single track for The Gap.

§

Milepost 197, Snow Shed 47:

> *"Mayday...mayday! This...is...Amtrak City train...we're wrecked...need help. Anyone! Can you hear me?"*

Marcus spun around in surprise, staring at the radio like he'd seen a ghost. "Jesus! They're alive!" He grabbed the radio mic. "Amtrak! This is a work train at Shed 47! We hear you! What's your situation? Over?"

Earl stared in stunned dismay for a moment, then leaned out the door of the office caboose. "Hey!" he shouted to the people nearby. "The Amtrak crew is alive! They're on the radio!"

148

"Snow...we're hurt. Karl...hurt bad...need help..."

"We're right above you on the embankment, Amtrak! We got the whole crew here. We're coming t' get you!" Marcus was sobbing with relief, as were all of them.

§

Milepost 198, aboard the 'City Of San Francisco':

The lounge car was never designed to be a maternity ward. Two rows of swivel seats lined a narrow central corridor, with a winding stairwell in the middle leading to the snack bar on the lower level. The place was packed with riders displaced from the single-deck section, who were well and truly traveling 'SRO', and weren't thrilled to reenact the bygone days of wartime railroading.

Reggie scanned the room as best he could; his quarry should be easy to spot even in this mob. "So? Where is she?"

Parkhurst gestured to the narrow stairwell. "Down there."

"Wha? What the hell's she doing down there?"

Parkhurst shrugged. "Getting a nukeburger."

The snack bar was essentially a concession stand with only a small area for customers. The only accessible furnishing was a cabinet used to store condiments, with bins for the same on the counter top.

Those bins and the two microwaves were moved to the cashier's counter. Olivia Bumarris, massive and massively pregnant, lay sprawled on it munching said nukeburger and complaining, while her husband Franklin strained to support her upper half and Barbara dug around below.

"It's a shame we couldn't take th' tax break *this* year," she griped between bites. "Lord knows we could use it. My sister'll be *impossible* after having to watch the kids this long." She looked up at her husband. "*You* wanted t' visit *your* family for the holidays! And now look at us!"

Franklin evidently had the wit to keep his mouth shut.

The nukeburger met its gristly fate, and Olivia chucked the wrapper at the trash bin, but missed. "How long is this gonna take?" she demanded. "My back is killing me!"

149

"I don't see any sign of dilation yet," Barbara said, soothingly. "Are you sure your water broke?"

"I know how this works. This ain't my first," Olivia grumbled. "So how many kids have *you* had, huh?"

Barbara straightened up and looked her in the eye. "About thirty." That shut off the complaints for the moment.

"Well? What's happening?" Reggie asked.

Barbara took him aside as best they could in the tiny space. "I'm not sure. It *could* be false labor induced by stress."

"Or?" Reggie sincerely *didn't* want to know 'or'.

"Or...she could be in early stage labor. It's too soon to say yet."

"Aw...fer cryin' out loud! This can't be happening!" Reggie felt like the walls were closing in on him, bringing on a rising sense of doom.

"She's two weeks short of term. If the baby is coming now, it'll be alright."

"I'm not sure I'll be!"

Barbara gave him an impish grin. "Relax. Women have done this for millions of years, and we've never lost a conductor yet!"

Reggie did the Frustration Tango trying to find some answer to this impossible situation. "She can't have a baby in here!"

"No, she can't. We need more room. We need to put her in one of the compartments."

§

Milepost 142, Colfax, California:

The weather was going to hell, fast. The weather service was making noise about a 'trailing edge front', but as far as Murphy was concerned this storm was getting worse and wouldn't be over soon. *Why* didn't matter. Right then all he cared about was a lost hi-rail truck somewhere between here and Fulda with two badly hurt men aboard. Looking out from the hi-rail he commandeered, all he could see was white darkness. He lividly cursed every snowflake; every last white, sticky, rubbery, bitterly cold one of them.

The radio crackled once again:

"This is th' Signals hi-rail to Murphy at Colfax. Over?"

That voice was scared. Murphy hefted the radio mic. "This is Murphy, read you loud and clear. How you guys doin'? Over?"

"We just passed Milepost 149. We're still moving, but we can't see a thing. Hell, we can't even see th' damned track! We're socked in solid, got no idea where we are. We're gonna need help when we get there, Murphy. Over?"

Murphy vented his frustration with a livid curse. "Copy that, Signals. We'll have somethin' for you by time you get here."

A local ambulance was parked right next to his hi-rail, which was parked right next to the cafeteria building in turn. "So what are you going to do?" the driver asked after Murphy hung up.

Murphy was momentarily lost. He'd just come back on duty only to find conditions were hopeless. The road was shut down for the time being, in fact, between the weather and the wreck up near Summit. "We got t' set up some sort-a barricade, someone t' flag 'em down when they get here."

"In this? You can't see your hand in front of your face!"

He was right about that. Murphy turned to him. "If we get 'em to you, can you get 'em to the hospital?"

"Yeah, sure. We got Navstar in our wagon. But you send people out there and they'll get lost for damn sure!"

"Yeah. Can't argue that." Murphy pondered the swirling blankness in front of him, and the mess hall door behind...

§

The crew cafeteria was busy with trainmen and Maintenance workers ready to go back on duty but with nothing to do since the railroad was shut down.

Murphy climbed on a chair in the middle of the room where everyone could see him. "Alright! All-a you!" he bellowed. "We got a hi-rail with casualties comin' down th' Hill. They should be here any minute, but nobody can see shit out there! I want all-a you t' line up from the front door to track two. Arm in arm! We gotta flag that hi-rail down. Let's go, people! We got t' help some of our own!"

§

151

Getting Olivia Bumarris to some place where she could have her baby in peace proved easier said than done. Getting her on her feet took their combined efforts, and navigating her up the winding stairway was an adventure in itself. Nor was that the end of the saga. She parted the crowd like a pregnant icebreaker, griping and cursing all the way to the next car, where George Reinsbach intercepted them. "What th' hell is this? Is she really in labor?"

"It looks like," Barbara said. "We need to get her into a compartment."

"Aw...jeez..." Now it was Reinsbach's turn to do the Frustration Tango. "Alright. Reggie, take charge here. I'll send Otis with the aid kit."

"And a bottle of whiskey," Barbara said.

"Rum," her husband added. "She prefers rum."

"Some peppermint schnapps," she demanded. "You and your rum, Franklin! I swear!"

Reinsbach shook his head in disbelief and headed forward. Reggie and O'Brian took on the delicate task of evicting a couple from their compartment while Franklin and Charlie Parkhurst propped Olivia up, and Barbara kept tabs on her heart and respiration. Getting her in through the narrow doorway was something best not discussed, and she settled in with Barbara in attendance and Otis as an unhappy assistant.

"It's a shame Mighty Mouth doesn't have a compartment," Parkhurst said after they retreated into the corridor. "I know how much you'd *love* to evict him!"

"I swear, once this is over, I'm gonna write a book," Reggie grumbled. "It'll be a best-seller!"

O'Brian shrugged. "You gotta admit, there's never a dull moment around here."

Reggie turned to him in anguish. "*Please* tell me I've gone crazy!" he begged. "Tell me I'm in the nut ward, even if I'm not."

O'Brian gave him a solemn look. "I'd lie to you if it'd make you feel better, Reggie, but I'm not sure I'd be lying."

§

Milepost 201, Horseshoe Curve:

They came up on the rear of the stranded single-deck cars without warning. Herb was so numb from the icy wind that he barely managed to stop in time. The second Sno-Cat pulled up next to him, and they huddled out of the wind in the partial shelter of the car.

'This may have been a bad mistake,' he thought as he tried to collect himself and decide what to do next. The weather was deteriorating. Visibility was almost nil, and the wind was hitting them head-on with punishing force. They only just reached the first wreck site after a miserable trek, and they had at least two more miles to go.

"You alright?" Jamie Kirk yelled to him.

"Managing!"

She dug in her pack and came up with a small jar. "Here! Rub this on your face! It'll help protect you from the cold!" She needed to shout to be heard over the rising wind.

Herb fumbled the jar, managed to get it open, and daubed some of the sticky goo on his cheeks. Whatever it was, it must have stung, but his face was too chilled to feel anything.

She turned her attention to her passenger. "How you doing, doc?"

Doctor Menendez was clearly suffering from the cold. His face was raw and bleeding from tiny cuts inflicted by wind blown ice, his breathing was rapid, and he was trembling. "Not so good! Is it much farther?"

"About two more miles!" Herb could hardly hear the others over the wind noise even though they were at arm's length.

"I can't do this! We need to get out of this cold!"

He was right about that. Herb was exhausted and stiff from their long ride; clearly Menendez was in worse shape. They all could use a breather. "Alright! Ten minutes! Everyone into the train!"

He struggled to his feet and turned his Sno-Cat off. "No!" Jamie shouted. "Leave 'em running! We can't risk a non-starter!"

§

153

They collected the packs of priceless medical supplies and struggled painfully up the steps into the last car. Inside was no warmer, but at least they were out of the wind. They left the backpacks in the vestibule and groped their way inside. Even the emergency lights were dead, leaving them stumbling blindly in the gloom. Jamie dug in her belt pack and came up with a glow stick, which cast a sickly blue light on the scene allowing them to find seats in the first row.

"Good thinking on that." Herb gestured at the glow stick lying on the window sill between them.

"It's a wonder you men survive without our help." She dug in her belt pack again, came up with hand warmer packs, kneaded them to get them working, and handed them to the others. "Here. Warm your hands and faces."

Painful as they were, the hand warmers were heavenly. Herb was embarrassed to admit he never would have thought of them. Maybe she was right.

"I don't think I can do this." Doctor Menendez was despondent and hurting from their long exposure to the hell out there. "We have to go back!"

"We can't go back! They need us!" Jamie was adamant about that, much to his dismay.

"And it's five miles back, and only two miles further up," Herb added. "The worst is past us, doc. We can do this."

He shuddered, hunching his shoulders and clutching the hand warmer in dismay. "Good Lord! I don't know why I let you talk me into this."

"Because there's people hurt up ahead," Jamie said. "You're on the front lines now, doc. We do this all the time."

"We'll make it," Herb assured him. "We just follow the tracks like we have been. It's not much further."

Jamie studied him gravely. "How's our fuel supply?"

It couldn't be good. The trip thus far was an endless slog through minor avalanches and snow drifts; the right of way would have to be dug out again before help could reach the stranded train. They were overloaded and crawling through thick snow against a bitter head wind, which meant they were burning fuel like

154

nobody's business. As for how much was left...those Sno-Cats were the cheap models not meant for roughing it long distance in the wilderness. He kicked himself mentally for not bringing a spare gas can.

"We've got enough."

The look in Jamie's eyes said she wasn't convinced. "Well, we better get moving. Those people need us." What she didn't say was the sooner they got going the closer they'd be to their goal, just in case.

§

Milepost 171, Emigrant Gap:

They were reorganizing the various elements, preparing to head up to Norden when the radio crackled to life:

"Maintenance Of Way at Milepost 197 to the Roseville dispatcher, over?"

"Roseville dispatcher."

"Roseville dispatcher, we've received a radio transmission from the missing Amtrak locomotives! Both crewmen are alive!"

"Jesus!" Walter gasped. "That's great news!"

"No, it ain't." Gus grabbed the radio mic. "Wreck train to rotary 207. You heard that message? We gotta get moving, pronto!" He turned to Walter and Parker Lee. "They ain't out of it yet, and won't be until we get there, so we need t' *move!*"

"Copy that, wreck train! Keep up with us if you can!"

§

Milepost 197, Snow Shed 47:

Marcus dropped the radio mic and turned to Earl. "You know what we have t' do. Your boys need t' dig out the end of the shed so we can get t' those two."

Earl was in an agony of indecision. "We can't do much against that mess, Marcus!"

155

"It'll take *hours* for the rotary t' get back here! Minutes can count. We all have t' do the best we can with what we got."

Earl pulled himself together. "Yeah, okay. We're on it." He headed for the dorm car at a fast trot.

§

Milepost 206, Truckee, California:

Dean Nakamura, Herb's replacement as crew caller, rapped on the door frame to his boss's office. "You wanted t' see me, Jim?"

Jim Mortensen was watching the snowfall through his office window, and didn't answer for a moment. "It's beautiful," he said at last, and turned to Dean. "So damned beautiful, like a picture postcard. I just wish we didn't have to run in it."

"Yeah. Well, that's the price of glory, I guess." Mortensen's pensive mood said something was coming down. Everyone knew he *sincerely* looked forward to retirement. Nothing pleased him more than for life in Truckee to go along at a relaxed, predictable pace. He tended to come unglued when things went to hell; winter was *not* his favorite time of year.

"How many warm bodies can you get me?"

Dean was expecting this ever since hearing the 'City' was in trouble. "Off the top of my head, I'd say maybe twenty, quick. A lot of our guys are already out on the line doing snow removal. I can pull maybe ten off there, and we can do hires for perhaps another ten soon enough to matter."

Mortensen sighed. "Okay, give 'em a heads-up. According to the weather, that Amtrak may be in too bad a spot for Gus to help 'em. If they can't get them out, we'll have to get those four cars cleared, and bring the train down ourselves. To do that, we need to set up a special snow removal run to clear track two."

Dean knew the real reason was Mortensen was feeling the heat; this was too big to look the other way and let Roseville deal with it. Omaha would be sure to notice before long, if they weren't already breathing on his neck. "Okay, boss. Thankfully we have that spreader from Colfax." Spreader 4032 led a freight down the Hill right before the Amtrak departed. They were lucky they had any snow removal gear in reserve at all.

156

"Yeah. I'll need a crew for the spreader, and the rotary will be going up the Hill shortly. We need crew changes all-round. We should also get a crane from Sparks before long."

That was news; Mortensen must be getting antsy. "Right. I still got some people 'off the law'. Let me see what I can find."

§

Milepost 142, Colfax, California:

The line of shivering railroaders stretched from the door of the crew mess to the main line, each holding the hand of the next to keep them linked to safe shelter. Every man in the mess, including two of the volunteer servers, joined the effort. Murphy anchored the line just beyond track two, and the last half-dozen men held switchman's lanterns or flashlights. The ambulance was parked next to the track, its headlights shining and its emergency blinkers going. All it did was surround them with a glowing fog. They still couldn't see the track for more than fifty feet or so.

The hi-rail came out of the gloom with no warning and skidded to a halt, just avoiding the men in its way who retreated in panic. The two Signals guys were out of their vehicle almost before it stopped. "Come on!" the driver yelled as he yanked the rear door open. "These guys are hurt bad!"

A dozen hands turned to, gently lifting the injured men and placing them on the stretchers. Davy Burns was out cold, but Pietro was semi-conscious. "What happened, Pietro?" Murphy asked as they carried him to the ambulance.

Pietro thrashed about weakly, moaning in pain. "Too much..." he mumbled. He was delirious from shock, not entirely aware of where he was. "...too...fast...hit ice..." He lapsed into senseless mumbling as they loaded him in the ambulance.

Murphy straightened up and gave Davy Burns a look of pure hatred; this was no surprise, and no more than what he could expect. Two good men—one, anyway—injured and a priceless spreader out of commission *just* when needed most, all due to that slacking jackass. *This* time he'd write Burns up for *damned* sure!

*****

157

Midnight, January 2:

Milepost 244, Maintenance of Way Office, Sparks, Nevada:

Bret Johansen caught Phil Collins as he was heading home at the end of his trick. "I don't know how we did it, but we got that piece of junk ready t' go," he said. "It's about as close to serviceable as we can get it, but it's dicey at best."

"Great work, Bret. How about a service train?"

"We got the tender flat and a caboose. The rest'll be up to Truckee to provide."

"Good luck with that! See the grave shift caller to get a crew. As soon as they come in, they can get moving."

"Like hell! I'll take her over there."

Collins studied him doubtfully, noting how worn he looked. "Bret, you're already on the law. Let Jim Meyers or Ed Holland handle it."

Bret shook his head. "That thing is going t' need constant babying to keep in working. "I'll rest up in the caboose until we reach Truckee."

"Well..." They were bending the hours of service law, at best, and nobody who knows railroading would be happy with sending an exhausted man up the Hill. But if anyone knew cranes, it was Bret Johansen, and this was no time to be picky. "Alright, we'll give it a wink and a nod. But you're signed off for now, so get moving, and *try* to get some sleep!"

§

Milepost 197, Snow Shed 47:

Visibility was nil beneath the overcast which blanketed the hills around Shed 47. The gandy dancers labored in the harsh light of spotlights powered by a portable generator. What little light they had was diffused and obscured by the continuing torrent of snow. Needless to say, the arrival of the Work Extra was a welcome sight for the men.

Getting there involved a monumental game of musical chairs at Norden, where they paused to sort out the varied collection of equipment and plan their assault once they arrived. The wrecker and its train were parked way back under Norden's snow shed, five miles from the scene of the action, since they wouldn't be needed for some time. It was hard to say which was the more welcome: rotary 207, the relief train's bulldozer, or the fresh manpower.

Any way you cut it, their arrival was a Godsend for the weary work crew, who labored for hours in bitter cold to dig out the end of Shed 47 with precious little to show for it. No one told them to board the camp train for food and warmth—likely no one could have stopped them—leaving Gus and Parker Lee to sort things out with Fred Roth.

The laborers' efforts did manage to clear enough space so they could climb up to find open sky. What greeted them was an ugly scene: a smooth slope of drifted snow as high as the snow shed's roof. Even with the aid of a couple flares, visibility was dismal. The cloud cover was barely above the rails, and the snow was so thick it was hard to say where sky started and land ended. Within the short distance they could see there was no hint of the right of way or even the cut it ran along.

"I'll say this for Mother Nature," Parker grumbled. "When that bitch decides t' jack us around, she does the job."

"How far is it to the wreck?" Gus asked.

"A bit more than half a mile," Fred told him.

"Alright, we need t' bring the rotary up and dig all this out. Then we can see about the wrecker."

"There's no way in hell we can risk taking the big hook out there," Fred said. "And I don't recommend we send the rotary out there, either. There's already a real danger of another slide, with how its been coming down."

The newcomers pondered that with no enthusiasm. At the rate it was snowing Fred's concerns were all too realistic. Gus scooped up a couple hands full and squeezed them into a ball: rubber snow, as thick and heavy as wet cement. "So what d'you recommend?" he asked at last.

"As I see it, we'll have to pull the train out from the other side. Truckee'll have to clear those two derailed cars, then they can bring the train out eastward."

Gus fixed him with a hard look. "They got avalanches on their side too. Why give them the job?"

"Because the snowfall isn't as bad east of here, usually, and the line below Tunnel 13 is more open than here. Less risk of slides, plus from what I hear they can get those two cars rerailed a lot easier than us recovering the baggage car."

That wasn't what they wanted to hear, but Fred had been on the scene for hours and knew the situation better than they did. "Yeah, but they don't have a crane," Gus objected.

"Um..." Fred hesitated, stymied for the moment. "Can they use tractor mounts?"

"From what I hear, there's no way they can get 'em in there."

Fred pondered that. "Then they'll just have to find a crane somewhere. If nothing else, they can call for one from further east."

"Yeah, but the nearest big hook is likely Salt Lake City; it'd take days t' get it here."

"We don't know that. It can't hurt to ask, and we really need t' sort out our options before we commit to anything."

As much as in burned Gus to admit it, Fred was right. Anyone who knew the Hill in all it's ugly moods would agree. "Yeah, I guess so. What about the locos? The baggage car?"

"The locos will have to wait for spring; too risky to try recovering 'em. Their diesels are froze up already anyway. The important thing is t' get the crew out. As for the baggage car, we tilt it off the right of way so we can clear the line. Once the train is clear, we set off a series of slides with dynamite and dig the track out over and over until these hills are stable."

Gus and Parker mused on it for a bit. "Sounds like a plan," Gus said at last. "But we need t' send the rotary out there anyway in order to rescue those crewmen."

Fred considered, then nodded reluctantly.

§

Milepost 198, down slope:

Bobby lay on his back for a time, too weary and sore to do anything else. At least he got through to the outside world; they

160

knew about their predicament; they were coming. He took comfort knowing the railroad would move heaven and earth, bend any rule, take any risk to reach them. All they needed to do was stay alive until help arrived.

He lay staring up at the ceiling, fading in and out for what seemed like hours before he remembered Karl. That poor bast'd was stuck, helpless, all alone. If he wasn't already dead, he soon would be. He had a right to know help was on the way.

That goaded Bobby into the superhuman effort of getting to his feet. He stood for a bit, looking vaguely around the cab, trying to decide what to do next. It took an effort to pull his thoughts together, he was so wasted, and he finally decided he needed to return to see how Karl was doing.

That took more labored thought to pull together a plan of action. Resolved, he staggered to the cab door and slid down into the snow; too far gone to realize he was abandoning their only radio link to potential rescuers.

§

Milepost 198, aboard the 'City Of San Francisco':

"Word is the folks from Truckee are gonna come up t' get us," Reinsbach told Greenbaum and O'Brian. "The people up ahead say it's too dangerous to bring their heavy gear up, so we'll have to go out back east."

"Any word on how soon?" Greenbaum asked.

"It better be right quick." The auxiliary generator in the baggage car finally ran out of fuel a few minutes ago, having lasted longer than expected, plunging the train into semi-darkness. Already the air was turning chill and damp, and a thin film of condensation was forming on metal surfaces.

"How long can we hold out with the batteries?" Reggie asked.

"I don't know. We better limit power usage to the emergency lights and communications."

"Even that won't help unless they get here soon," O'Brian said. "We better give them a hollar and see if they can come up with something."

§

161

Milepost 197, Snow Shed 47:

*"Our auxiliary generator just quit. We'll freeze unless
we can get more diesel. Is there any way you can get some
to us?"*

Gus gave Fred and Parker a dismayed look. "Auxiliary
generator?" Until that moment they hadn't realized the 'City' was
on auxiliary power.

"They'll freeze in short order unless we can get them out of
there," Fred said.

"Or we can get some more fuel to them," Parker added. "Do
we have any jerry cans?"

"Yeah, we got a dozen or so in the supply car."

"We need to send a locomotive down to Norden t' bring the
fuel tanker up," Parker said in disgust. "We should-a brought it
with us when we came up."

"Yeah, you should-a," Gus growled.

"Once it gets here, we'll transfer some to the cans and man-
porter 'em over to the train," Fred said. "But with the way its
snowing, we'll need t' send the rotary."

That meant bringing the rescue effort to a halt again, but there
was nothing for it. Without the auxiliary generator, the passengers
would freeze long before help could get to them. Gus pounded the
desk in frustration. "Dammit! I wish we still had the spreader!
We'll never get anything done like this!"

"Any idea on how soon we could get it back in service?"
Parker asked. "If they can't do anything else, we could send
Walter's hook to recover it."

"I'm not sure they can unless we divert the rotary to dig all the
way down to Emigrant Gap," Fred said, reluctantly.

"And our priority has t' be to reach those two crewmen, not to
mention getting supplies t' the passenger train," Gus added. It
burned him to face choices like this, but they simply didn't have
the equipment they needed. "The rotary goes t' get the fuel tanker,
but then it comes right back here, and *stays* here!"

"Any word on the 211?"

"Nothing. Last I heard, it'll be another week before they're up and running again." Without the third set of rotaries, and with their spreader out of commission, their only snow removal ability was right there under the shed.

§

Milepost 198, aboard the 'City Of San Francisco':

O'Brian was making another patrol to the rear of the train when he ran into a man dressed in heavy winter gear and an orange UP safety vest coming the other way. He gaped at this apparition in surprise. "Who are you?"

"I'm Herb Mokowski, from Truckee." The stranger jerked a thumb back down the aisle. "We just arrived with a doctor and a load of medical supplies."

"Thank God!" O'Brian keyed his portable. "Reggie! George! The relief train is here from Truckee!"

"No, hey, man, it's just three of us. We came in on Sno-Cats."

O'Brian blinked at him in surprise. "Sno-Cats?"

"Yeah. Look, we got a surgeon and a trauma EMT plus a shit-load of medical stuff. They need t' get to work on your casualties."

That shook O'Brian out of his stupor. "Okay." He keyed his portable again. "George! My mistake; it's not a relief train, just a work party, but they brought a load of medical supplies. I need you to send a couple porters back here t' help."

"Thanks for dashing my hopes! We're on our way."

By then the newcomer was joined by a heavyset middle-aged man and a petite woman lugging several heavy knapsacks and an oxygen bottle. "What's wrong with the lights?" Herb asked.

O'Brian grabbed one of the knapsacks and led them forward through the curious crowd. "The auxiliary generator must have run out of fuel a few minutes ago. We're on battery power now."

"Well I hope you can do something," the man complained. "Operating in freezing temperatures increases the risk of shock."

Herb turned to look at him. "We're workin' on it, doc."

§

Milepost 197, Snow Shed 47:

"We need for you to head down to Norden and bring the fuel tanker back.   "The Amtrak needs diesel for their emergency generator."

"Aw, fer cryin' out loud!" Margret grumbled. They progressed a whole four car lengths after returning from Emigrant Gap with the wrecking train, and now they were supposed to go galavanting off on *another* wild goose chase. She snatched up the radio mic. "Can't you send one of the diesels?"

"Ah, no.   The way this is coming down, the track'll likely need clearing again."

He was right about that, at least. The snow was coming thick and hard, even building up on her rotating clog-proof viewports. The right of way would be a jungle of minor slides and drifts. "Well, can't you syphon some from one of the diesels?"

"Have you ever tried to syphon chilled diesel? It's like syrup. In any case, we'll likely need the tanker for our units before long."

There was no arguing that, either, and as annoyed as she was, Margret *was* concerned about running out of fuel. She mumbled a curse and keyed the microphone. "Copy that, but I hope you know this is one Righteous Cluster Fuck!"

She dropped the mic, braked the rotary to a halt, and they collected their gear to move to the rear unit.

"Damn-fool way t' run a railroad," Willy griped.

She gave him a frustrated glare. "You don't know half of it!"

§

Milepost 201, Horseshoe Curve:

A track torpedo left behind by O'Brian was the only warning rotary 209 received before plowing into the back of the single-deck

164

section of the 'City'. Fortunately, that was all they needed since they were crawling along at a walking pace. The engineman killed his power, and the rotary consist stopped just like that without needing the brakes as the last car materialized out of the gloom.

The two crewmen sat uncertainly for a bit, before the engineman said, "Well? You know what we came here for."

His partner gave him a jaundiced look. "We?" There was nothing for it, so he sighed, made a great show of bundling himself up as best he could, and climbed down to the right of way. He was no more than a dark blur in a swirling white nothingness, outlined by a powerful battery pack lantern as he struggled forward into the gloom. The glow of his lantern faded into the distance, and it was some time before he appeared again and climbed up to the relative shelter of the rotary's cab.

"God, I'm glad to get back!" He crowded the radiator, trying to absorb all the heat in the cab. "Colder'n hell out there!"

The engineman handed him a cup of coffee. "So what's the situation?"

The brakeman gulped the coffee before answering. "The last two cars are good; we can couple up and haul 'em away. The next two forward have one truck each off. And I found this in the last car." He produced a used glow stick. "Looks like Herb made it this far, anyway."

"Good! I'd hate to think..."

"Yeah."

"The rest of the train...tried to head west." In a subdued murmur. "I hope they made it there."

"Yeah. I heard it's only a couple more miles. If they made it this far, they should be okay."

"I heard the Amtrak got hit by a slide right beyond Tunnel 13. Word is they can't see the locos. No one knows what happened to 'em."

The brakeman sagged on his seat, staring into the distance in dismay. "That's some scary shit, man," he mumbled.

"Yeah." They were shaken by the very real possibility that it could happen to them, too.

Just then the radio crackled to life:

"Maintenance of Way at Truckee to rotary 209?   What is your status? Over?"

"His master's voice," the brakeman grumbled as he hefted the radio mic. "Rotary 209 to Truckee, we've reached the first part of the 'City' train. It looks like the first two cars can be cleared, then you'll need to send up a hook. Over?"

"Copy that rotary 209.   Come back down ASAP, and we'll get a switcher up there.   In the mean time you can start to clear track two so we can get the wrecker in there. UP dispatch has given us local control, so we'll provide clearances. Over?"

"Wonderful," the brakeman said. "Track two is hopeless! We haven't cleared it in nearly a month. I don't know how we can do it now."

With the line from Emigrant Gap to Summit so deeply buried that the Colfax snow forces were hard put to keep a single track cleared, the Truckee force let the double track on their side of the Hill go. Up to now it was adequate for the limited traffic the Hill could manage. The single track they had ran along a deep, narrow shelf of snow higher than the locomotives which was compressed under its own weight into near-solid ice.

"That snow must be twenty feet deep!" the engineman protested in dismay. "It'll be like plowing concrete! We may have to blast the whole length."

"Yeah, and that could take weeks!"

"Maintenance Of Way Truckee to rotary 209, did you get our last transmission? Over?"

"Shit," the engineman muttered as he grabbed the radio mic. "Ah...copy that, Truckee. Rotary 209 starting down the Hill."

They climbed down reluctantly, and headed back along the consist toward rotary 17223, their paired companion at the other end, walking along the narrow cleared shelf dug through the deep

166

snow by their trip up here. Cold Creak Canyon opened out to their left, its rapidly descending slope lost in the swirling snowfall. To their right, beyond the snow removal consist, a sloppy, ragged wall of packed snow soared twenty feet high or more.

"Track two." The brakeman gestured with his flashlight, running the beam along the dirty white cliff. "That's an embarrassment."

"It sure is," the engineman sighed. "Mortensen should never have let Sparks steal our equipment and men. He must-a figured Colfax was having a hard time, so he could slack off."

"He really screwed the pooch on snow work," the brakeman said, morosely. "We'll play hell getting that passenger train t' safety because of it. Big time."

"Th' wreck made the network news, so sure as shootin' Omaha'll be down on us like a duck on a junebug."

The brakeman sighed. "Yeah, looks like. We can thank our boss for that, too. I don't know *how* we'll get out of this one!"

"Hey, this is on Mortensen. They can't blame us for his fuck-ups!" They contemplated the future in silence for a bit. "There'll be some lively discussion when *this* hits the fan."

"Yep. I *wish* I was a fly on the wall when Mortensen has t' explain it all t' Omaha."

"Shit, I'd pay good money to listen in on *that* conversation!"

They finally reached rotary 17223 and climbed aboard, thankful to be out of the wind at any rate, even if the cab wasn't much warmer. "I swear, once this is over, I'm gonna move t' Florida," the brakeman muttered.

"Yeah, well, hate t' burst your bubble, but they get cold weather down there, too." The engineman fired up the huge rotor, and the Truckee rotary began crawling east, down from the Hill.

"My luck, yeah." The brakeman slumped in his seat and stared out the window at the frozen hellscape. "I just hope Herb made it."

§

Milepost 198, aboard the 'City Of San Francisco':

Things had settled down somewhat in the dining car, but it still looked like a scene from a disaster area. Their eight seriously

167

injured were laid out on tables at one end of the upper deck while the less seriously but still largely immobile casualties—another dozen—sat or lay wrapped in blankets at the other end.

"Damn, you were hit hard," Doctor Menendez muttered. He turned to Barbara. "You handled this all by yourself?"

"With some first aid help."

Jamie considered the ghastly scene for some time, then turned to Barbara. "You did a great job," she said, softly. "You get some sleep; we'll take it from here."

"There's no time for that. You need to come up to speed on our worst cases." Barbara directed them to her two most critical patients. "Seventy-eight year old woman with what appears to be a compound fracture of the left hip, with probable internal injuries."

The old woman was semi-conscious by then, still clearly in pain, and a brief examination showed her left hip blackened and swollen. "I figure she needs drainage at a minimum, and I've tried to immobilize her hip without much luck." The patient's hip was looped with layers of duct tape.

"Yes, I concur on the drainage." Doctor Menendez was clearly worried. "Start with ten units of morphine, then see if we can improvise an abdominal catheter." Jamie was already digging their supplies out of the knapsacks, and grabbed one of their limited supply of morphine field ampules.

"Our other crisis is a fifty year old male with severe blunt force trauma to the occipital lobe. He has been unconscious and unresponsive, which makes me think there's more severe damage."

Doctor Menendez felt gingerly around the back of the patient's head. "I think you're right. He may have a depressed fracture."

"Yeah," she mumbled. "How soon can we get them to a hospital?"

"Well from what I saw on the way here, I'd say not any time soon. And I don't think we can expect much help, either."

Jamie joined them as Barbara pondered that uneasily. "So how do we proceed, then?"

Doctor Menendez was neither happy nor optimistic about either patient's chances. "We can't do much for the old woman beyond pain management and drainage. As for the man...if we have to...we can try a subdermal incursion to check for bone fragments. I'm not sure what we can do if we find anything, though."

"Let's just hope help gets here soon," Jamie said.

§

Milepost 198, down slope:

Bobby finally reached the rear of the lead unit, standing waist deep in snow, and tried to decide what to do next. He was numb with cold, and couldn't feel his legs, but at least his broken arm didn't hurt any more. He was slowly succumbing to hypothermia, and while he was in no shape to understand what was happening to him, he knew instinctively he was in danger.

It took monumental effort and several tries to scramble up onto the side of the locomotive. He stopped then on hand and knees, too worn to continue. The bitter wind buffeted him, nearly knocking him flat. He managed to look around, but there was nothing to see except a brief piece of the silver-and-blue carbody. Everything else was formless gray, constantly in motion. Even through his pain and exhaustion-induced haze, he could see the blizzard was getting worse. If he didn't reach shelter soon, an impossible forty feet ahead, he would die in this frozen hell. After regaining a bit of his strength—he was about played out—he started crawling forward along the side of the locomotive toward the cab door.

§

Milepost 198, aboard the 'City Of San Francisco':

A check of the rest of the injured revealed a couple who needed further treatment well within the rescuers' limited capabilities, and several who would benefit from further attention. The rest were doing well, and could be left to themselves for the time being.

"Our intermediate patients come first," Doctor Menendez said. "Once they're taken care of, we treat our less critical cases." He paused to ponder their two genuine emergencies. "As for those two, we keep them stable, but we won't try anything until the power is restored, and then only if we have no choice."

Barbara and Jamie took that news quietly. They were both trauma specialists, they understood the harsh truth of 'triage': those with the best chance came first. Their critical patients would have to hang on until help arrived, since there was little more they could do for them.

§

Milepost 197, Snow Shed 47:

> *"As a matter of fact, we do have a crane. We found one over in Sparks, and it's on its way here now."*

That was unexpected and welcome news to Gus and his team. "That's great, Jim! Hopefully our problems are over."

> *"I'm not so sure they are. Sparks told me it was out of service, headed to Cheyenne for overhaul. Their people got it running, but they aren't sure how reliable it'll be. We'll know more once it gets here."*

"Great," Walter grumbled. "It's never that simple, is it?"
"It's better than nothin'," Gus snapped.

> *"And it's only a dinky little forty tonner, but they sent a good crane operator, so they should be able to handle those single-decker cars."*

"Great! A utility crane!" Walter threw up his hands in despair.
Gus ignored his gripe, although he felt just as let down. "Well it's good t' hear you're making progress from your end, since we can't risk our heavy wrecker with the shape these hills are in. How soon can you get it up there?"

> *"Well...first we have to clear track two so they can reach the site. That may take some doing. We're putting together a snow train now."*

That caught Gus off guard. "What's wrong with track two?"

170

"We...hadn't been keeping it cleared since the traffic was so light."

It took Gus a moment to absorb that; his first reaction was an obscene volley which should have melted the snow off the caboose roof. Only when he had himself under control again did he key the radio. "Dammit, Jim! What have you been *doing* over there all winter?"

"We have to budget our resources. We're getting hit hard too, plus we gotta keep bailing Reno's ass out. We can only do so much, and thus far its been enough for the traffic you send us."

Yeah, well, that was likely true enough, although his explanation did Mortensen little good in Gus's opinion. "How soon will you be able to get track two cleared?"

There was a lengthy hesitation, no doubt because Mortensen was trying to think of something to report which wouldn't bring on another blast. Then:

"We're putting together an all-out assault on the Hill now. It should be ready to go in the next few hours."

Gus sighed in resignation; he'd believe it when he saw it. "Alright, Jim, keep at it. There are five hundred lives on the line!"

"What *is* it with that guy?" Fred griped. "Why can't he keep his end up?"

"He manages well enough in ordinary situations," Parker said, philosophically. "But this winter has just been too much for him, I guess."

"The last several winters! He's worse every year!"

"Don't sweat it," Gus said, sternly. "We got more immediate problems t' deal with, and I'm thinkin' he'll take his retirement soon." His tone suggested *retirement* would come sooner than Mortensen realized, if Gus had any say about it.

§

Milepost 206, Truckee, California:

Jim Mortensen hung up the radio mic with an embarrassed curse, grabbed his phone, and dialed the Mechanical office over in Sparks. He'd dithered over this idea long enough; Gus's condemnation rankled, pushing him to act. "Yeah, Mark? Jim, over in Truckee. I need a dozen road units to go up the Hill on a snow removal run. Can do?"

Mark, the third trick Mechanical Department super in Sparks, was skeptical. *"That'll cost, big time. What about your local stuff?"*

Right then cost was the *least* of Mortensen's problems. "We need to put together a special operation to clear track two up to Horseshoe curve. It'll take all the power we can get."

"So...how many crews will you need?"

"Looks like I'll need three, plus possibly relievers later."

"Uh huh." His tone clearly revealed his opinion of Mortensen's operations, to his embarrassment. *"So why do you need us? You've got the power we sent last fall for snow duty."*

"It's all old stuff, not much kick left in 'em. And we don't have all that many anyway. I really need some more horses, Mark."

"Is this about that passenger train?"

"Yeah. They evacuated to the forward part of the train, which is stuck over in Gus Vincincegorough's turf. I'm sending our switcher to recover two passenger cars at Horseshoe Curve. Then we need to clear track two so we can send our hook up to take care of the other derailed cars." It burned him to have to admit how he'd slacked off. Time to get it in gear. "I need the extra power for that snow removal job."

"Yeah, well, I got plenty of power now that nothing's moving, and I got some guys who'd love some time. So how soon d'you need 'em?"

Mortensen knew the passenger train would be his trump card. "Another couple hours, as soon as our switcher comes off the Hill. Dispatch gave us local control, so you have the road to here."

"Well, alright. You got it. I'll have 'em on the way shortly."

"Thanks, Mark."

He hung up the phone with a sense of annoyed satisfaction. At least *something* was going right around here.

§

Milepost 198, aboard the 'City Of San Francisco':

"*When* are they going to come and rescue us?" Wilbur Harkness, the regrettable Mighty Mouth, was not so much complaining as whimpering. The last twenty-four hours, especially with the present chill permeating the train, left its mark, reducing him to a cantankerous, whining nuisance. "I'm liable to catch pneumonia! How much longer is this going to take?"

George Reinsbach was too drained by exhaustion and cold to argue with him, especially since Harkness was also too weary to keep up his bluster. "There's no way to say for certain," he said, reasonably. "What with the conditions like they are. The railroad is doing everything possible to reach us. You'll just have to be patient."

Harkness huddled against one wall, clutching the bed sheet he'd been issued tightly around his shoulders. "Wonderful. You could at least give me a blanket! It's freezing in here!"

Reinsbach would have appreciated a nice warm wool blanket himself, not that he had a choice in the matter. "There aren't enough to go around, so we have to give priority to those needing them the most."

A few unfortunates didn't even have an ordinary bed sheet despite the thin sheen of ice on windows and metal surfaces. The crowd in the lounge car was subdued, cold and exhaustion having drained away their earlier agitation. Most of them huddled singly or in small groups trying to rest and keep warm. Conversation and movement were minimal. At least there were few signs of panic as yet; the mood seemed more apathy and even despair.

Harkness was the exception, although even he was not his old self. "This is pathetic! I'm supposed to be in Tokyo by now, but here I am, stuck on a mountain top in a snow storm! None of you people appreciate how much I do for the world economy!" He received precious little sympathy for his histrionics, and discovered to his amazement that none of the others would sell

173

their blankets for any money. Some were decidedly rude about it, too. The idea that the common masses couldn't be bought left him distracted and peevish.

"Well all your money and influence buys you squat right now, so you might as well get used to it." Reinsbach was well aware of his earlier attempts at bribery.

"Why am I not surprised? This has been a miserable trip! Worst of all this...hippy!...grabbed my seat! Not that I expect any better, but you can at least make *him* move."

Harkness glommed onto a choice lounge seat early on and clung to it like a barnacle until need utterly *forced* him to seek the nearest restroom. As luck would have it, he returned to find Charlie Parkhurst took it over and was trying to get some sleep amid the bustle and confusion.

"He has as much right to a seat as you do." More, in fact, in Reinsbach's opinion, since he and his girl friend Barbara were such tremendous help. "As crowded as we are, everyone has to share and share alike."

The dining car was reserved for the injured, and the restrooms were constantly patrolled to keep people from camping in them. About the only seating left was the lounge car, which couldn't begin to absorb all the refugees from the single deck section. The competition for the few available seats was fierce, with most of the refugees having to find an unoccupied corner out of the traffic.

"But surely you can..."

"Amtrak policy on lounge seats is first come, first served," Reinsbach told him, sharply. "Use it or lose it." With that he headed forward, determined not to put up with any more of Mighty Mouth's 'importance'.

Parkhurst opened one eye and gave him a sardonic look. "Even Monkey Kings have rules, man."

§

Milepost 206, Truckee, California:

"Now that the rotary is back, you need to make run up the Hill," Mortensen told the crew of the local yard engine. "We need you to recover the last two passenger cars at milepost 201. After

174

that, we can start clearing track two, then we can get a crane up there to rerail the other two cars."

The three local men weren't thrilled with going up the Hill in this weather, but orders are orders. "Okay, boss. We'll get on it right away," the conductor said.

Mortensen was well pleased with himself. His efforts thus far were coming together better than he'd hoped. A doctor was delivered to the train, the two good cars would soon be removed, his snow removal special would soon be ready to roll, and the crane from Sparks was due shortly. All in all, despite a tardy start, he'd handled the crisis nicely. Too bad they were playing catch-up, but once track two was cleared, they'd be able to keep things fluid with a little extra effort. He reminded himself sternly that he got himself into this mess, and that he needed to be more on the ball in the future—at least until this winter was over. He'd dug himself out from under at any rate, which pleased him no end.

His phone rang as the yard crew were leaving; he picked it up automatically. "Mortensen."

"Mister Mortensen? Please hold for Mister Oliver, the Vice President of Operations..."

*****

Mid-Morning:

Rotary 207 arrived back at the work sight after a couple hours with the fuel tanker coupled in between their two road diesels. By then Margret and Willy were ready to go on the law, and Dan and Jesus were called to take over.

"Alright, we're through futzing around," Gus Vincincegorough told them. "Our priority now is t' get those two trainmen out, and second, to get supplies to th' Amtrak. I want you to dig: *nothing* else, *nothing* less! Get that track cleared no matter *what* it takes!"

One thing about Gus Vincincegorough: he had the force of will to stir men to do the impossible. "We're on it, boss!" Dan said.

"Alright, good. Grab some hot chow and get to it."

Actually some progress had been made in the rotary's absence. Between the bulldozer and the track gang's shovels they cleared the end of the snow shed and advanced maybe a hundred feet despite endless snow trickles which threatened what little progress they'd made. The bulldozer was a blessing, but suffered the handicap of having to back the length of the snow shed to dump each scoop full at the far end before taking another bite. Worse, it was running low on fuel. The arrival of the tank car was none too timely. The only real answer was rotary 207, and now that it was back, Gus had no intention of allowing any more side adventures.

Walter Karns and Parker Lee came into the caboose as Dan and Jesus left. "How are things on the other side?" Gus asked.

"It's hell!" Walter was not happy. "Snowing like a sumbitch. We'd never get th' hook out if it wasn't under that shed." He helped himself to a mug of coffee from the pot simmering on the caboose's stove, and plopped in a chair. "Word we got was Colfax is shut down altogether. With the rotary up here being our only snow gear, we're losing the fight."

None of them were happy about the news. "Yeah," Gus grumbled. "We'll be playin' catch-up for weeks."

"The sooner we get that wreck cleared, the better. So what's progress here?"

"We're half-way between 'nada' and 'diddly-squat'. Right now we're tryin' t' get some diesel over to the Amtrak to power their auxiliary generator. Hopefully, now the rotary's back, we can make real progress."

"That would be a pleasant change of pace," Parker said, wistfully. "My people are gettin' pretty worn down."

Gus gave him a stern glare. "They'll know the *meaning* of 'worn down' before this is over!"

Parker sighed. "Probably."

§

Milepost 198, aboard the 'City Of San Francisco':

The rotary's return was welcome news for the stranded passengers as well.

> *"Our fuel tanker just arrived. We're filling jerry cans with diesel, and will man-porter 'em over to you."*

"That's great news," George Reinsbach replied. "We've about frozen our asses off over here."

Things went to hell big time in the three hours since the generator quit. Despite their insulation, the cars weren't much warmer inside than outside. The kitchen quit turning out what little warm food they were producing, and the passengers were miserable. What was worse, the batteries were running low; the lights were starting to dim, and George Reinsbach worried about how much longer their communications would last. O'Brian, on the other hand, wondered if there was still enough power to crank the generator. It was a near-run thing last time, and if they couldn't get it started again, they'd be in a desperate fix.

Paul came by shortly after the radio conversation ended, and Reinsbach cornered the two of them. "They're sending some diesel over for us. You two need to get things set up for 'em, and to get the generator back on line as soon as you can."

"Okay," O'Brian said. Paul nodded.

Reinsbach studied their steward for a moment. "How are things with the casualties?"

177

"Well..." Paul pondered the situation uneasily. "I'm no doctor, but I'd say our new arrivals from Truckee are making a real difference. Still, we need t' evacuate some of the worst ASAP."

"Yeah." Reinsbach brooded over that. "Any chance we could walk 'em over to Shed 47? We got the stretcher..."

Paul vetoed the idea emphatically. "No way! It'd take forever, and you add exposure to what they've already gone through, and you'll lose at least a couple of 'em!"

"Looks like they're stuck until help arrives," O'Brian added.

"Yeah." Reinsbach wasn't happy, but there wasn't any alternative but to wait. "I just hope someone *can* reach us!"

§

Milepost 201, Horseshoe Curve:

"Can't see a damned thing," the engineer of the Truckee yard engine grumbled. "I'd hate t' try driving in this."

"Yeah, well the highway department shut the pass, so it looks like you're not th' only one," his brakeman said.

They were well up into the mountains, somewhere near Horseshoe Curve, feeling their way along by blind luck and their borrowed GPS unit. The storm leaking over the pass from the west was now in full fury; they could hardly see the end of their unit. There was nothing beyond but swirling whiteness, leaving them to grope blindly along on slippery ice-clogged rails in a one hundred ton locomotive. The yard engine never went anywhere, so they never received a GPS installation, and the conductor wasn't entirely sure how to read the one they had. "This damned thing's gettin' wonky," he complained. "Th' battery's likely dyin. If we don't find something soon, we'll have t' go back."

"Shit," the engineman muttered.

"Just hope we don't hit no ice," the brakeman said. They were all haunted by the prospect of a derailment way out here in this frozen hell.

Fortunately the yard engine was fitted with pilot plows, which was all that kept them moving through the buildup from the last few hours since rotary 209 passed this way. The snowfall was manageable, but there were countless minor slides as the wall of

178

snow towering on their left crumbled under the stiff wind. They were able to dig through everything they'd come across thus far, but it was an ominous portent of the near future.

"This is impossible," the brakeman griped as he strained to spot any detail through the storm. "You better slow down some more." They were creeping along at a walking pace, trying to feel their way to their objective.

"Hell, we're barely moving as is."

"Yeah, well, watch your step." The conductor was trying to keep one eye on the white blindness ahead of them while simultaneously puzzling out what the unfamiliar machine was telling him. "We're getting close..."

Closer than he realized: the last Amtrak car appeared out of nowhere all of a sudden, and before anyone could react they hit. Fortunately their front coupler was open; the two units came together with a 'BANG', the coupler closed, leaving them neatly coupled to their objective, and the yard engine stalled.

The unexpected impact left them shaken. "Shit..." the brakeman mumbled after a tense moment.

"Damn it," the engineman added. "Everyone okay?"

"Yeah." Actually that was no worse than a hard coupling in the yard, but the shock spooked them all.

The engineman was the first to recover. "Okay, th' only thing left is to unhook the last two cars from the derailed ones and pump up the brakes. Then we can get th' *hell* off this Hill."

Neither the conductor nor the brakeman was thrilled by the prospect, but there was no way to get around it. After a round of grumbling and arguing, they decided to go together for safety's sake. They dismounted, and after fiddling with the heavy brake air hoses to link the locomotive to the cars, they vanished into the storm. It was a good forty-five minutes later before they came plodding back.

"Jesus, it's raw out there!" the conductor griped as they hovered over the heater vent.

"Yeah, well, don't get too comfortable yet," the engineman told them. "I've been pumping the brakes, but th' pressure's not coming up t' speak of."

Their weary cursing was matched by the steady pounding of the air compressor from back in the engine compartment. "It's the damned hoses," the brakeman grumbled. The heavy hoses which link between cars tend to leak in cold weather.

"Likely. I'm getting some pressure; let's wait and see what luck we have."

No one argued the matter since none of them were anxious to go out there again. In fact it was another thirty minutes before the pressure was enough—provided they kept the compressor running —and were able to start back down the Hill.

§

Milepost 206, Truckee, California:

Jim Mortensen made the mistake of letting Bret Johansen see his disappointment at the 'crane' newly arrived from Sparks, and Johansen was not one to hide his feelings. "You wanted a crane, you *got* a crane! And this is all you're *gonna* get, so you better suck it up and like it!"

Mortensen offered a pacifying gesture. "Hey, we're grateful for anything you can send...it's just...we were expecting something a bit bigger."

"We don't got cranes just sitting around! You want her or not? 'Cause if you don't, I'll take her back t' Sparks and you can whistle up a brand new wrecker out-a your ass!"

One thing Mortensen hated was confrontation, and one thing he didn't need was to stand out here in a blizzard arguing with an irate crane operator, so he tried to head this one off. "I'm grateful, of course, but can that crane handle a passenger car?"

Johansen came down a notch. "It should, with careful handling."

Mortensen had his reservations: UPMW 903052 was dirty and streaked with rust, and a couple struts in its lifting boom were buckled. It *looked* about as weary as he felt right then. Maintenance of Way equipment lived hard lives. "It'll have to do, I guess." He turned to Johansen. "What do you need?"

"I'll need a work crew and a load of ties for cribbing."

"Well that I can give you."

"And we need to get right up next to the cars in order to lift them. This light crane will only be able to lift that much weight up close and personal."

"Ah...well...that's not so simple. The cars are on track one. Track two is still snowbound."

Johansen looked askance at him. "Why do I get a bad feeling about this? How much snow you talkin' about?"

"About...twenty feet."

"*Twenty feet!?* What you people been doin' here all winter? Playin' grab-ass and passing the buck?"

"We're setting up a snow train to clear track two. It should be ready to go within the hour."

"Aw, fer cryin' out loud! How th' hell are you gonna clear twenty feet of snow!?" Johansen was starting to realize the sandhouse gossip about doings here in Truckee were all too accurate. "I don't see *how* we can get those cars out of there now!"

Mortensen was embarrassed by his condemnation: thus far in this emergency his department was repeatedly found wanting. Worse, Omaha was breathing on his neck, demanding real progress sooner. VP Operations clearly was not convinced by his evasions, and he, Mortensen, knew the heat was on. "We have an idea which should work. We'll send a spreader up track one with it's wings fully spread. That should undermine the snow pack, causing it to collapse onto track one, where the rotary will come along behind to scoop the debris up and clear it. We'll break the rotary pair and send the other one up track two to clear what remains."

Johansen eyed him skeptically. "You really think that'll work?"

"It should. It'll be slow going. They may need to make several passes, but it should."

"If the snow pack doesn't bury the spreader altogether!"

Mortensen hesitated. "Yeah, it might. We'll put some extra diesels on to drag it out by main force, if necessary."

Johansen shook his head in dismay. "*This* is your plan, eh?"

"We don't have much of a choice. You'll need track two if you're going to get your hook right up next to the derailed cars. It's only six miles to Horseshoe Curve, and the snow won't be all that bad the first couple miles."

"And who's gonna ride this Valhalla run? Whoever's on that spreader will be taking some very real risks."

"We'll...find some volunteers."

Johansen threw up his hands in disgust. "Helluva way t' run a railroad!"

§

Milepost 198, down slope:

It took more than a mortal human should be asked to give, but Bobby finally crawled the length of the first unit and reached the cab door. He was only semi-conscious by then, but knew instinctively he must to keep moving or die. Where he found the strength to keep crawling was beyond comprehension, but he managed to inch his way painfully along the side of the diesel. He wasn't sure where he was going, but he needed to get there.

He gradually became aware of something blocking his path: one of the vertical handrails by the cab door. He couldn't understand what it meant, but he was running on instinct by then. He groped blindly; felt something which fit the palm of his hand. He pulled, and the cab door gave way, revealing a dark chasm. A gust of slightly warmer air came up to meet him. Instinct served him one last time: he scrabbled around and managed to half-fall-half-drop through the door, landing in a painful heap on the engineman's console.

There was a faint gasp of pain. "Bobby..."

Karl was still alive, for which Bobby mumbled a prayer of thanks. He tried to rise to his knees, but his strength finally gave out. "Karl...I got through...on the radio...they're coming..." It was all he had. He sagged on his back, rolled off onto the floor, and passed out.

§

Milepost 197, Snow Shed 47:

"Aw, crap!   How soon can you get moving?"   Gus Vincincegorough was not amused by the foul-up at Truckee. The weather was appalling, and if they didn't get to it soon, there would likely be no way to clear the wreck.

182

"We'll be another hour or so. Prepping the wrecker is almost done, and putting together a work party is going well, but we have to clear track two so we can send them up."

"Well, you need to get a move-on. The weather up here is something awful, and it's headed your way."

"Word from our rotary is the snow isn't bad on the east slope. I'll keep after them nonetheless."

"How soon will you have track two cleared?"
"If they ever do get moving," Fred muttered.

"It's hard to say, but I'm throwing everything we have at it. I'd estimate we'll be clear up to the first wreck site in twelve hours."

"Copy that. Thanks, Jim. Out." Gus dropped the radio mic on his desk and sagged with his head in his hands. "Good Lord!" he groaned. "We'll never clear the line at this pace!"
"It don't sound too bad," Walter said, soothingly. "They had a crane after all." He turned to Fred. "Good call on that."
"Took 'em long enough," Fred grumbled.
"It takes time to pull a major operation together," Harper said. "They moved fast, for them."
"And their weather never is as severe as we get," Walter added. "They can still do this."
Gus looked up at them, his face contorted with anguish. "How can we say *anything* based on what went on in the past? This freakin' weather ain't natural! We can't assume anything!"
As seasoned and pragmatic as these men were, Gus's angst worried them. If even Gus Vincincegorough—'Old Railroad Iron' himself—was losing it, could they count on anything or anyone?
"All we can do is do our best, Gus," Walter said. "They're our best bet unless proven otherwise. And assumptions are the only thing we have t' go on."

"They got good people over there," Fred insisted. "Even if Mortensen is a screw-up, the troops on the ground know their stuff. They'll pull through."

Gus signed and rubbed his aching eyes. "Yeah, I know. It's just..." He sagged in his chair and stared out the caboose window into the black nothingness under Shed 47. "...it's getting worse, year after year. There's gonna have t' be some big changes, or someday we won't be able t' keep the Hill open."

"That's Omaha's lookout, Gus. They can't blame us for being overwhelmed by this weather."

§

Milepost 206, Truckee, California:

"I checked the snow pack as we came down, and I'd estimate it as twenty-two feet up near the Curve. Packed solid, too." Rotary 209's engineman was upset since it was their job to keep the tracks dug out. This sorry state of affairs was starting to attract attention from upstairs, and blaming this on Mortensen's poor leadership would only go so far in Omaha.

"And it's snowing like a sumbitch up there," his brakeman added. "I don't see *how* you can clear track two. We'll be doing good t' keep one open!"

This was hardly news; it was snowing hard in Truckee, and the wind was blowing up to gale force. The storm which plagued Gus's crews for so long was pounding them now, and they were no better equipped to deal with it than the people at Shed 47. What was worse were the forecasts which said they hadn't seen the worst yet. Mortensen's carefully hoarded gandy dancers were draining away as more of them were being diverted to keep the turnouts in Truckee clear. What's more, the delays in getting the snow extra ready was eating into everyone's time. Unless they moved soon, the recovery effort would collapse.

"My plan is almost ready to go," he assured them. "Now the switcher is back, we can put it into operation."

The engineman greeted his assurance with a rude noise. "Your *plan* is a setup! Whoever's riding that spreader will be in for a rough ride at best!"

"So who you stick on it?" the brakeman asked.

"I'll put Bill Borden on it, as soon as he's in off the law."

"Borden? He's road crew. He got lassoed into this too, eh?"

"Operations let him loose, huh?" the brakeman grumbled.

Mortensen was about at the end of his tether from the strain, not to mention Omaha was on his neck again. "Well for *your* information, until we get the Amtrak off the Hill, there won't *be* any road operations!" he snapped. "Borden will do whatever is needed, as will you two!"

The rotary's engineman shook his head in dismay. "You think this is gonna work, you gotta be fuckin' nuts!"

§

Milepost 198, on the grade:

"I gotta be nuts t' think we'll ever get this track cleared," Dan muttered.

Having gotten past the latest distraction, rotary 207 was back to digging its way toward the wreck, lost in the distance. That involved digging forward a bit at a time, backing off to clear the scoop when it overloaded, then trudging forward again to gain few more feet in an endless, seemingly hopeless process.

The whine of the rotor's drive bogged down again as the rotor became clogged. Dan shoved the throttle in, then sagged in his seat. "Damn," He muttered as he massaged his sore wrist. "This is gonna ruin me."

"I don' *believe* this, man-o," Jesus said. "I ain't never seen so much snow. This can't be natural."

Dan gave him a sour look. "Who said this was natural? I always heard the Devil liked fire, not snow."

Jesus shuddered and crossed himself. "*El Diablo*, he's the trickster, man. Maybe you right."

Dan sighed, and sat up straighter as the motor whine lightened. "Alright, here we go."

The snow was actually deeper than the height of the rotary's scoop in spots, the result of several avalanches. Each time they pressed forward, the overburden would spill over the top of the scoop housing, burying the cab, which forced them to back off while some of Parker Lee's gandy dancers loitering on the roof shoveled and swept it clear.

"Shit! We're stuck again," Dan complained when their view was blocked once more. He hit the brakes and sagged in his seat with a frustrated sigh.

"What scares me is what if this don' melt next summer?" Jesus waved vaguely at the world outside their cab. "This winter, what if it don' end?"

Dan considered him somberly. "My guess is we'll dig tunnels through it and use it for snow sheds."

"Let's hope it don' come t' that, *amigo*."

"You got that right!" Dan leaned back in his seat and stretched to relieve the ache in his shoulders. "Well, one good thing: if there's another avalanche, it'll slid right over us since we're already buried in it up t' our noses."

"Let's hope we don' find out, *compadre*."

There were faint scraping and banging sounds as the workmen standing on the cab roof dug away the latest overflow. The forward windows cleared abruptly, and before long the cylindrical rotor housing was as clear as it ever got. One of the gandy dancers gave them a thumbs-up, and disappeared toward the back of the rotary to wait the next mishap.

"Alright." Dan vented the brakes and nudged the throttle up a couple notches. "Here we go again."

Jesus gunned the rotor up to full speed—the only way to keep from bogging down was to hit the snow pack at a dead run—and they inched forward once again.

§

Milepost 198, the baggage car:

O'Brian and Herb Mokowski were hard at work digging away the snow around the baggage car fuel tank when the first gandy dancer arrived lugging one of the large five gallon jerry cans, which he dropped as soon as he arrived. "Damned thing weighs a ton!" he grumbled as he sagged in the snow.

"You okay?" O'Brian asked. As tough and enduring as these men were, this one looked beat.

186

"Yeah, I guess, but I'm not sure this is such a good idea. Those damned things'll break your back, and its way too easy t' get lost out there."

O'Brian knew all too well the hell this guy went through, lugging a seventy pound jerry can a half-mile or more through waist deep snow in this Godawful weather. "Well...we don't have much of a choice. We got t' have juice t' keep these people from freezing."

"So we gotta freeze instead, huh?" He staggered to his feet and dusted the snow off his legs. "I could-a been in th' movies," he muttered, and trudged back into the storm.

Over the next half-hour three more porters came in, and their offerings were eagerly added to the meager fuel supply. With that on board, they managed to get the auxiliary generator going again, although it sputtered and gasped a few times. They went back to draining the jerry cans one by one as they came in at lengthy intervals. "This'll take forever," O'Brian groused as he hefted the latest contribution. "We'll never get this thing filled, and we'll freeze our asses off trying."

"You got that right." Herb paused and looked around at the blinding gray-white nothingness. This was hopeless. At best they were barely keeping up with the generator's voracious fuel demands, and they couldn't stay out here forever wrestling these heavy cans. They needed a new approach. He racked his mind trying to find a solution. "Um...do you think they have any gasoline over there?"

"Huh? Why?"

"I got two Sno-Cats. If we can get fuel for 'em, they'll make all the difference."

"Th' hell you do!" O'Brian dropped the half empty jerry can and grabbed his portable. "Maintenance of Way at Shed 47, do you copy?"

"Ah, yeah, we copy. Who is this?"

"This is O'Brian, from the 'City' train. D'you guys have any gasoline?"

"Gasoline? Wait one."

"Jesus, I hope this works," O'Brian grumbled.
"Yeah. We can use a break."
"You know it!"

"Ah, Maintenance of Way Shed 47 to O'Brian, we got some gas for our light power equipment. What you have in mind?"

"I'll fill you in when we get there. Break out that gas, and have a shit-load of those diesel cans ready!"

§

Milepost 197, Snow Shed 47:

Rotary 207 and the gandy dancers withdrew to Shed 47 as Antonio prepared to blast two more fallen trees blocking the right of way. O'Brian and Herb arrived with the last stragglers, bringing Antonio with them. Gus, Walter and Harper Lee were there to meet them, since they were curious as to what was up.

"Snow bikes!" Gus exclaimed when he saw them. "Just what we need! Where'd you find 'em?"

"We used them to bring a doctor and some medical supplies up from Truckee," Herb explained. "We can use these t' move two, maybe four cans of diesel at a time. It's the only way we'll ever get caught up."

"It'll mean less risk for our people, too," Harper said as he admired the battered Sno-Cats. "We need t' get some of these for the maintenance force."

"Yeah, we should." Gus was all gung-ho for the idea. "As soon as we get back down th' Hill, we'll..."

BOOM!

...The shed reverberated from the first of Antonio's charges; they looked up just in time to see a large pine tree flying in pieces.

"Wait for it," Parker cautioned.

BOOM!

The second was more distant, obscured by the blowing snow except for a brief flash. A moment later there was a subdued rumble as another avalanche came pouring down the hillside. Most of the rotary's progress to date—maybe three hundred yards —was wiped away by the torrent.

"Awwww...SHIT!" Parker muttered.

"Dammit! We'll never get this done!" Gus complained.

"Sorry about that," O'Brian said. "Still, we need t' get moving. We need more diesel for our generator."

§

Milepost 198, aboard the 'City Of San Francisco':

Doctor Menendez rapped on the door to the compartment where Olivia Bumarris was confined. "How is your labor case?" he asked Barbara when she answered.

It took her an effort to pull her thoughts together. "She seems to have stopped for now. She's been on-again-off-again; I can't tell if this is a false labor or not."

"So what's her condition in general?"

Barbara pulled herself together with an effort. "She's resting comfortably. Good pulse and respiration. Blood pressure spikes, but is good on the whole." She gave Olivia a furtive glance, then added softly, "I'm worried about her obesity. Once she gets going, the labor will put a severe strain on her system, and her health isn't all that great to begin with. I don't know what we can do if she goes into a crisis."

Menendez could see how bad Olivia was, and agreed with Barbara about the risk. "There isn't much we *can* do. I'd hate to try a cesarean under these conditions."

"It's just not do-able. We don't have the blood we'd need."

"I hate the idea, but if it comes right down to it, we'll jury-rig some sort of direct transfusion setup."

Barbara pondered that wearily: it violated every principal of modern medicine, but they might not have a choice. She nodded at last, too tired to properly to express her opinion of their dire straits.

Menendez turned his attention to her. She seemed strung-out from fatigue, and he was worried about her ability to function in a crisis. The one thing they couldn't have was for any of them to lose the medical picture at a critical moment. "How about you? You look beat."

It took her a bit to answer. "I'll manage."

"You should..."

"We get used to the long hours. I've done worse, and right now there's no one else."

There was no arguing the plain facts, and as a medical professional, Doctor Menendez approved of her dedication. "Still, try to pace yourself. If I can I'll send someone to spell you for a while so you can grab a nap."

Her answer was slow in coming. "Thank you. How are things in the dining car?"

Doctor Menendez sighed. "Most of them are stable, but the old woman with the broken hip is slipping. Our head trauma is still non-responsive, and I may have to go into the internal injuries case. If so, I'll have to pull you in to assist."

Barbara stared vacantly while she absorbed the implications. "God, I hope it doesn't come to that. We simply aren't equipped for major surgery."

"Yes, well, the next twelve hours will tell."

§

Milepost 142, Colfax, California:

It hardly seemed possible, but the weather was getting worse. According to the weather reports, this particular storm was supposed to be playing out, but if so it intended to go out in style. Second to the dispatcher in Roseville, who had his hands full, Murphy was the de-facto head of operations on the Hill, which was proving an impossible task since his one reliable asset was the radios. All that amounted to was trying to help the wrecking crew at Shed 47, and it was to a point where even that was impossible.

"I got fifty guys here, but there's no way we can get 'em up there," he reported to the troops at the front. "Unless you send the rotary down, we can't move anything up to ya."

190

"There's no way Gus will agree to it. The weather up here is awful, and he wants t' get the train out before it's froze in solid, if it ain't already."

Murphy knew Fred Roth from long experience, and didn't doubt his word on conditions at Summit. "I hear you, good buddy." He silently cursed Davy Burns: reportedly both of them would live, although Pietro would likely pull full retirement for his injuries. Their priceless spreader might as well be in China for all the good it would do, *just* when it was needed the most.

"Any word on the weather?"

"Yeah, but I don't like using that sort-a language." If the people at Shed 47 thought they were in it bad now, they were in for a rude awakening. "I hope you got your crying towel handy."

"Hell, we're all cried out up here."

§

Milepost 197, Snow Shed 47:

Gus Vincincegorough, Parker Lee and Walter Karns stood at the back of the column of wrecking equipment, just inside the cover of the shed, watching the weather with mixed feelings of despair and frustration. The cloud cover barely cleared the mountain peaks, and was thick enough to reflect their lights back at them, casting a perpetual twilight gloom over the scene. The snow was coming down thicker than ever, blown sideways by a stiff arctic wind so it was piling up under the end of the snow shed.

"God, what a mess!" Walter complained. "I never seen the like in all my years on the Hill. We'll never reach those two crewmen in this."

Parker nodded gloomily. "Yeah. We'll likely find their bodies next spring, when we get the pass open again. For now all we can do is focus on getting that train out."

"I hate t' say it, but you're likely right."

191

None of them were happy with the thought of leaving two of their own to die in this frozen wilderness, but there was nothing they could do. Rotary 207 was back at it, digging its way forward a few yards, backing off to clear its rotor, then trudging forth a few more paces. At the rate they were going, it would take over a day to dig their way to the 'City' train, assuming no more avalanches. Only the wildest optimism would buy that. Until they reached their goal or the weather let up it was impossible to even try a rescue. Even then, they lacked the gear they would need, and as much as they wanted to reach those men, the risks were too great.

Fred Roth joined them just then. "Any word?" Gus asked.

"I was on the horn to Colfax. Murphy said they're socked in solid; nothing's moving. The weather report has this storm ending, but there's another one coming right behind with four feet more."

"Dammit! How we supposed t' move trains in this, even if we can keep the track clear?"

"How th' hell we supposed t' keep the track clear t' begin with?" Fred replied, heatedly. "Even the rotaries can't keep up in this weather!"

"What's worse, this-here is January," Parker said, morosely. "We're only now gettin' into th' bad part of winter. It can only get worse fo' the next month or two. Ain't no way we can keep up."

Walter contemplated the snow which was piling up visibly as he stared at it. "It wouldn't do any good anyway," he sighed. "Even if we clear the track, the risk of avalanches is too great." They pondered in silence as the snow grew deeper at the entrance to the snow shed. "It's no good," he said at last. "We can't win against this. The only thing we can do is focus on getting those people to safety. We'll have to regroup and come back to reopen the Hill another day."

Gus turned on him. "Th' *hell* we're giving up! This road stays open no matter *what* it takes!"

"How?" Walter cried. "We got equipment down, our people are exhausted..."

"And what about those two crewmen?" Fred insisted.

Gus was silent for a long time. "We can't get to them. They're likely already dead."

"We don't know that!" Fred protested. "They may be unconscious. Their radio might be broken..."

Gus turned on him angrily. "You think I wanna leave 'em out there?! We don't got a choice! We're not set up for rescue work in these conditions. We'll be doing good t' get ourselves out-a this, not t' mention them passengers!"

"But...we can't just give up on them..."

...The last thing any of them expected was an armored personnel carrier to come careening in out of the blizzard, setting off a minor panic as they scrambled out of its way. It almost plowed into the supply box car before grinding abruptly to a halt. Before they could recover their wits, the rear hatch opened, and four military types came out. Their sergeant was a big, burly man with a lantern jaw and handlebar mustache; the very image of an old time Canadian trapper. His men were perhaps of lesser stature, but no less impressive. "I'm DeBeers, National Guard," he announced. "We're a mountain rescue unit sent up to help you with your missing people."

"God, you guys are a welcome sight!" Gus said. "We didn't expect to see anyone up here until the storm passed."

"Yeah, well, we heard it's not *gonna* pass, so we put one track inside the rails and drove blind. I don't know how you guys can run in this. You can't see shit out there!"

"We have our moments."

DeBeers considered the heavy equipment filling the snow shed, then turned to Gus. "So, whadada got?"

Walter was the first to answer. "We got two guys missing down slope in a pair of wrecked locomotives. Both are bad hurt. Our last contact was by radio, several hours ago."

DeBeers nodded. "Right. Let's get to it."

*****

193

Dawn, January 3:

Milepost 197, Snow Shed 47:

It took a number of false starts and do-overs, with progress repeatedly set back by blown snow drifts and minor slides, but rotary 207 finally reached the baggage car after an epic journey of a half-mile. At that they were lucky not to be hit by any more avalanches or run into any fallen trees—evidently the pressure was relieved somewhat by recent slides—so they managed to finish a lot sooner than expected. But they knew it wouldn't last.

"Damn," Dan muttered. "We did it."

"*Si, compadre*," Jesus said. "It took us long enough. Maybe we get some sleep now, huh?"

"God...another whole day of this shit. Let's hope its enough."

It was a good omen nonetheless, and the rescuers made the most of it. The first order of business was to refuel the baggage car's auxiliary generator again. At the same time Doctor Cummings, from Roseville, was delivered along with their medical supplies, and Jack Whitacre was detached to assist.

After which, all thoughts turned naturally to the two missing Amtrak crewmen, which was Sergeant DeBeers' moment to shine. They'd waited impatiently through the night, and were eager to get to it. The bulldozer was brought up to a point not far from the baggage car to dig out the displaced snow on the downhill side, giving the rescuers a window to operate in. They parked the APC right next to the baggage car where it would have at least a bit of shelter, and DeBeers, his three, Walter and Parker met O'Brian on the right of way to plan their next move. Whatever they did, it wouldn't be easy. Dawn brought nothing but more snow and a howling wind; even the faint morning light soaking through the clouds didn't help.

"God, I don't like the look of that sky," DeBeers grumbled.

"It can only get worse." Walter needed to shout to be heard over the keening wind. "The latest is there's supposed t' be a break in the weather before the next storm hits. It should'a been here by now, but I wouldn't count on it."

"Maybe you should hold off until the storm passes," Parker said. Perhaps it was their imagination, but the already bitter wind seemed to be picking up.

"No, we can manage, so we need to go now," DeBeers said. "Hypothermia can kill, especially when they're already hurt. We have medical supplies, rations and a heater, which could make all the difference for them. If we must, we can take shelter in their locomotive and wait out the storm." A blast of wind buffeted them, sending them reeling. "You guys do this for a living?" DeBeers shook his head in disbelief. "And I thought *we* were crazy mo-fo's!"

"Trust me: at times like these we have our doubts about that," Walter said, bitterly.

DeBeers looked around, trying to pick out some landmarks in the gray hell. There was nothing: total white-out conditions. They could hardly see half the length of the baggage car. Finally he turned to Walter. "Can't see a thing! What's the lay of the land around here?"

Walter gestured vaguely off to their right, up hill. "There's a steep rise on this side." He gestured to their left. "It drops off down to Donner Lake on that side, a mile or so. Our people are down there, somewhere."

DeBeers pondered the emptiness swirling around them. The wind cut like knives, chilling them to the bone through their heavy arctic issue. Those two men wouldn't last long in this, even if they had shelter. Finally he gestured off to their right. "That's where the slide came from? Any chance of another any time soon?"

"I'd say a good chance, yeah, with all this coming down. You'll have a little time what with the minor slides we've seen recently, but it's gonna happen eventually."

DeBeers considered for a time. "Right. Let's get this done, then. We'll tie our lines to the rails. Get your people back under cover. No sense putting yourselves in danger."

"Is there any hope for them?" Walter asked, plaintively.

DeBeers tried to break it to them gently. "From what you told me, I'd say their odds aren't good. But if anyone can get 'em out, it'll be us."

Which was some reassurance, at any rate. Their APC was packed to the gills with rescue gear, and all four of them were seasoned professionals. "Well, good luck." Walter and the others retreated.

Once they left, DeBeers turned to his crew. "Alright people, let's get on the stick. We'll need climbing gear, the portable heater, some extra fuel canisters, some MREs, Doc's medical supplies, and the heavy extraction tools. Lash 'em to the Stokes." The others were already breaking out equipment and the rigid Stokes stretcher, which they piled with the rest of what they'd need. DeBeers grabbed one of the heavy coils of climbing rope and a pair of snow shoes, worked his way back to the open gap the bulldozer cleared, and tied his line to the near side rail. "Form a line abreast," he told the others. "I'll anchor the left flank. We'll spread out to form a search line at ten yard intervals."

"How far we going, sarge?" one of them asked.

DeBeers pondered that: being ever-cautious is just good business in this line of work, especially with that sky. No, that sky didn't look good at all. "We'll go out the first hundred yards. If we don't find something by time we reach the end of these ropes, we'll regroup and try another angle."

The four of them spread out along the right of way, with DeBeers on the left, then Corporal Cranston, their medic, then privates Langsdorf and Chase on the right. They were equipped with ropes and snow shoes, Cranston carried a pack full of medical supplies, and Langsdorf and Chase carried various supplies and tools they'd need early-on once they found the locomotives. The rest was secured to the Stokes stretcher, which was bolted to a child's plastic toboggan and fitted with its own rope. They left it sitting at the edge of the drop off where it could easily be pulled down to them.

"Alright everyone," DeBeers said. "You know the drill. We take it slow and easy, keep your alignments, and if you find anything, sound off."

They hesitated a moment to adjust their equipment and get their bearings, then moved off down slope under an ugly sky.

§

Milepost 206, Truckee, California:

"I see the Screw-up Fairy visited us again." Bill Borden was not pleased to be 'volunteered' to serve as engineman on spreader 4032. No sooner did he sign on after a few hours sleep at the local Motel 6 then he was informed of his part in this suicide mission, and he was not amused by Mortensen's grand plan. "This is just plain stupid," he complained to Mortensen. "You know this, don't you? You expect us t' move *twenty feet* of snow with a *spreader*?" Like everyone else roped into this cluster-fuck, he wasn't sure whether the sheer improbability of it working or the risk they would be taking was worse.

"We'll have to improvise methods, but it should work," Mortensen assured him. "All you'll do is break up the snow pack. The rotaries will do the heavy lifting."

"'We', huh? Yeah, right. 'We' undermine that mess and it'll come right down on us!"

"We put extra power on to haul you out if need be. And the rotary will be right behind you on track one to dig you out."

"If they don't get buried alive themselves!"

Dean Nakamura, Herb Mokowski's successor as crew caller, shared his dismay, even though he wasn't part of this scheme. "We pretty much have to. It's the only way we can get the Amtrak down off the Hill."

Borden pondered him with no enthusiasm. "There's no chance we can clear twenty feet of snow off track two! You'll need t' blast the entire length."

"That'll take weeks; we don't have the time."

"All you'll do is break up the snow pack," Mortensen added. "We'll split the rotaries and send them up both tracks at the same time. You knock the snow pile down to something the rotaries can handle, and they'll clear it."

Borden expressed his doubts about this brilliant scheme in the same terms used by the rotary crew earlier. "You're fuckin' nuts! How they gonna dig backward if they get buried?"

"We'll have to hope for the best. The diesels we received have pilot plows, and we'll have a work party to dig you out if needed."

197

"Pilot plows, huh?" This was madness, but there was nothing he could do: one doesn't walk off an assignment on the Union Pacific. Borden glowered at Mortensen, then sighed. "I gotta tell ya' this is come kind-a *piss-ant* operation!"

§

Milepost 198, aboard the 'City Of San Francisco':

"We got some National Guard guys here t' go looking for your two crewmen. Don't know if they can get them out, or if they're even still alive."

Conductor Reinsbach wasn't thrilled by Walter's lack of optimism, but at least some effort to find their two missing was *finally* getting under way. "That's good. How soon do you think you can get this train out? Over?"

"I don't think we can. There's too much danger of another slide for us to risk our big hook, plus this weather is too rough for major wrecking work. Truckee will have to come up and get those two derailed cars, then they can bring you out back east. Over?"

Reinsbach wasn't impressed. "Any word on how they're doing?"

"Nothing yet, but they can call people in from Reno and Sparks. They should get to you pretty soon."

"Alright, fine." It wasn't fine, but griping about it wouldn't help. "We're just about out of food, but we can hold out for a while longer." Which about said it all, so they signed off. "This is taking forever," he grumbled after the radio conference ended.

"You got that right!" Greenbaum said, fervently. "This is simply too tedious for words!"

"It's the stress," O'Brian added. "It gets to you after a while. We really need to carry a hot tub on this train."

"Yeah, plus a massage therapist."

198

"Female, of course. An athletic blond."

"Sounds good. And *think* of all the seniority we're building up waiting around like this. We'll be able to bid on assignments in Hawaii: palm trees, tropic breezes, and no snow. They'll owe us, big time!"

"Sounds great, but I'm not sure I have the figure for shorts and an Aloha shirt."

"We'll need to learn to play a ukulele, too."

"Can we include surf boards in our travel kits?"

Reinsbach answered their attempts at morale boosting with an icy, short-tempered glare. "I'd bite your legs, both of you, only we have more important things to worry about right now!"

The two put kidding aside. "The docs aren't happy about our serious cases," O'Brian said. "I wish we knew how much longer this'll take."

"At least we got more help on hand now," Reggie said. "I'd say everyone's odds have improved now we got proper medical care for them."

"Some of those people need t' be in the hospital. Some kind-a *ad hoc* field effort ain't gonna cut it."

Reggie sighed in frustration. "Yeah. Hopefully the docs can buy 'em some time, at least. Still, they need rescuing."

"Hell, don't we all?"

§

Milepost 198, on the grade:

"Okay, Albert," DeBeers' voice came from somewhere off to the left, lost in the swirling gray. "You know the drill. We take it slow and steady, by the numbers."

Cranston studied the white nothingness before them for a long moment, but couldn't see anything. Frankly, he was scared. He had enough experience in these conditions to know exactly how dangerous what they were doing was, and being linked by a rope to the right of way above didn't matter much. He shook off his unease and hefted his backpack. "I'm okay, Sarge." He wondered if he telegraphed his uneasiness to the sergeant somehow.

"Good man."

Cranston gathered his bundle of rope and tossed it ahead to lay it out, then trudged down hill face first, playing the rope out under his left arm. Progress was painfully slow; doing the 'Eskimo Boogie' was hard enough on the flat, but these snow shoes were a major headache on this steep grade. It didn't help that he couldn't see squat, either.

Something emerged out of the nothingness: a young pine tree, snapped off at the roots like something large came rolling down this grade. This was promising.

A voice came faintly from his right: "Hey, sarge? I got a broken pine tree here."

Even more promising. Cranston relayed the report. "Sarge? Langsdorf found a broken tree. I got one too. It looks like our locomotives came this way."

"Good work, both of you! Keep your eyes open!"

Cranston stepped gingerly over the fallen tree, flicked his coil of rope out ahead, and trudged on into the white-out. Despite their discovery, he wasn't optimistic about those two missing men.

§

Milepost 206, Truckee, California:

'Damn-fool Snow Extra 4032', as Bill Borden dubbed it, sat on the number one main line while rotary 209 maneuvered into position a hundred yards back. Rotary 17223 was already in position next to them, with the work train close behind.

Kareem Shabaz was a recent engineman hire, still in training, called up from the extra board to act as brakeman. He was not thrilled when he learned the details of this assignment. "How did this happen? I thought you Maintenance of Way guys were sharp."

Borden was in no mood to be diplomatic. "That's an ugly rumor, and completely untrue! We work for Mortensen, God help us, so throw away your rule book. We operate strictly by Murphy's Law! Besides, I'm road crew, and thankful of it. You'll be good enough t' remember I'm just passing through."

Kareem was duly impressed. "Do you think this'll work? I've been over the Hill lately. That snow pack is something awful. There's no way we can clear it with a spreader!"

"Yeah, well, you can thank our Fearless Leader for this, and a whole bunch of other problems."

Jeff Karns, another brakeman assigned to handle one of the huge spreader arms, muttered, "*Shee-it!* How does he get away with it? You'd think Omaha'd be *all over* the snow ops here."

"Errors have been made. Others will be blamed."

Kareem pondered the dozen road diesels strung out around them four each on the two rotaries and the spreader. "That's an awful lot of power. What'll happen if we run into something solid, like a rock slide?"

Borden glanced down the line of locomotives; it truly was an awesome array. "Best guess, we get crushed like a tin can."

He was *seriously* not happy with this jury-rigged operation, and was venting his frustrations, but the danger was real nonetheless. He couldn't control those road units from his perch here in the spreader like he could with the dedicated units, which meant they didn't have the swift reaction time needed to avoid problems. More than that, their road crew was not used to how the Maintenance forces operated. There would be inevitable confusion and delayed reaction times, but the regular M o W crews were mostly dead on the law, so the commoners needed to step in. They wouldn't really be crushed like a tin can if they hit something, but this was still a recipe for serious damage.

"Rotary 209 to the spreader, you guys ready?"

Borden hefted the radio mic. "This is the spreader. To answer your question, no, but let's get on with it."

"Yeah, I hear you, Bill. Rotary 17223, how about you?"
"About fucked is how about us. Let's get it over with."
"Ain't we all? Okay people, let's roll this muther."

"So what do I do?" Kareem asked. "I've never run on a spreader before."

Borden looked at him in surprise, then muttered a weary curse at how fucked up this operation was. "That figures." Kareem gave him a hurt look. "Okay, you drive." He gestured the newby to his center spot at the controls. "Watch for anything which could hurt us, like tree or a rock slide. If you see something, hit the brakes and sound off to the engine crew, in that order." He gestured to the radio on the bulkhead between them. "Don't wait for instructions. Jeff and I'll run the spreader arms."

Kareem took his place reluctantly. "I'm sorry..."

"It's okay, kid," Borden said, gently. "It's not your fault you got roped into this stampede."

There was a lurch as the road units shoved from behind, and Spreader Extra 4032 was on the move.

§

Milepost 198, aboard the 'City of San Francisco':

"Word is the folks from Truckee are gonna come up t' get us," Reinsbach told Doctor Cummings. "The people up ahead say it's too dangerous to bring their heavy gear up, so we'll have to go back east."

"Any word on how soon?" Doctor Menendez asked.

"It better be right quick," Jamie said. "Our critical cases need more than we can give them."

Menendez was slightly annoyed at her presumption, but he had to agree with her. "We have our critical cases stabilized for now, but their conditions are still worrisome. The sooner we can evacuate them, the better."

Reinsbach wasn't happy, but there was nothing for it. "All we can do is hold on until this storm passes. After which, it's a matter of time and effort. They'll just have to hang on, doc. The railroad's doing their best."

§

Milepost 197, Snow Shed 47:

"So what now, *compadre?*" Jesus asked once they'd parked the rotary under the snow shed again.

Dan sagged in his seat and fought off a jaw-breaking yawn. He was weary in ways mere sleep couldn't cure, and it took him a moment to collect his wits and ponder Jesus' question.

202

"I dunno. They don't need us for now, so maybe we can get a break."

"We getting near t' outlawing, too."

Dan yawned again, and glanced at his watch. "Yeah, we sure are." After a bit, he picked up the radio mic. "Rotary 207 to the super at Shed 47, over?"

"Yeah, 207, whatja need?"

"We're gettin' close t' outlawing. D'you want to relieve us now since we're not busy?"

"Ah...negative on relief for now. Stand by in case we have another slide, or something else comes up. We'll relieve you when your time ends."

Dan cursed that under his breath. "Ah, copy that. 207 out."

"*Mierda*," Jesus grumbled. "I was lookin' forward t' being warm again."

"I hear you." Dan recalled something Murphy told him way back in Colfax. "There's no telling *how* long we'll be stuck here since they extended the hours of service."

Jesus greeted that with some choice Spanish invective. "Then let's hope they don' decide t' make us plow back to Norden."

"Shit," Dan mumbled gloomily. "I wouldn't be surprised."

§

"We don't need them right now," Parker Lee said after Gus cut off the radio. "Those boys have put in their time. Now's a good chance t' relieve them."

Gus pondered the idea for a bit. He knew full well those 'boys' were cold and weary. Everyone was, but none of them could afford the luxury of slacking off; not until that passenger train was moving. "Yeah, I know," he said, reluctantly. "But we got t' keep on our toes in case something comes up. We may need the rotary at a moment's notice."

"They're tired and cold, likely hungry too. I'd feel better if our only snow gear had a fresh crew."

"Margret and Willy need their sleep too," Gus snapped. There was a tense silence in the office caboose, broken by the faint sound of idling diesels, then he backed down. "I understand Trudy'll have lunch ready in about an hour." He paused to consider his watch. "When she's ready, we'll call 'em in for beans."

Parker Lee brooded on that, then nodded reluctantly.

§

Milepost 205, Hwy 89 overpass:

Spreader 4032 made good time thus far since the land hereabouts was still fairly open and the snowfall, while severe, was manageable. Rotary 209 came this way on track two earlier, making all of a mile and a half before bogging down. From that point, now a half mile ahead of them, the real challenge would begin. They reached the County Highway 89 overpass before Borden announced, "It's gonna get hairy in the next mile or so, so keep your eyes open."

The land on their left was rising while it fell away to the right as they started up Cold Creek Canyon. Beyond, four miles ahead, the canyon came to an end and the track bent back on itself to climb along the opposite face: Horseshoe Curve.

The spreader shuddered as a gust of wind hit it. "Hey, turn the heat up a bit, will you?" Jeff asked. Borden gave the line ahead a quick glance, and seeing his chance he turned to the control panel on the cab's rear bulkhead. "There. That ought t' keep us."

"I don't like the look of this weather." Kareem looked askance at Borden. "We're in for a rough time as is; this storm will make coordinating with the others impossible."

"Yeah, I know," Borden said, regretfully. If this was a normal winter, we'd have some clear skies t' work under. Only this ain't a normal winter, not nohow."

"Hell, this likely *is* a normal winter any more!"

"Yeah, if the last couple years are any clue," Jeff added.

Borden brooded over that while the spreader trundled along, throwing several inches' worth of snow to either side. "Let's hope it doesn't get any worse. It's about all we can hope for, I guess."

§

Milepost 142, Colfax, California:

"Hey, Murph, wake up."   Someone was shaking his arm, dragging Murphy out of an exhausted daze. He looked around in confusion, and realized he'd drifted off to sleep sitting at the mess hall table. "Roseville's on the phone for you, man."

"Uhhh? Ah...yeah. Thanks." He wasn't popular around here, and could well imagine the crews snickering at his display of mortal weakness. Iron Man Murphy, with feet of clay. He swore to himself that once his relief arrived, he'd get some solid sleep.

He shouldn't feel embarrassed: these endless days were wearing everyone down. He hated to admit that mere mortality applied to him as well. But Roseville was calling, which meant something was up.   He struggled to his feet, which took more effort than he liked to admit, and headed for the sign-in desk where the phone was waiting.

"Yeah, Murphy here."

"Hey Murphy, I got some bad news for you." It was the field dispatcher recently activated at Roseville to handle the crisis on the Hill. *"We just got a weather report, and you aren't gonna like it..."*

§

Milepost 198:

Perhaps it was his imagination playing tricks on him, but the wind seemed more shrill and bitter than ever. Corporal Cranston struggled against the blast, utterly lost in the gray-white nothingness.   The only way he could orient himself was by following the steep downgrade, using the rope stretched out behind him and leaning into the wind to keep his feet on the treacherous snow pack. The clumsy snow shoes kept digging in, threatening to trip him, but without them this would be impossible.

"I can't see a damned thing," someone, Private Chase perhaps, said from somewhere to his right.

In fact, Cranston could barely make out his snow shoes and the coil of rope at his feet in the swirling white-on-white. There were supposed to be two *railroad locomotives* somewhere near by, but they might as well be on the moon for all he could tell.   That

205

disturbed him. He was an avid skier; his girl friend, Patricia, was an enthusiastic snow bunny; but this...*emptiness*...got on his nerves to where he was starting to think this wasn't a good idea.

"Alright everyone. Watch your pace and keep alert. If you take a fall, hang on to your rope. You'll need it to get reoriented. By the numbers, people."

"Right, sarge," someone said.

'The sarge must be feeling it too,' Cranston thought. It seemed like he was trapped in some gigantic surreal snow globe. There was no up, no down, no direction, nothing to see. And the rising wind tore at him, flinging snow in his face, making the steep slope all the more treacherous. Honestly, he couldn't tell which way he was going, or even if he was right side up. He was starting to get scared.

The exertion and the thin mountain air were getting to him, making him pant. He paused for a moment to catch his breath...and caught a faint whiff of something. He puzzled over the scent; something familiar but not something he would expect to find out here. He sniffed the air, trying to catch that illusive odor again. Nothing. So he did the next best thing; he reported what he found.

"Hey sarge? I can smell something."

§

Milepost 204:

The snow removal extra's progress ended abruptly another half mile on when Spreader 4032 reached the place where rotary 209 ran into more than they could handle. Ahead of them lay a partly drifted track one and a solid wall of packed snow taller than the fifteen foot height of the rotaries where track two should be. The menagerie ground to a halt as they paused to size up the task ahead.

"You gotta be shittin' me," Jeff Karns said as they studied the scene. "How th' *hell* we gonna deal with *that* with a spreader?"

Borden favored him with a grim smile. "So much negativism! You gotta think positive."

"We are *positively* screwed!"

"We are *positively* in deep shit!" Kareem added.

"Deep snow, too."

"Alright, you two worry-warts." Borden felt the same way, but refused let it get to him. "We got us a job t' do, so let's get on it. The sooner this circus falls apart, the sooner we can all go back to Truckee."

The two brakemen considered that glumly. "So how do we do this?" Jeff asked. "These wings won't take it at full extension. You'll buckle the left one if you're not careful."

Good point, for which Borden had no firm answers. "Likely all we can do is extend out slightly, try to shave the stack and get it to collapse," he said at last.

Jeff and Kareem exchanged uneasy looks. "You say so," Jeff mumbled.

"Yeah, I say so. Extend your side t' full width, Jeff. We'll need the pressure t' keep from tipping over. I'll stick the left one out just a little, and we'll try shaving that mass bit by bit until we get results."

Jeff gave him a glum look. "I could-a signed up t' be an astronaut." There was a steady hiss of the hydraulics as the right wing spread out and lowered to right above the ballast. "All set."

"Yeah." Borden used his controls to move the left wing outward until the end overlapped the snow bank by perhaps a foot. "That's about all we dare try, I guess." He glanced at Kareem. "Okay, tell 'em to go ahead, dead slow."

Kareem stared at him in confusion until Bill gestured at the radio, then picked up the hand mic. "Spreader to engine crew, move us ahead, dead slow."

"Copy that."

There was a rising rumble from behind, the spreader lurched, and moved forward, its wings digging into the snow pack. "Let's just hope this works," Kareem said, bitterly.

"And we don't get buried," Jeff grumbled.

Neither was promising. The left wing dug into the wall of packed snow, causing the spreader to shudder and twist sideways

207

at the uneven resistance. Their *first* big worry was the massive machine might be lifted off the rails, which would leave them in one hell of a fix. "How you doin', Jeff?"

Jeff was studying the sight out his side window. "I'm digging right down t' the ballast, can't go no further. We better slow down a bit before we get pushed right off the track."

Borden agreed with him, seeing how the spreader shuddered and tried to roll to one side. "Show us down a bit, Kareem."

Kareem already had the radio mic. "Spreader to diesels, ease up a bit." The rumble of their diesels dwindled slightly, and their pace slackened. "How we doing?" he asked Borden.

Borden craned his neck to look back down the line: they'd gone perhaps a hundred yards. The spreader wing was digging a ragged gash in the wall of snow, causing the overburden to crumble onto the track practically at their feet. The wall of snow was crumbling behind them, rotary 209 was digging into the pile, making fair progress while rotary 17223 labored further back.

"It looks good. We may need to make a couple passes to clear track two, but it seems t' be working so far." So far: but any miscalculation could bring the wall of snow down on them.

"Shit, I don't know why we bother," Jeff sighed. "At the rate this stuff is coming down, the whole line'll be buried shortly."

Borden glanced at him. "I heard there's supposed t' be a gap in the weather after this storm quits. Maybe we can get ahead."

"Hell, I'll believe it when I see it."

"I'm not sure I'll believe it even then. Mortensen'll screw it up somehow."

"You got that right!"

"We're still riding awfully rough," Kareem said.

He was right: the left wing looked like it wanted to buckle under the strain. Borden retracted it a few inches, and it dug in more readily. The spreader steadied as the uneven pressure eased.

"Looks like we maybe found a balance," Jeff said.

"Yeah, looks like..." There was a muted rumble, and a mass of snow came down on them, shaking the spreader and burying their cab.

§

Milepost 198, down slope:

"What you got, Doc?" Sergeant DeBeers called from somewhere off to his left.

Cranston took a deep breath, trying to recapture the scent. There it was, weak but unmistakable: a heavy, oily smell. He puzzled over it before he realized what it was. Diesel fuel.

"Sarge? I got a smell of diesel. It's really faint."

"Good work, Doc! They must be close..."

...The rope in Cranston's hands jerked abruptly, slipping from his grasp. As he grabbed for it he was slammed from his right and thrown bodily forward, his arms thrashing desperately in surprise. He was swept off his feet, tumbling head over heels, pounded from all sides, leaving him completely disoriented.

The next thing he knew, he slammed up against something hard, stunning him. The tide of snow pressed against him in turn, smothering him, triggering panic as he flailed helplessly. The last thing he realized was he was being buried by an avalanche..

§

Milepost 204:

The crew of the spreader were nearly rocked off their feet as the spreader abruptly reversed. They stared at each other in panicky confusion for a moment, then Borden said, "Jeff, raise your wing." Jeff hit his hydraulics as Borden copied him on the left, and the spreader seemed to steady. Then the radio kicked in.

"Locos to spreader, you guys alright?"

It took Borden a bit to recover his wits and grab the radio mic. "Ah...yeah, we're okay. How's it look?"

"It could-a been worse. We'll have you backed out in just a moment."

As soon as they came to a halt, the three of them turned out to inspect their charge. The roof and walkways were heaped with

209

snow, the left side cab window was cracked, and the headlight was ripped loose, but otherwise they were intact.

"Damn, this shit's gettin' real, ain't it?" Jeff muttered.

"It'll do." Borden turned his attention to the hundred yards or so they'd cleared before being buried. The snow bank was partly collapsed onto track one save where they were dragged out backwards by main force. "Hmph! This might work after all!"

Track one was a mess, but nothing a rotary couldn't handle. Track two...was still buried pretty deep, but the snow bank was collapsed enough so a rotary could peck away at it. Mortensen's grand scheme might work after all, provided they could avoid being buried alive.

"You guys okay?" The conductor of their power was standing above them on the lead locomotive's front walk. "Can your unit still move?"

Borden pondered that for a bit as he surveyed the damage. Aside from their spreader, the left catwalk of the lead diesel was heaped with snow, and the cab roof partly buried. "Yeah, it could-a been worse. How about you?"

"I don't mind tellin' ya that gave us a scare! I'm glad no one was hurt. So what now?"

Good question, since Borden could already see a glitch in Mortensen's plans. "We gotta get the 209 ahead of us somehow so they can dig out what we've cleared. Don' know how we're gonna do that unless we back clear down to Truckee to use their crossover."

The locomotive conductor pondered the scene in turn. "Yeah, dammit. Looks like that's our only option."

"Right. We need t' go down anyway so we can make some repairs. Give us a bit to get squared away." The three of them headed back to the spreader's cab, kicking as much of the accumulated snow off the catwalk as they could. Back in the cab, Borden got on the radio. "This is the spreader to the two rotaries. Us and the 209 need t' back down to Truckee so we can trade places and they can dig out what we got thus far. Rotary 17223, you go ahead and start in on track two. That'll keep you busy until we can get back."

210

"Rotary 209, I guess that's all we can do.
"You leaving us up here all by our lonely?"

"Yeah, 17223, 'fraid there's nothing for it. You got the work party t' dig you out of need be, so take it slow and careful. Th' 209 should be back in an hour or so."

"Damn-fool way t' make a living!"

"That's a big Ay-firmative, good buddy! Okay 209, let's head on back to Truckee."

"Best idea I've heard all day!"

§

Milepost 198, down slope:

It took Corporal Cranston a while to shake off his stunned disorientation before he realized he'd been caught in an avalanche, and another minute or so to get over his panic. He was still alive and was head and shoulders above the snow slide. Right: it was just a minor one. He pulled himself together and focussed on his body to see if he was hurt. Aside from a bloody nose, an aching left knee, and feeling like he'd gone ten rounds with George Foreman, he seemed to be alright.

"Shit, boy," he grumbled to himself as he started digging his way clear. "You're one lucky sumbuck." It took some doing, but he was able to extract himself enough so he could turn around, lean on the barrier he'd come up against, and dig for his snow shoes...

...That barrier...

He turned around again and pondered the mystery, and was confronted with what seemed like a curved wall of dark-colored steel. It took a moment, but he finally realized he found one of their missing locomotives.

"Hey! Sarge!" His words were lost in the rising howl of the storm. "SARGE! I FOUND 'EM!"

No answer.

§

211

Milepost 198, Aboard the 'City Of San Francisco':

> *"We filled the fuel tank and transferred as much diesel as we have jerry cans for, so you should be in good shape for a while. There's no telling how long this blow will last, but there's supposed to be a break in the weather coming. We'll see about refueling you again at that time."*

"Wonderful," Reggie Greenbaum said as they monitored the conversation between George Reinsbach and the rescuers at Shed 47. "Who knows how long this storm will last!"

"Yeah. Refilling the fuel tank in these conditions is a miserable job under the best of conditions," O'Brien said, sourly.

Reggie glanced out of the narrow vestibule into their dining car cum hospital ward. "What worries me is two refills are good for about eighteen hours," he said softly; not that anyone was likely to hear them over the steady howl of the wind shaking their car. "So what do we do if this storm hasn't quit by then?"

O'Brian offered a resigned sigh. "We freeze, I guess."

*****

Mid-Morning:

Milepost 198, down slope:

It took Corporal Cranston a few minutes to dig himself clear of the avalanche which half-buried him, but finally he was standing knee deep in the snow, back against the curved roof of the Amtrak diesel. He looked frantically around for the others, but the wind-whipped snow blanked out everything. Then he remembered his utility belt, and dug out the flashlight he always carried. Its beam faded into nothingness within yards.

"HEY!" he yelled over the rising wind. "SARGE!" There was no response. "SARGE! WALLY! JERRY! ANYONE!" Lost, alone, disoriented, he was starting to get really scared. He stumbled back and forth, wading through knee-deep snow trying to see anything. At one point he almost wandered away from his only landmark, then carefully retreated to the overturned diesel.

"HEY! ANYONE!" There was nothing, and he was beginning to wonder if he was the only one to survive. If so, he wouldn't last for long lost in this frozen hell. Then, after what seemed like a lifetime, a vague figure materialized out of the gloom, almost blundering into him. It was Langsdorf; Cranston grabbed him in a desperate bear hug. "God, you okay?"

Langsdorf was shaken, with a bleeding scrape on his forehead, but he seemed alright otherwise. "Wha-happened, man?"

"We got caught by a slide, but we're alright. Check this out!" Cranston pounded the steel wall with his fist. "We found 'em!"

Langsdorf wasn't impressed. "Let's get out-a this damned wind, man!"

Good idea, now that Cranston thought about it. The wind was a lot worse than he remembered when they started down from the railroad grade. The weather was turning down rapidly. "The sarge and Wally are still missing!" he yelled. "Plus I lost my rope! D'you still have yours?"

"No! What do we do?"

"We call for help!" That was when Cranston realized his portable man-pack radio was missing. "You got your radio?"

213

"No, man!"

Great: they were on their own, lost in a growing blizzard.

"What are we gonna *do*, man!?"

§

Milepost 206, Truckee, California:

Bret Johansen was waiting for them trackside when the spreader returned to Truckee. "So how's it going up there?" he demanded.

Borden considered him and his ad-hoc crane extra parked on a siding nearby. The sight was a real letdown; that dinky utility crane hardly seemed worth all the flop-sweat they were going through. "It's working, after a fashion," he said. "But you might wind up taking your retirement before we can get you there."

"Bad, huh?" To Johansen the spreader looked like it'd been through hell: piled with loose snow, headlight dangling. The whole unit seemed weary and sore.

"You got no idea. We're catching Hail Columbia up there. I hate t' think what they're going through up at the main wreck. You got it soft down here!"

Even as Borden spoke, rotary 209 crawled through the crossover and started back up the Hill, leaving the spreader to await events. Johansen watched it vanish into the snowy gloom, then sighed. "Yeah. I should know better."

§

Milepost 198, down slope:

It took Sergeant DeBeers a few minutes to recover from his rough ride. He lay half buried, trying to collect his wits as he pieced together what happened. Obviously he was hit by an avalanche. It must not have been a big one, or they'd have found his body next spring after the snow melted. For all that, he ached all over from the pummeling he took, and the side of his head stung. He tried to feel his face, and came away with traces of blood. There were scattered rocks laying nearby, which explained that. A few anxious minutes' self-examination showed his injuries were bloody and extensive, but superficial.

His immediate situation assessed, he turned his attention to his men. He couldn't see more than a few feet in this white gloom, and his rope was missing. He must have been carried some way down slope by the avalanche, and there was no sign of the others.

"HEY!" he yelled; a hoarse croak. "Cranston! Langsdorf! Anybody!" Nothing. His words were carried off on the wind and buried in blowing snow. "HEY!" he shrieked with all his strength. The storm hardly noticed, other than to swallow his words as if he had never spoken. "Where's a goddamned St Bernard when you need one?" he grumbled.

After several futile minutes of calling, he gave up and focussed on his own plight. His injuries weren't severe, but he'd lost most of his gear in the slide. One snow shoe was missing, as was his man-pack headset he'd been wearing when the slide hit. He dug in his pockets, but his cell phone was missing too, as were most of the contents of his backpack.

There was no sign of his rope, his one lifeline to the outside world. But there was no sense in crying over it, so he pulled himself together and wondered what to do. The sky was ugly, and the wind was picking up: clearly the forecast of a break in the weather was a load of bull. He struggled to his feet, bracing himself against the wind, and tried to see some sign of a way out of this mess.

He had one thing going for him: he was standing on a steep slope, which at least gave him some orientation. The railroad must be that-a-way, but how far? It didn't matter. He knew there was no hope of climbing this mountain without his snow shoes. That left only one alternative...

§

Milepost 197, Snow Shed 47:

"You better watch out. The weather report says this storm developed a trailing edge front with high-altitude winds, or some-such. They say you're gonna get hit with hurricane force winds before this one ends. It's already getting bad here. Thankfully we're down below it, but we're being pounded anyway."

215

Despite coping with an ever-increasing traffic backup, the Roseville dispatcher found the time to follow the news and weather reports, and forward them to Murphy over in Colfax, who passed them along up the Hill to the work site. What he had to report wasn't comforting. "Any idea how long we got?" Gus asked.

"No idea, but it can't be long. You best watch your step. They're sayin' high-altitude winds as great as a hunnert-mile-an-hour."

"Jesus!" Walter muttered.
"No way!" Fred was equally appalled.
"Thanks, Murphy! We'll take it from here." Gus signed off the caboose radio and turned to the other two. "We can't take that kind-a weather. Th' wind chill will be deadly. Walter, you get on the horn and warn them National Guards. Fred, you and me need t' get our people in."

§

Outside, at the end of Shed 47, the wind buffeted them harder than ever, forcing them to brace themselves against the snow shed walls. Gus pondered the sky with deep misgivings; the clouds were churning, whipped into a frenzy, and the snow was flying horizontally. Already they were having a hard time keeping on their feet, and from the look of things the worst was yet to come.

Half their force of gandy dancers were standing a one-hour shift trying to keep the drifts from building up too badly. The other half were in the dorm car warming up, and would replace this lot shortly. Although they couldn't see him, Parker Lee was ramrodding his shift from a position about half-way down the line to the wreck site.

Gus keyed his radio. "Gus to Parker. You there, Parker?"

"Right here, boss."

"Word from down the Hill is this weather is getting worse. We're gonna get hit with a major blow any time now. We need t' get everyone in, right quick!"

"Copy that, boss!"

The two watched briefly as Parker's people started drifting in, fighting the wind as they came. It was already worse than they realized earlier. This evacuation might already be late in the game.

Then Gus remembered something, and turned to Fred. "I want you t' check the equipment t' be sure everyone's got plenty of fuel. Who knows how long this'll last, and we don't want t' have t' refuel in a hurricane!"

Fred looked down the dim interior of the snow shed in dismay. The stiff wind coming over the pass was trapped by the open shed, accelerating it to a punishing force. Snow blown in from the far end was already building up around the equipment, and it was hard to keep one's feet. How bad would it be when the wind speed doubled or even tripled?

"Okay!" He had to shout to be heard. "Let's hope it holds off a while!" He headed down the snow shed, bracing himself on the side of the dorm car and hunched into the wind.

§

Milepost 204:

By time rotary 209 returned, rotary 17223 had caught up with what they accomplished thus far and pushed on another two hundred feet or so. That wasn't saying a whole lot, but it was at *some* progress, anyway. Having done all they could, rotary 17223 retreated while the 209 cleaned up their limited gains on track one. Then everyone backed off and they went into a huddle.

"Damn if this isn't working," the lead engineman on rotary 209 said.

"Ol' Mortensen got somethin' right, for once," the MoW foreman added. "Who'd-a-thunk it?"

"Yeah, right. He may be flying high now, but that just makes for a bigger crater when he crashes."

"As long as we don't have t' clean up his wreckage," the foreman grumbled. "Okay, times a-wastin'. Let's get th' 209 back down th' Hill so the spreader can to it."

§

Milepost 197, Snow Shed 47:

"Gus, I can't get hold of them National Guards," Walter reported when the two returned to the office caboose.

Gus gestured at the walkie-talkie the Guardsmen lent them so they could keep in touch. "That thing got good batteries?"

"Yeah. I tested 'em, and I can hear calls on other frequencies. Our guys aren't answering."

"Wonderful. I hope they're alright." The roar of the wind was deafening, and the caboose vibrated steadily. The snow shed was acting like a wind tunnel, funneling and accelerating the icy blast. "There's not a blessed thing we can do if they're in trouble." There was a faint rumble, and one of their locomotives crept past dragging the fuel tank car. Aside from refueling the equipment, and it must be a miserable task for Fred and his people, the rescue effort was shut down.

§

Milepost 198, down slope:

Right then all Corporal Cranston could think of was to retreat to shelter in the locomotive and try to sort things out. As far as he could see their rescue expedition was a bust; they needed to focus on getting reorganized and rescuing themselves. Langsdorf's head injury seemed superficial, and when he tested his knee it was sore but functional. They were both lucky.

He pondered how to climb up on the side of the locomotive—it was clearly capsized and there were no ladders on the roof—then decided they could pull themselves up using the mesh grilles. He got a good grip on one and started to climb...

...but his right leg was tangled in something. A rope.

He climbed down and tried to untangle the rope, and it took him a moment to realize it was blue; they used red ropes for themselves; the blue ones were for equipment. "Hey! Help me with this!" he yelled. Langsdorf joined him, and they hauled the rope in eagerly until the Stokes stretcher materialized out of the white nothingness. It was upside down, but for a miracle their equipment was still firmly lashed in place.

218

"Thank God for small favors!" Langsdorf said, fervently.

"Yeah, you got that right!"

They were distracted by a faint voice: "Sarge! Anyone!"

"It's Chase!" Cranston and Langsdorf started yelling at the top of their lungs, and before long, Chase came stumbling out of the blizzard along the side of the second locomotive. "You okay?" Cranston asked, but the man was too shaken to answer, tears flowing down his face.

"What about the sarge?!" Langsdorf cried.

"Don't know!" Cranston yelled. "We'll never find him in this!" The wind was blowing harder than ever, tearing at their arctic gear and chilling them to the bone. It was hard to hear each other over the steady roar. "The weather's picking up! We got to get out of this wind!"

"Where do we go? We got no ropes!"

Cranston turned and pounded the locomotive again to focus their panicked minds on it. "In here! We hole up inside until the storm passes!"

§

Milepost 206, Truckee, California:

Someone shook Bret Johansen out of a sound sleep in the 'wreck train' caboose when rotary 209 returned after it's second try. By time they switched off onto the next service track over, leaving the spreader free to get back to work, he was dressed and had set a pot of coffee to heat on the caboose stove. "So how's it look?" he asked the rotary's engineman.

The man offered a bemused look. "It's working, believe it or not. The spreader got buried, but we're able to pull 'em out, and we've cleared maybe a thousand feet thus far."

"That's all?" Johansen was disappointed but not surprised. "This'll take forever."

"Yeah, well, seeing what we're up against, I'd say we're doin' okay. At least it's working."

"Yeah. All we can do is do our best, I guess."

"Let's just hope those people up there can hold out til then."

§

Milepost 198, down slope:

They turned to, determined to get out of what was starting to look like a nasty blow. Cranston carefully tied the Stokes stretcher to the overturned lead unit's horns while the others dug the portable heater and some propane bottles out. The locomotive was half buried, laying on its left side, but it still took an effort to scramble up on top of it. Once the three of them made it, it wasn't long before they discovered the open cab door.

Cranston dug out his flashlight and explored the dark cavern. The first thing he recognized was a body lying ten feet below. "Hey, I found them!" He jumped down and knelt by Bobby's prostrate form. "He's alive!" He turned to check Karl, and hesitated when he saw the man's predicament. A quick check of his pulse was reassuring. "They're both alive!" He started digging through his backpack of medical supplies. "Jerry, get the heater going. Wally, grab those pry bars off the stretcher."

§

Milepost 204:

It took the spreader another half hour to crawl back up to the front lines, and when they got there, they were less than impressed with progress to date. Track two was cleared for another twelve hundred feet or so thanks to the concerted efforts of the work crew and rotary 17223, which left them three miles to go.

"Aw...shit," Jeff muttered as they pondered the task ahead. Kareem was silent, but clearly not looking forward to this. But then none of them were.

"Well, it ain't gonna get done unless we do it, so let's get on the stick." Borden picked up the radio mic. "This is the spreader. Take us ahead, slow and easy."

"Copy that."

The diesels revved somewhere behind them, and the spreader eased forward for their next go at the Hill.

§

220

"I swear I'm gonna quit once we get down off this damned mountain," Dan griped. "I am so damned *sick* of being cold!"

"I hear you, man-o," Jesus said. He pondered the scene outside their rotary: the wind was whipping snow the length of the snow shed so they were slowly being buried from behind. "Maybe we ought t' try to reach the bunk car? It'll be warmer there."

"Well it sure as *hell* can't be any colder!" Without the heat exhaust from the traction motors which turned the massive rotor, idle for the moment, the steam generator couldn't keep up against the raw arctic wind. Despite its best efforts they were miserable, but both were reluctant to risk the torrent between the two rows of equipment. It was their own stupid fault they were stuck here, he reminded himself. They'd hesitated to leave their charge when the gandy dancers were called in, and by time they were refueled, the scene outside was not inviting. Gus's orders be damned, they should have taken the recall as their cue to dive for cover. Too late now. The massive rotary was trembling from the tornado wind buffeting them. Maybe they could cross the narrow gap to the dorm car, but neither of them was eager to risk it.

"They got hot food, too," Jesus said, wistfully. They'd both gone for some time before the weather kicked up.

That reminded Dan of the sack of sandwiches he picked up back in Colfax. He grabbed it and started rooting through it. "I got some sandwiches here." He offered a couple to Jesus.

"*¡Muy gracias, compadre!*" The ham and cheese were a bit stale but still good from being in the chilly cab all this time. They both dug in with a will. "How long you think we be stuck here, man-o?" Jesus asked after a bit.

"God...I dunno." The massive rotary was rolling like a storm-tossed ship, and the windsong had become a shrill roar. "Until this weather breaks, I suppose. How long it'll be is anyone's guess."

"At least we got some food, thanks to you, man!"

Food wasn't the only thing they needed. The raw wind was draining the heat out of the cab, and them.

§

221

"How's he look?" Langsdorf asked as Cranston worked on the body they found on the floor.

"He's alive; that's about all I can tell you."

They both jumped as one of the heavy steel pry bars landed near them. "Hey!" Langsdorf yelled as Chase lowered the second pry bar and dropped it to the cab deck. There followed another propane bottle (handed carefully to Langsdorf), a rucksack full of MREs, and a heavy tarp which could serve as a blanket.

"That's about it for now," Chase said after he clambered down. "It's getting ugly out there."

He made to close the cab door over their head, but Cranston stopped him. "Leave it open. We'll need the ventilation with the heater going." Their portable propane camp heater cast a pale blue light in the confined cab. Its use against the bitter mountain cold was problematic, but the wavering light was a blessing and every bit of warmth was cherished right then.

"Let's just hope our gas supply holds out," Chase said as he clambered down. "Let's get this other guy loose."

The three of them turned to with the two pry bars, struggling to find the right leverage to shift the massive console. They really didn't have the room they needed, but by dint of major straining they were able to pry it around enough for Cranston to drag Karl free and lay him on the deck next to Bobby.

"He alive?" Langsdorf asked.

"Kind-a, but he's in bad shape." Cranston studied his vitals for a long moment. "The other guy is probably okay, but I'm not so sure about this one." He continued his examination, then gave Karl a morphine tab. "It looks like he's got some busted ribs, and he's deep in shock. We need t' get both of them to a hospital right away, this one in particular."

"Yeah, well, nobody's going anywhere until this storm lets up," Langsdorf said, gloomily.

"Yeah, and who knows how long that'll be," Chase muttered.

"Hell, someone screwed up right from the get-go."

§

It wasn't long before the storm was raging in full fury, forcing the rescue to a halt as everyone took shelter from the terrible wind. Conditions in the snow shed were horrific; the rescue party hunkered down under siege. The labor force spent the time eating or playing cards or sleeping, thankful to be indoors. Gus and the supervisors were gathered around the caboose stove engaged in the time-honored practice of chowing down on beef stew and griping about the situation.

Needless to say, the big topic was how the *hell* they were supposed to fight this battle when they were so short on equipment. "I don't see how we can deal with this weather with only one rotary," Parker said. "Shovels and bulldozers ain't gonna do it. At the minimum we need the 211, and we got to rescue the spreader as well."

That was a gloomy topic all round. "Damn shame about them wrecking," Fred muttered.

"I don't get it. They derailed from a standing start," Walter protested. "Those spreaders are designed for these conditions. I don't understand how it could happen."

"You should ask the crew," Joey said.

"No can do," Fred said. "They were the two injured men evacuated down to Colfax."

"This doesn't add up, Gus grumbled. "Why would a spreader derail? The snow wasn't all that deep, was it?"

"Not to speak of," Fred said. "It needed plowing, but it was nothing a spreader couldn't handle."

There was a brief silence as they mused on the mystery. "Unless there was somethin' wrong with the track?"

That got under Fred's skin. "I gave Ernesto clear orders to work on those turnouts!"

Gus shot him a hard look. "D'you trust him?"

That put Fred in a bind. "Not...entirely. But I don't see what he might have done which could wreck the spreader."

"But I know how we can get to the truth of it."

§

"Jeez, it's blowing like a sumbitch out there!" Private Chase clambered down from the overturned control console, and rubbed his hands in the exhaust from their portable heater. "We're gonna be stuck here for a while if this keeps up."

"Yeah, and if this was Hawaii we could go skinny-dipping!" Corporal Cranston was more than a little wired between the endless cold, the unknown fate of Sargent DeBeers, and the all-too-likely fate of his two patients, which Chase's endless chatter didn't help. There was a brief silence, broken by the howling wind and the hiss of their propane heater, before he glanced at Chase. "Sorry," he mumbled. "Could you fix us something t' eat?"

"Yeah, sure." Chase began digging through the rucksack of MREs. "What would you like, Jerry?"

"We got any of the Curried Chicken meals?"

"Uh...yeah." Chase made a face and handed the foil packet to Langsdorf by one corner with two fingers. "How about you Al? You up for some international cuisine?"

Cranston considered Langsdorf's obvious enthusiasm for the meal he was preparing, and shuddered. "No way! I'll take a minestrone, if you have one."

"Don't know if it makes a difference." Chase dug up another of the white winter ration packs and handed it over. "They'll rot your guts out any old how."

"Yeah, well, they're better than nothing." The next few minutes were devoted to prepping their first hot meal in twenty-four hours. They settled in to eat and reflect on their present unhappy circumstances.

"What d'you think the sarge's chances are?" Chase asked at last.

"Face it, man, he's dead!" Langsdorf said. "If he isn't already, he might as well be, and there's no way we can search for him in this slop."

"We don't know he's dead! The sarge is a survivor; if he can find shelter somewhere, like in a cave or something, he might make it."

"Maybe," Chase said, reluctantly. "But even so, we'll have to call for more help to search for him. We got our hands full already."

Cranston's stomach was tight with worry from agonizing over the sarge and their present plight. As he was discovering, the weight of command was not an easy burden to bear. "Look, let's not dwell on it, okay? We got enough to deal with as is."

There was nothing they could do about the sarge or their two patients or the weather, so they let the matter drop by mutual consent, and went back to eating and worrying. The only sound was the howling wind and the hiss of the propane burner.

§

Milepost 204:

This time the spreader managed to go some quarter mile before the wall of snow collapsed on them again. Against that, the left cab window finally shattered, and the loose headlight parted company with them.

"Aw fer Christ sakes!" Borden griped as he fought his way clear of the piled snow and shattered bits of glass filling the cab. "This is a damn-fool way t' make a living!"

"What? You call this living?" Jeff was nursing a cut on his forehead from when the window imploded on them.

Kareem abandoned the central station, grabbed the first aid kit on the rear bulkhead, and began cleaning the blood away with some wet wipes. "You will survive, my friend. It's not so bad."

Jeff sighed and applied a large sticky plaster to close the cut. "Yeah, this is about par for the course around here."

"Spreader, what's your situation? Over?"

Borden grabbed the radio mic. "Fuckin' disgusted is our situation!" he growled. "We need t' make some repairs, so take us back down t' Truckee."

The spreader began moving in reverse, and they hastily retracted the wings. "This is a sorry state!" Jeff groused. "Our luck, they'll take the damages out of our pay."

225

"Naa, out of Mortensen's pay: he created this fuster cluck t' begin with."

The spreader reached open ground and picked up speed as they rolled downhill. "This is going to take forever," Kareem sighed. "I hope they're managing up there at the wreck site."

"They can't be any worse off than we are!"

§

Milepost 197, Snow Shed 47:

Pepe Rodriguez was in the crew car napping after a quick lunch when Fred accosted him. "Pepe, we need t' talk with you."

Back in the office caboose, Pepe found himself standing alone surrounded by all *Los Jefes*, which made him nervous. "You're not in any trouble, Pepe," Gus assured him. "But we need some answers about how the spreader got derailed at Emigrant Gap."

"*Si, Jefe,*" he mumbled. Gus tried to make this seem like a harmless discussion, but all the heavyweights would intimidate anyone. He eyed the rank of *Patrons* uneasily, then nodded.

"We need to know if a problem with the track caused the derailment. Did Ernesto have you guys clean the turnouts like Fred told him?"

"*¡Si, Jefe!* We worked on them for maybe an hour. We only came in about fifteen minutes before *Señor* Fred and the others came back." That wasn't what Fred ordered, but better than he expected.

"An hour, huh?" Gus gave Fred a skeptical look. "What about the flangeways on the detracking points? Did you clean them?"

Pepe froze, and his face turned pale. "I was up the line at the crossover, *Jefe*."

"Did *anyone* clean those flangeways?"

"I...don' know, *Jefe*. We couldn't see nothin' in that snow."

Gus pondered him in silence for a long moment. "What about Ernesto? What did he do?"

Pepe reacted angrily. "That *perezoso*, he ain't no good, man! He sit in the truck all the time!"

"That must be it," Walter said. "Ernesto dogged it, and the others didn't think to do the flangeways."

"Yeah," Fred added in disgust, remembering too late how Ernesto only did the minimum he was specifically *ordered* to do, and then only when ridden constantly.

"But why did it derail?" Walter asked. "Them spreaders are designed for these conditions."

Pepe fielded that one. "Well, *Jefe*...after we got on the train, they take off real fast. Some of us fell down, they was goin' so fast. Maybe that do it."

"They did, huh?" Gus pondered this bit of news in surprise. "Why'd they take off like that?"

"It was likely the guy running it," Parker said. "They were having trouble with him all the way up the Hill. Him and the rest of the crew were bickering constantly."

"Really? What's his problem?"

"From what I gathered, he's a slacker. They had to push him no end to keep the train moving at all. He's got a real temper too, he does; got into it over the radio with his conductor. The Roseville dispatcher had to step in and break it up."

"I wondered why it took them so long t' get t' Emigrant Gap," Fred muttered.

"But how'd the wreck happen?"

Parker brooded for a time. "My guess, he finally lost it there at the Gap. Like Pepe said, they really peeled rubber out-a there. That's when the wreck went down."

There was a brooding silence, broken by the roar of the wind and the hiss of their oil stove, while they pondered these revelations. "So..." Gus said at last. "The flangeways were packed with ice..."

"...and the spreader was under heavy acceleration..." Walter added.

"...and it pigeon-toed, at the worst possible moment!" Gus concluded. "Great! A slacker decided t' play cowboy, and put half our equipment out of commission!" The standing orders to be extra cautious in bad conditions were there for a reason.

"I'm sorry, *Jefe*..." Pepe had been listening, all but forgotten, all this time.

"Don't worry about it, Pepe," Fred assured him. "You didn't do anything wrong."   His worry was understandable: people were fired for less, and the Union Pacific *never* rehired. "You can go on back to the dorm."

Pepe mumbled something and beat a hasty retreat.   "Tell Ernesto we want t' see him," Gus called after him.

"And the other two as well," Walter added. Pepe nodded and got out of there.

Gus turned to Fred. "This Ernesto any good?" he demanded.

"Not really. He does what he's told, but he bears watching."

"So why'd you make him straw boss?"

Fred found himself on defense. "That was his doing! He struts it every time I turn my back on him!" In truth, he let Ernesto be in charge on his truck down south because someone needed to ramrod that crew, and the others didn't argue, and he was too tired at the time to work it out. Right then he was kicking himself mentally for not remembering how little Ernesto could be trusted on his own when the weather was foul and a warm truck cab was handy. He was dismayed by how such a minor decision could go so wrong, and how it put *his* job in jeopardy.

Gus gave him a skeptical look. "We'll see about that."

§

Milepost 142, Colfax, California:

"Yeah, I got a hard-on for him," Murphy snarled at the mention of Davy Burns. "According t' his brakey, he was goin' way too fast when th' derailment happened." This report from Gus up the Hill confirmed his earlier suspicions about the incident.

"What's his condition?"

"They're both gonna live, but his number two is likely t' get retirement 'cause of his injuries. Good man; I hate t' lose him. I already wrote Burns up, and I'll be go-t'-hell before I'll let him back on *my* rotation!"

"That's what we figured. Thanks, Murphy."

§

Johansen made a point of meeting the conductor of the spreader train when they came down the hill again. "We're makin' progress," the man reported. "But by time we reach those passenger cars that spreader'll likely be pounded t' scrap."

"Yeah, I saw the damage." The earlier cracked cab window was shattered altogether, the headlight was missing, and it looked like the left wing was slightly bent. The idea bemused him; those wings were meant to take a pounding.

Bill Borden came in just then. "So how's it going?" Johansen asked.

"We're still alive," he grumbled. "We got any plywood? I got a window t' board up. We could use some wire brooms, too."

"There should be some in the MoW warehouse. I hear you're doing good."

Borden greeted his remark with a contemptuous snort. "Shit, we might as well lay new track on top of th' snow. It's solid enough."

"How long d'you think it'll take t' reach those cars?"

"Hell's already froze over, so there's no sayin'," Borden groused as he turned and left.

The conductor had no joy to offer. "I'd say at least another day at this rate, assuming we don't have any setbacks."

"Yeah. Well, you know what you do when you 'assume'."

"Ain't that a fact." The conductor was silent for a moment as he pondered the scene outside with something akin to dread. "I'm thankful you're down here to back us up if..."

Johansen eyed him, noting how unsettled he seemed. These road crews weren't used to facing Nature at its most feral. But then, any sensible person would be shaken by conditions up there on the Hill. "Yeah, well, we'll do what we can of course, if it comes to that." Not that his dinky utility crane and a handful of Mechanical Department people could do much.

Outside rotary 209 trundled through the crossover and crawled into the gloom, heading up the Hill once more.

§

In fact it was some time before Ernesto showed up in answer to Gus's summons, and Gus had plenty of time to get the truth out of Juan and Miguel, the other two on his truck, before he showed. Their stories, plus Murphy's report, were conclusive. They stood off to one side looking apprehensive when Ernesto arrived. No doubt Pepe warned him *Los Jefes* were angry about the spreader mishap, and Ernesto spent the time pumping him for details. He seemed properly subdued when he appeared, far different from his usual flippant nature.

"Fred here told you to clean the trackwork at Emigrant Gap," Gus said, sternly. "So what about it?"

"We did, *Jefe!* We cleaned them turnouts for over an hour."

"Like an hour matters in this weather!" Parker grumbled.

"But what about the flangeways on the detracking points? Did you clean them too?"

"*¡Si, Jefe!*"

Gus slammed his fist on the desk. "These men tell me otherwise! They say you dogged it while they did all the work, and *none of you* touched the detracking points!"

Ernesto got heated over that accusation. "They a bunch-a lyin' *perros, Jefe!* I cleaned them flangeways good!"

"Then *why* did the spreader *derail* when we were able to use the crossover with no problems?!" Gus roared.

Ernesto hesitated, with a trapped look in his eyes. "It was jus' bad luck, *Jefe!*"

"Bad luck, my ass! Two men are in the hospital and half our available snow gear is wrecked thanks to YOU!"

"That ain't so, *Jefe!*"

Gus bored in relentlessly. "You set yourself up as straw boss on your truck. Who told you to take charge?"

"I had to, *Jefe! Señor* Fred, he was with the other truck, and none of them wanted the job."

Gus waved one fist at the other two. "So why didn't you tell 'em t' do the flangeways?"

"I did, *Jefe!*"

"You just told me you cleaned 'em yourself! So what is it?"

Ernesto hesitated, caught in another lie. "I *did* tell 'em, *Jefe!* But they didn't, so I had t' do it!"

The others started to protest, but Gus overrode them. "That's a pretty sorry straw boss! In fact they say you dogged it in your truck while they did all the work!"

"That ain't so, *Jefe!* They lyin' on me!"

"Frankly, I don't believe you. Your story has too many holes, and the others *all* say different."

Walter and Fred watched in stony silence as Ernesto fidgeted nervously. Parker Lee gave him a look of outright contempt.

"This railroad doesn't need a slacker like you," Gus said, coldly. "Under the circumstances, we can do without your services hereafter. You are to remain in the dorm car until we head down to Roseville."

Ernesto fumed in speechless rage, with a look like he was about to boil over and loose a tirade against his former coworkers. Then he seemed to sag as reality caught up with him. He stared at his former coworkers for a bit, then turned without saying anything and left.

After a moment, Gus turned to the other two. "You two can go on back to the dorm." They left hastily, no doubt preferring the storm out there to the one here in the office caboose.

There was a brief silence broken by the relentless howling wind as they absorbed what happened. "Actually this does raise a good point," Walter said to Fred at last. "It looks like you need a good straw boss on your team. You got anyone you can trust?"

"Elwood," Fred said without hesitation. "He's a steady sort and popular with the men."

Gus nodded. "Alright, then. Give him an extra two bucks an hour and tell him he's your number two."

"Right, thanks." Fred wasn't about to argue since he really did need a straw boss on the second truck, and because he still had his job.

*****

231

Noon:

Milepost 206, Truckee, California:

> *"They're out of food and running low on fuel for their heat and lights. We're pinned down by this damned hurricane, and can't do anything for them until the weather clears. It's all up to you. You need to get to them as soon as possible."*

"Ah, copy that, Gus." Jim Mortensen was dismayed by the latest word from the wreck site; the radio transmission was all but drowned out by the roar of the storm. What was even worse than having this rescue come back on him was his grand plan to clear track two wasn't progressing like he hoped. "We're pushing ahead as fast as we can, but it's slow going. We're being hit by this storm too, and it's tying everything up." The damaged equipment didn't help either, nor did all the extra equipment moves as the rotaries and spreader traded places, and his carefully hoarded labor force was melting away as they went on the law. No, this wasn't working out nearly as well as he intended.

> *"They're counting on you and your people, Jim."*

That hurt. Mortensen *hated* being stuck with the responsibility in this crisis, what with it gaining national news coverage and Omaha breathing on his neck as a result. He was much more comfortable ramrodding the annual tie replacement and grade-leveling work, which *never* meant a life-and-death crisis and rarely drew attention from further up the feeding chain. "We'll keep at it, Gus. We'll be there as soon as we can."

> *"Copy that. Good luck, Jim."*

"We're a long way from getting to those two cars," Dean Nakamura said once the radio conversation ended. "From what I hear, we're looking at a minimum of two more days."

232

"Dammit! Why'd this have to happen?" Mortensen pounded his desk with both fists in frustration. He had to fight back tears of anguish as he struggled to come up with some sort of answer.

"Hey, don't take it so hard, Jim," Dean offered. "These things happen. We're dealing with a crisis here."

Mortensen have him a poisonous glare. "A derailment is a crisis; this is a freakin' disaster! Omaha is already giving me hell over it!"

There was no denying that, nor Mortensen's fault in letting things get so out of hand in this side of the Hill.

"Perhaps we should get a load of food and fuel together and get 'em, up the Hill in a hi-rail so they can be delivered as soon as possible," Dean said after a bit. "Herb can transfer some of it to the wreck site with his two sno-cats."

Mortensen was appalled at the idea. Maybe they could get a hi-rail truck up there, but it was a long way from where the snow clearing effort was to where the 'City' was stranded. "That's a long way to go on sno-cats. Herb couldn't carry much on those bikes anyway. Plus there's no way to know how much longer this storm'll last, or what shape the right of way will be in by then."

"It's a calculated risk..."

"It's a damned-fool's errand." As much as he wished for some solution, the prospect of such a desperate expedient chilled him. His stomach was churning with frustration and worry, and he realized his hands were trembling. He was too weary, too short on sleep to think about it. "Unless we get a break, we may be too late to save all those people."

Nobody would have thought to take a poll on the matter, but such was not an option for the men of the Union Pacific. "God...I hope it doesn't come to that," Dean muttered.

There was an awkward silence, save for the roar of the wind and the monotonous tick of the old-fashioned clock on the office wall, and an occasional snatch of garbled radio static. The roar of the wind chilled them, even in this overheated office.

"There is another option," Dean said at last. "We can tip those two cars off the right of way; clear the line so we can bring the train down. We can recover them later."

It might be their only real option, Mortensen thought, morosely. They could bring up a big Cat D-Niner and tip those two off the line, but that would pretty well wreck them. Omaha would not be amused if they did it, nor would Amtrak, who would hold the railroad answerable for repairs. Like all tough decisions, the responsibility chilled him.

"Let's see how things go for the next few hours," he said at last. The nearest big Caterpillar was in Sparks anyway, if it was even available. "In the mean time, we'll hold off on your hi-rail and see see what develops. Maybe Herb can scout the wreck to see about shoving them off the line."

As usual, Mortensen confronted a hard decision by prevaricating. Dean sighed in frustration, nodded and left. He had phone calls to make.

§

Milepost 198, aboard the 'City of San Francisco':

"I'm worried about his vitals," Jamie said quietly, so no one could hear their conversation. "His BP is dropping and his pulse is becoming thready and erratic. He seems to be developing lung congestion, too."

Their unconscious head trauma case was still unresponsive after all this time, and now his vital signs were slipping. Doctor Cummings listened to his heartbeat, then examined the patient's eyes. "Retinas are differentiated, too. This doesn't look good."

"So what do we do? He sinks much more and we may not be able to save him."

Doctor Cummings brooded on the medical picture for a long moment, trying to come up with some answer other than the obvious one. "We need to consult with Doctor Menendez," he said at last.

Doctor Menendez was hot-bunking in the dining car crew's dorm when Jamie shook him out of an exhausted slumber. "We need you," she said.

A few minutes later, after a much-needed cup of coffee, he met with his colleague. "Our head trauma is slipping," Cummings reported. "I'm afraid we have no choice but to operate."

Menendez was dismayed at the idea. "Neither of us is a neurosurgeon!"

"We have a depressed skull fracture: all we need to do is open the scalp and realign the fracture."

Even that simple procedure was intimidating, as it would be to any medical professional. "There's so *many* things which could go wrong! I'd hate to risk it. Can't we carry him over to the rescue train? They could take him on to Roseville."

"It's blowing a full hurricane out there! Even if we could carry him through that, the cold would kill him." As if to drive home the point, the ninety ton diner was shaking from the wind blast, and the roar of the storm was a steady, unnerving shriek.

Jack Whitacre was kibitzing nearby. "It wouldn't do any good anyway, doc. It'd take them at least a day to get down the Hill in this weather, if not longer."

"I'm afraid there's no choice," Cummings insisted. "We need to act now before he gets any weaker."

"Our supply of oxygen is low." Jamie gestured to the gauge on the portable oxygen bottle, and confronted the two doctors. "We only have two units of plasma left, and no whole blood. Plus all we have are a few hemostats which need to be resterilized."

"This will be a superficial incision," Menendez said. "That should be enough."

"Incision? With what?"

That thwarted Menendez for a moment. "Um, perhaps a steak knife? All we need is to peel back an area of scalp."

"Yeah, right. It'll be a freakin' *miracle* if nothing goes wrong! We need a suite of instruments, oxygen, a load of antibiotics, and more plasma at minimum before you try anything. Without them, this would be an act of desperation. Odds are you'll kill him!"

Doctor Cummings spread his hands in a helpless gesture. "You're right, but what can we do? The patient is critical, and slipping!"

"And we need to get a drain into our hip fracture, too," Menendez added. "She's already in distress." Their other 'grave' patient, the old woman, needed drainage and a massive infusion of antibiotics. Time was running out for both of them.

235

"Then we need to get them to send up more supplies." There would be no arguing with her. "Without that, you're gambling with your patients' lives."

Cummings was not happy at the prospect, but there was no alternative. He hesitated for a long moment, then nodded.

§

Milepost 198, down slope:

"How are they doing?" Langsdorf asked as Cranston tended to their two injured men.

Cranston gave him a frustrated, worried look. "Not good," he said, softly. "This guy..." he indicated Karl Olsen, laying unconscious between them. "...he has internal bleeding and a couple cracked ribs, and I think he may have a ruptured spleen, too. The other one isn't as bad off, but he'll be in trouble if that arm becomes infected."

Langsdorf studied their two patients for a bit. "There's nothing we can do for them right now, anyway."

"Yeah, we need supplies we don't normally carry, like antibiotics. Plus I don't know *what* to do about internal injuries beyond immobilize and transport. In any case, there's nothing we can do until this storm quits."

"Even then we're all in trouble unless we can find a way to get back up to the railroad."

"Can't we turn the heat up a little?" Chase whined. "It's freezing in here!"

"That's our only bottle of gas," Cranston told him. "We need to make it last." The only thing between them and the storm was a single twenty pound propane bottle like those used for bar-b-ques. Their other one was empty.

"D'you think they'll make it?" Langsdorf asked, softly. "They can't hold out much longer."

"Hell, d'you think *we'll* make it?" Chase added.

"Honestly..." Cranston couldn't feel sure of anything, especially with the sarge missing and probably dead. "I...don't know."

§

Milepost 197, Snow Shed 47:

"It looks like the docs need to operate on at least two of their critical patients, but they need more supplies. At a minimum, they say they need more plasma, some oxygen, some antibiotics and some surgical instruments. They said to check with their hospital for specifics. Over?"

"Wonderful," Gus grumbled. He fought off a yawn before complaining. "What th' hell do they expect from us, anyway?"

"That we save them," Fred said, bleakly.

Gus winced at the reminder, and hit his radio mic. "Ah, Amtrak, I'm not sure what we can do. We don't have anything left over here. I'll have to call down the Hill to see what can be done. Over?"

"Is there any way you can get this stuff to us? They say it's critical. The way things look, they stand to lose two people unless we get help. And there are several others who need attention, too. Please do whatever you can."

"Copy that, George. I'll get back to you ASAP."

"Please hurry!"

"Great," Fred muttered after Gus ended the radio conversation. "How th' *hell* we gonna get supplies to them in *this* weather?"

"If I knew, I don't think I'd like the answer," Gus growled.

"Well if we're gonna bring up more supplies we'll have t' send the rotary down to Colfax. Should I call Margret and Willy?"

Gus pondered that wearily. "Naaa. It'd take 'em all day to make the trip, even if they could do it in these conditions, and likely as much again coming back. I don't want us stranded up here without a way to retreat." He reached for the radio again. "We'll just have t' come up with a better idea."

"Let's hope there is one."

§

Milepost 197, in the kitchen car:

"I don't know *what* we can do any more." Despite needing sleep, Margret was burning through her precious few hours 'on the law', something railroaders *never* did these days, to seek comfort from the only other woman at the scene. "It's just too much. I don't see how we can cope with weather like this." Her weary angst, fueled by sleeplessness, cold, and strong coffee, put her in a full-blown depression; something she carefully hid from her fellow workers and the railroad.

Trudy leaned on the counter opposite to speak privately with her. "The railroad will bring in more equipment; we just have to hang in until the stuff can get built and delivered, is all." She could see Margret was hurting, and her grandmotherly instincts reached out to comfort her.

Margret greeted that with a contemptuous snort. "This road? They've let snow removal go for the last twenty years. There's so many patches on this old gear it's a wonder anything works." She contemplated her coffee mug with no joy; the caffeine was making her headache worse. "It'll take more than new rotaries. They'll need motive power, crews, doctrine, the works. It'll be years."

"Then we'll take years."

"We can't do another winter like this. They need t' build more snow sheds, a lot more."

"No doubt they will, next summer."

Margret gave her a frazzled glare. "If we even *have* a next summer!" She sighed in frustration. "They need t' either abandon the Pass, cover the whole thing with concrete, or drill a tunnel from Sacramento clear over to Reno."

"Sad to say, none of those were viable options." Trudy paused to renew Margret's coffee mug. "That reminds me of when I was forced to choose between a large rock, a rusty knife, or a pissed-off rattlesnake to solve my root canal issue."

That got a chuckle from Margret despite her angst. "Do you offer a Dental Plan?" After a moment, reality returned to trouble them. "I don't know *what* we can do for those people."

§

Milepost 197, Snow Shed 47:

"Don't...know if I can do this, man-o." Jesus was cowering next to the steam generator wrapped tightly in his coat and shivering uncontrollably.

It took Dan a moment to understand him since he was groggy with the cold and fatigue himself. "Ah...yeah. How...long...we been on duty?"

Jesus didn't answer for some time. "Don' know, man. Too long." They were both wiped out by the cold. "Too long."

Dan tried to focus on his control station at the other end of the cab, but it was too impossibly far away. The radio mic dangled on its cable, out of reach.

§

Milepost 206, Truckee, California:

"I'm afraid we're out of options. If you can't get those medical supplies to them, they're set to lose at least two people, perhaps more."

Mortensen was horrified by the prospect of people dying on his watch, especially if he failed to deliver in a crisis which was to some extent his making. "Ahh...Alright, Gus. We'll see what we can do."

"It's all up to you, Jim."

That was the last thing Mortensen wanted to hear. "Alright, Gus. We're on it. Truckee out."

"I guess that settles it," Dean said once the radio call ended. "We need to send the hi-rail. Herb can at least transfer some medical supplies."

"What good can we do?" Mortensen spread his hands in a gesture of helplessness. "This is hopeless."

"A hi-rail can still make it, one with a dozer blade anyway. The line isn't *that* bad yet."

"It'd take 'em half a day to get there!"

239

"And it'll take Gus at *least* a day to reach Colfax, maybe more, plus the trip back again. You heard him; they've been pounded far worse than we have, and they have further to go. In any case we need to see if those two cars can be tipped off the right of way."

Mortensen ignored him for the moment, lost in his own sense of helplessness, bitterly regretting being saddled with the responsibility. *Why* did these things have to happen, especially to him? It seemed so terribly unfair how the weather contrived to make *his* job a living hell! No one deserved to be dumped on like this, forgetting his own fault for letting track two go for so long. And now *he* was supposed to come up with answers for something confounding Gus and his experts...

"Jim?"

But Dean was right; there was nothing for it, and it was up to him to unscrew the inscrutable. Mortensen came reluctantly back to the here-and-now, and nodded in despair. At least Dean had a plan, however unlikely it was. "Alright, but if we're going to do it, let's send up some food too. Might as well make the trip worth the risk."

"Got it." Dean turned to go, then paused. "You need to get some sleep. They don't have enough numbers for all the time you're putting in."

His words pulled Mortensen out of a drowse. "I'll be able to sleep after this crisis is over."

"Next June, then." Dean nodded and headed back to his cubby hole to push the effort already under way.

§

Milepost 204:

"Damn, I'm tired!" Kareem sagged against the sill of his forward window, his weariness showing, but kept a close eye on the white chaos ahead. "How soon we gonna go on the law?"

Borden already knew the answer to that one. "We're due right now." He flogged his weary mind to try to come up with an answer. "My guess, we'll be relieved the next time we go down the Hill."

"I hope so, man."

240

Privately Borden wasn't optimistic; he'd seen the same FRA bulletin and knew without saying that they were in for the long haul. Truth was the routine discipline of times and duties was all blown to hell by this weather crisis, not to mention the rescue effort. Borden saw it all before, more often than their young trainee realized. They could be stuck out on the road, 'on the law', for hours—days, in theory—until relief could reach them. In fact, they'd be bending the rules to take their spreader down to Truckee rather than parking here and waiting.

"How much longer d'you think this'll take?" Jeff asked. "I am getting sick and tired of being cold all the time."

That took a lot of mental effort, which none of them could afford. "My guess, another day, day and a half," Borden said. "If we're lucky..."

...A massive gust of wind caught them just then, staggering the spreader and forcing their four locomotives to a halt. They held on in near panic as the wind caught their wide-spread plow blades, causing the spreader to dance like it might be lifted bodily off the track. Their boarded up window burst in as they were buried under another snow slide, knocking Borden down and sending Kareem sprawling. A moment later the rocking died as the wind settled down again.

"...shit..." Kareem mumbled.

"You guys okay?" Borden asked.

"Yeah."

"This is way too real, man!" Jeff was nursing a bruised forehead where the sheet of plywood smacked him. "We can't keep going if this weather's getting worse!"

"It can't get any worse...can it?" Kareem was shaken after being shoved against the rear bulkhead by the flying sheet of plywood. "How we gonna keep going if it gets worse?"

Borden managed to pick himself up and felt all over; there was no evidence of injuries. "I heard storms will get like this when they're dying down." He lied outright; his team needed it. "They start acting wonky. We may be seeing the end of this mess." In truth he was spooked by the imploding window and by the way the wind tossed the heavy spreader around.

"God, I hope so!"

Their radio crackled to life:

"Hey spreader, you guys okay?"

Borden grabbed the radio mic. "Ah, I guess so. We gotta fix this window again. Can you look t' see if we're still on the track?"

"We'll let you know once we get dug out. The whole section came down on us so you got plenty of time t' fix that window."

"Copy that." Borden hung the radio mic carefully on its hook. "Ain't this some kind-a shit?"

Jeff and Kareem were wrestling with the sheet of plywood, trying to force it back over the window opening against the stiff wind. "Damn, man," Jeff grumbled. "I don't see how we can make it if this keeps happening."

Borden grabbed the roll of stove pipe wire, rammed the plywood home with his shoulder, and started lashing one corner in place. "We'll just have t' hope for the best."

§

Milepost 198, Aboard the 'City Of San Francisco':

Despite his exhaustion and the massed woes in the dining car, Doctor Cummings took a few minutes to visit the compartment where Olivia Bumarris was confined. It took a moment for Barbara to respond to his knock, and she looked frazzled.

"How's she doing?" he asked, gently.

She had to ponder that before answering. "She's stable for now. Her contractions have stopped again. She's resting comfortably."

"And how about you?" He was not pleased with the strung-out look of their RN. "You've been pushing nonstop from the get-go."

"I'm managing." He noticed the mattress from the upper bunk was leaning up against the wall; at least she was getting what catnaps she could. "We get used to these long hours."

"Yeah, but not like this." There was only so much the human mind and body can take, and she was clearly pushing her limits. "Since your patient is stable for now, you need to get some sleep." He overrode her protest. "You can't function like this. She needs you to be with it when her time finally comes. Doctor's orders."

There was no answering that, so she nodded reluctantly and pulled the mattress down onto the floor. As he headed back to the diner he decided to have her friend bring her something to eat.

§

Colfax, California, Milepost 142:

"Hey, Murphy? Phone call for ya, man. It's Roseville."

Murphy looked up from his plate of chicken nuggets and cole slaw, and gave his assistant an annoyed glare. "How'd you like t' take a little trip up t' see Gus at Shed 47? On foot?"

"Hey, man, I'm just doin' my job!" His assistant backed away cautiously; Murphy was known for his temper.

Murphy reined in his frustration with an effort. Roseville? That couldn't be good. "Yeah...okay."

It was the Roseville dispatcher, alright. *"How they doin' up there on the Hill, Murph?"*

"They ain't *doin'*. They're hunkered down t' weather this damned storm."

"Yeah, well about that, the latest weather report says this storm is gonna go on for at least another day. Word is we may get a brief break afterwards, but there's plenty more where this came from."

On top of *everything* else, it was just too much. "How th' hell we supposed t' operate like this, huh?"

"I dunno, Murphy. My yard is choked with cars; we got trains parked on the main with nowhere t' go. Omaha's talkin' about putting an embargo on movements all up and down the coast."

He didn't need to say that all came down to the blockage on the Hill. Donner Pass was one of the major choke points for traffic on the west coast. With them out of action the only alternative was to haul cars south and give them to the Santa Fe—but they had their problems too from what he'd heard, as did the Burlington Northern, out of Seattle. There were no answers.

243

"I don't know what t' tell you. Gus and his crew will get the Hill cleared as soon as possible. When that'll be, you need t' ask the weather bureau."

"I hear ya, Murphy. Give my best to Gus and his boys."

"I'll do that."

Murphy stood brooding at his office window for some time after hanging up. The weather was thick out there; snow blowing sideways, all but obscuring the lights of the flanger trying to keep the yard tracks cleared. It was all a fool's errand. Even if they could clear the wreck, there was no way they could keep ahead of this weather with their limited assets. He stared into the blinding whiteness, lost in its formless depth, and cursed Davy Burns for trashing their only spreader. And how much longer would it take rotary 211 to come back from the shops? Right then it all depended on rotary 207, stuck up there with Gus and his rescue party.

But there was no sense in worrying about it since he couldn't do anything for it. He had his own problems: his increasingly lean manpower roster as road crews stranded by the lack of movements were drained away to Roseville and beyond. He picked up his clipboard and studied it with a sigh. Time to rotate the crews working to keep the yard open. Not that it mattered.

§

Milepost 198, down slope:

"Jeez, that sky looks ugly." Langsdorf was perched on the overturned control console trying to see out through the unburied part of the windshield, with precious little luck.

"D'you see anything?" Cranston asked.

"Nothing but blowing snow. Those clouds can't be more than a hundred feet above us, and I can hardly make 'em out." He turned to Cranston. "I don't think I've ever seen it this ugly before."

"Probably not," Cranston sighed. "I tell ya, this weather is getting to be too much."

Chase was curled up in one corner, wrapped in one of the mylar thermal blankets, using Cranston's backpack for a pillow, trying to get some sleep. Their two civilian patients lay on the wall which was now the floor, taking up almost the entire available room while Cranston frog-walked awkwardly about tending to them. As for Langsdorf, he decided to remain on the overturned control console rather than trying to squeeze into the little space they had. The effect was claustrophobic, made all the worse by the darkness and the endless howling of the storm.

"Are we gonna get out of this, you think?" Langsdorf was scared by the weather and their isolation, and by the likely fate of Sergeant DeBeers.

Cranston pondered him for a long moment. "I don't know, Jerry, honest. We know where we are, so we just have to wait for this storm to quit, then we can make a break for the railroad. We just have to hold out til then."

"If this damned storm *ever* ends!" They both knew the weather up here in the high Sierras was not like the wimpy weather down there in the civilized world. Storms usually went on for days, and lately they came so fast, one after the next, that it was all but perpetual.

"It'll end." Cranston wasn't sure of that, at all. "Anyway, they know we're here and we got their two crewmen. If we can't get to them, they'll come for us."

"I hope they can figure some way out of this before we run out of gas," Langsdorf said, gloomily. "We can't hold out until next spring."

"We'll hold out as long as we have to."

§

Milepost 204:

> *"Yeah, you guys are still on the rails, although how you lucked out is beyond me."*

The much-delayed report from the gandy dancers digging the spreader out from the latest snow slide was a relief in a way, but then it wasn't since it meant they were back at it. Borden keyed the radio mic. "Yeah. God looks after fools and children."

> *"And railroaders!"*

245

"Thank heaven for big favors!" Jeff muttered. "I'd hate t' be stranded up here in this mess!"

"Yeah, that'd make this job even more hopeless!" Kareem added.

"It can't *get* more hopeless," Borden grumbled.

The rumble of their four diesels came over the roar of the storm. Borden could see them out the rear window: running lights barely visible, a cloud of exhaust whipped away by the wind. The spreader lurched, then limped backward as they were dragged bodily out of the snow heaped around them.

"Thank God we're not stuck," Jeff mumbled.

"Not this time, anyway," Kareem answered.

"You guys are runnin' up a pretty big tab with the Almighty," Borden said.

Jeff gave him a frustrated look. "Hell, He owes us for this!"

§

Milepost 197, Snow Shed 47:

> *"The weather people are sayin' this storm'll go for at least another day. Also there's no word on th' 211 or any other snow gear, so it looks like you're SOL for any help."*

This was bitter news, not that Gus was surprised. Their caboose was parked just inside the end of Snow Shed 47 where it caught the full blast of the storm trying to roar through their shelter. "Okay, Murphy. All we can do is hang on for now."

"Damn," Walter muttered as he studied the sky through one of the end windows. "When we get fucked over, we get fucked over in style."

"Yeah, the Hill's good for that," Parker grumbled.

Gus ignored them and keyed his mic again. "Any word from Truckee, Murphy? We haven't been able t' raise 'em for some time."

> *"Last I heard their spreader was stuck again. That was a while ago, so I don't know what's goin' on now. "I'll try t' reach 'em on the land lines, if they're still running."*

"Thanks, Murph. Let me know when you hear anything."

"Well that tears it," Walter said, bitterly. "This means our two crewmen are likely dead, and maybe those National Guards, too."

"Not to mention them people over there in the Amtrak," Parker added. "We'll lose a couple at least, from what I hear."

"Dammit! Even the communications are going down! I hate t' say it, but it looks like we're whipped."

"We ain't done yet." Gus tried to be positive, even though he was starting to despair. "Truckee will come through."

"Gawd! We're in a world of shit if we're counting on Truckee, ain't we?"

§

Milepost 197, aboard rotary 207:

"Jesus?" Dan pawed his arm vaguely, trying to get some response. "Come on, man. You with me, dude?"

Jesus stirred and mumbled something, but didn't respond otherwise. The raw cold was getting to them both, and the steam generator, by itself, couldn't begin to cope. Dan gave up trying to get a response from his brakeman, and focussed on staying awake.

§

Milepost 206, Truckee, California:

"We're gonna send up a hi-rail with a load of food and medical supplies for th' wrecked Amtrak." Mortensen considered the two dozen men called as relief crews for the snow fighting effort. They seemed passive about the prospect of going up the Hill in this godawful weather, but who could say what their feelings really were? "This is critical. They're out of food, and they have some medical emergencies to deal with. They need this stuff."

They stood around his desk silently, listening, impossible to read.

"I know this isn't your usual work, but all our Maintenance people are committed to the rescue effort, so I hope we can get a couple volunteers..."

"What about the contract?" one of them said. "This crosses union lines."

"...I know. This is an emergency; lives are at stake. I hope maybe we can bend the rules a bit in this one instance."

There was an uneasy silence broken by the roar of the wind outside and a garbled burst of static from Mortensen's two-way radio. Finally, the local Shop Steward spoke up. "We all want t' help them people, but we can't *officially* bend the rules, you know that," he said to Mortensen. He paused to look around at the others. "But if anyone wants to *volunteer*, it'd be on your own hook."

The protestor spoke up again. "What? Go up there without pay?" That produced a subdued rumble among the men; none of them were looking forward to the next twelve hours to start with, and as much as they agonized over the crisis up there the unions have a long tradition of jealously guarding their contract rights.

The Shop Steward glanced at Mortensen, then offered a wry grin. "Well, I *suppose* ain't nobody gonna complain about bending the rules t' *pay* someone."

Dean Nakamura grabbed the opening. "Anyone interested in *volunteering* for some 'extra movement road duty'?"

Every man in the room raised his hand, including the protestor.

*****

Mid-Afternoon:

Milepost 198, down slope:

"Damn, it's not gonna quit, is it?" Langsdorf was back on his perch on the overturned control panel trying to see out the partly exposed windshield. "They *said* it would quit. We're getting buried!"

Chase was awake, hovering as near the heater as possible across from Cranston over their two casualties. "We're gonna freeze t' death!" He was trembling from the cold and fear. "That gas'll run out and we'll freeze!"

"No, we won't!" Cranston rebuked him, sharply. "We got shelter and our thermal blankets, so we can hold out. You need t' keep a grip, man!"

"Shit, man! They gotta rescue us!" Those thin sheets of thermal mylar were miraculous, but could only do so much, and two of them were already committed to their two casualties.

"None of us got radios, man. Without 'em, there's no way they can know where we are."

Cranston was surprised when something brushed his pants leg; it was one of the crewmen lying between them, reaching up with a trembling hand. "Radio..." he whispered. "...second...engine..." He was semi-conscious at best, features distorted by pain, his eyes glazed. "...second engine..." His hand slipped from Cranston's leg as he sagged in a dazed stupor.

Cranston and Chase looked at each other in consternation. "The second engine?" Cranston muttered.

"That must be how they heard from these guys before!"

"Ya gotta go call 'em!"

Cranston hesitated. "I can't. These guys need me. You'll have to go."

Chase took the news badly. "I can't...I'm in no shape...I'd get lost out there..." He was likely right: Chase was short and heavyset, and was frequently gigged for his physicals. Odds were he'd have a hard time even climbing out of the overturned locomotive.

After a moment, both of them turned and looked up at Langsdorf...

"Aw, shit, man! Why me?"

"Cause you're fitter than I am, plus you're already half-way there." Chase gestured at the hatch over their heads.

"And because you have your orders," Cranston added.

Langsdorf sighed, and reached up to grab the rim of the open hatch. "And I wanted t' be a hero," he grumbled. "It's my own damned fault!

"Look at it this way: you could be down there in th' delta stacking sandbags in th' freezing rain."

Langsdorf paused and gave Chase a frustrated glare. "Deal!"

§

Milepost 197, Snow Shed 47:

> *"This is National Guard rescue to the UP rescue party on Donner Pass. You guys hear us? Over?"*

Walter stared at the caboose radio like it had turned into a snake. "Jesus!" he muttered as he grabbed the mic. "This is the UP rescue at Shed 47! We hear you! What's your situation?"

> *"We got hit by an avalanche. Our sergeant is missing, and we lost some of our gear, but we found your two missing men. Both are badly hurt, but alive. You got me?"*

Walter was weeping with relief. He glanced at Fred. who was lounging by the stove. "Tell Gus!" Fred jumped up and headed for the dorm car. "We hear you, Guards! How long can you hold out?"

> *"For a little while, maybe. What th' hell's with this weather? It's blowing like a sumbitch down here!"*

"The tail of this storm is a real muther. We got hurricane force winds and sub-zero cold, everything's shut down until it passes. D'you guys have shelter?"

"We found the two locomotives. We're holed up in them with your guys."

Gus came in just then, followed closely by Parker Lee. "They found our people!" Walter told them, then turned back to the radio. "There's no way we can get to you right now. The only thing you can do is hunker down until this storm passes."

"Yeah, copy that. Your guys are in bad shape, but we'll do what we can for 'em. Also our sarge is missing. Can you put the word out for him?"

Walter hesitated for a long moment. Anyone lost out there in these conditions was probably already dead. "Ah, yeah. We'll spread the word." They all knew it was a futile gesture.

"Thanks. I gotta leave this radio and return to the first engine. I'll try to contact you after the storm passes. National Guard, out."

"Ain't that something?" Fred said, fervently. "Maybe there's hope for 'em after all."

"Yeah, hope, maybe," Gus said. "But they're a long way from being rescued, and it's hell out there."

Fred contemplated with storm somberly The bitter sub-zero wind shook the caboose with a steady dull roar. "God...what must it be like for them?"

§

Milepost 197, aboard rotary 207:

"Jesus?" Dan pawed vaguely at his brakeman's arm, trying to rouse him. "Come on, man. Wake up."

"Uh? Wha?" Jesus thrashed around, weak and uncoordinated.

"It's no good, man." It took all Dan had to focus on waking his partner. He wasn't exactly rational by then, but knew instinctively the cold was killing them both. "Got to...get up, man. Gotta go."

§

Most of the work crew were busy digging accumulated snow from around the spreader after another cave-in, and were surprised when a pair of dim headlights came out of the gloom from back east. They watched in amazement as a hi-rail truck clawed its way off the rails onto the ballast, honked at them as it crept past, and vanishing into the storm ahead.

"What th' hey?" Jeff muttered. "Where they going?"

"T' hell, likely." Borden hefted his wire broom and went back to work.

§

"And I thought railroading on this Hill was a damn-fool way t' make a living," the hi-rail driver grumbled as the lights of the spreader faded in the distance. "Can't see a damned thing."

"It just goes to show you learn something new every day," his partner said. "We're doing good, so far."

"So far." The trip up from Truckee went fairly well since the right of way was recently cleared by the spreader, but now they were leaving civilization behind and setting off into the wild. Their plow dug into the snow until the accumulation brought them to a stop. "We won't get nowhere in this," the driver said. "We need t' get back on the rails."

"I was afraid you'd say that." The passenger pulled his coat tight, scrambled out into the storm, and beckoned the driver forward onto the track. Their hi-rail bucked and skidded as it fought its way even with four wheel drive. It took way too much effort, but they managed to get the rail wheels reengaged.

"Let's hope we don't have t' do that again!" the passenger said as the hi-rail dug into the drifted snow and moved on up grade. He was shivering from the cold, which the truck's heater couldn't entirely deal with.

"How far to them two passenger cars?"

"I heard about two miles or so."

The driver sighed. "This'll be a muther-long two miles."

"Imagine what th' guys who laid these tracks must-a felt."

§

Milepost 142, Colfax, California:

"Hey, Murphy? Phone call for ya."

Murphy contemplated his freshly drawn mug of hot coffee with a resigned sigh. "I gotta tell ya, I'm gettin' sick and tired of phone calls." He turned to his assistant, who didn't look happy at interrupting his first break this day. "Roseville, huh?"

"Fraid so."

He stared at the far wall of the near-empty cafeteria, too weary and too fed up to care who wanted to talk to him. The place was all but deserted: anyone not on duty was upstairs in the dorms getting what little sleep they could.

But there was nothing for it. Duty called, hot coffee or no.

§

"I hope you're calling t' tell me the sun's shining where you are," he greeted the Roseville dispatcher.

"Sorry, Murphy. In fact it's worse. The weather people say this storm is being overtaken by the next in line. They say it looks like hell for the next twenty-four hours at least."

"You're no fun at all!"

"Yeah, well, I don't like it either, but them's the breaks. You need t' pass it along to Gus and his crew."

"Any word from Truckee?"

"Yeah, as a matter of fact. I heard from them briefly before the line went dead. They sent a hi-rail with food and medical supplies for the Amtrak, and their snow clearing effort is going along steadily."

"Damn. Ol' Mortensen got his shit t'gether, eh?"

"Looks like. Right now the best bet is for them to reach the Amtrak and pull them out east."

"Yeah, okay. Thanks."

"Good news?" his assistant asked after he hung up.

Murphy pondered this news compared to what he'd seen lately. There were too many things which could go wrong to have much confidence in the near future.

"We'll see."

§

Milepost 197, aboard rotary 207:

Somehow—it was hard to say how since Dan was delirious—he found himself on his feet. Jesus was on all fours, completely out of it, trying vaguely to pull himself up by Dan's arm. All Dan could comprehend was they needed to get out of there. Where 'there' was, or where they could go was beyond him. All that mattered was the killing cold had all but finished them. His hands and face were numb, his breath burned, he was trembling so hard he could hardly move his legs for fear of collapsing.

Instinct was all Dan had left; he was beyond reason. They *must* reach safety—somewhere—before their dwindling strength gave out. He managed to get Jesus on his feet, and they leaned on each other as he tried to figure out what came next. There was a door...

The blast of arctic wind knocked both of them down as the door slammed open. He lay on his back, stunned, then instinct took over once again. He struggled to his knees and crawled toward the open doorway...

The next thing he knew he was laying on his face. There was pain. He pawed at his face but couldn't see or feel his injuries. He struggled to his knees and tried to crawl, but something landed on him, knocking him flat again. It was Jesus, who followed him out the door and took his same tumble to the hard ground below.

It took more effort than tired men should have to make to get untangled and on their feet again. Jesus was mumbling incoherently, his face a bloody mess and one arm dangling. Dan was no better. He couldn't feel the cold or his injuries, was only vaguely aware of where they were, but the one thing he was aware of was they had to find shelter.

"Come on, man," he mumbled. "Gotta move."

His words were lost in the howling wind sweeping through the snow shed, but Jesus followed him instinctively as he started limping in some random direction. He had no idea where he was, lost in the gloom, pushed relentlessly along by the wind down the length of the snow shed toward the far entrance...

§

254

Milepost 198, down slope:

Langsdorf was gone so long that Cranston was starting to worry about him when he appeared in the cab door overhead. He lay on the locomotive's side for some time, fully exposed to the savage wind, before half-climbing-half-tumbling through the doorway. Cranston and Chase had to catch him as he fell.

"Come on, man." Cranston massaged his arms vigorously to get his circulation going again. His issue arctic parka was encrusted with ice and snow, his face was raw, and he trembled uncontrollably. "I thought we'd lost you, man!"

It took Langsdorf a few minutes to recover enough to make sense. "Almost got lost." He paused for a gulp of lukewarm ration coffee before going on. "Can't see a damned thing."

"Did you find the radio?"

It took Langsdorf a minute to reply. "Yeah. I got through. Real bad storm. They're all bunkered up...can't help us...til the storm breaks."

It was clear that was all they could expect from him for now. They shook and brushed off as much of the snow and ice as they could, then wrapped him in one of the mylar thermal blankets and laid him next to the two railroaders.

"God, it must be hell out there," Chase complained.

"Yeah." Cranston was shaken by Langsdorf's state as much as by what he reported. He sat staring at the gas heater, listening to the roar of the storm, and wondered how long their gas supply would hold out.

§

Milepost 201, Horse Shoe Curve:

Like everyone else who made this trek, the hi-rail was blinded by the storm so they came up on the two passenger cars by surprise and barely managed to avoid ramming into them. It was a rough ride getting this far as they fought their way through various drifts and minor cave-ins, so both were a bit punchy by then.

"Damn, we made it," the driver said.

"This far, anyway."

There was a brief, nervous silence as the wind shook their hi-rail. "Now what?"

"I guess we see if Herb can come down t' meet us."

"In this weather? No way! We're in bad enough shape; no chance a snow bike could do it."

As much as they hated the idea, he was right. The storm was going in full fury, shaking their hi-rail like a terrier shaking a rat. They were both bitterly disappointed by what seemed like the failure of their urgent mission. "Well...at least we can scout these two cars," the driver said. "See if they can be shoved clear."

"Yeah." The passenger pulled his coat tighter, grabbed a couple fuzees, and made to climb out of the hi-rail.

"Watch yourself out there!"

§

Milepost 198, Aboard the 'City Of San Francisco':

"How's your labor case doing?" Doctor Cummings asked when he stopped by the compartment once again.

Barbara was so groggy it took her a moment to answer. "She's still on-again-off-again. I don't know what to make of it."

Cummings wasn't thrilled by her bleary-eyed expression. "Maybe her weight is influencing her labor. She may be a slow starter, is all." In fact Olivia Bumarris was asleep at the moment, snoring softly.

"I...hope so."

He noticed the room was littered with empty styrofoam coffee cups. "Have you been getting any sleep?" he demanded.

"I took a nap a little while ago." Truth be told, she couldn't remember when, and wasn't entirely sure she did.

"You're in no shape to be on duty! Call her husband in here to keep an eye on her, and you get as much sleep as you can!"

She started to protest, but his stern look rode her down. She sighed, and nodded. As he turned to leave, she asked, "How's everything up front?"

"Same as always. We're hoping some supplies will come through, but there's no sign of help yet."

§

Milepost 203:

"How you guys doing?" the spreader train's conductor asked. They were gathered in the cab of the first locomotive where at least they could stay warm.

"We're dug out, again," Borden said, sullenly. "I guess we can move."

"Right. We'll head back, then, so th' 209 can take over."

The thought of another endless retrograde move wasting still more precious time was too much to bear right then. Borden turned and gave him an icy glare. "Th' hell we will! This is taking way too long! We can go on ahead, so we need to push on forward."

"But..."

"We got the dancers t' dig us out when needed. We gotta quit dickin' around and get this show on the road!"

It was a risk. The farther they went, the greater the danger of the spreader becoming irretrievably stuck, but Borden was right; this was taking way too long, and those people up on the Hill needed them.

"Well...alright, you say so," the conductor said, reluctantly. "Let's just hope nothing bad happens!"

"Too late," Jeff muttered.

§

Milepost 206, Truckee, California:

Word came down from the hi-rail some time later, and it was not reassuring news:

"You can forget about tipping these two cars off the track. They're wedged up against a rock outcropping; ain't nothing gonna move 'em."

Another wishful hope vanquished. Mortensen didn't even waste the energy cursing his ill-luck, since everything he tried seemed to backfire. He vented a weary sigh, and his head sank in his hands, still clutching the radio mic. This was hopeless.

Nothing he tried worked. This weather was simply too much for feeble men and machines to cope with. He felt sick to his stomach knowing they would probably lose those two critical patients, and the rest of them were in dire straits as well.

Dean came in just then, and noticed Mortensen holding the radio mic. "Any word from the hi-rail?"

That brought Mortensen back to the here-and-now. "They reached the two derailed cars; they say we can't tip 'em off the right of way."

Dean took the news quietly. "What about those supplies?"

That shook Mortensen to action. "Ah...Truckee to hi-rail, what about linking up with Herb?"

"No way in hell! We're hard-put as it is. No way a snow bike can make it in this mess!"

Mortensen sighed. "Copy that." He dropped the mic, and his head sank in his hands again.

"What now?" Dean asked, softly.

"God...I don't know." Mortensen sobbed in bitter frustration. "If you've got any bright ideas, I'm fresh out."

§

Milepost 203:

"Alright everyone, let's move out!"

There was a garbled chorus of affirmatives over the radio, all but drowned out by the roar of the storm. A moment later the spreader shuddered as the diesels pushed it forward once more.

"How long will it take to reach those two cars?" Kareem asked.

Borden glanced at the speedometer, which was barely registering. "Well, *assuming* we don't have any more delays, I'd say another three or four hours."

"Yeah, assuming." The wind was bodily shaking their heavy flanger, visibility was maybe fifty yards, and the snow was even building up on their rotating clearview screens, it was so thick and heavy. "If this storm doesn't make an *'ass'* out of *'you'* and *'me'*."

§

"Shit, I should know better than t' expect any help from *them*," the driver groaned. He dropped the radio mic in disgust with a vivid curse for the rear-echelon fuckups in Truckee.

"Now what?" his number two asked at last.

The driver pondered the blowing snow for the longest time. "If Fred can't come down, we have t' go up to them," he said, evenly.

"Can't we go back?"

"We...don't have a choice. We're all they have left." There was a painful silence, both men cowed by the fury of the storm. "They need this stuff." That was the crux of the matter. Despite all common sense—despite their urge to cut and run before they wound up in a mangled heap at the bottom of the canyon—they needed to get those supplies through to the wreck site. It was all down on their shoulders. Lives depended on them.

"I...dunno. What about that rock outcropping?"

"We might be able t' dig our way past with the blade." The passenger gestured at the dozer blade projecting out in front of them. "I'm sure th' service road runs around this."

That was a risk. The service road—a mere gravel path—ran right next to the tracks, but they could hardly see the right of way in the dim light, and what they could see wasn't comforting. The snow along the track was at least a couple feet deep, and it was impossible to tell where the right of way ended and the steep drop off into Cold Stream Canyon began. If they strayed too far, they'd wind up in a pile in the woods down slope.

"Yeah, but do you want t' take the risk trying t' find it in this? One wrong move and we'll be down in the valley. They likely won't find us til next summer."

"Yeah, there is that. So what do we do?"

"We'll have to climb over it."

The rock outcropping wasn't very high, and from what they could see of it, which wasn't much, it looked fairly shallow. Still the idea was appalling in this weather.

"This is suicide, you know? We're gonna get stuck, or blown off the right of way t' hell and gone."

That seemed likely, as much as they might wish otherwise. The storm was shaking their hi-rail, threatening to shove them off the rails. Both men were terrified by the power they faced.

"Maybe," number two said, reluctantly. "You wanna try?"

"No. But the only alternative is t' go back."

Neither of them said anything for the next few minutes, but it was a given that those supplies go up the Hill. "Damn," the driver muttered at last, and grabbed the radio mic. "This is the hi-rail to Truckee; we're gonna go on ahead and try t' reach the Amtrak." There was nothing more to say.

"Good luck, guys."

"Damn-fool way t' make a living," number two grumbled.

"Yeah."

Neither of them were happy with the prospect, but there was no alternative other than to turn back. They couldn't do that in good conscience. The brakeman climbed out, raised the small rail wheels, thus freeing the hi-rail, and climbed hurriedly back in. "Muther *cold* out there!"

"So I heard." The driver turned the wheel hard right and gunned the engine. The hi-rail staggered over the rails and down onto the access road, its plow digging in and shoving a mass of snow ahead of them. "Shit," the driver griped. "T' think I volunteered for this." Since there really was no choice, he screwed up his courage and gunned the engine. The hi-rail crawled ahead, piling snow up in front of them as they went until the load got to be too great and they were forced to a halt.

"Swing right. You got room."

"You hope."

The driver backed up a bit, steered hard right, and they plowed into the snow again, passing their earlier pile and advancing another fifty feet or so before they were stopped again, their wheels spinning futilely. A shift to the left brought them to the edge of the rock outcropping.

"Great. Now what?"

§

Milepost 197, Snow Shed 47:

"What th' hell?" One of the gandy dancers was looking out a dorm car window at the hurricane-force hell in the snow shed. "There's some damn fool out there!"

That brought on a rush of curious onlookers to the windows. "Sucker's gonna freeze," someone else said.

"Hell, there's two of 'em!"

Walter Karns happened along just then. "What's going on?" he demanded.

"There's two guys out there!"

Walter peered through the window and uttered a livid curse. "They're in trouble! Come on!"

§

Milepost 198, Aboard the 'City Of San Francisco':

"His vital signs are weak, but steady." Doctor Cummings was filling George Reinsbach in on the state of their critical passengers. "It won't take much to push him into a downward spiral. I'm surprised he lasted this long." He gave Reinsbach a somber, worried look. "Still no word on any medical supplies?"

"No, nothing. Our communications are awful spotty; the storm must be affecting the relay towers."

"I had no *idea* it was so bad up here." The dining car shook from a gust of wind, causing him to blanch. "How do you guys..." He was interrupted when the lights flickered and faded again, evoking an undercurrent of panic among the patients. After a moment, the lights came back up, flickered, faded again, then came back. They stood frozen for an endless time waiting to see what would happen next.

"What's causing that?" Cummings asked at last.

"Water in the fuel, probably." Reinsbach didn't want to think of what other possibilities there could be.

The doctor pondered him somberly, his misgivings plain, then turned back to his two critical patients. "I hope somebody does something soon. Otherwise we may lose both these people."

§

261

"I don't like the look of that rock," the driver said as they pondered the rock outcropping dimly lit by their high beams. "Can we get over it?" From what little they could see, the rock outcropping had a fairly gentle slope; enough so a four-wheel drive could climb it anyway, under normal circumstances. But these were not normal circumstances.

"It's the only way."

They sat in the hi-rail for the longest time, frankly terrified by the raging storm and the risk they were about to take. The tension finally reached a breaking point. "Alright, we either go back t' Truckee or we go over that damned rock," the brakeman said. "Whatever we do, we gotta do something before we get snowed in."

The driver was not thrilled. "Okay, but I'll need you to scout ahead for me."

"Yeah." The brakeman grumbled a curse, climbed out, lit a fuzee, and struggled ahead up the slope. Soon he was invisible in the driving snow except for the red glow of the fuzee he carried. The faint red glow faded and climbed into the distance, then finally stopped and motioned a 'come ahead' signal.

"Here goes nothing," the driver said. He shifted down into first gear, hit the four wheel drive, and the hi-rail crawled up onto the outcrop, bucking and skidding on the rough, icy rock. It seemed to take forever, but they managed to reach the crest, roughly level with the coach windows barely visible to the left. As soon as he came to a stop, the brakeman dropped his fuzee and scrambled back into the relative sanctuary of the heated cab.

"Jeez, it's muther-cold out there!" he griped as he huddled near the heater vent. "That wind's a sumbitch, too!"

The driver anxiously searched the darkness ahead while his partner recovered from the chill. "I can't see anything," he said after searching the gloom. "Do we chance it?"

The brakeman gave him a harassed look. "Better not. We don't know what the ground ahead is like, and we don't dare risk getting wrecked in *this* hell!"

That was the understatement of the year since their present perch made movement in any direction a calculated risk. "Fine time t' learn these things! It's as dangerous to try backing down off this rock as going forward."

The brakeman greeted that with a weary curse at his own stupidity which put him here. "Yeah. In for a penny, etc. Guess I better scout some more," he said at last. "My penance for my sins."

He grabbed another fuzee, braced himself for the bitter cold, managed to force the door open against the wind, and slid out onto the rock. In moments he vanished into the wind-whipped darkness save for the faint red glow of his fuzee. Even that vanished after a few seconds.

It seemed like forever—the driver was starting to worry about his partner's safety—before the faint red glow reappeared, the brakeman clawing his way along the side of the derailed buffet car. His fuzee burned out as he reached the truck, and he not so much climbed in as crawled into the cab again.

"You okay, man?" The driver noted a streak of blood on his partner's forehead with genuine misgivings.

"*Hell no!* I refuse t' be okay until we're down off this *freakin'* mountain!" He hovered in front of the heater, rubbing his hands vigorously amid a steady stream of subdued grumbling, before he poked at his injury, then glanced at the driver. "Took a tumble. I'll be alright."

"Yeah, well, be careful, man. We can't afford t' get hurt out here."

§

Milepost 197, Snow Shed 47:

It took a major effort to rescue the two lost men, but most of the gandy dancers in the dorm car pitched in to retrieve them. By time they were safely on board and tucked into berths, Gus and the rest of the leadership were on the scene.

"How they doing?" Gus asked.

"They're both half-froze," Walter told him. "They're out of it, but my guess is they'll be alright once they warm up."

Dan and Jesus were laid in lower berth cots wrapped in extra blankets, semi-conscious and delirious from exposure. One of the section hands was using a warm washcloth to clear away the blood on Dan's forehead. "Jesus has a broken arm, and they both got bad cuts," Walter added. "I'd say they fell trying t' get out of th' rotary. I can't say if they got frostbite or not."

"Gawd, it must be hell in that rotary!" Fred muttered.

"Yeah," Gus said. He was appalled that his two best operators were out of commission. "We need t' call over t' ask the docs about these two. And wake Margret and Willy up."

"You're not gonna send 'em over there!?"

Gus wasn't happy about it either. "We gotta have those units manned in case they have an engine shut-down or something." If one of the aged diesels in the rotary consist quit and froze up, their only snow fighting gear would be out of commission.

Walter didn't like it, but there was no real choice.

§

Milepost 202:

They made it nearly half a mile before the spreader was rocked to one side by another avalanche and ground to an abrupt halt. Borden was on the radio almost instantly. "We're stuck again. Get those gandy dancers up here!"

"Did you ever stop to consider the one constant thing in all these avalanches is you guys?"

"Oh, sure, blame us for all the world's woes!"

"At least we're making progress," Kareem said as he studied their GPS unit. "I make us at Milepost 202. There's only one more mile to go."

"Yeah, you make better time when ya keep goin' in the same direction!" They were making good time, in fact. Borden glanced at his watch and was surprised by how the time was going by. At this pace, they'd reach their destination after only about fifteen hours on duty.

§

264

Milepost 201, Horse Shoe Curve:

After a few more minutes nursing his nicked forehead, the brakeman got back to business. "The far slope looked a bit steeper, what I could see of it. It's do-able, but it'll be no picnic getting down."

"This is the *last* time I volunteer for *anything*," the driver muttered as he put the truck in gear.

"You and me both."

The driver pressed gently on the throttle, trying to ease the hi-rail forward without gaining much speed. The vehicle hesitated, spun its wheels, then dug in and inched ahead into the storm. They were in trouble almost at once as the hi-rail skidded and fish-tailed over the ice-coated rock.

"You call *this* do-able?" The driver fought the wheel with a livid curse as they bounced over some unseen obstacle, rolling faster as they slid on the packed snow.

"You want flat, transfer t' Kansas!"

A gust of wind caught them just as they bounced over an outcropping, sending the truck into a wild skid.

"I'm losing it!" The driver steered wildly as the hi-rail slid sickeningly to the left, bounced off the side of the buffet car, spun away from the track toward the edge of the canyon, and finally skidded to a halt when one wheel dropped off the right of way.

*****

Sunset:

Milepost 199, Tunnel 13:

The two volunteers in the hi-rail were punchy with fatigue and cold and fighting the relentless wind when two red lights materialized out of the nothingness ahead of them. It took the driver a moment to realize what those lights were, and he slammed on his brakes just in time to avoid rear-ending the 'City' train. They sat for a time staring at the blank steel end of the last car towering over them before the brakeman muttered, "We made it."

That shook them both out of their torpor. "Damn, we did it, didn't we?" the driver said. "Come on, we gotta get this stuff delivered."

Even here, in the lea of Schallenberger Ridge, right up where the track dove into Tunnel 13, the storm all but knocked them flat so they were forced to stagger blindly along the track, holding each other up. Even when they reached the partial shelter of the last car, the wind still pummeled them, cutting them like knives. They were both in agony by time they reached the door to the last car.

The car's entrance area was jammed with a half-dozen people sitting or laying along the walls. They looked haggard and cold, some of them huddled together to share a blanket and body warmth. The air in the room was clammy and thick with the odor of unwashed bodies. The new arrivals and the passengers stared at each other in confusion for a moment, then the reaction set in as the icy wind from the open door hit them, evoking a chorus of complaints. The brakeman hastily pulled the door shut, and only then did the passengers realize help was at hand, setting off a minor storm of hysterical relief.

"We're just bringing up some food and medical supplies," the brakeman told them as the driver used the intercom to reach someone in charge.

The first to arrive was conductor Greenbaum, followed closely by Parkhurst and Jack Whitacre. "Thank God you made it!" Greenbaum greeted them. "We didn't think anyone could reach us until this storm quit."

"Yeah, well, it was no joy, I can tell you," the driver said. "We got the medical supplies you ordered, plus we brought as much food as we could pack in our truck."

"Great! I hope you brought plenty of coffee." He didn't wait for an answer, but hit his portable radio. "George? Jeff? We got a truck here loaded with food and medical supplies. Shake the kitchen staff out and let's get this stuff in."

"Copy that!"

"God, I was never so happy to see you Maintenance of Way guys before!" Greenbaum said, fervently.

"We're road crew, actually," the driver said. "We volunteered for this, if you can believe it."

"What's the story about your engine crew?" the brakeman asked.

Greenbaum turned somber at the mention of their missing men. "There's no word. Some National Guards showed up and tried to reach them, but they're missing now, too."

"Not good, huh?"

"No. It doesn't look good at all." None of them held out much hope for the missing men after all this time in this weather.

Reinsbach turned up just then along with Otis and several of the stewards, with O'Brian not far behind. "Alright!" the driver said. "We got a hi-rail parked right behind this car with a cooler full of medical supplies and whatever food they were able to scrounge there in Truckee. I gotta tell you, it's muther-nasty out there, so be careful."

It was muther-nasty, indeed. The crewmen cringed under the raw cold, and fought their way blindly through the wind, drawn by the headlights of the hi-rail shining faintly in the distance. The rear seat of the hi-rail yielded a large plastic cooler full of medical gear and a tank of oxygen on the rear floor. They grabbed these and beat a hasty retreat.

The lamentable Harkness was waiting when they returned laden with their priceless medical loot. "I hear you arrived in a truck." That was not a question.

The brakeman sized him up suspiciously. "Yeah. We brought some medical supplies up from Truckee."

"This railroad can't do anything right, but at least *some* of you are on the ball!" Harkness grabbed the brakeman's arm. "I want you to take me down to San Francisco, right now."

The brakeman threw his arm off. "Not a chance! We were lucky we made it this far. Plus we're not here to provide *you* with private taxi service."

"I insist!" Harkness was getting heated. "I've been stuck in this Godforsaken hell for *days* now! I have a major business deal in Tokyo, and I won't wait any longer for you people to get it together!"

"Enough, Harkness!" Greenbaum snarled. "We got more important things t' do than put up with your shit! You'll reach San Francisco when this train gets there, *not* before!"

"You owe me!" Harkness ignored Greenbaum and turned on the two newcomers. "I paid good money to ride this botched abortion, and by God I'll collect! Since you two are the only ones who seem to have your act together, I *expect* you to deliver what this fucked-up railroad can't!"

The driver was too tired and too wired to endure this jackass with good grace. "No one gives a damn *what* you want, mister! We're not going anywhere, and neither are you in this weather!"

Harkness retreated under his tirade, which just made him angrier. "You don't realize how important I am!" he yelled. "I can get all of you fired, which is *exactly* what I will do unless you get your act together! *We are going to San Francisco!*"

"Like hell!"

"The only place you're *going* is back to your seat!" Greenbaum grabbed the cooler of medical supplies and shoved it at him. "And you can do something useful for once by taking this to the diner."

Harkness stared at him in incoherent rage for several seconds before recovering his wits. "You'll never hear the end of this!" he snarled, then turned and stomped off, leaving Greenbaum holding the cooler.

"Who is that sumbitch?" the brakeman asked after a moment.

"He's the punishment for our sins," Greenbaum muttered.

"Real sweetheart," the driver grumbled. "What's his problem, anyway?"

"He's discovering the world doesn't revolve around him, and he's not taking it well."

"He's likely t' give arrogant SOBs a bad name," the brakeman added in disgust.

"Yeah, he's good at that." Parkhurst scowled in the direction of the retreating Harkness. "He's a genuine 'New York' asshole, as opposed to your garden variety asshole."

"Enough gossip." Greenbaum shoved the cooler at Parkhurst. "Get this stuff to the diner. The rest of you get your coats and let's get that food in here," he said to the others.

It took a few minutes for the diner staff to collect their coats, and make ready to venture out into the storm once again.

"Everyone stay together!" the driver told the reinforcements. "It's hell out there. If you get separated, you'll be a goner. The truck is parked right behind this last car, so follow the headlights and you'll be alright."

It wasn't anywhere near as simple as described; the dozen volunteers were only able to stick together by holding onto each other's arms, fighting their way blindly over the slippery, uneven ground against the roaring storm. They made it to the hi-rail by sheer endurance, and each grabbed as many of the cardboard cases stacked in back as they could carry. If anything, the trip back was worse, and the two volunteers had to work up and down the group to keep them moving and prevent them from wandering off.

Mercifully they all made it, although all of them were shaken by the experience. "God, that was awful!" Greenbaum sighed.

"Yeah, and we'll need t' make at least two more trips t' get the rest of it, too."

"That can wait a few minutes," the driver said. "Th' stuff lasted this long, it'll keep a bit longer til we can warm up."

"You got that right! So what's for dinner?" O'Brian began checking the labels on the cartons stacked by the door. They all read the same. "Canned beef stew over rice," he said, disgustedly. "I should know better."

§

Milepost 198, down slope:

"I don't mind telling you I'm getting sick and tired of MREs." Chase was poking at a field ration with little enthusiasm.

"A *heated,* winter MRE," Langsdorf admonished him. "We need every heat source we can get, so eat up before it turns cold."

"The Swedish Chef." Chase wasn't thrilled by MREs. "Truly we are blessed."

"Ja-sure, youbetja!"

"Alright you guys, we only got a few of those things left, so make the most of 'em."

The others quit their grumbling and went back to eating. After a bit Langsdorf asked, "How long d'you think before this storm will quit?"

"What makes you think it'll *ever* quit?" Chase grumbled.

They finished the last of their MREs and sat staring at each other, listening to the roar of the storm. "D'you think they'll ever find us?" Chase asked, plaintively.

"We're not dead yet!" Cranston scolded him. "We're safe enough in here for the time being, and they know where we are. If nothing else, they can bring up another rescue team t' come for us."

"What good would they do in this weather?" Langsdorf was still agonizing over their predicament, to Cranston's annoyance.

Their argument was interrupted when one of the casualties laying between them moaned and stirred. It was the one with the broken arm.

"Hey, you awake, man?" Cranston shook his good arm. "Come on, dude!"

The casualty blinked aimlessly, then focussed in on the anxious faces around him. "Thought...you were a dream," he whispered.

"It's no dream, we're real enough."

"It's a nightmare," Chase muttered.

Cranston gave him a sharp look, then went back to their semi-conscious patient. "How do you feel?"

"...Shit, man. Hurts."

Cranston glanced at his watch. "I'll give you a shot in a little while." They only had two morphine tabs left.

270

"...Radio? You get through?"

"Yeah, man, we got in contact. They know you're alive." The roar of the storm made it hard to hear each other. "There's a big storm going, we're trapped right now. Soon as it breaks, we'll get you out of here."

He was silent for a bit, then, "Karl? He's trapped. Is he...?"

"We got him loose. He's alive."

The casualty nodded faintly, then closed his eyes, seeming to sink into himself with his pain.

"Well that's *some* good anyway," Langsdorf grumbled. "Although he'd be better off if he didn't regain consciousness."

"What good's it gonna do him?" Chase whined. "We're all gonna freeze in here!"

Cranston could see their morale was starting to crumble under the relentless onslaught of ill-fortune. "You two need t' buck up! All this pissing and moaning won't do any good, so put a sock in it! We'll make it; you just gotta hang in there."

"Just hope we don't run out of gas," Langsdorf said.

That put an end to the complaints for the moment. They settled in to wait out the storm, which continued to rage outside. The faint hiss of the space heater was lost in the wind roar.

§

Milepost 197, Snow Shed 47:

"Dammit!" Gus muttered. "I wish this...*freakin'* weather would quit!" He was staring out one of the end windows of the caboose trying to tell whether they could go out there again.

"It must be down t' zero out there!" Earl said.

"Th' glass says ten below." Fred gestured at a thermometer bolted to the side of the car just outside the bay window. "But that don't take into account for th' wind chill."

"It's cold enough for me, thanks!"

"We could call Colfax t' see if the weather guys can tell us," Gus said. "I want t' get back out there as soon as we can."

"We got a chart here." Fred dug through the track diagram package he always carried, and came up with a multi-colored card. "What d'you think the wind speed is?"

"Last we heard from Colfax it was a hunnerd-mile-an-hour."

"Damn, this chart only goes up t' 60...and at that rate it says minus forty-eight!"

Gus shuddered. "Damn! That must make it sixty, seventy below. Ain't no one can survive out there for long."

"No wonder Dan and Jesus got froze! We just aren't equipped for this." The brooding silence returned, except for the steady roar of the storm.

§

Milepost 201, Horseshoe Curve:

At long last the first of the two derailed passenger cars appeared out of the snowy gloom. "Damn, we did it," Kareem said as Borden brought the spreader to a halt some fifty feet short of their long-sought goal.

"And we're still alive," Jeff added. "We must lead charmed lives, or something."

"It ain't over yet," Borden snapped, then picked up the radio mic. "This is the spreader to rotary 17223. We've gone as far as we can go. It's up t' you guys now."

"Copy that, Bill."

"Spreader to diesels, pull us back."

"Well do. Good work, guys."

There was a lurch, and they began crawling backward as Borden and Jeff quickly retracted the spreader blades. Soon they passed rotary 17223 which was pushing doggedly forward against a solid wall of snow which towered over them.

"What now?" Kareem asked. "We need servicing and repairs."

Borden pondered that for a long moment. It took some effort to pull his thoughts together, he was so weary. "We go back t' Truckee. Let someone else worry about repairs. We're on the law as soon as we get back."

§

Milepost 142, Colfax, California:

"I don't care *what* it takes, you've got to get the 211 back in service!" It took Murphy no small effort and more than a bit of luck to connect with the Roseville Shops, what with how communications throughout the region were crumbling under the weight of the endless storms. Having finally made a connection didn't improve his overworked temper. "We've got nothing for snow removal up here! Unless you get that rotary back on line, there's no way we can even rescue our own people up at Norden and at Summit. If anything happens to th' 207, they're screwed!"

"Look, I know its bad, but you'll just have to manage. We're working as fast as we can." The Roseville Shop super was another sorely tried soul, and Murphy wasn't the only one riding his back. *"We're bogged down ourselves, and we have dozens of locomotives to turn around..."*

"*FUCK* YOUR DAMNED LOCOMOTIVES! The only thing that matters is SNOW GEAR! We *need* that rotary!"

"What about the spreader we sent you?"

"It got wrecked! It's on its side up at Emigrant Gap. and your wrecking train is stranded at Shed 47."

"Dammit! You guys are breaking equipment faster than we can fix it!"

"Yeah? Well you shop pukes need t' allow for wear and tear! It's hell up there on th' Hill. We've had four feet of snow here in Colfax, this storm, and its *still* coming down. Stuff's gonna get damaged!"

"You think I don't know it? Look, we're doing the best we can. You'll just have..."

It took Murphy a moment to realize he'd been cut off. "Hello? Hello? You there?" Nothing but a faint crackling noise. Not even a dial tone. "Dammit!" He slammed the phone down in an agony of frustration.

"Not good, huh, Murph?"

He gave his assistant such an evil glare that the man took a step back. "This railroad's going t' hell!"

§

Milepost 201, Horseshoe Curve:

Bill Borden and his two were so groggy with fatigue and cold that the arrival of three strangers caught them by surprise. "Bill?" their leader asked. "Nate Cochraine. We're here to relieve you."

Borden stared at the three for a long moment while he collected his wits. "*Now* you show up?"

"Sorry about the delay. Things are hectic down in Truckee."

"You got no clue," Jeff muttered. "They got it easy down there."

Cochraine eyed the boarded-up window and the left side blade, which was clearly bent. "Yeah. You guys took a pounding, huh?"

"You can bet on it."

"Well your troubles are over!" Cochraine's number two said. "You guys can go on the law now. We'll take care of things from here on."

"Perfect timing! We got the job done, and you show up just in time to take 'er down the Hill and collect all the glory!"

"Hey!" Cochraine protested. "We sat on our asses *forever* waiting for you t' come down th' *freakin'* Hill, except you didn't show! We had t' hitch a ride on the Truckee switcher!"

That quashed any further complaining since Borden realized his decision to push ahead was what kept them from a timely rendezvous with their relievers. He was dismayed not only by how his diligence backfired on them, but by how these poor schmucks had to do hours of dead time as well. "Uh...yeah. Sorry," he mumbled. "We just got done and are waiting t' head down the Hill."

His reliever greeted that with a derisive snort. "Ain't that the sad and sorry way of it?"

"Come on, Bill. Let's get over to the dorm car," Jeff grumbled. "We're due a hot meal and some sack time."

"Yeah, you got that right." Borden pulled his gloves on and tightened up his coat zipper. "She's all yours," he said to his reliever. "What's left of her, anyway."

"Pleasant dreams."

§

274

The arrival of the medical supplies felt like Christmas for the weary medical team, and unpacking the cooler gave them all hope for their critically ill patients.

"It looks like we got everything we need," Jamie said as they sorted out the loot. "Instruments, plasma, antibiotics..."

"And insulin!" Barbara grabbed several small white boxes taped together, plus a box of syringes. "We need to get these to our diabetic cases right away." Two of those diabetic cases were running low, one was nursing her supply, and one was out. "I'm headed back to take care of my childbirth case, so I'll distribute these along the way."

"How's she doing? Doctor Menendez asked.

Barbara brushed back a loose lock of hair with a weary, frustrated expression. "I'm not sure what's going on with her. She still starts having contractions, and then they stop. I can't make rhyme or reason of it."

"False labor, you think?"

"Maybe. But her water broke, so she should be active."

Doctor Menendez pondered the case glumly. "As large as she is, she might be in complications. I hope we don't have to do a caesarian."

Barbara shuddered. "Lord, no! We don't have any whole blood."

"All we can do is hope for the best. Keep monitoring her, and let me know if she's in difficulty."

"Right." Barbara collected the priceless insulin and headed back to the rear of the train.

"In the mean time, we better get to work on these two," Doctor Cummings said. "They can't hold out much longer."

"Let's just hope this stuff got here in time," Jamie added.

"Yeah, that's the question. Both of them are critical. Can we risk battlefield surgery in their condition?"

That was the question indeed, since their head trauma case was slipping in and out of cardiac seizures and the old woman's infected hip would normally rate a stay in Intensive Care.

"We don't have a choice," Doctor Menendez said. "It's now or never for both of them, regardless of conditions."

"I'm afraid so." Doctor Cummings studied their two critical cases. "So which do we tackle first?"

Menendez pondered both their patients with no joy. They were both critical, both on the clock, and time was running out. "Jamie and I will set the drain in the old woman," he said at last. "In the mean time, you prep the head trauma. As soon as I'm through with her, we'll go in on him."

"Right."

One thing they agreed on quickly was they couldn't operate in the general dining room where everyone could watch. After some debate in which they ruled out moving the patients down stairs to the kitchen or into the next car to take over a compartment, Jack Whitacre scrounged up a roll of duct tape, a hammer and some nails, and tacked some of their priceless bed sheets up across the dining section, driving nails into the car walls with abandon. By time he sectioned off the tables where the patients lay, the two doctors had scrubbed up as best they could, and Jamie sorted through their gear to collect what would be needed.

They hesitated before starting on the old woman. "I hate to do this," Menendez said. "This is damned chancy."

Cummings paused to consider. "We don't have a choice." She was fitted with an IV drip of glucose and an antibiotic cocktail, but it wouldn't be enough unless they drained her abscess.

Menendez took a deep breath and gave Jamie a searching look. "Alright, let's do it."

§

Milepost 197, Snow Shed 47:

"How do these two guys look?" Gus asked when Fred came back to the caboose.

"They're better. They're both awake and soaking their fingers and toes like the doc said." Fred wasn't happy with Dan and Jesus' condition. "Only time will tell if they got any frostbite."

"God, I hope they're alright!" Those who work the snow trains were painfully aware of the risk of frostbite on the Hill.

276

"What about Margret and Willy?"

Gus came to a decision he'd been debating for some time. "Get all the train crews together and work out a rotation. I want the rotary manned at all times, but just four hours a shift. I don't want t' lose any more good people!" Unlike the diesels, the rotary's old steam boilers weren't adequate for these conditions. The extra shifts would play hell with the train crews' rest, but railroaders were used to it.

§

Milepost 198, Aboard the 'City Of San Francisco':

"How does she look?" Doctor Cummings asked. His tone was hushed even though neither of their patients could hear them.

Jamie ran her blood pressure again while Doctor Menendez studied the vile off-white goo dripping from the drain tube. There were traces of blood, and more infectious mass than he was happy about. "I wish we could do a white cell count on her," he said. "But this can't but help her situation."

"Her BP is rising slightly," Jamie reported. "One-oh-five over fifty-six. It's up five points since the drain went in." That was still seriously low.

"It's all we can do," Menendez said. He turned to the next table and Doctor Cummings' patient, stripping off the disposable surgical gloves as he examined their next job. "You ready?"

"Yes." While Menendez worked on the old woman, Cummings had shaved the back of the head trauma's scalp and scrubbed it liberally with bright orange disinfectant. With the hair gone, they could see the depression where a part of the skull was driven inward.

"He's lucky to be alive with that injury."

"Let's hope we don't make it worse."

Jamie poured alcohol over Menendez' hands, helped him put on a new set of disposable gloves, then poured alcohol over them in turn. It wasn't proper sanitary procedure, but it was all they could do.

"Alright, let's begin. I'll be the primary, you my backup. Jamie monitors the patient's vitals, and Jack holds the light."

"Agreed," Doctor Cummings said.   "The instruments are ready."

"Ready here," Jamie added.   She took a seat next to the table with her blood pressure cuff, being careful to stay out of Menendez's way, while Jack took station opposite her with an emergency flood light borrowed from the train crew.

"Alright..." Menendez paused to consider Jack closely. "Are you going to be okay?"   As their only non-professional, he was worried about Jack's reaction to what he was about to see.

"I'll be fine, doc."

"Very well, let us begin. Antiseptic wipe."

"Antiseptic wipe."   Doctor Cummings handed him a hemostat with a gauze pad soaked in orange disinfectant, which he used to scrub the wound area.

"Scalpel."

"Scalpel..."

§

Milepost 201, Horseshoe Curve:

"Gawd, I'm glad that's over!" Jeff grumbled as the relieved spreader crew enjoyed their first hot meal in nearly a day. "I don't envy the Maintenance of Way types, especially at their pay scale."

"Yeah, hopefully we'll be back to life as usual," Kareem said, wistfully.

"Don't count your chickens," Borden told him. "Keep in mind what passes for 'usual' around here!"

That was not a happy thought to ponder. "Yeah, well, they're gonna have t' do something about these winters. We can't keep going like this."

Borden looked askance at Kareem.   "That's the railroad's problem. Right now our priority is some sack time."

"You got that right! That and hot grub!"

The kitchen car for this work train was another retired caboose fitted up with a makeshift galley. It wasn't as elaborate as the one enjoyed by Gus and his crew on the other side of the mountain, but at least it provided them hot servings of pork and beans and plenty of coffee.

"I sure could do with a steak, though," Jeff said, wistfully. "Smothered in onions, with a huge baked potato with butter just oooozing down..."

"I love it when you talk dirty!"

The bunk car was crowded with track laborers waiting for the next call, but they were able to find three bunks—all uppers—which weren't marked by someone's bed rolls. They climbed up and were asleep in minutes.

§

Milepost 198, Aboard the 'City Of San Francisco':

"Hemostat."

Menendez held his hand out without taking his eyes off the surgical incision while Doctor Cummings fished another clamp out of the sterile bath and handed it to him. Menendez used it to clip a fold of the patient's scalp back, exposing the fracture. There was surprisingly little blood.

"Disinfectant."

Cummings handed him another hemostat with a cotton ball soaked in alcohol clamped in it, which he used to gently scrub the wound area.

"More light."

Jack held the flood light closer illuminating the wound which Menendez examined carefully.

"It looks like the fracture was pressed in, then slid under the rest of the skull, which is why it didn't rebound."

"We need something to pry the two apart. Will a scalpel do?"

"I don't think so. This will require something more substantial."

Cummings was anguished by the setback. "We don't have anything!"

"I might be able to find something. Hang on." Jack set the light down, disappeared down the narrow stairway to the kitchen level, and reappeared a few minutes later. "Here." He displayed a small screwdriver. "Will this do?"

Menendez pondered it for a moment. "It'll do. Scrub it, thoroughly."

Jamie took the screwdriver and attacked it in the instrument tray, scouring it with a steel wool pad also borrowed from the kitchen. When she was finished, Menendez dipped it in the orange disinfectant, then turned to Jamie. "Monitor his BP continuously."

"Right."

Once they were ready, Menendez carefully worked the tip of the screwdriver between the skull and the displaced fracture, then pried it around. The fracture shifted slightly and popped back in place. The patient convulsed, and they spent the next few minutes anxiously watching to see if there was any further reaction.

"Damn," Menendez muttered at last as he stepped back and pulled the gloves off. "I don't want to go through *that* again!"

"You and me both!" Cummings said, fervently.

Menendez took a deep breath and tried to steady his trembling hands, then turned to Jamie. "Go ahead and close."

§

Milepost 206, Truckee, California:

"Hey, man, wake up." Someone was shaking Bret Johansen's arm, rousting him out of an uncomfortable sleep. "Word just came down from Horseshoe Curve: they got the track cleared."

That brought him fully awake. He stared at the caboose wall for a bit, then rolled over on his back with a groan and the protests of muscles forced to sleep on hard caboose bunk pads. He stared up at the laborer who rousted him, not recognizing him as one of his people. "What time is it?"

"About four-thirty, boss. The snow trains are coming down, and should be here in another hour or so."

"Right. Is everyone ready to go?"

"The caller here is shaking them out from a local motel. They should be ready about time the line is clear."

He struggled to sit up and stretched to get the kinks out of his back. "What's the weather like?"

"Ain't nothing *to* like about it! It's still snowing, but the wind is dying down a bit."

Johansen clambered to his feet and peered out the nearest window. The Truckee rail yard was buried under a blanket of new snow at least four feet deep. The only signs of civilization were the recently plowed main line and a few lights in the Maintenance of Way office nearby. The rest of Truckee was hidden by the steadily blowing snow.

"Shit! That sure is a mess, ain't it?"

"If it ain't it'll do 'til the mess gets here."

Johansen retreated to the oil burning stove and rubbed his hands in the welcome heat. "Do me a favor? Go over and bite Mortensen's leg and have him chase up a 'dozer to dig us out."

"You got it, boss."

The man headed out, allowing a brief blast of icy wind in through the open door. Johansen pulled his coat tighter, then looked around to see what was left of the food he brought with them from Sparks. He settled on a can of beef stew, which he set on the stove to heat, and dug a stale roll out of its plastic bag. He was out of coffee.

§

Milepost 198, Aboard the 'City Of San Francisco':

Reggie Greenbaum found Jamie and Jack Whitacre on duty in their 'critical ward' when he came by on one of his routine patrols. "How you doing?" he asked.

She greeted him with a vacant stare and a deep sigh. "I'm managing. Any word on our rescue?"

"Nothing firm lately, but last I heard they were making progress east of here." He paused to take in the oppressive silence of the diner-cum-hospital ward. They were down to a half dozen cases still under their care; the rest of the diner was largely unused since they'd run out of food again. "How's our critical cases?"

"Our hip fracture is stable. We've got a drain in her, and the swelling seems to be going down. I just wish we had more antibiotics, and we could use more sedatives, too." She pondered the old woman for a moment, then turned her attention to their head trauma case. "He's still unconscious, but his vital signs are improving slowly. Unless he develops an infection or has a stroke, he should recover." She turned to confront him. "Still, all these people need to be hospitalized as soon as possible."

Reggie nodded, ruefully. "I know. We're doing everything we can. You'll just have to be patient and hope for the best."

"That's all we can do now, hope."

She seemed to be on her last legs, her usual fiery personality faded. Reggie didn't know how long she'd been on duty, but he couldn't recall when he hadn't seen her here in the diner. "You need to get some sleep."

That reignited a spark of her spirit. "We *all* need some sleep!" She sagged again, then said, "One of the docs will be by soon. I'll turn in then."

"It goes with the territory," Jack said. "Same as us railroaders."

Reggie was in no better shape than either of them; all of them driven to superhuman effort by their professionalism. "Yeah, it sure does," he sighed.

Jamie stared at him without speaking for a moment, then went back to checking their head trauma's blood pressure. Reggie watched for a bit, wondering how much longer they would have to endure, then moved on.

*****

Mid-Evening:

Milepost 201, Horseshoe Curve:

Approaching the stranded passenger cars meant an unnerving crawl along a narrow passageway with a solid wall of snow towering over Johansen's crane. The trickles and patches of snow raining down on them as they passed didn't help his apprehension; nor did the steady snow fall being blasted in their faces. The glare of their spotlights was enough to reflect faintly off the storm clouds passing overhead. The worst of the storm pouring over the ridge up ahead merely brushed against them as it passed, but the sky was menacing and muther-ugly, and the radio reports from Gus and his people were alarming.

"Shit, I am not a happy camper," Johansen muttered. The crane's mechanic caught part of his gripe, and looked at him curiously. "I don't like the look of that sky," he added.

"Nobody asked our opinion, boss," the man said. "We just got t' go out in this shit and clean up other people's mess."

"You got that right!"

The wind whipped at them, chilling them both as they stood in the crane's drafty open cab. Up ahead a group of his mechanical department people and some gandy dancers were stacking railroad ties to create beds for the crane's outriggers. This was hazardous work in the blinding glare of their spotlights, made all the worse by the bitter cold and their chronic exhaustion.

"Let's just hope th' take-up clutch holds. I don't wanna strip that sucker down again!"

"You and me both!" The take-up drum clutch needed a complete rebuild, not shims made of bits of sheet metal. It wasn't the only aching joint on this rig, either.

They moved gingerly up next to the two cars, Johansen gauging his position by eye until he brought it to rest just short of where they joined. Once in position, his laborers extended the outriggers and lowered their jacks to rest on the railroad ties, while others prepared to chain the crane down to the rails. Even with the close-in lift they needed to make, there was a very real danger of the heavily loaded crane tipping over. If that happened, they would be royally screwed. While the crew worked, Johansen climbed down and studied the wreck. Aside from some sheet metal damage, the derailed cars didn't seem bad off. The trucks appeared, at first glance, to be undamaged, but they needed to make a closer inspection once the crane was ready. Thankfully the two cars weren't badly snowed in. If they could get them back on the rails, dragging them down off the Hill wouldn't be a problem.

By time Johansen finished his inspection, his lead mechanic had the crane's diesel running (rough, but steady), and the laborers were installing the last shims under the outrigger feet and dragging the steel lifting cables forward. He pondered the scene for a bit, going over the lift in his mind to be sure everything was accounted for.

"We'll need the spreader bar," he said at last.

His lead mechanic nodded, and the crew set to work wrestling the massive fifteen foot I beam—needed to keep the lifting cables from crushing the car sides—out of the tool car so it could be added to the hoist.

The last outrigger was snugged down, and he raised the boom to its maximum height. The only way this light crane could shift so much weight was to get the greatest leverage possible, but that meant his radius of action was next to nothing. He'd have to get right up to the derailed cars to do any good.

Once the crane was at full height, he rotated to the right, bringing its heavy hook directly over the first derailed car, and realized he'd come up a bit short. "Alright," he called to his lead mechanic. "Shift her forward about two feet!"

That meant slacking off the outrigger screws so the whole crane could be moved, which stuck in his craw, but the error was understandable in these conditions. The work train foreman signaled with a lighted fuzee, their locomotive shoved gingerly, and the crane crawled ahead, swaying unsteadily in the high wind. "That'll do! Lock her down!" The laborers jumped to reset the outriggers and tighten the rail clamps while several more dragged the heavy cables into position and carefully threaded them under the first car.

Finally everything was ready—as ready as could be, anyway. This was hardly an ideal setup. They cleared the snow wall by inches on one side and the cars being rescued by inches the other way. There was precious little room to swing the crane, the light was bad, the footing treacherous, and they were all suffering from the cold. That, and by rights their ad-hoc wrecker should be in the Cheyenne back shop. But there was nothing for it, so Johansen greeted the task with a weary sigh, and gunned the crane's engine.

§

Milepost 197, Snow Shed 47:

Dan and Jesus were taking a well-deserved sleep in the bunk car since they were on the sick list at Doctor Cummings' orders. It still wasn't certain if they suffered frostbite or not, so the order was to keep them warm and let them get plenty of rest. Margret and Willy were off duty as well since the 207 was not needed at the moment, while an unenthusiastic team of 'volunteer' enginemen stood abbreviated duty aboard the rotary.

At least everyone else was taking advantage of the storm to get plenty of sleep. The engine crews did solo watches on their charges, but other than that, and the kitchen crew who kept busy hustling up hot coffee and soup, life was easy.

It was also frustrating, especially for Gus Vincincegorough. "Dammit, *when* is this weather gonna quit?" he muttered as he peered out one of the caboose windows.

"The weather does its own thing in its own good time." Walter and the others were busying themselves with another round of their interminable game of poker. "You just need t' go with the flow, man."

"I swear I'll do a Victory Dance when the last snowflake melts off this damned mountain!"

"Well I hope you live that long, Gus."

That earned Fred an icy glare. "Maybe I'll stick you out there to clear the right of way. The way you run your mouth, we won't *need* a rotary!"

"Hey, chill out, Gus! There's nothing we can do but wait, so there's no sense getting all up in a tizzy over it."

285

"Right now you owe me the eastern Nebraska Division and ten years seniority," Walter added. "You in, or do I call your marker?"

"Yeah, I guess." Gus returned to his jealously guarded seat next to the stove and palmed the deck. "The game's Texas Hold-em. The stake is two bits or a month's seniority, nothing's wild, and hell's froze over!"

§

Milepost 198, Aboard the 'City Of San Francisco':

"Hey, Reggie?" O'Brian was studying his old-fashioned pocket watch when Conductor Greenbaum happened on him in one of the sleeper vestibules. "It's been near fifteen hours since the generator was fueled last. It's liable t' quit any time now."

Greenbaum stared at him in confusion while he tried to force his weary mind to understand. "Ah...Jeez, it's been that long?"

"Yeah. We're gonna have t' go out there and refuel right soon. That generator quits, it'll set off a panic."

Not to mention it would come at the worst possible moment for the doctors trying to treat their critical patients.

"Well," Greenbaum sighed. "Nothing for it, so let's get to work."

§

The raw wind cut them like a million knives as they climbed down from the first sleeper. Even here on the lee side, where they were forced to exit since the car was tilted sharply over, the storm was blinding. Paul had been dragooned into this joyless effort, and was the only one with the wit to bring one of the emergency lanterns.

"God! This is awful!" He shone his lamp ahead of them, but even the powerful beam couldn't do much more than show them the next ten feet of the car side.

"We got no choice!" O'Brian said. "Let's get 'er done!"

They stumbled through the storm, trying to keep together and hugging the car side to keep their feet and avoid getting lost. It took forever to reach the end of the sleeper, then grope blindly down slope along the baggage car. They finally found the fuel tank, and O'Brian scraped the snow away from the fuel gauge.

286

"It's not showing!" he yelled. "We're almost out!"

Paul used the pry bar to open the baggage car door, which was sealed with ice and snow. Reggie and O'Brian boosted him up into the car, where he found the two dozen jerry cans lined up neatly by the wall. It took a major effort with his flagging strength to drag the heavy cans to the door and hand them down to the other two, who needed all their strength in turn to empty them into the fuel tank.

None of them knew how long this went on, but they were all numb with cold and fatigue, and had trouble handling the heavy cans with frozen fingers before the last one was drained. By then they were all so worn and cold that rational thought was almost impossible.

"'T' think I always wanted t' work on the railroad as a kid!" O'Brian was shivering from the cold and exhaustion. "I was an idiot!"

"Ya like playin' with your trains?" Paul grumbled. "Let's get out-a this!"

§

Back inside, in the *blessed* warmth of the first sleeper, it took the three some time to warm up enough to ponder what came next. "We added..." O'Brian had to pause to laboriously work out the math in his head. "...one-hundred-twenty gallons to th' tank. How long will that last?"

Paul was the only one who knew enough about the generator to hazard a guess, and he was too weary to even try. "Several hours...maybe half a day. Can't say f' sure."

"Damn, I hate this!" Greenbaum said.

"That's all the fuel we had," O'Brian said. "We need t' check with the rescue people and see how soon they can get some more to us."

§

Milepost 206, Truckee, California:

"I got ten guys coming in in the next hour, and another fifteen due off the law anywhere from three to six hours." Dean Nakamura checked his clipboard again with a mournful

287

expression. "And we've had no response to our call for new hires. It looks like the locals aren't fool enough to go up the Hill in this weather for Company money."

"Two dozen? Is that all?" Mortensen was dismayed by how few warm bodies he had left. Truckee could absorb that many and more just clearing rooftops to keep the buildings from collapsing. What he'd do for the right of way, not to mention relievers for the rescue effort was beyond him.

"That's it, Jim. Sorry." Not that Dean sympathized since he knew why they were hurting. "Most of our people are on the law since you sent 'em all out earlier."

"Could...we call for help from Reno?"

"I doubt if they have anyone to spare, plus getting them here would be a huge effort."

He was right. The whole road was suffering. There likely wasn't a free hand anywhere west of Omaha. "Alright," he sighed. "We'll just have to make do as best we can." His phone rang as Dean was leaving; he picked it up automatically. "Mortensen."

"Mister Mortensen? Please hold for Mister Oliver, the Vice President of Operations..."

"Oh, shit," he muttered. Dean caught it, and stopped in the doorway to listen. There was a click on the phone.

"Mortensen? What the hell's going on up there? Why haven't you reached that passenger train yet?"

He gave Dean a panicked glance. "We're making real progress, sir! We expect to reach the first wreck site in the next few hours..."

"How long does it take to plow five miles with a rotary?"

"It's this weather..."

"Even in this weather! You should have cleared those cars by now and brought the rest of the train down. So what's the holdup?"

Mortensen felt like the walls were closing in. There was no way in *hell* he could admit to the condition of track two, but what other explanation could he give? "...Mister Oliver, I don't think you realize how bad it is here. We've been hit with over a hundred feet of snow, and right now there's a full-blown hurricane pounding the mountain..."

"I didn't just fall off the turnip truck, mister! I got my start on the Hill, right there in Truckee in fact, so don't try to shine me on! I want that Hill cleared! Pronto!"

"Yes, sir! I'll...hello?"   Mortensen stared at the phone in confusion before realizing the line was dead, then hung up and cradled his head in his hands in utter despair. Dean watched him for a bit without saying anything, then left.

§

Milepost 198, down slope:

"Hey, I think he's awake!" Chase shook Cranston to wake him out of an exhausted slumber. "Check him out, man!"

He was right: one of their patients, the guy with the broken arm, was stirring feebly.   Cranston stared in confusion for a moment before the reaction kicked in, then rolled up on his knees. "Hey pal, you with us?"

His answer was an agonized groan, then the man opened his eyes and stared aimlessly at them.

"Come on, dude. You hear me?"

The man focussed on him. "...Wha...?"

"Come on, pal! What's your name?"

He was having trouble focussing between the cold, his semi-shock and the last dose of morphine, but managed a weak answer. "...Bobby...Mayfield...who...?"

"We're a National Guard rescue unit. We're here to get you and your buddy out."

"...Karl..."

"He's right here next to you. He's alive." Even through his groggy state Bobby's relief was plain, then he winced when Langsdorf bumped his injured arm.   "We're snowed in for the moment, but we'll get you out of here as soon as the weather eases up."

Bobby managed to focus on the sound of the storm. "Always like this," he mumbled.

"Naa, man, this is something special whipped up just for us. It's a *muther* out there, so we have to wait for the storm to wind down. You just take it easy. We'll have you out ASAP."

Bobby pondered that as best he could, then nodded and closed his eyes. They went back to waiting.

§

Milepost 201, Horseshoe Curve:

It took several hours for the car toads to string cables under the first of the two derailed cars, but everything was ready for their first lift. "Now we find out if this'll work," Johansen muttered to himself. His lead mechanic couldn't hear him over the roar of the wind, but he must have been thinking the same thing. This dinky forty-tonner was barely enough to lift one end of one of these cars, presuming the thing was properly stabilized, which they couldn't really do in this limited space. And then there was the wind, which could set the car swinging dangerously once airborne.

He gingerly eased back on the lift clutch, and hauled on the lift handle. Their diesel sputtered and increased its tempo, the lift drum started turning, the cable slack came in, and the car reluctantly shifted.

"Damn, this might work!" his mechanic said.

Maybe, but they were a long way from home. The car came up, and swayed awkwardly as the wind caught it. They held their breath in agonized suspense as the track crew and car toads fought to stabilize the swinging mass. It took most of their crew to corral the beast, but the foreman finally gestured to Johansen, and he gingerly tried the traverse lever. The crane rotated as the foreman guided him with his fuzee. After stabilizing it once again, the foreman gestured, and the car inched down, hung up on one rail momentarily, then dropped onto the track.

"How's it look?" Johansen asked the foreman when the car toads were through inspecting it.

"A bit of sheet metal damage, and that busted door, but she's good t' go otherwise."

"Alright, let's get it out out-a here and get on the other one before we're socked in solid."

A switch engine was standing by for this. It moved in to couple to the errant coach, and hauled it clear to await the remaining one before heading to Truckee where it could join the other two cars. With it in the clear the car toads promptly got to work to advance the crane a few more feet to tackle the buffet car. Despite the urgency, they moved slower than before, and it was obvious they suffered from cold and exhaustion. The snow was getting heavy, and word was another monster blizzard was raging a few miles distant, right on the other side of Summit. No one wanted to be caught in that mess, but they simply couldn't move any faster.

It seemed to take forever before the outrigger jacks were reengaged and the rail clamps tightened down. Johansen had watched all the while, but it took an effort to shake off his half-frozen bemused state and man the crane's controls for the second lift.

§

Milepost 142, Colfax, California:

The latest crew trying to keep the yard clear with two Bobcats came trudging into the cafeteria, shaking the snow off their coats and boots. They looked thoroughly worn and miserable despite only being out there for four hours. Bobcats have open cabs and no heaters.

"You guys alright?" Murphy asked.

"About as alright as we can be, I guess," one of them said.

"It's freakin' *cold* out there!" another one complained. "And we're doing damn-all good with them Tonka toys!"

"I know, but they're all we got." Murphy knew full well how hopeless this was, but their last piece of heavy snow gear was still on its side at Emigrant Gap. Absent a spreader or rotary, all they had were the pilot plows of a hijacked road unit and the two Tonka toys. "We have t' do the best we can t' keep the yard open." Right then these four couldn't care less. "Go get some chow, then you're down for eight." He had three shifts rotating that thankless, miserable duty. At least they could get some adequate sleep.

One of them paused as they headed for the chow line. "Hey, Murph? Maybe I'm crazy, but it seems like th' wind is dying down a bit out there."

"Yeah? Good. Thanks."

After pondering the weather for a bit—he couldn't tell if things were improving or not—he called the Roseville dispatcher.

"Hang on a minute, I'll check the latest bulletins." It was no surprise Roseville wasn't keeping a close eye on the weather lately. They were up to their ass in troubles as the traffic kept piling up, and even the lowlands were suffering from the relentless storms. *"Ahh...yeah. Latest word is the wind is down to about eighty-five. They're saying this storm is starting to wind down. No idea on how soon, though."*

"Yeah, good. Thanks." That wasn't the greatest news, but at least it was something. Maybe he should call that up the Hill to let Gus know.

His thought was interrupted by one of the section hands. "Hey, Murphy, we're out-a coffee in here."

Murphy shot him a sizzling glare. "Do I have 'Starbucks' tattooed on my ass? You're a big boy; you ought-a know how t' make coffee by now!" The man retreated post-haste.

§

Milepost 197, Snow Shed 47:

"We managed to transfer the fuel in the jerry cans, but that was only one-hundred-twenty gallons. We got nothing left, and that won't last long. How soon can you refuel us?"

Gus silently cursed this latest crisis. "Ah...I can't say for sure. Word from Colfax is this storm is starting t' fade, but there's no way t' say how soon we can make a move."

"We're guessing we might have another six hours or so, but that's only a guess. If you got any ideas, we'll be needing them soon."

"Yeah, George, we're doin' everything we can think of." Even though they never met, the MoW Supervisor and the Amtrak conductor were fellow professionals, bonded over the radios during this crisis. "Keep me up to speed, and we'll try t' figure something."

292

"Thanks, Gus. Amtrak 15, out."

"Damn!" Walter muttered. "I hope we can come up with something." Gus wasn't the only one pulling for their stranded comrades a mere half-mile away.

"I wish we could get to that personnel carrier," Parker said. "It ought to be able to make it."

"I'm not so sure about that, deep as this snow is. In any case, it's over there where we can't get at it."

"Plus who knows how t' drive it?" Fred asked.

Parker paused to study the storm through the window. "We could send the rotary."

Gus gnawed his lip as he listened to the storm's roar. "If we have to, but I don't want t' risk it unless we got no choice. Let's see what this weather does in the next few hours. We still got time yet."

§

Milepost 201, Horseshoe Curve:

Their crew finished stringing the cable to the derailed truck of the second car, and their foreman gave Johansen a thumbs-up. "About damned well time!" the lead mechanic grumbled. They were all suffering from the bitter cold in a job which went on far too long already.

"Yeah." Johansen knew full well how his crew was suffering— they were all suffering—but he was too cold and too weary to hold much charity in his heart right then.

First the take-up. The drum rotated—skipped—running by fits and starts as the clutch slipped—and the car lifted reluctantly. The wind interfered again, sending all hands to the ropes to steady it. It took several minutes, during which the massive car slammed against the crane's chassis, bringing down a minor avalanche before they got it stabilized.

Almost there. Johansen took a firm grip on the traverse clutch handle, gingerly eased his foot down on the transverse brake pedal, and carefully moved the handle.   The rumble of their diesel deepened, and the crane started to rotate...

...the clutch gave a nerve-wracking *'CRUNCH'*, and the traverse froze as the handle kicked against his palm. "Dammit!" Johansen muttered as he and the lead mechanic attacked the cover over the broad ring gear used to pivot the crane's superstructure. It took forever to undo the sixteen bolts holding the cover in place, and their effort confirmed their worst fears.

The drive gear already had one broken tooth when they got the crane; now a second tooth was sheered off, leaving a gap too wide for the ring gear to jump over. Without that drive gear, the crane couldn't pivot, rendering it useless.

"Shit! What do we do now?" the mechanic asked.

§

Milepost 206, Truckee, California:

"Well I've got good news," Mortensen said when Dean Nakamura came to bring him the latest crew availability figures. "I just got word from up the Hill that those two cars are being cleared. The line should be open any time now."

"Thank heaven for small favors!" Dean said, fervently. Still, he had to marvel that the rotaries and spreader trains returned over two hours ago, and only now was Mortensen getting the word. It said a lot about his reputation with the MoW forces.

"The weather's getting better, too. We should reach that Amtrak shortly and end this damned crisis." Mortensen was already celebrating. "That'll show Omaha we can do the job!"

Dean knew different. A friend at Reno called a short time ago to let him know the weather there had cleared enough that the airport was letting a few flights in to ease the backlog. According to rumors, Reno Operations were told to send a car to meet an unscheduled flight from Omaha. He didn't like to think what that flight must be like; it was still raw and blowing out there. The fact that a corporate jet was coming from Omaha, in these conditions, was ominous, the implications plain. He thought for a moment of giving Mortensen a heads-up, but decided not to. It was no skin off *his* nose, not that he cared anyway, and Mortensen had enough to worry about. Besides, it ought to be an entertaining show.

§

The poker game broke up eventually and various players scattered in search of food or sleep, leaving Walter and Fred on radio watch. It was a deadly dull ritual, but it had to be done, so like watch standers everywhere, they killed time by talking.

"Honestly, I don't know what to do any more." Fred sat next to the rear windows of the caboose watching the storm blow in under the end of the snow shed. "We simply can't handle this much snow. We don't got the equipment, and our guys can't take this cold all day long."

"We got no place t' dump all that snow, too," Walter added. He was manning the radio while Fred hung around as his runner. "What scares me is how it's gotten worse every winter these last few years. Th' weather's goin' t' hell. What'll it be like in the future?"

Fred gave him a dismayed look. "I don't even want t' *think* about it!"

"Well you should. You gotta go out there and work in it!"

Silence returned, save for the relentless howling of the wind and the faint hiss of the oil stove. The silence was oppressive, wearing on their nerves. This old caboose had a forlorn feel to it, like something left over from another age. It left everyone who felt it feeling a bit lost.

"Well we gotta do *something* t' keep the Pass open," Fred said at last. "More rotaries, maybe."

Walter hook his head. "That wouldn't help enough. There's too many spots on the Hill where there's no room to clear so much snow off to."

Fred offered a contemptuous snort. "You got that right!" His own turf, between Mileposts 171 and 178—'The Gap'—wasn't unique. "Plus there's too many places can get hit by slides when the snow's this bad."

Silence returned, except for the howling wind and the hiss of the stove. There was a brief burst of inintelligible noise from the radio.

"What *can* we do?" Fred asked at last.

Walter pondered for some time. "The only thing I can figure is to build more snow sheds, all the way across the Hill."

"That'll be a hell of a project! I can't see it being done next summer."

"The road likely can't afford it anyway. Between all the lost traffic and the extra cost of snow removal, I'll bet Omaha'll be feeling the pinch."

"No bet here!"

More brooding silence.

"It'll take 'em several years t' build all them sheds," Walter said at last. "Start with the most critical spots and spread out to cover the entire line."

"Yeah, we'll have to." Fred *sincerely* hoped they'd start with his hell-hole at Emigrant Gap. The radio crackled to life:

"This is Murphy at Colfax to the rescue party at Shed 47. Over?"

Walter turned and keyed the mic. "Shed 47 to Murphy, how's things down your way? Over?"

"Well it ain't exactly balmy, but I wanted t' let you know the weather people are sayin' this storm is starting t' play out. The wind is down to maybe sixty, and the snow is getting less."

"That's good to hear, Murph."

"How are things at your end?"

"Just fine and dandy. We're having a regular ski holiday up here." That earned him a crude retort. "Yeah, love you too, Murphy. Bye for now."

"Well that's good news! It looks like the crisis will soon be over. Today's crisis, anyway."

"Yeah, but the day ain't done yet, and tomorrow's likely t' be a mutherfucker." Walter noted the time and entered the message in the radio log. "You need t' go wake Gus up. I don't know *how* he can sleep when there's so much joy to be shared."

"Thanks. It's not like this job isn't dangerous enough."

§

Milepost 198, down slope:

"How's he doing?" Bobby was awake again, but his voice was so weak it could hardly be heard over the roar of the storm.

"He's still alive," Cranston assured him. He was busy taking Karl's blood pressure, which wasn't good. From all the indications, he had internal injuries and was slowly bleeding out. Moreover his breathing was raspy and labored; signs of a possible ruptured lung or bleeding into the chest cavity. Whatever he suffered from, he wouldn't last much longer without treatment Cranston simply didn't know how to give.

What's more, their supplies weren't adequate. He gave Karl their last unit of infusion glucose several hours—or was it days?—ago, and they were out of morphine. The events seemed strangely compressed, and he, Cranston, only knew the date from his digital watch.

"How is he?" Langsdorf asked, quietly.

Cranston glanced at Bobby, who was laying quiet wrapped in a mylar survival blanket, his eyes shut. "He's not good. I *wish* we brought more supplies!"

"I wish we could get to the APC. Our troubles would be over."

Cranston shook his head. "Fraid not. There's nothing we need there. We brought all the morphine with us, and the extra plasma and glucose will be froze solid by now. If we could reach the APC we could get these guys out, which won't happen in this storm."

Langsdorf sagged where he was sitting with a weary sigh and stared at nothing as the storm raged outside. "I just hope those railroad guys are hard at it," he muttered at last.

§

Milepost 201, Horseshoe Curve:

"Alright, lock it down." Johansen and his lead mechanic started tightening the bolts holding the gearbox cover down.

Providently, the tool car included a MIG welder, and Johansen was able to build up the broken gear teeth enough to engage the ring gear. The work was sloppy, the welds were not hardened steel, and his effort used up the last of the unit's welding wire and the special inert gas mixture, but hopefully it was enough to get the crane back in commission. They tightened the last bolts, and retreated to the work train caboose to warm up.

"How's it look?" the work train foreman asked when they arrived. They ignored him long enough to help themselves to the coffee pot bubbling on the caboose stove, and sagged on the folding chairs.

"We did what we could," Johansen said. "Hopefully it'll be enough; the welder's used up."

"We'll have t' baby it," the mechanic added. "But she's ready to go."

"Yeah, well I'm pulling my men in for th' time being. This storm is just too much."

That caught them both off guard. "We gotta clear that car!" Johansen protested.

"I got some guys pretty well ruined by this cold. There's talk of 'em walkin' off the job, it's so bad. You wanna get that car cleared, you gotta give these guys time t' warm up."

Johansen had to admit he was right. The weather was horrible, even by the usual standards, and he was pretty well beat. The thought of their track force pushed to the point where they'd go out on a wildcat strike was warning enough. "How long you talkin' about?" he asked, tensely.

"A few hours. We overheard a call to Gus, over the Hill, sayin' this storm is starting t' give out. Give it a little time, let my guys get warmed up and rest a bit, and we'll be able to tackle that last car."

Johansen didn't like it, but there was no choice, really. They were all worn down by the last few days. "Well...alright. A few hours."

"Right. And you two get somethin' t' eat. You look like you could use it." The foreman set the remnants of a box of fried chicken and biscuits, carry-out likely a day old now, in front of them.   Johansen felt divided by the offer.   Greasy cold fried chicken was hardly his idea of fine dining...but he realized he was trembling, his arms almost too heavy to lift.   The foreman was right: the cold and hard work and long hours were exacting a toll. Right then, as urgent as it all was, he was too tired and too worn to care.   He had to eat *something*, and then he needed a nap in the worst way. *'Okay, a few hours'*, he promised himself, and dug in.

*****

Midnight, January 4th:

Milepost 142, Colfax, California:

"Well I'll be go-to-hell," Murphy said. "Somebody screwed up. That ain't natural."

"Don't knock it, Murphy," one of the group standing in front of the crew dorm looking up at the sky cautioned him. "Ya don't wanna curse it."

The wind was still cutting and bitter, tearing at their heavy coats, but for a wonder stars showed through rents in the cloud cover overhead. The snow had all but quit, save for that being blown around by the wind, creating massive drifts such as the one threatening to bury one wall of the crew cafeteria. Still, to all appearances the weather was *finally* moderating.

"God," someone said. "D'ya think its over?" A half moon emerged from behind drifting clouds, illuminating Colfax yard with its pale, silvery light. Aside from the faint glow of signals and the headlight of their borrowed road unit still fighting to clear the line, there was no sign of activity.

Murphy tore himself away from the almost hypnotic sight. "Th' hell its over! We got us a break, is all. We better make the most of it!" He turned abruptly and headed back into the cafeteria where a motley assortment of men lounged at the trestle tables. Once again he climbed up on a chair to confront them.

"Alright everybody!" he yelled. "We got a break in the weather, and we're gonna make it count! I want work crews on the turnouts, I want the flanger manned, and I want a detail clearin' snow off the company roofs. We got maybe a few hours before the next load drops on us, so let's hustle!"

§

Milepost 198, down slope:

Langsdorf had the watch while the others tried to get a bit of sleep. He couldn't sleep in any event since the endless roar of the wind was getting on his nerves. *'How long is this gonna go on?'* he thought in frustration.

That raw cold—waiting out there like some hungry predator—unnerved him. He huddled close to the space heater which was their only defense against nature on a rampage, trying to absorb as much heat as possible. It wasn't much, but every little bit helped, especially in his mind.

"I got myself screwed crude," he said. He couldn't help but think of the sarge, lying dead out there in the snow somewhere. "Hell, we'll never get out of this!" He'd been obsessing over it all evening, in fact, and his morale was starting to buckle under the strain.

That gas heater... It kept them alive for nearly a day now. One of their two gas bottles was already empty; how much longer could the other one hold out? How much gas was left? The thought preyed on his mind. The cold...out there...waiting... He shuddered in horror at the thought of freezing to death. On impulse, he reached for the heater valve for the umpteenth time, promising he would turn it up just a little...

...No. He forced his hand away and tucked it under his arm pit to conserve his body heat and to keep himself from doing something suicidal. "Dammit," he mumbled, embarrassed by the thought the others would see him. How much gas was left?

He sat huddled by the meager heat source and prayed; for rescue, for a break in this damned storm, for help from somebody. Anybody. His eyes blurred with tears of anguish. Somebody. Anybody.

There was no answer, except for the endless roar of the storm.

§

Milepost 197, Snow Shed 47:

Things were quiet aboard the camp cars as well. The endless storm left everyone depressed and frustrated, so there was little enthusiasm to be found. Aside from an endless game of penny-ante poker, most of the workers were in their bunks. A few were actually sleeping; many lay wrapped in their blankets, listening to the roar of the wind, wondering if they would ever rescue the Amtrak, wondering if they would make it safely off this damned mountain.

The word from Colfax changed all that abruptly:

"Believe it or not, we actually got clear skies here, for the moment anyway.   But don't count on it lasting. Roseville says the next storm is already coming in, so you got a few hours at best."

Fred was on watch monitoring the caboose radio. "Ah, copy that, Murphy. Thanks for the good news." This was welcome news indeed to the weary men who spent so much time and labor to get this far. Their struggles were far from over, and this break in the weather would finally let them get their job done.

"I hear-tell the weather people say the next several storms are starting t' pile up. T' hear them say it, we're in for a non-stopper going on for a week, maybe ten days. This may be your last chance t' rescue that Amtrak."

"*Jesus*, a week or more?" Joey muttered.
"Yeah, copy that, Murphy. Thanks. Be sure t' give our regards t' them weather guys. Shed forty-seven, out."
Joey was freaked by that forecast. "A *week?* Ten days? We're gonna get buried!"
Fred wasn't pleased either, and he had a much better picture of what a week-long blizzard could do. "You got that right! But there's nothing t' do but suck it up and take it." Joey seemed to be coming a bit unglued by the idea. "It's not as bad as it sounds. We been hit with major storms all th' time. We'll make do."
Joey pulled himself together. "So what's the drill?"
"We need to let Gus know about this. Go wake him up."
"Right."

§

Milepost 206, Truckee, California:

"Things are going well for once."   Mortensen paused for a yawn and rubbed his aching eyes. "End of my little day. I need some sleep."

"Yeah, you do look beat." Dean Nakamura had precious little sympathy for his boss. He was the one doing all the running around here, and as tired as he was, he planned on continuing for at least a few more hours until the situation on the Hill was clearer. There was a break in the weather coming, to hear the local radio news, which meant things would finally get moving. Mortensen, on the other hand, was already bundled up, and his car was warming up where he parked it in the MoW garage. And here it was scarcely midnight.

"If anything comes up about the rescue...no, don't bother calling. We've done all we can here, and it's up to the guys on the Hill now. The morning should bring some pleasant news." He made a show of pulling on his gloves and headed home.

"*We*, huh?" Dean groused. His contempt for Mortensen was complete by then, and he drew cold amusement from knowing tomorrow would bring some pleasant news indeed for their erstwhile Maintenance of Way Superintendent—direct from Omaha. But for now he needed to update the duty list for all the hands recently released from the rescue party. The railroads have a long tradition of epic paperwork. *'It never ends around here,'* he thought, philosophically. *'Job security, I guess.'*

§

Milepost 198, Snow Shed 47:

As soon as everyone was up and the kitchen car working on getting them all fed Gus, Walter and Fred headed out to check the current conditions. The weather was still brutal by any rational standard, but it seemed like Paradise after what they'd been through. The snowfall was down to a thin dusting, but the wind was bitter and still blowing nearly gale force.

"This don't exactly look like a 'break' t' me!" Walter grumbled. Even so, compared to what went before, the scene was almost balmy.

"Yeah, but its already easing up," Gus said. "If its only now hitting Colfax, we got maybe two hours until it gets here."

The sight which greeted them at the end of the snow shed was of the road bed buried under three feet of new snow. "Hmph!

Could-a been worse." Gus activated one of the portable searchlights they used for illumination at night, and turned it upward to reflect off the cloud cover. It seemed a lot higher than before, but no less menacing. "Maybe it is breaking up."

"If this is 'breaking up', I say good riddance to th' real thing," Fred said.

"Th' timing is good," Walter said. "It'll give us a chance t' feed our people, and with luck this'll hold until dawn. I'd rather work in th' daylight."

"Yeah, plus we need to plan our work so we can get the most out of this break in the weather," Gus added.

"First thing we gotta do is help them National Guards," Fred said. "We gotta get our people out first."

"Yeah, but we got no contact with them."

"If we can find one of their radios in their vehicle, someone can take it down to them. Then we can work out a plan."

Gus pondered him doubtfully. "That's risky."

"We know where the locomotives are now, and our two guys need help. Hell, I'll go."

"Well...alright. If you think you can do it safely. But we don't need any more rescuing t' do!"

"I'm with you on that one, Gus!"

"What about the Amtrak?" Walter asked.

Gus shifted his searchlight and studied the 'City' train, faintly visible in the distance. "That baggage car is hardly worth trying to salvage, and we can't take any unnecessary risks with what those slopes must be like."

"Yeah, we can't risk th' big hook out there," Walter said. "So how do we handle this?"

"We'll wait until the rescue party is in the clear, then we'll bring the bulldozer up and shove the car off the line. Everyone else will be back in the snow shed."

Walter considered the scene. "Yeah, right." Then he recalled how the first cars were heeled over by the fringes of the original avalanche, which wasn't good news. "Those first two cars got snow packed under 'em; it's a wonder they didn't tip over. We'll have t' dig 'em out. We can't risk rolling 'em back on the rails."

"Yeah. We can do that while those Guardsmen do their thing." Gus keyed his portable. "This is Gus to th' dorm. We need t' get organized for the final push. We'll need t' dig those last two cars out in particular. Parker? You up? Your turn."

"Ah...yeah...copy that, Gus."

"Woke the poor bast'id up," Walter grumbled.

"Amtrak, did you copy that? You need t' evacuate those first two cars so we can safely work on 'em."

"Uh...yeah. This is the 'City' train, we copy. Don't know where th' hell we'll put 'em, but will do."

Once he finished, Gus turned to Walter. "It's time t' wake a whole bunch-a people up!"

§

Milepost 198, Aboard the 'City Of San Francisco':

"Well, this sounds promising," Jack Whitacre said after Gus signed off. "Hopefully they can refuel the generator before it quits."

"That's all fine and dandy, but how long will it take for them to get here from Truckee?" Jamie was standing watch over their two critical cases while the doctors managed a few hours of urgently needed sleep. "These two are in bad shape, and public health in general is deteriorating."

George Reinsbach happened to be checking on them when Gus's radio call came in. "There's no way to tell at this point. From what we've heard, they're making progress. If this storm is breaking, they may be able to get in here fairly soon."

"*Fairly soon* isn't going to cut it with these two," Jamie insisted. "They're stable for now, but if anything comes up, there's nothing we can do for them. They need to get to a hospital ASAP, even if the rest of the train remains here."

The old woman was improving. She was semi-conscious although feverish and groggy, and the swelling in her hip was

305

going down. Their head trauma was still unresponsive, but at least his vitals were a bit better. The doctors weren't happy with the state of either of them.

"My guess is if they can take advantage of a break in the weather to move those two cars at Horseshoe Curve, they can have us out-a here in ten-twelve hours."

"Maybe," Jack said. "*If* this weather clears, and *if* everything goes to plan. I'll believe it when I see it."

"Anything more than another ten—twelve hours and it won't matter," Jamie said, grimly.

§

Milepost 201, Horseshoe Curve:

The latest news from Colfax also made a splash with the Truckee force:

> *"Th' word from Colfax is we got a break in this weather comin' in a couple hours. After that we get hit for a week or more, so this is our last chance t' get this rescue done."*

Being woke up out of a sound sleep to receive such news was *not* how the track gang foreman liked his day to start, especially as he was running on about three hours' sleep. Still, news of a break in the weather was welcome, since he like everyone on the Hill was eager to get that Amtrak to safety. "Ah, thanks for the heads-up, Gus. We'll be ready for it here."

> *"How's it look for you?"*

"We were hit pretty hard, but we can manage." At least they had Colfax's borrowed spreader and rotary 209 to dig them out. "We're ready to go after this last car, so we should have the line cleared by dawn." If the damned crane didn't break down again, or any of a hundred other things go wrong.

> *"Good work! We'll get this done yet. Hang in there, guys. Shed 47, out."*

306

"Thank heaven for small favors!" the radio watch-stander said, sincerely.

"Yeah. Th' Good Lord watches over fools and children, and railroaders."

"You want me t' wake Johansen?"

The foreman pondered the matter through his fatigue. "Naa. Let him sleep until the kitchen is ready t' serve breakfast. Th' poor bast'id needs it."

§

Milepost 198, Snow Shed 47:

"This is our chance t' rescue those two crewmen and get the wreck ready t' move," Gus told Margret and Willy. "We need you t' dig over to where the wreck is so we can get started."

The two rotary crewmen had been called from a sound sleep, and weren't thrilled to go out there again. "We're supposed t' be on the law!" Margret protested. "Why don't you get Dan and Jesus for this?"

"They're both still on the sick list, at least that's what the doctor ordered. Plus Jesus has a cracked arm. He wouldn't be much use out there. It's only a half mile run; you should be able t' do it in no time."

"Plus this is our last chance," Walter added. "And we gotta jump like quick little bunnies to take advantage of this break in the weather."

Margret had no answer for that. Union rules are one thing; life and death is something else entirely. She fumed for a moment, that being her nature, then they headed out.

§

"I'll be glad to see the end of this weather," Trudy said, fervently, as she dumped a load of scrambled eggs in the serving tray. "I don't see *how* you folks manage in conditions like this!"

"We mostly don't," Willy grumbled. Despite the urgency, they were taking a few minutes to grab a hot meal in the kitchen car since their promised break in the weather hadn't materialized yet. "Honestly, I don't see how we can go on like this. There'll have t' be some big changes if these winters keep up."

307

"Hey, th' 207 is a tough old girl!" Margret said. "She can do the job!"

Willy greeted her rebuke with a snort of contempt. "That 'tough old girl' is an antique. She belongs in a museum."

"Yeah? Well she's all we got, so we'll just have t' make do."

Willy sighed, and helped himself to a scoop of hash browns. "I really hope we get one of them new rotaries." Word came down a little while ago that the Union Pacific had just placed an order for a dozen powerful new rotary plows. "I hate t' think what next winter'll be like!"

"Yeah. Well, I'll believe it when I see it, knowing this road. Until then we have t' make do with what we got."

"Hey, ya wanna move th' line?" The gripe from one of the gandy dancers set off a rumble of complaints from the backup behind them.

Margret gave him an icy glare. "Hold your water, lil cowboy. We'll leave you some snow t' dig!"

§

Milepost 198, Aboard the 'City Of San Francisco':

The Amtrak crew soon learned that when you wake people up out of a sound sleep and tell them you're evacuating the car, you need to choose your words carefully. Half the passengers were convinced rescue had arrived while the other half were near-panicked thinking some new disaster was upon them. The result was chaos as the exhausted, emotionally wasted civilians milled around in the narrow corridor trying to decide what to do; who to listen to; what the *hell* was going on.

"I swear I'm gonna quit railroading and become a cowboy!" O'Brian swore when he ran into Greenbaum in the second car.

"What? You think herding livestock will be any easier?" Reggie grumbled.

"No, but at least I could use an electric cattle prod!"

"I like it. You should send it in to the home office."

The two of them paused to catch their mental breath, pondering the chaotic situation around them. People sat everywhere, on the seats, in the aisles, in the vestibules, crowded together shoulder to shoulder wrapped in whatever blankets or towels they could find. For all the world they looked like so many refugees. The atmosphere matched the mood. The air was foul, the car littered with trash and discarded food wrappers, and there was a general tone of misery over the sound of the wind. Despite everything the generator could do, the car was chilly and dank. People were already showing signs of respiratory distress.

"Gawd, this is one hell of a mess, ain't it?" O'Brian said at last.

"Yeah. I don't know how much longer these people can hold out, but it can't be for long."

Their worse fear was that the passengers would try to leave the train and strike out for some imagined safety in the worst storms in living memory. There was no way the crew could guard all the entrances, or go after someone who tried to leave.

"I heard the doctors say they're seeing signs of colds, maybe even pneumonia. We could be looking at an epidemic." The way everyone was crowded together, once disease got a foothold, it would spread rapidly.

"Yeah. Being cold and hungry doesn't help, either."

"Let's just hope that bunch from Truckee gets their act together soon. We're running out of time."

§

Milepost 206, Truckee, California:

"Well this is good news," Dean Nakamura said. "How soon do you think we'll get them?" The caller was the grave shift Maintenance of Way supervisor over at Sparks, who called to share the good news about new rotaries with Mortensen.

"They just put the order in, so my guess is we won't get 'em til spring."

"Just in time to moth-ball them for the summer. Why am I not surprised?"

"Yeah, well, you might want t' keep those thoughts under your hat. You never know who might be listening."

309

The radio connection was dicy, but all they had since the telephone lines were still out. Their conversation could be monitored the width of the system. *"Omaha might not be impressed with your enthusiasm."*

"Yeah. Well if they're listening, I hope they'll send us a new heavy wrecker, too."

"That would be nice. You should ask Santa Claus."

"Hey, I work for UP MoW; we don't believe in Santa Claus." Dean sighed and pondered the stacked paperwork on his desk. He needed to get back at it. "I'll pass the good news on to Mortensen when he comes in."

"Yeah, speaking of which, Mortensen better watch his step. This guy from Omaha is a scalp-hunter. He's kicking ass and taking names big time."

That was no surprise, although it was discomforting news. "Yeah, well I suspect Jim's a bit late to start worrying, as usual. Truckee, out."

§

Milepost 198, on the grade:

A mere three feet of fresh snow was child's play for rotary 207, but the snow on the mountain above them was what had their attention. Margret kept their progress slow and steady, keeping her diesels at low power to minimize their noise. It must be working: the mountain didn't come down to bury them.

"I swear I'm gonna transfer to Southern California," Willy grumbled. "I am freakin' *sick* of snow!"

"You'll have t' wait your turn," Margret said, sharply. "Seniority."

"Yeah, and I got time on both of you, so I go first," Fred added.

Willy offered a derisive snort. "We can have our reunions there; bring down a rotary and plow the desert sand."

Margret gave him a sharp look. "And get heat stroke? Not me, lil' cowboy! I'll do my reunioning at the swimming pool!"

Despite their cautious pace, they made steady progress since the new snowfall was free of tumbled rocks and trees. The baggage car could be seen up ahead, and they were just coming up on the area where the bulldozer cleared away the displaced snow so the National Guards could make their fateful effort...

"Hold it!"

Margret slammed on the brakes and killed the throttle in one swift motion. "What?"

"Something I remember." Fred grabbed one of the shovels leaning against the cab wall and climbed down onto the right of way.

§

Wading through three feet of snow takes monumental effort, especially after laboring like a mule for three endless days. Fred needed to dig his way forward, and by time he reached the leading edge of the huge rotary scoop his arms were aching.

"Let me, I'll take over." Fred was a bit surprised to see Willy had joined him. He commandeered the shovel and worked his way forward past the scoop and inward toward the track.

"We gotta find the rail," Fred called to him.

"Here it is!"

Fred took over and dug a narrow trench wide enough for their legs along the railhead. He was getting tired again when the shovel struck something under the snow. It was a rope, tied around the rail.

"We got four of these!" he called to Willy. "We need t' find 'em. They're how we can get t' those National Guards!"

He dug out the rope enough so he could untie it and loop it *under* the rail and retie it so it wouldn't be cut when the rotary came up. By that time he was tuckered out again, and surrendered the shovel to Willy. "You can figure another ten yards or so to the next one."

"Right!" Willy dug in, tossing shovel-fulls of snow off side which were promptly scattered by the stiff wind.

§

Milepost 201, Horseshoe Curve:

While the foreman shook his people out, Johansen gathered his handful of Mechanical Department people and got their crane ready. The first challenge was getting the damned thing to kick over, which it definitely did *not* want to do in this cold.

"Come...ON!...dammit!" he muttered as the starter ground futilely. More often than not the battery would drain before the main diesel did more than backfire a few times. His people were already stringing the jumper cables, in fact.

The diesel kicked once and kept on grinding.

"She should be hot now." His lead mechanic was back in the engine compartment trying to coax the balky motor. "Try it again."

Another brief kick. More grinding. The motor sputtered a few hesitant beats, then quit. The battery was running down. More grinding. The diesel kicked, sputtered, then started running on maybe two cylinders, shaking the crane. One by one the cylinders came on line until the diesel was running ragged but fairly steady.

"Alright, let her warm up a bit."

His crew watched until the diesel was running steadily, then began stowing the jumper cables again.

§

Milepost 198, Aboard the 'City Of San Francisco':

The evacuation of the first two cars took more time and frustration than expected, but somehow the crew got the passengers herded together and moved further down train. After three days they were exhausted, hungry, and at the ends of their emotional tethers. The cars they went to were packed, and the people there did not welcome their fellow sufferers.

"Find a seat wherever you can," was the Amtrak mantra of the hour. "The rescue is getting closer. You just have t' hang on for a little while longer."

The air was thick with the odors of unwashed humanity and overflowing toilets, everyone's nerves were raw, and the Amtrak crew were staggering with fatigue. A handful of passenger volunteers were all that made continued order possible.

Chief among those was Charley Parkhurst, who had been on his feet for most of their misadventure, save only for a few brief naps. He caught up with conductor Reinsbach as he was struggling to settle the refugees in the lounge car. "So what's going on?" he asked.

"Word is the storm is dyin' down, so the bunch up ahead are gonna try t' reach us t' refuel the generator." Reinsbach was wasted; it took him a bit to pull his thoughts together. "They're gonna dig those first two cars out, too, so we needed t' clear 'em."

"That so? So what about getting us out of here?"

"The bunch from Truckee are working t' clear those two derailed cars, after which they'll pull us back down th' Hill. They were held up by this storm, but hopefully they'll reach us soon."

"Uh huh. How bad is it out there right now?"

More weary pondering. "Well at the moment it's *only* blowing about thirty miles an hour, it's *only* five below zero, and there's *only* three feet of new snow for them t' dig through."

Parkhurst winced. "Sounds like a walk in the park."

"Yeah. Easy as pie."

"You there!" They were confronted by Wilbur Harkness of painful memory. "How much longer is this going to take? I am getting *sick* and *tired* of your incompetence!"

Reinsbach was too tired and too frustrated to tolerate this jerk with good grace. "You again," he grumbled. "We haven't seen you for a while. You been avoiding us, or what?"

"We all wished he'd chill," Parkhurst said in disgust. "Seems even an arctic blizzard couldn't do it."

"He managed for a while. It was so peaceful and quiet, too. Don't give up now; you were doing so good."

But Harkness was in no mood for sarcasm, not that he ever was. Like everyone else he was cold and hungry and hadn't showered or changed in days, which did his temper no good. "No, I will *not* be quiet! This train is a disgrace, and the railroad is no better! Why haven't they reached us yet?"

"It's this weather; they take snow days off."

"We don't need your attitude! *When* are they going to get here to rescue us?"

"You can quit your worrying," Reinsbach snapped at him. "Now that this storm has quit, they're movin' again. They'll get here soon enough."

"A likely story! And *look* at this place! It's like a tenement! Why is everyone crowded in here like this?"

"We came up with a new strategy," Parkhurst said. "We're going to move everyone to the back of the train, one car at a time, until everyone's crammed into the last car."

Harkness stared at him in confusion. "Then what?"

"Then they're going to bring up a huge dirigible and float that car over the mountains direct to San Francisco."

"We should arrive on the advertised, depending on the headwinds," Reinsbach added with a straight face. "There'll be no extra fare, too."

Harkness was tired enough that it took a moment before he realized they were ridiculing him. "That's nonsense! This is no time for juvenile humor! *When* are they going to get here?"

"They'll get here when they get here, and your noise won't make 'em go any faster. So you might as well do us all a favor by *sitting* down and *shutting* up!"

"I swear I'll get you all fired!" But there was clearly nothing for it, so he stomped off in search of a place to sit.

Reinsbach confronted Parkhurst with a jaundiced look after he left. "Dirigible, huh?"

Parkhurst offered a smug grin. "You never can tell. It might work at that."

"Yeah. You never can tell."

§

Milepost 198, on the grade:

"There! That's the last one." Willy held up a loop of the fourth rope. "So what's next?"

It took them forever to trench their way thirty yards, and they were both staggering from exhaustion by time all the ropes were accounted for. Fred tied the last one off, then straightened up with an effort. "What's next is you have Margret clear up t' here while I get the *hell* out-a this wind!"

314

"Right!" Willy shouldered his shovel and started trudging back to the 207 while Fred turned his attention to the National Guard's APC. It took some doing to clear the rear door, but once inside he discovered a wealth of rescue gear.

"Damn," he muttered. "It's like fuckin' Christmas!"

There was so much, in fact, that he wasn't sure what to take. At least he was out of the miserable wind, so he could afford the luxury of taking his time. He thought about maybe firing the APC up to get its heater going, but had no idea how to do it. In any case, there was a job to do.

After exploring for a bit, he commandeered a canvas backpack and filled it with a spare portable radio, some batteries, and as an afterthought some MREs. He spotted a pair of snow shoes, and despite having never worn such before, he took them along. While he worked, he heard the sound of the 207 coming closer. But he was still a bit shocked when he emerged to discover the massive rotary had stopped a mere five feet from the APC.

'Cut that kind-a fine,' he thought.

Maybe the sky looked better after the few minutes he'd spent in the APC, but he couldn't tell. The weather was still miserable. He managed to get the snow shoes on and trudged around the rotary to reach the spot where the National Guards started their fateful journey. Margret met him in the cab door as he passed. "You going down?"

"Yeah." The less time he spent in this frozen hell the better.

"We're gonna move back so they can bring the fuel tanker up. Is there anything you need?"

He paused and gave her a weary look. "A winning lottery ticket'd be nice. Other than that, nothing."

"Good luck."

That about said it all. He fished one of the ropes out of the snow and started down slope.

*****

315

Early Morning:

Dean Nakamura was busy working on his roster in his cubby hole when he realized someone was standing in the door. "Where the hell is everybody?" the stranger demanded.

Dean was tired enough that it took him a moment to shift mental gears. This stranger wasn't one of their usual workers. He was dressed in a suit and wool coat, and carried a brief case. "Um...who are you?"

"I'm Caruthers. I was sent here from Omaha to find out what's going on with that Amtrak wreck." This Caruthers was not a happy camper. "Where's Mortensen? Where are all your people?"

"Jim's at home, off shift. Most of our people are on the law, and a few are with Bret Johansen and the wrecker up at Milepost 201."

"Don't you have anyone to clear this yard? I had to leave my car at the end of the public road." Caruthers' trousers were soaked and his coat encrusted with snow. His having to tramp the distance through three feet of snow probably explained his current mood.

"Most of our people were committed to reaching those two derailed cars. They're on the law now. I sent everyone else up with Johansen."

"And who are you?"

"Dean Nakamura. I'm the day shift caller filling in for the night man."

"Where's the regular crew caller? Is he at home too?" Mister Caruthers was not pleased with the answers he was getting. Worse, he was clearly a go-getter to be up at this hour. This didn't look good.

"He volunteered to run a load of medical supplies up to the Amtrak two days ago."

"Really? How'd he do that?"

"On a pair of sno-cats."

Mister Caruthers seemed impressed, which reassured Dean to a small degree. "Have you been able to get any more help to them?"

"A couple of volunteers took a load of food and medical supplies up in a hi-rail. I can't recommend it as a solution, seeing what they went through."

"Well, it's good to see *some* people around here are on their toes!" Better yet; at least they weren't *all* found wanting. Mister Caruthers sat his brief case on Dean's desk. "Now, what's all the holdup on getting the Amtrak cleared?"

"Yes, well, *that's* going to take some explaining." *'So, it begins,'* Dean thought. Rumor had it the Union Pacific was cracking down on slack like never before in response to the ongoing weather crisis, and it appeared the rumors were true. How many heads would roll in the next day or so? And here he was planning to head home soon.

§

Milepost 198, Aboard the 'City Of San Francisco':

"What's the situation with your labor case?" Doctor Cummings was making his rounds after an all too brief nap, and was calling to see about Olivia Bumarris.

Barbara greeted him with a bleary-eyed stare. "She's on-again-off-again," she managed at last. "Right now she's off again. She's slightly dilated, but its nothing significant." She had to pause for a jaw-breaking yawn. "She's resting comfortably. Vitals are slightly up." She offered a diner napkin with a series of penciled readings on it. "Fetal heartbeat and movement sound normal."

Cummings studied the crude log. "Good. Hopefully we'll be able to get her out of here soon."

"They're here?"

"The storm is breaking. The word is they will make a final push to reach us soon. It won't be much longer." Cummings pondered her blank expression with concern. "You look wasted. Are you getting any sleep?"

She labored over that for a bit, then gestured vaguely to the mattress she pulled from the upper berth. "I do what I can."

"Uh-huh. You need to sleep. You look like you don't even have your own medical picture, to say nothing of hers." He turned to go. "I'll send someone to relieve you. You get some rest."

317

"I can manage..."

"No, you can't," he lectured her sternly. "You know how important it is to pace yourself! You should get at least a few hours' sleep, and I'll see if we can scrounge something for you to eat, too."

Barbara tried to protest, but her weariness was too much. She sagged on the chair borrowed from the diner and nodded numbly. After Cummings left, Olivia looked at her. "It's alright, dear. I'm doing fine. You go ahead and take a nap. I'll call you if I need anything." Barbara didn't respond; she was sound asleep.

§

Milepost 198, down slope:

The three Guardsmen were killing time and worrying about their two patients when they were startled by something banging on the diesel's shell. "What th' hell's that?" Chase asked.

"Another avalanche?"

The banging came again along with a faint call.

"There's someone out there!" The three were on their feet instantly. "In here! We're in here!"

A light appeared in the doorway overhead. "Hey you guys! You alright?"

"Jesus! We're glad to see you!" The three of them were sobbing hysterically in relief.

"I brought you a radio and some batteries from your truck." The vague figure behind the flashlight started to climb into the doorway.

"Wait! Hold it!" Cranston called. "Is our stretcher still out there?"

The figure hesitated. "Yeah, but it's pretty well buried."

"Before you come down, there's a chain saw and a can of gas. We'll need 'em to cut our way out of here."

"Oh. Okay." The shadowy figure disappeared again.

"Damn! Looks like we're gonna make it after all!" Chase said.

"Well don't get your hopes up yet. We're not out of this, not by a long shot." Langsdorf was having trouble throwing off his bleak pessimism of earlier.

"Alright you guys," Cranston said, sharply. "We got our work cut out for us, so let's get on the stick." The arrival of help from outside didn't mean their predicament was any less dire. "As soon as we know the score, we'll make our move."

§

Milepost 201, Horseshoe Curve:

"Colfax says this storm is playing out, although you couldn't prove it by me. At least th' weather's starting t' improve here. I'd say if you're gonna get them cars out, your time is coming."

Good news indeed to the weary men trying to clear the right of way, and it gave them hope this nightmare would end soon. Already the murderous wind seemed to be dying down; the endless roar left them all agitated and half deaf, and it was a relief to be able to hold a reasonable conversation again.

"That's great, Gus," Johansen replied. "We were starting t' get bored up here." The improving communications alone said the worst was passing, for now.

"Yeah, well don't sit around congratulating yourselves. Word is th' next storm is already movin' in. No word on how long you'll have, but you'd best make the most of it."

"Yeah, we copy that, Gus. Thanks." Johansen signed off the radio and turned to the work party foreman, sitting comfortably next to the stove. "Looks like we're in business again."

The foreman was less than enthusiastic. "A few hours' window with only a regular blizzard storm t' worry about? Ain't this some kind-a shit?"

"You know it, but that's life on the Hill." If the weather was breaking in Colfax now, it would reach Gus at Milepost 198 in about two hours, and get there to Horseshoe Curve an hour or so later. "We need to get your people up and running. Get 'em fed, get 'em organized. I want t' hit this thing hard when we make our move."

His chief mechanic came into the office caboose just then. "I been out lookin' at the weather. The wind's dyin' down, and the snow's a lot less."

"Yeah, we got us a breather comin' soon." Johansen turned to the foreman again. "Shake your people out and let's get the Hill cleared!"

§

Milepost 198, down slope:

"He's right, the weather does seem to be clearing," Chase reported from his position atop the locomotive's control panel where he could look out the forward windscreen. "The visibility's improving, and the snow is a lot less."

"Thank heaven for small favors!" Langsdorf muttered.

"Yeah, we can see the weather appears to be improving," Cranston spoke to their portable radio. "Do you want to start rescue operations now, or wait a bit?"

"We better get on it now. There's no telling how long this lull will last."

"Yeah, we copy. We're gonna start things from this end."

Cranston switched off the radio to save its batteries. "Okay, Jerry, you need to get on that chain saw and cut us an exit. Fred, see if you can climb back up there and strip the extra gear off our stretcher. Don't worry about the stuff; we'll abandon everything we don't need. As soon as Jerry has a hole cut, pass the stretcher through to us, then stand by to help pull it out from that side."

"Yeah, well first lets have us some food!" Langsdorf insisted. Fred's MREs were welcome since they ate their last ones long ago.

Cranston hesitated for a bit, wondering if they could afford the delay. "Th' weather's not *that* much better," Fred said. "Even a half-hour will improve things, so grab a hot meal while you can."

That was a powerful argument. They were all depleted by cold and hunger, and needed the extra energy. "Alright, but let's make it snappy."

§

320

Milepost 198, on the grade:

With rotary 207 safely back under the snow shed, the fuel tanker was brought forward. It turned out the hose was just barely long enough, requiring several men to hold the thing taut so it could reach the baggage car's fill spout. While that was going on, Gus and Parker Lee examined the two sleepers to see what they were up against.

"It could be worse," Parker said after a bit. "At least it don't look like there's any rocks or trees mixed in."

"Still, this'll take hours t' dig out," Gus said. "And we're hurting for time."

Parker glanced at him. "Then me and my boys best get on it."

The first two cars caught the fringe of the avalanche, which tipped them over at a twenty degree angle and piled up against them nearly to the roof line. More snow was packed underneath, so they would need to be undermined as well. Neither of them liked the thought.

"We'll have t' crib up before we can dig 'em out." There were jacks and railroad ties in the supply car, but it would mean more time-consuming, back-breaking work.

"Yeah." Gus was not thrilled with all the hard labor ahead of them. "But I don't think we got the time. We may have t' risk dragging them clear and hope they land on the rails."

"I hate the idea, but you're likely right."

"But before we try that, we better give it our best. You need t' turn both your shifts out, and I'll send you some of Earl's people too. We can't afford t' waste a moment."

Parker pondered the task ahead of them with a glum expression. "Well...at least they didn't derail."

Gus gave him a disgusted glare. "Th' only bit of good news we've had thus far."

§

Milepost 198, Aboard the 'City Of San Francisco':

"At least the generator is taken care of," O'Brian said. "Lets hope this weather holds until Truckee can get here."

321

Conductor Reinsbach didn't answer at first since he was in the grip of a jaw-breaking yawn. "Yeah, lets hope" he sighed at last. "All these sick people are gonna get worse, and I'll bet things'll go t' hell fast." Colds and sinus conditions were spreading rapidly in the desperately over-crowded cars, and the doctors reported seeing the first signs of possible pneumonia. "If we don't get down off this mountain soon we're looking at most of these people winding up in a hospital."

"If Truckee has a hospital big enough for so many."

O'Brian was too weary to answer, but the facts needed no explanation. Everyone on board, passengers included, were at the end of their rope. Between hunger, cold, and the crowded conditions many were starting to succumb to exhaustion and depression. All they could do was wait, and hope for the best.

§

Milepost 198, down slope:

They were just finishing their hasty meal of MREs when their gas heater dimmed, sputtered, and quit. Despite the steady roar of the wind, the absence of the heater's soft hiss was painfully obvious.

"Okay," Cranston said. "All bets are off. It's time to make our move. Jerry, get on the chain saw."

"Right." Langsdorf scrambled to his feet and hefted the heavy saw.

"Fred, we need you to get the stretcher ready."

Fred nodded. "You got it." He managed to scramble up on the overturned console and pull himself through the overhead door.

"Wally, you help me with these two guys."

"Yeah."

The two of them got busy preparing to move Karl, who was still unconscious, while Langsdorf pulled on the saw's starter rope. He needed a dozen hard yanks and a lot of swearing before the frozen machine kicked over. It finally started amid a cloud of blue exhaust, and the roar of the storm was drowned out by the roar of the saw as it bit into the locomotive's roof.

§

Milepost 198, on the grade:

There are few tasks in the Maintenance of Way worse than digging snow. Between the cold and the endless wind and the sheer mass of frozen water to be moved, the work was tedious and miserable. One dilemma was whether to use the broad snow shovels, lifting massive weight with each scoop, or to rely on smaller regular shovels. Those weren't as unwieldy, but the work took far longer. Either way, the labor was back-breaking, and it didn't help that there weren't enough of either type to go round. Even the relatively fresh workmen were struggling, and everyone was concerned about some of the older men maybe suffering heart attacks. It'd happened before.

"This'll take forever," Parker Lee muttered. His people were in charge of digging the two cars out, and progress was painfully slow.

"We're moving again, finally," Earl said. "I was getting plum tuckered out from sleeping so much."

They were quiet for a time, each absorbed in their thoughts, before Parker glanced at the sky. "Damn!" He gestured at the breaking cloud cover overhead. "That don't seem right somehow."

Earl pondered the unusual sight of high, patchy clouds broken by patches of clear sky with stars shining faintly through. "This *is* a change of pace. I could get t' liking it."

Parker offered a snort of disgust. "Well don't get too comfortable with it; it won't last."

That about summed it up. Silence returned as they settled into their respective tasks, each of them determined to get the job done in the narrow window remaining, but neither of them holding out much hope.

§

Milepost 206, Truckee, California:

"You guys better watch your step," Dean said softly so, hopefully, Caruthers wouldn't overhear from the next room. "We got a real hatchet-man here, and he's having a hissy-fit. So if anything goes wrong up there, *don't* call it in!"

323

"Ah...yeah, copy that, Dean. Thanks for the heads-up."

Having done what he could to warn their people about the new broom from Omaha, Dean hung up the radio mic and concentrated on his manpower roster.

Caruthers appeared in his office door a moment later. "Did you get through to Milepost 201?"

"Um...yes, briefly. The communications are still pretty bad. They said they're making progress on the last car, and should have it cleared shortly."

That seemed to mollify Caruthers to a degree. "Good. I want to hear the moment they're clear. Also, have you had any luck contacting the work party at Shed 47?"

"Not as yet. This weather has jacked communications up something awful."

"That won't do, mister! I want to speak to whoever's in charge up there!"

Dean backtracked hastily. "I heard one of the relay towers was damaged in the last storm. We were hit with hurricane force winds up there. I'm sure a Signals unit is already responding to correct the problem."

"Lets hope so for their sake!" He gave Dean a stern look. "I want to hear from you as soon as you make contact." Having had his say Caruthers stomped off.

It took Dean a moment to realize his hands were shaking. This Caruthers was a holy terror, and Dean couldn't help but feel sorry for the roasting waiting for Jim Mortensen when he came breezing in in a few hours. One thing he already knew was the Union Pacific would soon be in the market for a number of new hires, and not just for grunt force, either. Dean sighed and went back to work on the radio. Tomorrow would be interesting, indeed.

§

Milepost 197, Snow Shed 47:

Gus returned to the office caboose where Walter was manning the radio in response to an urgent summons. "What you got, Walter?"

324

Walter offered him the radio mic. "It's Dean Nakamura, from Truckee. He says there's a new broom sweeping righteously in their shop."

"That a fact?" Gus grabbed the mic and settled comfortably on the corner of the radio desk. "This is Gus at Shed 47 to Truckee, over?"

"Hey Gus, Dean Nakamura here. I'm calling to get the word on your progress, and to give you the heads-up."

"Yeah, howdy Dean. We're doin' okay here. Any word from Mortensen?"

"He's due in a few hours. Right now we got a..."

There was a brief inaudible interruption, then a new voice came on line:

"This is Caruthers, from Omaha. What's going on up there? How soon will you get that Amtrak cleared?"

Not the right tone to take with Gus Vincincegorough! "We're doing fine and dandy except some *hot rock* keeps interrupting us on th' radio!" Gus snapped. "How soon we'll get done depends on how many interruptions we gotta put up with!"

That seemed to take Caruthers by surprise, as it took him a moment to respond:

"I'll have you know I'm a special representative from Omaha! I want the latest information on your rescue efforts!"

"Well for your *information*, we delivered th' relief supplies, rescuing th' two crewmen is under way, and we're putting th' last touches on gettin' the Amtrak ready t' go down th' Hill; all of it in a hurricane blizzard! And as for Omaha, unless you're prepared t' *special represent* a shovel I got no time for you! This is th' *rescue party* at Shed 47! Out!" He threw the mic down. "Only one way t' deal with them clowns," he said to Walter. "Tell 'em where t' get off!"

"He's an *official* clown, Gus; straight from Omaha," Walter said, dubiously.

"You got that right!"

§

Milepost 201, Horseshoe Curve:

Once the Truckee switcher left with the two passenger cars, the maintenance force went to work tidying up. First thing was an inspection of the track to be sure it wasn't damaged by the derailment. It wasn't long before they made an interesting find.

"Damn, that'd do it," Johansen muttered. The track gang foreman held what looked like the answer to the pretty riddle of this derailment: a flat piece of stone split in two, with deep gouges where the break occurred.

"Yeah. I found it right where th' wheel marks in th' ties start. It must-a lifted those two cars right off th' line."

"But how'd it get there?" That was a good question since the spot it was found in wasn't near any overhanging bluffs. It didn't seem likely it was put there by vandals, either.

"No idea," the foreman said. "Unless maybe it was wedged in the underbody gear of one of the cars and got shook out right there."

Johansen nodded ruefully. "I've heard of weirder shit happening. Damn! This was sheer dumb luck!"

"Dumb, yeah. Luck, I dunno." The foreman handed the two broken halves to Johansen. "Here: you get the trophy."

§

Milepost 142, Colfax, California:

"Hey, Murphy? You might wanna check out th' weather." One of the road crew assigned to a diesel doing temporary snow work between Roseville and Colfax jerked a thumb over his shoulder at the dorm entrance. "Looks like your break in these storms is playing out."

326

Murphy was weary enough by then that he merely gave the fellow a disgusted glare. "Yeah, that's what I'm hearing." He gestured at the small TV propped up on the sign-in desk:

"The latest report from the National Weather Service says that the incoming front is losing speed after combining with the storm front behind it. The combined front is already hitting San Francisco with heavy rain turning to snow and ice. This new storm is due to hit Sacramento shortly, and expected to reach the mountains within the hour. Due to the front's reduced speed, the Weather Service anticipates this new storm will last at least ten days, with severe flooding in the low-lying areas and as much as sixty inches of snow in the mountains."

"Damn! It never quits, does it?" the crewman muttered.

Murphy turned to confront him. "No, it don't, and neither do you. So get back on your rig and get t' humping. You got five feet of snow t' keep ahead of!"

The man grumbled something and left. Murphy sighed in resignation then headed for his office to warn Gus and his people up the Hill.

*****

Dawn:

Milepost 197, Snow Shed 47:

The work went on feverishly through the night as they raced against time and the weather, but there was so much to do that the first faint light of dawn filtering through the high clouds found the situation little improved.

"It looks like the weather's startin' t' turn down again, like Colfax said." Gus just returned from his rounds of the work site, and what he had to report wasn't pleasing. "Th' wind is picking up, and there are clouds off to the west. It don't look pretty."

"How long do we have?" Walter asked.

"I'd say another hour or so, maybe."

The end of their weather reprieve not only got things moving faster than ever, but also stirred controversy about how to proceed. They were pressed for time with the next storm pending, and knew they must leave the Pass in condition where they could keep it open through the worst the weather could do.

"So what are we gonna do about that train? How soon can we move it?"

"Hard t' say," Parker Lee said, reluctantly. "We still gotta dig them two cars out, not t' mention clearing the baggage car."

"That could take hours, and from what you say we don't have hours," Walter said to Gus.

"We'll have t' tip th' baggage car off th' line and dig them two cars free for as long as we can, then we'll have t' try dragging them clear."

"And hope they come down on th' rails! If they derail, we'll have a helluva mess t' clean up!"

"There is that." Walter mused on the dilemma. "But we got no choice if we're to reopen th' Hill."

"Yeah." Gus scowled at the uninviting prospect of a new derailment to clear up in what promised to be a godawful storm. "And we gotta worry about all them hurt people. If it comes down to it, we uncouple the derails and send the rest down to Truckee. We may have t' close the Pass until the storm clears."

"We're gonna have enough trouble getting Summit open again even if that train can be removed."

"Our priority is getting them passengers out, plus we still have t' get our guys up from those wrecked engines."

"What's keeping them, anyway?" Joey asked. "This weather's been good for the last several hours. We should'a heard somethin' by now."

Gus turned to Walter. "Have you tried calling them?"

"Yeah. They don't answer."

"Wonderful!" Parker grumbled. "It looks like Fred went to all that trouble for nothing. Should we try again?"

"I'm not happy about sending anyone down there," Gus said.

"Aside from them, what about us?" Earl asked. "We should pull everyone out, too. We're about used up."

"At least back down to Emigrant Gap," Walter said. "We can focus on getting th' spreader rerailed."

"Which puts us back to square one."

There was a period of brooding silence as they pondered a seemingly intractable problem. "It'll depend on how soon Truckee can clear them two derailed cars," Gus said at last.

"*If* they can get those cars cleared."

"They will...eventually. I guess it's a race t' see who gets here first: them or the weather."

§

Milepost 201, Horseshoe Curve:

While the brains in Shed 47 debated and the work gangs dug, Bret Johansen and his team were hard at it. With only one car left to rerail, they could sense that well deserved victory was within reach. All they had to do was lift the last car—and hope the crane would hold up for a few more minutes.

"How's it look?" Johansen asked the car foreman as his people threaded the lifting cables into place.

"We'll be ready in just a bit," he was told. "It all depends on whether *your* wreck will manage."

That was the question. The repaired drive gear was a desperate improvisation, and that wasn't the only problem with this beast.

329

Johansen and his lead mechanic poured their blood, sweat and tears into getting this wreck to function, and they knew it was iffy at best. One more lift...

The car toads finished connecting their turnbuckles and pulled clear. Their supervisor gave the rig a thorough once-over, then turned to Johansen. "She's all yours."

"Yeah. Here's hoping."

The crane's diesel was running rough, as always, as he took station at the controls. He exchanged anxious looks with his lead mechanic, then eased down on the lift drum handle. The diesel sputtered, wound up reluctantly, belching black smoke, and the take up drum started to reel the cable in.

§

Milepost 198, down slope:

The ear-splitting racket of private Langsdorf's chain saw quit abruptly, and there was a minor crash as part of the locomotive's cab roof fell to the floor. "There! That ought t' do it, Al."

"You took long enough," Chase grumbled.

"You ever try cutting sheet steel with a chain saw? It ain't easy." Langsdorf had cut part of the cab roof away to make an opening wide enough for them to slide the rigid Stokes stretcher out onto the snow pack. Wrestling that saw left him aching from the strain and vibration. He set the heavy saw down and turned to Corporal Cranston. "How're they doing?"

They weren't doing at all well, in fact, although he wasn't about to say so where they could hear. "They're okay for the moment, but we need to get them out-a here."

"Yeah," private Chase added. "I'd say it's now or never."

Cranston looked up at him with all the stern authority a twenty-two year old corporal could muster. "Then it better be now."

Fred peered in through the newly cut opening. "How you guys doing in there?"

"We're all set. Feed the stretcher through and we'll take the first guy out."

"Right. The weather's looking to turn bad again. Any word from up top?"

330

That reminded Cranston of the portable radio Fred brought down, and the fact that they hadn't heard anything from the rescuers on the grade above. He grabbed it...and discovered it was turned off. He'd done that from force of habit to save the batteries. "Dammit," he griped at his own carelessness as he fired it up again. "This is Rescue One to Shed 47. You guys hear us? Over?"

§

Milepost 197, Snow Shed 47:

"It's about time they showed up," Gus grumbled as he keyed his radio mic. "Yeah, this is the rescue party at Shed 47. Nice t' hear from you guys."

"Sorry. We've been kind of preoccupied. We're ready to bring your two guys up. You ready at your end? Over?"

"Yeah, we'll be ready. You need t' hustle up; this weather is starting t' go sour on us again."

"Copy that. We'll be ready with the first stretcher in a few minutes. Out."

"Damn! We may pull this off yet," Joey said.

Gus gave him a hard look. "Maybe, if we can keep ahead of this next storm. I need you t' pass the word along t' Parker Lee; we need a team t' haul that stretcher up."

"I'm on it," Joey muttered as he headed out.

§

Milepost 201, Horseshoe Curve:

"Alright, that's it!" Bret Johansen shouted and waved to the work party supervisor after the last car settled on the track. The heavy steel cables slackened, and the car toads set to removing them while his chief mechanic examined the car.

"It looks good," he reported at last. "There's some minor sheet metal damage, and that busted window, but the truck looks okay. I'd say we could put 'er right back t' work after a quick fixup."

"Good." Johansen could take the satisfaction of at least doing *his* job well and quickly. "Let's secure the crane and bring up th' switcher. We need t' get the Hill cleared."

According to the latest word from Truckee, a brace of diesels off the *'California Zephyr'*, annulled at Reno, were waiting in the yard to come up and grab the forward part of the Amtrak as soon as the Truckee yard switcher could get the last car off the main. Everything other than their crane was in the clear, medical was standing by in Truckee, and assets were in place to house the stranded passengers. Reading between the lines, this sudden burst of diligence suggested there was considerable heat from Omaha blowing on Jim Mortensen's head. Couldn't happen to a more deserving guy, in Johansen's opinion.

He watched for a bit as the last material was secured, then headed to the crew car to contact Gus Vincincegorough.

§

Milepost 198, down slope:

Langsdorf and Chase made a production of dragging the bulky Stokes stretcher through the cut-away opening while Cranston checked his patients once again. Karl needed to go first. He was semi-conscious and feverish, thrashing weakly from the pain of his injuries. "How's he doing, really?" Bobby mumbled.

Cranston gave him a measured look, wishing he had just one more morphine tab. "I think he'll make it," he said, softly. "But we need to get him out of here. How you doing?"

Bobby shifted a bit, and winced in pain. "I'll manage. Take care of him."

Even with the hole cut in the locomotive's roof, it took a lot of effort for the four of them to wrestle the Stokes stretcher and their first casualty out onto the open slope. Once outside, Cranston climbed up on the locomotive's pilot and scanned the lower slope anxiously for any sign of DeBeers. Nothing. The snow stopped for the moment, and the cloud cover was thinning. There was a fleeting patch of blue sky, but the sky to the west was dark with new clouds sweeping in. There was no time to hang around if they were going to get these two out of here, and it didn't look like they'd be able to come back and search for him. He felt an ugly pang of regret, but there was nothing they could do. They had urgent matters to attend to.

Langsdorf must have shared his misgivings. "What about the sarge?" he asked, softly.

Cranston searched the lower slope again, then pondered that ugly western sky. "There's nothing we can do," he said at last. "We got to make a move before that shit hits."

"I sure as hell don't like the look of it!" Chase gestured to the scudding clouds, the first outliers of the oncoming storm. The sky was lowering again, and the wind was picking up. They didn't have much time.

Langsdorf wasn't happy, but he could see the obvious. They had two critical cases, not to mention saving their own hides, and precious little time. If they didn't get out now, these two would likely die waiting for the next storm to pass. Their chances wouldn't be good either.

"We're all set, Al," Chase said. The dragline was attached to the stretcher, and they were ready to guide it up-slope.

There was nothing he could do. As much as leaving DeBeers somewhere out there pained him, he had his duty. He was in command of a team caught hip deep in a life-or-death crisis. He needed to save what he could.

"Right. We abandon everything except what we need to get back up to the railroad, and we move now." For the first time in his young life, he felt the true weight of command; it was an ugly feeling which bore on his soul.

That sky wasn't going to wait. He climbed down and grabbed the walkie-talkie. "Rescue One to Shed 47, we're ready to bring the first casualty up." Langsdorf and Chase hesitated for a long moment as they absorbed the situation, then turned to without a further word.

§

Milepost 197, Snow Shed 47:

"Good work, rescue! We're ready for him." Gus's relief at the pending rescue was interrupted by another radio call:

333

"This is the Truckee wrecker to Shed 47.   You there Gus? Over?"

Gus keyed his mic. "Yeah, Bret. How's it going at your end? Over?"

"We got the last car rerailed and on its way down. We should be able to retrieve your train within a couple hours. Over?"

"Good work, Bret! Thanks a lot."
"Well: they did it!" Walter said, admiringly.
"Yeah. Now we'll find out if th' damned train can be moved or not."

§

Milepost 198, on the grade:

As tired as the Gandy Dancers were, a dozen of them turned to eagerly to haul on the drag line bringing the stretcher up from the wrecked locomotives. The sun broke through the thinning cloud cover briefly as the National Guardsmen brought the first stretcher up to the grade. It seemed like a final, brief Benediction to the weary work crews.

"How's he look?" Gus asked Doctor Cummings as he examined Karl's injuries.

Cummings straightened up and turned to the anxious faces crowded around them. "Broken ribs, a punctured lung, blood loss and hypothermia; he needs to get to down the Hill right away. He's in bad shape, but he should recover." He carefully tucked in the thermal blanket. "Let's get him in where it's warm."

"Put him on the 'City' train. The line is clear, and they'll be moving shortly."

Doctor Cummings gave him a curious look.   "They will? Good! It's none too soon for some of our critical cases." He led the National Guards and some track men back to the dining car with the stretcher.

"Welcome back to th' living," Gus said to Fred.

334

"Yeah, thanks. That was a bad scene down there."

"Okay, we'll leave this t' them National Guards. You report to Earl; we're gonna wrap this up ASAP."

§

Milepost 201, Horseshoe Curve:

About an hour later, two large Amtrak road units hove into view and stopped where Johansen waited for them. "I see the heat's on down in Truckee," he greeted the crewmen.

"You know it!" the engineman said with obvious satisfaction. "There's a smoldering crater where the Maintenance of Way office used t' be. I heard Operations, in Reno, caught some flak too."

"We were told to shag our butts up here, PDQ," the second engineman added. "Some big-shot came in from Omaha, and things are a whole lot-a humpin' down in Truckee all of a sudden."

"Good! There's been too much slackness around here lately."

"So where's your train?"

"It's right at Tunnel 13." Johansen climbed up into the cab; the two crewmen gave him curious looks. "I want t' see this damned train, after all the hassle we went through t' rescue them!"

The engineman nodded and released the brakes. "You got it."

§

Milepost 198, down slope:

Bobby was semi-conscious when the rescuers came back for him. "How you doing?" Cranston asked.

It took all his concentration to focus on answering. "Hurts. Gotta...take a leak..."

"Alright. We got your pal to safety, and now we're gonna take care of you. We'll have you up topside shortly."

Bobby mulled that over wearily. "Good. Wanna get warm."

"Soon enough, my friend." Cranston carefully tucked the thermal blanket around Bobby as they gently loaded him into the stokes. By then Bobby was out of it from pain, cold and fatigue. He was only vaguely aware of being hoisted out through the hole in the locomotive's roof, and the long slow trek up to the grade.

§

Milepost 197, Snow Shed 47:

Despite their best efforts over the last several hours the first two Amtrak cars were only partly cleared of the wall of snow inundating them.

"We're making good progress," Walter reported to Gus in the office caboose. We won't beat th' weather, but I think we're good enough t' haul those two cars clear."

"Good! There's some road power on its way. Hopefully we can clean this up, then we can get the *hell* out-a here." He turned his attention to Joey, who was monitoring the rescue effort. "How's it going?"

"Pretty good." Joey was monitoring one of the National Guard walkie-talkies. "They should bring the second guy up any time now."

"Right." He turned back to Walter. "Start getting our gear loaded. I want us to move ASAP once the train is gone."

Joey looked up in confusion. "What? They're here already?" The way he said that made their departure seem anticlimactic.

"They will be soon enough." He followed Walter out onto the caboose's platform. "Bring up the bulldozer t' shove that baggage car clear, then get everything else secured, and load up everyone we don't need for the moment. I want as much of a head start on this weather as we can get."

"Right." Walter headed back to the work site.

"Hey Gus?" Joey called after them. "They're on the way up with the second crewman."

§

Milepost 198, on the grade:

A few minutes later the second stretcher was hauled up to the right-of-way with Corporal Cranston roped to it in turn.

"Well thank heaven you finally got 'em out!" Gus said, fervently. "How's he doing?"

Bobby stirred faintly. "I been worse," he whispered.

"Okay, let's take him back to the *third* car, that's the first one all the way on the rails."

336

The three National Guards, helped by some of the work crew, hefted the stretcher and headed down the lea side of the train. The third car was the diner; the two casualties were laid on the floor since Doctor Menendez didn't want to risk trying to haul them up the narrow stairway to the upper level. At least they were warm for the first time in days.

"What about our sarge?" Cranston asked Gus. "He's still down there somewhere."

"Yeah." Gus had some bad news for them. "We got word from the Highway Patrol a little while ago; he made it all the way down to the lake. He must have been tryin' to find refuge in one of the summer cabins down there. A snow plow found him layin' in the road."

That hurt, even though Cranston was expecting it, even though they all knew the risks of this duty. "He made it further than I figured," was all he could think of to say.

§

Milepost 198, Aboard the 'City Of San Francisco':

"Hey! There's a train coming!" Someone in the last car pointed to a light approaching from behind. That set off a minor stampede as excited passengers crowded to the rear of the car trying to get a look. Except for a lucky few they couldn't see much since only one small window faced the rear. Still, the glow of the approaching headlight shone brightly off the snow, filling the car.

O'Brian was soon drawn from the next car, wondering what all the commotion was about. People were laughing, shouting, weeping, hugging each other in a riot of relief that their long ordeal was nearly over.

Once O'Brian understood what was going on, he keyed his portable. "Reggie? George? The rescue is here from Truckee! We're going home!"

"Well Glory-fuckin'-Hallelujah. Took 'em long enough!"

§

337

Milepost 198, on the grade:

The leading locomotive ground to a halt about twenty feet from the last Amtrak car, then crawled slowly ahead until the couplers touched. It took about five minutes to hook up the brake hoses and power lines, and they were ready to go.

"We still gotta uncouple the baggage car," Reinsbach told the engineman. "It's sitting cattywumpus across the track; there's no chance of rerailing it."

"Okay," the engineman said. "But let's get this done before you're snowed in, if you aren't already." The weather was closing down fast; already the light was fading and the air was hazy with blowing snow.

"Yeah, well, speaking of snowed in, the first two cars, at the far end, are undermined by the slide. You'll have t' drag 'em out and hope they come down on th' track."

"Why am I not surprised?" The engineman sighed. "Alright, let's get to it and hope for the best."

§

Milepost 198, on the grade:

"Locomotives to Shed 47, we're hooked up at this end. You can cut the baggage car loose."

This was welcome news to the weary men who spent so much time and labor to get this far, but the struggle wasn't quite done yet. Earl, who was supervising at the wreck site, keyed his portable. "Ah, copy that, engines. Give us a few while we make arrangements."

"So what's the drill?" Fred asked.

Earl pondered the scene before him. The battered wreck of the baggage car was hardly worth trying to salvage, and with the delicate situation on the slopes above, they couldn't take any unnecessary risks. Get it done, quick and clean. Right.

"We'll wait until those two crewmen are in the clear, then we'll shove this car off the line. Everyone else will be back in the snow shed by then."

338

The bulldozer was already crawling toward them and Parker Lee was sorting out his people and sending some to the rear. The sky was turning ugly, and the wind was already starting to pick up. There was snow in the air; light for now, but no one expected anything less than the worst Donner Pass could deliver. "Yeah, right," Fred said. He looked the last two passenger cars over, and was not pleased. "What about those two?" Both cars were still leaning hard over, their undersides packed with snow from the original avalanche. At least the last several hours' work had cleared much of the snow banked up against their sides.

"We're out of time for digging." Earl paused to ponder the oncoming storm, which was not a pretty sight. "We'll have t' risk trying t' roll 'em back on the rails."

"Whatever we do, we best do it now. We should send the last of our people back t' the snow shed."

"Right." Earl keyed his portable again. "We're getting set t' cut the baggage car loose as soon as the last of our men are under cover. It'll be a few minutes. After that the diesels'll have t' pull the train clear."

"Locomotives, we copy."

"Okay Fred, we're on the home stretch now." Make sure all th' work crew get safely back to th' barn. Then we'll have th' bulldozer deal with that baggage car."

"You got it." The wind whipped at them as he turned to go.

§

Clearing the baggage car off the right of way proved more of a challenge than anyone expected. A brief examination showed the coupler twisted out of shape by the tremendous force of the avalanche, which wasn't surprising: the one at the other end was ripped bodily out. It should have been a simple matter to pull the cut bar, but when Parker Lee tried it, the coupler was jammed. They tried prying the locking pin loose with a pry bar, but there was no luck.

"Alright," he said at last. "We'll have t' bring up a gas torch and *cut* th' sucker off!"

That took time which they really didn't have between the lowering skies and the risk of another avalanche. By time the bulldozer brought up the gas torch the new storm was already building in its fury.

The worst of the snow pack holding the two passenger cars had been cleared, so it was hoped the two diesels could drag them out by main force. Everyone fell back to Shed 47 while Parker took charge of the torch and started in. It took several minutes before the steel was hot enough to start cutting. Once it did, Parker worked methodically around the coupler shank, keeping a wary eye on it so he could jump aside when it let go. The last part of the shank deformed under the strain, then parted. The electrical conduit which kept the train supplied all this time whipped wildly, causing him to duck, and the baggage car slid down slope with a deep metallic groan. Parker hastily shut the torch off and retreated behind the last passenger car, waiting several minutes before deciding there wouldn't be another slide.

"Well, I guess we won't be needing the bulldozer after all," he muttered to himself.

§

Gus and his people gathered to decide what came next. Their brief Benediction of sunshine was gone as new clouds swept in over the pass. Already the new snow was building up, obscuring features on the ground, and the outlying streamers of cloud were at grade level or below.

"Word from Colfax is this next one's gonna be a mutherfucker," Gus said. "We got what we need, so as soon as the Amtrak clears we'll get out-a here while the gettin's good."

"What about the right of way?" Fred asked. "We've come this far, can't we finish the job and get the Hill open again?"

Parker stared into the distance for a time as his exhaustion overcame him. The view of the slopes was fading as the wind blown snow grew heavier. "We're in no shape fo' it. The men are exhausted, we're low on supplies, and that spreader needs t' be recovered. In any case, we can't take any more risks."

Fred sagged and rubbed his eyes with a weary sigh. "We're giving up, huh?"

"We have to," Walter said. "There's no way we can fight this weather. Corporate'll just have to make do without the Hill, I guess."

"The *hell* we will!" Gus shook his fists at them. "This is *our* railroad! I don't care *how* bad the snow is, we *will* keep the Hill open!"

"But how? We're exhausted, we need t' reorganize, the equipment needs servicing too."

"And we need more people," Fred added. "We need at least a hundred new hires if we're to keep up."

"And we gotta get the 221 and that spreader out of the shops, too."

Gus glared at them, his anger boiling down to the cold resolve which made him famous as a snow fighter. "Then we'll *get* reorganized. We'll *get* stuff fixed. We'll *get* new hires. We'll bring gear and people in from wherever we can find 'em. We may have t' lay off for a few days, but we'll be back. *Nothing* closes the Hill!"

§

Milepost 197, Snow Shed 47:

"I'll be thankful when this is over," Trudy said as she dropped the latest dishes in the sink.

"You're not the only one," Margret grumbled. "We could all use a rest." She was parked on a stool at the kitchen car's work table nursing a mug of hot soup. "I hope t' tell you I am *sick* to *death* of snow! I'll be glad when this winter's over."

Trudy set her dishrag aside and confronted her. "Remember how it was last summer? Six months from now you'll be longing for a bit of cold weather." Margret winced at the reminder about last summer's miserable, relentless heat. "It took you *forever* to get over that sunburn, remember?"

Margret sighed at the thought of the perpetual tormenting rash she developed. The sun at these higher elevations can be treacherous. "Yeah. This weather's going t' hell all round."

"It sure is." Trudy was already thinking of what next summer's fire season would be like. "We can't win, can we?"

§

341

Milepost 198, on the grade:

It's amazing how eighty-eight hundred horsepower of high-performance diesels can exert such a delicate touch to eight hundred tons of train, but the Amtrak crewmen were nothing if not good. The two locomotives rumbled and spewed exhaust, and the 'City Of San Francisco' reluctantly shifted. Gus and a few of the leadership defied the risk to witness the fruits of their long struggle, watching anxiously as the last two cars broke loose from the blizzard's icy grip. Their efforts to dig them out were only partly successful, but the weather was closing in fast. They were out of time, so they needed to take chances. The train crept backward with endless grinding and moaning sounds. The last two cars gradually slid off the piled snow and settled on the track. For a miracle, they hadn't derailed.

The car toads checked the two cars out briefly, then, almost without anyone noticing it, Amtrak 15 slowly moved back toward Tunnel 13, finally disappearing from view in the distance. Gus and Parker Lee watched the train vanish with solid satisfaction.

"Mission accomplished," Gus said at last.

"Feels damned good, don't it?" Parker added.

Gus pondered the emptiness where the 'City of San Francisco' was stalled for so long. "Yeah, it does." he said at last. The wind tore at them, flinging heavy wet snow in their faces. "Let's go home."

§

Milepost 197, Snow Shed 47:

"Doc Cummings, here, tells me you two are fit to return t' duty." Dan and Jesus were summoned to the office caboose a short time later to receive news which really was no surprise. "We'll be moving out shortly, so I want you two on the rotary."

"What about Margret?" Dan asked.

"She's been on duty since you two went down. I want my best men in that cab." No surprise, but unpleasant news nonetheless. Returning to the chilly cab of the rotaries was a poor second best to a comfortable bunk under warm covers on sick pay.

"That's gonna be a helluva trip," Dan griped. "How long's it been since the line was cleared last?"

"Too long," Jesus mumbled. "We be up against it, even with our rotary."

"Well the alternative is to hole up here for the winter and freeze," Gus snapped. "If you guys can't do it, who can?" His tone softened; these were two weary, worn out men facing another brutal trick on the Hill. "I know we can count on you. You'll get us through to Colfax."

Dan fought off a jawbreaking yawn. "Maybe we'll get some sleep, then." Without a further word he and Jesus headed for their rotary.

§

"Shit, what a miserable job," Fred grumbled as the last of his section gang boarded the camp cars. "All we can say is we broke even, and the line is in lousy shape."

"We got everyone out alive," Walter said. "It wasn't for nothing. We'll be back; the Hill won't whip us."

Fred sighed. "Yeah. Whatever." Right then he was so weary he just didn't care any more. Now that the crisis was passed, he was confronted with what Emigrant Gap must be like after being abandoned for four days. Those turnouts would be unworkable, and on top of *everything* else, they would have to clear away that spreader so the wrecker could come in and haul it out. All of it in a blizzard expected to last a week or more. "Shit," he muttered.

§

Rotary 207 was the first to move out, sending a thick arc of snow flying to one side as they went.

The work train followed the rotary after a few minutes, moving slowly to let them get ahead, the gandy dancers already celebrating their victory with a hot meal and exhausted slumber. The last to leave was the National Guard armored personnel carrier, crawling carefully along straddling one of the rails. The sound of the big EMD diesels faded into the distance and finally ended, leaving nothing but a trampled right-of-way covered with spilled diesel and bits of trash. Quiet returned for the first time in four days, leaving nothing but the whistling wind.

The wind blew from the west, clean and chill. The sky darkened, and the clouds sank down to the right of way once again as the next blizzard came rolling in from the Pacific. The temperature dropped and the landscape became obscured as the wind picked up, creating a blinding fog of blown snow. The world was silent, etherial, save for the steady moaning of the wind. The Big Snow came down, light at first, but quickly building into a deluge, even drifting under the end of Snow Shed 47, accumulating steadily. Soon the trash and spills, the trampled footprints, the forlorn baggage car, even the rails themselves—every hint of mans' presence in Donner Pass—were obliterated under a coat of pristine white.

*****

Epilogue:

The platform at Truckee was lined with emergency vehicles and, despite the ongoing snow, mobile TV news trucks when the tattered remnants of the 'City Of San Francisco' arrived.

"God...we made it," Reggie mumbled as the train ground to a halt with what seemed an all too human groan.

"Yeah, and we're famous, too." O'Brian waved vaguely at the glowing fog of TV klieg lights. "They look hungry."

"Gawd, this is the *last* thing we need right now!"

"Yeah, well you better suck it up. Your fifteen minutes of fame is coming right down on you."

Reggie stared for a bit until the thought registered on his tired mind. "Fame? Hell, I'll settle for a hot bath and a good night's sleep."

"In Miami."

"Hmph."

Reinsbach joined them just then. "Helluva mess out there." He watched the swirling snow for a bit, his own exhaustion showing all too clearly. "We need t' get started. We'll evacuate our seriously wounded first, then the less serious injuries, then the rest of them."

"Yeah, well before you do that, you'll have to deal with the reporters." O'Brian gestured at the seething lights and the press of figures vague in the gloom.

"Shit," Reinsbach grumbled. "That's the *last* thing we need right now." From the look of things, a stampede was in the offing. He turned to Reggie. "I could use some help with this. Gimme some backup, huh?"

"Hey, you're the conductor, you're the captain of this train, it's your problem."

Reinsbach gave him a hard look. "Coward."

"I'm too damned tired to be a coward."

The riot was starting in the background. "I'm no damned PR flack!" There was a hint of panic in his voice.

"You're the 'Public Face of Amtrak'." Reggie gestured at the oncoming rush of klieg lights. "Your public awaits. Besides, the trip is over so I'm signing off on the law as of right now."

Reinsbach glowered at him. "*You're a cold one!*"

§

Having thrown Reinsbach to the wolves, Reggie and the others started the evacuation with the help of the local fire and rescue volunteers who were equipped to take the seriously injured down the narrow stairway to the lower level. Their worst—the old lady with the broken hip, their two head injuries, and the two Amtrak crewmen—went first, followed one at a time by the others, helped gingerly along by the medics. Barbara's long vigil had paid off: everyone survived, and now there was plenty of help at hand.

Once the injured were down the narrow stairway, getting them into the ambulances and on their way to the local hospital—escorted by a caravan of news trucks—was fairly easy. The injured, even the severe cases, took the hassle calmly, thankful their ordeal was finally over.

"We have a problem," Doctor Cummings reported a few minutes into the effort. "That pregnant woman is into active labor; I don't want to try moving her in her present state."

"Of course," Reggie sighed. "Why the hell not? It fits."

"She's stable enough to remain here until after the delivery," Cummings said. "I can monitor her for now. The rest of you focus on getting the other casualties offloaded." He headed back to the next car and his patient.

"Hell...we'd need a forklift t' move her anyway," O'Brian grumbled.

§

Milepost 142, Colfax, California:

It seemed like forever before the parade made its way to Colfax, where rotary 207 paused momentarily to drop Dan and Jesus, leaving Margret to take the consist on into Roseville. The only way they could tell they'd reached their destination was the GPS unit and two hi-rails parked on either side of track two shining their headlights into the gloom. The weather was abysmal.

This new storm—or was this the old one? There was no way to tell. Did it matter?—the storm was going like gangbusters: total white-out conditions and a howling gale force wind which cut them like icy knives.

They stood at trackside peering about uncertainly as the rotary moved on. "This is some kind-a shit!" Dan yelled over the wind.

"*¡Si, amigo!* Thank God we be out of it soon!"

A figure came looming out of the whiteness: Murphy, following a rope tied to one of the hi-rails. "Come on!" he yelled. He shepherded them back down the rope to the entrance of the crew dorm, where they were finally able to speak.

"Helluva show, huh?" he griped as he shook the snow off his coat and boots. "If it's like this here, I hate t' think what it must-a been like up there."

Dan gave him a bleary-eyed glare. "God, Murph, you got no idea, no clue."

"It was hell, *amigo*," Jesus added, somberly.

"So I hear." Murphy pondered them for a long moment, noting their utterly beaten, worn down postures and vacant thousand-yard stares. These two were used up. He'd seen that look far too often lately. "You two look like hell."

It took Dan more effort to ponder it through his exhaustion than he could spare. "Yeah. We went ten rounds with th' Hill. It wasn't pretty."

Murphy nodded. "Right. You two are on the sick list until further notice. Get some hot chow and I'll have someone take you over to th' hospital."

"They need to recover the spreader," Jesus protested.

"Yeah, but that's not your problem." Murphy frowned at the memory. At least they would soon be rid of Davy Burns. "That's sumpthin' for Roseville t' deal with. You two are out of it for now, so count your blessings."

Dan nodded wearily and headed for the cafeteria. "Thank God for small favors," he muttered to himself.

"Yeah, man-o. Maybe we get some sleep now, huh?"

"Hell, I'll settle for being warm!"

§

Milepost 206, Truckee, California:

Conductor Reinsbach finally managed to escape the clutches of the press and turned up in the dining car as the last of the injured were being readied to go. "Gawd, I'm glad t' be out of *that!*" He gave Reggie a venomous look. "I almost wished we were back up there on the Hill, no thinks to you!"

"Yeah, sorry. Gotta cover ass, ya know. Hey, d'you have an extra hat?"

Reinsbach eyed him uncertainly. "Yeah. Why?"

Reggie jerked a thumb at Charlie Parkhurst and Barbara, who were attending to the last injured despite their obvious exhaustion. "Those two were a huge help during this mess. I made them a promise I'd like t' keep." Barbara was trying Reggie's spare hat on the two children in the group while Parkhurst took pictures and offered witty comments to lighten their mood.

Reinsbach pondered them for a bit, then headed for the crew dorm. "I'll be right back."

§

Milepost 107, Roseville Shops, California:

The wrecker ground to a halt, the switchman reset the points, and it was backed onto the siding near the shops. Even before it came to rest, the track gangs were peeling off and heading either to the crew dorm or, in a few foolhardy cases, for their cars.

"Damn, it's good t' be home!" Walter said as they climbed down from the office caboose. He paused and turned to Gus. "Sorry we weren't able to use the big hook; it was just too risky."

"Not a problem," Gus assured him. "But we need t' think long and hard on how we're gonna do this stuff from now on if this weather keeps up."

"You got that right! We need a whole new game plan. So how soon do we go after the spreader at Emigrant Gap?"

Gus pondered for a long moment, watching the snow as it swirled around them. "As soon as we can. If this storm doesn't break soon, we'll have t' go after it anyway. We need it back in action, and we need t' get the Hill opened again."

348

"Yeah. I'd say we likely move as soon as we get rotary 211 back from the shops."

Gus nodded. "That's a plan. Get your train serviced, and tell your people to be ready at a moment's notice. We'll start t' reclaim the Hill shortly."

They didn't notice one figure standing next to the crew car as they headed for the shop building. Ernesto watched them pass until they faded into the swirling blizzard, then turned and headed for his pickup parked nearby. There was nothing left to say.

§

Milepost 206, Truckee, California:

Once the injured were taken away by ambulances along with Doctor Menendez and Jamie Kirk, the uninjured passengers were herded into school busses bound for temporary lodging at railroad expense at the numerous ski resorts in the area. This influx was welcome news for local tourism hard-hit by the environmental crisis, although word was Omaha was wetting themselves over the cost, and Amtrak was feeling heat clear over in faraway Washington DC.

They were just wrapping up the last details when Charlie Parkhurst brought the latest word from Doctor Cummings: mission accomplished. Olivia Bumarris had delivered their newest passenger.

§

"Mother and baby are doing fine," Doctor Cummings informed the stampede when they arrived. "Give her a few hours rest, and we can transport her."

"Good," Reinsbach said. "They're taking the consist on to Sparks for overhaul; we can unload them in Reno."

Franklin was fidgeting in anticipation. "How is she, doc? Can I see her?"

§

Olivia Bumarris practically filled the compartment, threatening to spill off the narrow bed onto the floor. She was covered with an Amtrak issued blanket and was busily consuming a sandwich from the dining car.

"How do you feel, dearest?" he asked gently as he knelt by her side.

She finished her sandwich and gave him a dreamy smile. "The same as usual. You worry too much, love. I've got this down to a routine by now."

"I'm sorry we weren't able to get home in time so you could go to the hospital."

"It's not your fault, love, there was nothing we could do about the delays. But next time we'll stay home so there won't be any slip-ups. Your family can visit *us* for a change."

Franklin was embarrassed. "I'm...ah...maybe we shouldn't assume anything...seeing how many we already have..."

She gave him a sardonic look. "You forget I know you, you horny old coot! This won't be our last, I'm sure."

Franklin blushed. "Ah...well...I..."

Barbara returned just then from the next compartment, where she was using their restroom to clean up, and presented Franklin a tiny, wiggling bundle wrapped in a bath towel. "Congratulations," she said to him. "It's a girl."

Franklin's face fell. "Another one?" he mumbled.

Olivia turned to him with fire in her eye. "What d'you mean *'another one'*? I'll 'another one' *you*, you ungrateful whelp!"

Barbara took that as her cue to hand him the infant, herd the rest outside, and shut the door, leaving the happy couple to sort out their differences.

§

"God, I'll be glad when this is over," Reggie sighed once they were safely out in the corridor. "This has been one hell of a trip!"

"It's all over but the paperwork," O'Brian griped as he sagged against the bulkhead.

"Don't remind me!" Both of them were tottering from exhaustion. "There'll be hell 't pay for this mess!"

"Well, hey, you had some bad luck, is all," Parkhurst said. "It's a shame your train got banged up, but they can't blame you for the weather."

"Yes," Barbara added. "You pulled us through the worst of it. That has to count for something."

"Yeah, you're right," Reggie muttered. "We did our part. Where it's gonna come down is on the snow crews, I'll bet."

"But do we get a medal or th' chest t' pin it on?" O'Brian wondered.

Reggie fought off a yawn and rubbed his aching eyes. "At least we'll get plenty of down time. At best it'll take days t' get this schedule up again."

"Hell, I'll settle for that instead!"

They wound down through mutual exhaustion then, too weary to say or do anything more, leaving nothing but the faint hum of the train's systems. After a moment, the silence was punctuated by a shrill bellow; they were drawn in spite of themselves to the 'discussion' among the Bumarris family in the compartment next to them.

"So," Parkhurst mused as they listened to the tirade coming through the thin bulkhead. "The fat lady sings."

The End

*****

Postscript:
Some Thoughts On Climate Change

One question which plagued the men in this work of fiction was just exactly why 'global warming' could produce so *much* snow. It's counter-intuitive—one would think it would be exactly the opposite. But those who are confused shouldn't be embarrassed: the enigma escapes many intelligent people.

In simple terms, warmer oceans evaporate more easily, loading the air with moisture. With the melting of the polar ice caps, this moisture comes not only from the North Pacific, but from the vast Arctic Ocean and the Canadian tundra as well. Warm oceans are also the engine driving storms and hurricanes. Such a large-scale warming of the oceans means more evaporative surface, more moisture in the air, more heat to drive the engine, and thus more energetic weather. It's that simple.

Nature can absorb much of this temperature rise. Like all living things, the biosphere can adapt. But, like all living things, the biosphere can only take so much. Our weather is the result of a complex relationship of atmospheric, oceanic and terrestrial factors. It works the way it does because of the present balance of forces. Rising temperatures can upset that balance, triggering a chain reaction with devastating and unpredictable results.

Can these events really happen? Yes, of course they can, if the right circumstances occur. True, the biosphere is vast and its elements trend toward stability. But now a new factor threatens the health of our world: we humans. We have grown so numerous, and consume so much that we are altering the ecosystem. The evidence is all around us, and those who are wise do not dispute it. We are starting to repair the damage, but will our feeble efforts be enough? Can we stop the disaster in time?

This is hard to say. As was noted before, the biosphere can absorb a lot of damage, but there will come a tipping point where it all falls apart. How close we are to that tipping point—no one knows. The biosphere, for all its grandeur, is a fragile thing. Once it is ruined, there will be no turning back. It is a very real question whether we will survive in such a changed environment.

The all-time record for snowfall in Donner Pass is 884 inches —73 feet, 8 inches—and it was an unmitigated disaster. As in this novel, the real 'City Of San Francisco' became trapped, setting off an all-hands rescue effort which went on for days.

One critical difference between the winter of '55-'56 and today is the railroads have chronically reduced their snow fighting capability, relying instead on an aggressive policy of attacking any snowfall before it can accumulate. That may work for ordinary times, but it is a recipe for trouble if their calculations are upset. This scaling back is understandable since most wrecking and snow fighting equipment was built in the steam era, and can only be rebuilt so many times. But in an age of global warming, such blind optimism can lead to disaster.

The weather has always been hard to predict, driven as it is by never-ending combinations of environmental conditions, but there's nothing to say these events couldn't come to pass. It will be a national nightmare if it does, but who can say?

What we can be sure of is no matter how deep the snow or how bitter the wind, the Maintenance of Way crews will be out there fighting to uphold the time-honored tradition that the trains will always get through.

*****

Addenda:

Railroad Terms:

Balloon Track:
A loop of track which turns back on itself, used to turn equipment around.

Big Hook:
Heavy duty rail mounted wrecking crane.

Crew caller:
A supervisor who keeps track of available crew personnel and assigns them to various duties.

Car Toads:
Slang for rolling stock repairmen.

Crossover:
A set of turnouts designed to transfer a train between parallel tracks on the run; used to improve traffic flow by allowing trains to pass each other under the best conditions.

Dead on the law:
Train crews are legally limited to no more than 12 hours on duty, after which they are said to be 'dead' until they've had a chance to sleep.

Extra board:
The list of crew personnel with low enough seniority that they aren't assigned a regular duty, and have to take various odd assignments as needed.

Flanger:
A snow removal car fitted with small plows underneath to clear show from between the rails; often used for light snow removal or to back up a spreader to clear where they missed.

FRA

The Federal Railroad Administration; the government agency which regulates the railroad industry.

Fuzee

A bright pyrotechnic flare used as a signaling device. Also used for lighting in extreme conditions.

Gandy Dancer (or just 'dancer'):

Archaic term for track maintenance workmen.

Go for Beans:

Pause for food.

Head End:

The crew in the locomotive at the front (head end) of a passenger train; also the cars at the front of a train.

Head End Power:

Electric power supplied by the locomotives for heat, light, etc.

Helper Engine:

One or more locomotives assigned to a local base to help trains over especially steep grades. Trains on Donner Pass might have as many as a dozen modern locomotives assigned to them.

High iron

Slang term for primary main lines which are built with heavier rail, as distinct from sidings and yard trackage.

Hi-rail Trucks:

Standard motor vehicles equipped with extendable railroad wheels to run on the tracks; used by Maintenance of Way forces.

Points:

The moving parts of a turnout, activated either by a hand crank or remote control, which alter a train's course.

Rotary Snow Plow:

The 'big guns' of snow removal; these machines have a rotating blade in front to scoop snow up and throw it to one side.

Snow Shed:

A structure made of wood or concrete built over a track to protect it from avalanches or to protect key turnouts.

Spreader:

A snow removal car fitted with wide steel wings which can be set to shove snow clear of the right of way; the most widely used snow removal equipment.

SRO:

Standing Room Only; a condition not seen on passenger trains since the lean, high-traffic years of World War 2.

Torpedo:

An explosive device placed on a rail to give an audible warning when run over to trains approaching some unseen danger.

Trick:

A shift on duty, generally twelve hours, although the time actually worked may vary if an assignment is completed early.

Turnout:

A special piece of track which can be set to route a train in either of two directions. These are very susceptible to blockage with snow or ice, and much effort goes into keeping them cleared.

Wye:

A triangular track formation used to turn equipment around.

*****

A Brief Note From The Author

Thank you for reading this novel, which was a pleasant change of pace in my writing. I hope it was a good read for you. I would love to hear from you, my readers, to let me know how I am doing as an author. Every bit of input helps me to make my next effort a better product for your enjoyment.

All my best,

Bob Boyd

You can learn more about me, and keep up to date on my efforts through our Facebook Blog:

Facebook.com/The Written Wyrd

*****

Titles from The Written Wyrd
2017

The Diplomacy Trilogy - Science fiction humor.

First contact from the aliens' perspective in a trio of lurid tell-all memoirs written by a team of alien diplomats sent to earth to open an embassy.

The MacKenna Trilogy - Science fiction military drama.

He was earth's greatest soldier; they needed his skills once more, but they didn't realize how wrong bringing him back from the dead was.

Nature's Way - Environmental disaster / apocalyptic horror.

This is the last day of our last stand against Nature out for revenge!

Trial - Science fiction political thriller.

The aliens demand justice for their murdered ambassador while right wing extremists plot revolution; which is the greater threat?

Overland - Period science fiction drama / romance.

He was trapped between a beautiful genetically enhanced revolutionary from the distant future and the inhuman monster sent to destroy her. Can he survive caught up in their titanic battle?

Playing God - Apocalyptic horror.

Brenda discovers she is the Dream Girl of a mad scientist capable of altering the past. Can she find a way to undo the disaster he wrought and prevent a nuclear holocaust?

The Big Snow - Environmental disaster / adventure.

A passenger train is wrecked at the top of Donner Pass in the worst storms in recorded history. Can the railroaders get the passengers to safety?

(continued)

Young Adult Demi-Novels:

Diplomacy's Children - YA humor / adventure.
A young alien space fleet recruit faces his greatest challenge in a self-centered, foul-tempered human youngling he is ordered to keep in check.

Star Flight - YA adventure.
She was an outcast, cursed with supernatural powers.   She was offered a reprieve, a chance to start over, but could she survive the challenge?

Short Story Anthologies:

Deus Ex Machina - Humorous fantasy short story collection.
From bungling wizards to moronic barbarians to redneck elves, here are the old tales of epic adventure as we would love to see them told - just once.

Ghoulish Good Fun - Macabre short story collection.
Reality is a cruel practical joke. Laugh along with it if you dare!

*****

Available in print and Kindle from Amazon,
and in PDF and ePub downloads from Smashwords.
Visit our web site for details.

http://www.the-written-wyrd.org/shopping.shtml

70542312R00202

Made in the USA
San Bernardino, CA
03 March 2018